A PERIOD
OF ADJUSTMENT

Dirk Bogarde

VIKING

VIKING

Published by the Penguin Group
Penguin Books Ltd, 27 Wrights Lane, London w8 5TZ, England
Penguin Books USA Inc., 375 Hudson Street, New York, New York 10014, USA
Penguin Books Australia Ltd, Ringwood, Victoria, Australia
Penguin Books Canada Ltd, 10 Alcorn Avenue, Toronto, Ontario, Canada M4V 3B2
Penguin Books (NZ) Ltd, 182–190 Wairau Road, Auckland 10, New Zealand

Penguin Books Ltd, Registered Offices: Harmondsworth, Middlesex, England

First published 1994
1 3 5 7 9 10 8 6 4 2
First edition

Filmset by Datix International Limited, Bungay, Suffolk
Printed in England by Clays Ltd, St Ives plc
Set in 11/13½ pt Monophoto Sabon

A CIP catalogue record for this book is available from the British Library

ISBN 0-670-85559-6

For
FANNY BLAKE

With my love
and admiration

AUTHOR'S NOTE

There are no such places as Bargemon-sur-Yves, Saint-Basile or any of the other villages. They come strictly from my imagination and are, in some cases, composites of places which once I knew well in the late eighties, which is when this story is set – before a number of rules and regulations were altered in France, before the European Community existed, and when AIDS had only just started to wreak havoc among the young of both sexes.

I am grateful to Dr Peter Wheeler and Dr Jonathan Hunt for their advice and counsel, to my editor, Fanny Blake, for trying valiantly to control my excesses, and to Mrs Sally Betts who, to our mild surprise, typed this, our twelfth volume together, with her usual speed and skill.

D.v.d.B.

CHAPTER 1

Giles said, 'Well, now that you've found him and he's dead, what will you do?'

We had just turned into rue des Serbes down towards the sea.

'I don't know,' I said.

'Does it mean we'll have to go back? To England?'

'Not sure yet.'

'I expect so. I expect there will have to be a funeral, won't there?'

'I expect so.'

I turned right on to the Croisette, lights in my favour. People stood in impatient clusters waiting to cross to the beaches. Arms piled high with umbrellas, beach-balls, inflatable ducks and sea-lions, towels. Light breeze flicked and snapped the flags and pennants on the yachts sliding at anchor on the gently heaving water of the harbour. The sky was achingly blue: morning blue, clean, refreshed by the night. Men unravelled long skeins of net along the cobbles of the quay, stacked lobster pots, bawled and laughed to each other. They were still washing and sweeping the pavement and street outside the bars and restaurants along quai Saint-Pierre, sunlight sequinning the spilt water among the cobbles. It was still reasonably early; up on the clock of Le Suquet it said ten-thirty. But you couldn't be absolutely sure of that really. Inaccurate.

It seemed to me that I had been gutted. I felt transparent. Hollow. Tap me and I'd sound like an empty vessel. I was driving all right, no problems, automatic reflexes were all intact, it was just that my real mind seemed to be mislaid. Elsewhere. I could hear Giles's voice as if he were speaking into an empty bottle. A vaguely booming sound, far too adult for a nine-year-old boy to use.

'What is AIDS?' he said.

I turned left at the port, straight down to the sea and then right on boulevard Jean Hibert, and the Hôtel Méditerranée, along the coast road to La Napoule, past the Aérospatiale factory, the umbrella pines of the golf course. The traffic was already heavy.

'Will? Is it something really bad? Something like . . . an appendix?'

'Who said anything about AIDS?'

'You did. Talking to that man, your friend at the clinic place. The tall man in the blazer.'

'No such thing. I never said anything.'

'"So *that's* what AIDS does," you said. And he said, "Yes. I did warn you."'

'Little pitchers have large ears.' I *had* said it, I remembered. Just forgot to lower my voice, I suppose. I thought the boy was still in the car, but of course he'd got out and wandered about the *parking*. He was sitting in the shade under a mimosa bush – it was already hot – and he'd heard Aronovich and me talking. I'd forgotten. Naturally. I was not altogether used to having him around all the time.

'Yes. Pretty awful. Shut up for a bit, will you?'

'I thought it was. You look funny.'

'Do I? What sort of "funny"?'

He shook his head, dismissing thought. 'Nothing. Just funny. Nothing . . .'

'Do you want a coffee? Orangina? Something?'

'Well, we had breakfast ages ago . . . But I wouldn't mind . . . A croissant? Can I have one? Some honey?'

At a small café by the harbour in La Napoule we sat under an umbrella at a tin table. A girl in flip-flops set a tray of things before me, cups, pot, so on. There were two other people having a late breakfast. Probably German or English. She in a white cardigan and bright floral print, he in baggy cotton trousers and an over-washed Aertex shirt. He studied a folded map; she sipped her coffee or whatever, contented, smiling vaguely, peering fatly at a happy world through pink-rimmed sunglasses.

Giles was slowly unwrapping a butter pat. 'It's frozen hard. Silly. Terribly hard to undo.'

'Leave it in the sun for a bit. It'll melt. Get soft . . .'

'Was he a doctor or something? The man in white trousers and a blazer?'

'No. No, he was a friend of Uncle James. Knew him very well, nice man. Didn't you meet him once? At Jericho? When he came to collect some stuff? Paintings.'

Giles had unwrapped his butter and was pressing lumps of it on to a piece of warm croissant, with his thumb. He shook his head at my question. 'I don't think so. Perhaps I was with Dottie and Arthur or . . . I don't know. I didn't recognize him.' He stuffed a piece of croissant into his mouth.

'His name is Solomon Aronovich. Just keep your voice down. I think they may be English at that table there. *Don't* look! Just talk, if you have to, about "ill" instead of the other thing. Okay? "*Ill*".'

'Instead of AIDS?'

'Clever boy.'

'I suppose now you'll have to tell Florence, won't you? I

mean she's his wife and so on. Did she know he was . . .
"ill"? Well, dying really?'

'No. No. She didn't know. But she was sure that he was
dead. She said so . . . she had a hunch. You know? People
do get hunches like that. When he went away all that time
ago, she was pretty certain he'd gone for good. Wasn't
around . . .'

'But all the time he was at that clinic! Dead.' He pushed
another piece of honey-dripping croissant into his mouth.

The amazing insouciance of youth almost made me laugh.
Almost. Yes, now I'd have to tell Florence. I'd have to tell
my wife Helen – Giles's mother – as well. Not that she'd
care a jot, but she'd have to know that the 'job', my search
for a missing little brother, had ended this morning. Now I
would be free to return to family life and pick up the reins
which I had laid down on the reception of a small package
from France all those weeks ago. There on the kitchen table
in Parsons Green. No duty to pay, an old key and a
message: *Don't come to try and find me. I've gone away for
ever. My house is yours. Here's the key.*

Tempted by that challenge I had come here to find
him. And had. As Giles had so correctly said – dead. Up
in the clinic, the Villa Mimosa, by the Observatoire in the
hills above Cannes. Now all that I had to do was the
tidying up. A funeral, of course; first tell his French
family, and then decide just what to do myself. What to
do with myself was going to be difficult. Helen had
cleared off with her lover, a not frightfully savoury gentleman, big in commercial television, immensely rich, leaving
me with what she had called a 'sullen and sulky' son of
nine. I'd lived with him all his life but, frankly, hadn't
really bothered to get to know him. And here he was,
right now, stuffing himself with honey and croissant,
swinging his legs cheerfully, nodding about with
contentment.

4

I'd agreed to let him stay in France with me while I searched for his uncle. I didn't at all regret the decision: he was a pleasant companion, I didn't see anything sullen or sulky about him. But I hadn't actually ever seen Helen's friend lying in her bed with his pig-tail untied. Giles had. So.

But now what? Florence was the non-wife of his Uncle James. By that I mean they had actually never been married in a church but had gone through some kind of larky betrothal on a rock on some beach one blazing summer day (I had a snapshot of the silly event to prove it), when they exchanged vows and some cheap metal ring before witnesses, and mingled their blood from a couple of midget scratches on their wrists. All very fey and idiotic. But it had made shacking up together and having a child – she was pregnant it seemed – more acceptable to the people of the village in which she had spent a great deal of her life. A small village full of small minds. Naturally. But the child was ill-born. Down's Syndrome. Adorable, as they so often are, if you could handle it; desperate and ruinous if not. Florence could. James could not. He had eventually fled, convinced that he was guilty, shattered that his own secret and ugly predilections for being bashed to hell by a strong male before other gloating males might very well have resulted in this deformity in his child. Seeking 'punishment' for this hideous frailty in his infant, he had succumbed entirely to depravity, and died from the loathsome spores which his passions had spawned. I suppose it was all pretty predictable, and it was equally predictable that I, for my part, had of course fallen very much in love with his bewildered wife, Florence. 'Malchance', as they say in France. Florence had *not* fallen in love with me. Ah, well . . .

Giles accidentally kicked me under the table. I slopped coffee down my wrist. He apologized, wiped his mouth with the back of his hand. There was a golden fringe of crumbs stuck under his lower lip.

'Crumbs. On your chin. Wipe them off ... Want any more?'

He shook his head, poked about in the little basket covered with a red gingham cloth. 'No, thank you. What's this?'

'A brioche.'

'Would I like it?'

'I don't know. You have them for breakfast, don't you? At the hotel?'

He seemed to remember, nodded, pushed the basket aside, sat back in his chair squinting into the sun. 'I expect you'll have to say it all to Florence. Won't you?'

'I will. Yes.'

'I bet she'll be sad. Especially if she didn't know. Very sad, I expect.'

'Very sad. Look, do shut up for a bit. I really am trying to think things out and you go rabbiting on. Just for a little time? Look at the view, the sea, anything. Be a good chap. All right?'

He looked perfectly pleasant, nodded, swung his legs, sat on his hands, rested his head on his shoulder. I called the girl in flip-flops for the bill. The sunlight sparkled on the little puddles where she had recently washed down the terrace. The man in the Aertex shirt started folding his map; it cracked and rustled. The woman opened her bag, took out a compact, pushed the sunglasses high on her head, pursed her lips, bared them in a deathly plastic smile, snapped the compact shut, fumbled it into her bag. The girl brought the bill, I paid and we walked up to the car in the *parking*.

It only then dawned on me that we were on the wrong road. I was on the coast road, not the 'Provençal'. Old habits died hard. I was familiar with the coast road, but it would take a couple of hours or more to get to Bargemon-sur-Yves that way.

'We're on the wrong road. Got to turn back into Cannes, get on to the autoroute.'

Giles had started to stoop into the car. 'It's jolly hot. Burning. The car, I mean, don't touch it. I think this way is nicer. Must we go back?'

We must and we did; finally we got on to the slip road and started off again. James, the golden ewe lamb, my younger brother by about ten years, had not, as Aronovich had warned me on the telephone when he announced the death, looked remotely like anyone I had ever known. The sunken face, the dark skin, the grinning lips, stretched taut as thin elastic, the teeth like a mad beast's, the sores. Almost no hair; the fair tumbling fall, so very much a feature of his conceit and youth, once worn like a glittering cap, was now so sparse and thin that the speckled scalp showed through it like a bird's egg.

We had stood, Aronovich, his guardian and help, and I, silently in the small white room in the half-light thrown by the morning through tightly slatted shutters. There was nothing to say. Nothing at all. On a small glass shelf a shabby, canvas hand-grip, faded green, leather handles, an old label hanging still in the airless room. Aronovich nodded towards me across the thing on the bed, a sort of 'Enough? Seen enough?' look. I nodded back and he drew up the sheet and covered the deathly face and then took the hand-grip from the shelf and offered it to me.

'This was his. All that he had left. You'd better take it. It has an out-of-date passport, the remainder of what little money he had, and . . . I don't know . . . bits and pieces. Nothing much. A sketch-block, some pencils, a rubber . . .'

The bag was light, the things shuffled about. There was no clothing of any description, but the old family photograph from Dieppe which I had given Aronovich only the day before, and which he had begged for, was there. I took it out. It had been removed from its frame to copy. The copy which he had had done was not there.

'You asked to copy this. For James? Did you?'

'I did. I told you. I was just in time . . . he was very moved to see it, he had always kept it. He asked no questions, he had not the strength anyway. Just held it as close to himself as he could. He kissed it . . .'

'A reminder of a time of happiness. The family on the beach at Dieppe; Mama, Papa, our sister Elspeth, James and me. God! So long ago. Where is the copy?'

Aronovich shrugged gently, began to open the door into the corridor. 'I have it. You do not mind? I would like to keep it if I may? Everything else of his is in the bag you have . . . Shall we leave now?'

I looked down at the covered body of my younger brother. His nose thrust in a peak through the sheet, there was a vague outline of folded hands. I followed Aronovich into the polished, shadowy corridor.

'Of course, keep it. Thank you for this stuff . . . no clothing? Nothing?'

'Oh. Some bits. A couple of shirts, jeans, underpants. At my flat.'

'He lived with you?'

'Towards the end, yes. Before, some friends with a small villa gave him shelter. But when things became too difficult . . . I took him, until we got him here.'

We had reached the bright, glassy, light hall of the clinic. People in white, a girl behind a high ebony desk, telephones purring, a glass tank of darting tropical fish, flowers. It was almost like an hotel, not a place to which one came to die hideously from a vicious, untreatable disease. There was not the slightest sign down here of the crumbling destruction in the rooms above.

Aronovich pushed wide the glass doors into the sun-bleached gravel courtyard. The air was warm, scented, our feet scattered little stones. The car I rented from the mayor of my village sparked and glittered in the morning light. For a moment we stood together in silence. He sniffed the air, I took a deep breath, expelling the imagined odour of ether or formaldehyde from my nostrils. There was nothing, at that moment, left to say to each other. With his help I had located James, and with his help James had managed to die at the very least in comfort and with some tattered shreds of dignity. He was a good man. Thinking that, I smiled at him, one of those idiotic, embarrassed, very English smiles. Meaning a great deal more than I could at that moment say. Instead he shook his head sadly and murmured, 'Pneumocystis pneumonia. It sounds so simple.'

'So that's what AIDS does. God Almighty . . .'

'I did warn you.'

'I know, but you see now that it was essential? I mean, I had to *see* him. Thank you. Inadequate. I'll call you when I have –'

He interrupted me with a brief movement of his hand. 'Call when you have settled things. I will call you if there are any immediate problems. We will have to move reasonably quickly, you know? A funeral. Cremation? It would be wiser . . .' He smoothed his hair, fished a key ring from his pocket, smiled, nodded, turned away crossing back to the glass doors of the clinic.

I walked, carrying the battered bag, towards the car, baking in the sun, and heard Giles call out from under the bush in the centre of a raised bed in the courtyard.

'I'm here! Will! In the shade. The car's too hot. You've been *ages*.' He came scuffling through the gravel. The gently buffeting wind, the fag end of a mistral, ruffled his hair. 'I left the doors open, to get some air. All right?'

'Yes, all right. Probably run down the battery. However

. . .' I slung the hand-grip into the back seats. 'Come along, get in, let's get home.'

'Was it all right? In there? Did you see him? Uncle James?'

'Yes. We were too late, Giles. He was dead. But I saw him, yes. Paid my respects.'

'I bet it was a terrible shock. But you knew he was ill, so that was good.'

'Yes. That was good. Now we have to find our way back down to the town.'

I began winding slowly down the hill under a vast canopy of wind-tossing green leaves, shadows freckled and danced over the road. At the side a small milestone, red and white, indicated that Cannes was 4 kilometres ahead, and ahead of that I had some explaining to do. To Florence, to Madame Mazine who ran our hotel, to Helen in Marbella, to Arthur and Dottie who had been waiting for Giles to begin his French lessons. It was already after ten: it would be well after noon by the time we got back to the village. But at least my main job had been accomplished: I'd found James. All that was left to me now was a tidying-up job. No problem.

Except that, along the way, I had suddenly acquired the custody, as far as he was concerned anyway, of my neglected son. I had someone in my life after all.

He gave a great shout of delight suddenly as we rounded a bend: 'Bamboo! Look at it! A forest, huge, thick as your leg! It's so high . . . Bamboo! Awesome!'

I'd have to adjust to things now. Like Giles.

The mistral, which had been blowing hard when we left for Cannes earlier in the morning, had now exhausted itself and, apart from an occasional snarling gust, had drifted off to sea leaving a litter of branches, twigs and broken tile all along the way.

Dottie Theobald was tying up the lengths of vine which had fallen and now trailed across her terrace, a fat bunch of raffia in the pocket of her cotton pinafore. She looked up with some surprise, as I pulled into their narrow track leading up to the house, holding on to her straw hat, the little gusts of left-over mistral still puffing and tumbling into the rose bushes. She hurried down towards us, a pair of old secateurs jiggling in her hand.

'Terribly late! Goodness, I *have* been worried! It's almost lunchtime.' And as Giles scrambled out of the car, she said, 'Arthur's up at the aviary. If you have the energy, run up and see him.' She turned to me as Giles started up the little hill towards the ornate bird-cages and the vague shape of a man moving about beside them. I began to apologize, but she waved me silent, and started up to the terrace. 'Don't explain anything. Just so long as all is well. One does get such a fright at sudden changes. Do you know what I mean? Question of age. Unprepared in the midst of one's apparent serenity. Do sit down . . .'

I told her, as briefly as I could, what had happened since the telephone call from Aronovich at the hotel to alert me to the fact that my brother had been found, was dead, and to where I could find him. Search over. Mission accomplished. She didn't move all the time I was talking, just sat quite still, her pale blue eyes holding mine, wisps of her faded fair hair fluttering lightly under the brim of her hat in the little eddies of air. The sky above was sparkling blue, clean, wiped, infinite. It dazzled to look up into it. Then she put the secateurs on a tiled table before her, took off her hat, and fiddled with the untidy plait of hair coiled about her head.

'When the boy hadn't arrived by nine-thirty I guessed something was wrong. I called your hotel and they said you'd rushed off to Cannes together. A call at breakfast time? So I guessed you were off on the hunt. I'm most dreadfully sorry for you. What an appalling shock. Can you say what had happened?'

'He was in a clinic. A friend called me to say he had died in the night – well, early morning – from . . . pneumonia. Double pneumonia and pleurisy . . .' The lie fell sweetly from my lips. Dottie nodded sadly, sighed, put a hand on my knee and said, again, how terrible and how sorry she was.

'I gather from his mother-in-law that he was dreadfully headstrong, very stubborn.'

'You mean the daunting Sidonie Prideaux! A tough lady . . .'

'Umm, she was in despair of him, often. At bridge she used to be so very cast down . . . and then when he left his wife, for ever one gathers, to go off as he did . . . fearful . . . '

'I know. It was a dreadful shock to them all. Just going away, into the night –'

'No, no. I mean to go off in that manner! On a cycle! In nothing but a jacket and trousers, not even a coat! In January, in snow . . . Madness! No wonder, if you'll pardon me for saying such an apparently callous thing, no wonder he caught pneumonia! I mean, no wonder.'

'So Giles had missed a morning's lessons. But can I ask you a favour?' She nodded, twisting her plait gently to the top of her head, and sticking in a hairpin. 'Could you just keep an eye on him here for the afternoon? I have to get over to the village and tell Florence and Madame Prideaux. They'll have discovered that I left. Madame Mazine at the hotel has a hot line to the Prideaux house.'

For the first time Dottie looked lost. 'Hot line? What's that?' So I had to explain, and she laughed lightly, and said, 'Of course. Why not stay to luncheon? Just pâté, salad and cheese?' I accepted gratefully: there was no point in returning to the hotel now, and I was desperate for a drink, even if the thought of food was not terribly attractive.

Dottie had got to her feet and was removing her little checked pinafore as Arthur and Giles came down the path towards us, Giles chattering like a magpie, but, alas, not in French. Arthur waved; he looked comfortable, easy, his bony, bronzed legs sticking out of slapping khaki shorts, his laceless boots clattering up the steps to the terrace.

'Morning!' he called. Dottie said we were staying to lunch and would he get me a drink, I looked as if I needed it. Or would I prefer to wash my hands first? Giles said that *he* would, he knew where to go, and belted off. Arthur motioned me to sit.

'You've had a bit of a trip. Eh? Giles is starry-eyed about giant bamboo and seeing giraffes by the side of the auto-route. Amazed! I told him there was a wild sort of zoo at Fréjus. I'll get you a drink. Wine? Or a stiff Scotch? Or just water . . . what you will.'

The good thing about Dottie was that she really did just chuck things on the table. There was no fussing, no dainty teas caper. There were a bundle of forks and knives, a bowl of radish, assorted cheeses capped with fresh fig leaves, a huge bowl of lettuce and endive, a pile of odd plates, a jug of wine and, finally, brought from the cool of the kitchen, a crock of rich-looking pâté and a bowl of cornichons. Lunch was on the table.

'Sometimes English guests ask for butter with all this, but it really is criminally insane. Think of one's liver! Giles, get the baguettes will you? From the kitchen, *et de la moutarde pour votre Papa. Vous voulez de la moutarde, Monsieur Colcott?*' Giles had gone off, and she was smiling, and so was I, with a large goblet of Frascati handed over by Arthur.

'A brimming glass. Don't spill a drop. Nectar. I get this in crates from a chap over at Sainte-Brigitte. Deceptively good: like drinking lemonade with the ultimate kick of a Cretan mule. Giles seems quite unruffled by the events of the morning. Wouldn't it be marvellous to be that age again. He says he's staying on? Correct?' Arthur bit into a radish with strong teeth, raised an eyebrow. 'Are *you*? Here, I mean.'

'I'm not absolutely certain yet. A lot to sort out now that the main item in the treasure hunt, so to speak, has been found. Tragically. But, yes, Giles wants to stay on. Here. But more importantly, and a bit worryingly, he wants to stay on with me. Not to return to the UK and, I regret to say it, to his mother.'

Dottie was mixing the salad with a large pair of wooden forks, watching me carefully. 'To stay with you? I see, well, quite a responsibility of course. Is that something you'll be happy about?'

Giles came back with the bread and the jar of mustard. 'Take your shoes off, boy! Like I do,' said Arthur. 'Scuffing the polish!'

'Yes. It's something I'll be very happy about,' I said. 'Take a bit of getting used to, but I rather think it might work out. We'll see.'

And then I said no more, before Giles and Arthur started to push knives and forks about, and asked where the plates were, found them, and generally busied the table and we all set to and ate. It was relaxed, warm. I mean the atmosphere, not just the morning, and Dottie said that she had made the pâté a day or two ago and let it stand uncut so that the flavours would all blend deliciously. Her word. And they did. After lunch we three adults sat about comforted by simple food and, in my case anyway, a good deal of the Frascati, which dulled grief and worry. Giles had gone off with some fruit pieces for a perroquet or something up in the aviary, then Dottie was making coffee somewhere in the cool of the house.

Arthur said suddenly, 'Seems a very relaxed boy. Anyway, with you. Things not quite what they should be at home? I pry, forgive me. But he *has* mentioned it before. About hoping he could stay with you. Children do rather bash on if they feel one is being sympathetic. I try to keep him on French – he's picking it up quite well – but we tend to have to stick to English when he gets to the business of relationships, you know? His French vocabulary is very limited but he is quite loquacious in English. I do hope you don't mind.'

'His mother is a splendid person really, it's all rather my fault. I trapped her into marriage when really she was a career woman, if you follow. She had a very good job in the commercial television world. Thought she could give it all up and have a family. Before she was too old. Which, indeed she did. Brilliantly ... but I am afraid I didn't really help her much. Immersed in my world I left her to flop about being a mum. She got bored with that in time, some women do ... And there is a daughter. I have a daughter. Nice child, Annie, the eldest, but Giles and she don't really enjoy each other. *She* is her mother's child. Giles got slightly left out, and I didn't, I regret to say, notice it all happening, until I got here and he was sent out to me to "sort out". Sulky, sullen and rude, I was told ... Difficult.'

Dottie came through on to the terrace with the coffee. The clatter and clash of the bamboo and bead curtain, whispers in the sweetness of the afternoon, swung gently behind her.

'Arthur, move the things, the table is like a Harrods sale ...'

We collected plates, stacked, clutched cutlery, rattled it into a neat pile.

'Giles is staying on for the afternoon. So your nap will have to wait.'

Arthur poured the last of the wine into our glasses, said he was delighted, and that he only napped when he had nothing else to do and no one with which to do it. Giles would be very useful to him. They could clean out the small aviary.

'When will you collect him?'

'About five? Is that all right?'

'Perfect,' said Dottie. 'And don't try to give me a hand with the washing up or I'll kill you. I know where everything goes and it goes where it lives, in my own time. I don't want to have to search drawers, long after you have gone away, to find a pickle-fork.'

I left shortly after, hazed in Frascati comfort, not in the least drunk, merely eased – braver, if you like – to meet Florence, which was my next stop.

Before I left I called up to Giles, scrabbling somewhere up among the roses by the bird-cages. He half ran down the hill towards me, apprehension in his urgency, but I stopped him with a hand and shouted that I'd collect him very soon, about five. He came down a little nearer to me, shading his eyes from the sun. His feet were bare; he carried a little bunch of green feathers in one hand.

'Sure?' he said. Almost uncertainly. We went through this every time I left him anywhere. Even here, with Dottie and Arthur whom, I knew, he liked and trusted. Somewhere along the line in Parsons Green, when I had not been actually present, like abroad doing research, or merely up in the North for a few days doing Signings, someone had not been quite truthful, or perhaps just a little unreliable? Giles, I was discovering more and more, was terrified of being abandoned. Odd.

'About five o'clock. Okay? I have to go and see your Aunt Florence about this morning. It might take a bit of time. But I'll be back.'

He brushed his forehead with the bunch of feathers. 'Okay. But you will . . . ?'

'I will. Promise.' I crossed my heart.

That seemed to satisfy him. He turned and ran, a loping

sprawl, back to whatever he had been doing, and I drove over to Bargemon and Florence.

Waiting for Florence on an upright cane chair, in the conservatory stuck on to the side of her mother's house, I realized, I suppose for the first time ever, that even though I had been a visitor to the place for some weeks, I had never got further into the house than here: the conservatory, stuffed with creeper, ferns, a small banana tree, a tank of goldfish and pots of lilies and scarlet geraniums. Very French. I had never seen a sitting-room, a dining-room . . . nowhere else but here. Apart from crossing the hall, with its heavy banisters, solid staircase, vase of pampas grass, Turkey carpet, I had no territorial knowledge of Florence or her life and habits. And she had always made it quite clear that I never would. Keep-Off-The-Grass was writ large. I had obeyed.

Presently she came in, tall, slender, neat, good legs and ankles, clear grey eyes, hair in a fringe, a white shirt, open at the throat, grey flannel skirt. She'd never be noticed in a crowd. Deliberately, it seemed. And she was rushed, as usual, and as usual was trying to button a cuff, one arm stretched out, fingers fiddling. An impression, very distinct, that she had just finished washing up, painting a wall, or kneading dough, that there had been some compelling action before my arrival, and that I was interrupting something rather more important that she had to do.

We had not seen each other since, the day before, she had pleaded with me in this very place to drop my search for her 'husband', my brother, and save her and her family the 'pain' and 'distress' of his possible discovery somewhere. 'He's dead. James sought oblivion. His wish. Honour *that*,' she had said, in so many words. She had long ago resigned herself to his disappearance, and had come to terms with spending a life caring for her disabled child and her domineering mother. The typical only-daughter bit. The fact that Solomon Aronovich had promised to call me, when he had digested my threat that I would seek official help from the British Consul and the local police if he did not, had disturbed her greatly. I had refused her pleas to leave well alone.

So our meeting today was one of great concern to her, although this she was determined to hide. Fiddling with a shirt button was the only outward sign of confusion and apprehension.

'I was busy in the kitchen with Céleste,' she said, finally fastening her sleeve. 'So, what did Monsieur Aronovich have to say? Has he been quite amazing and finally discovered James? Is that it?'

We spoke together in French, easily and colloquially. My French was pretty slangy, her English good, but it always fussed her to use it. So we stuck to her formal French and my lightly accented efforts.

I pulled up a second cane chair, told her to sit down, that what I had to say was difficult and might be distressing. She obediently sat, a slightly mocking smile on her face trying to disguise the agony in her eyes. 'Oh, là là! We are to be lectured, is it?' She folded her arms in her lap; her hands were shaking.

'Florence. I found James. He was not in Tunis or Corsica or anywhere. He was in Cannes . . . he had been in Cannes ever since he left you in January.'

'Was! Had! Past tense . . . so?'

'James is dead.'

She flinched, shut her eyes, then looked briefly round the conservatory. Her fists were clenched on her lap, the knuckles white.

'Go on. You are certain?'

'I saw him.'

There was a longish pause. I could hear a pigeon cooing

somewhere up on the roof and someone clanged shut an iron gate in the street outside.

'Will you tell me where? Am I not to know?'

'In the Villa Mimosa, above Cannes.'

'I don't know this place. Should I?'

'It's a private clinic, Florence. He died from AIDS.'

For the first time she looked at me, her face white, bleak, expressionless.

'Aronovich told you this? Where he was?'

'Yes. He's been his guardian all the time. He got him into the place. He took me there this morning.'

She got up slowly, walked away from me, her arms swinging loosely, fingers splaying, as if she was at music practice. Then she stood quite still by a large pot of something, bowed her head, shook it from side to side so that her short hair flung wild, and began to weep helplessly. I made no move. I knew that to touch her would be disaster, her grief was not to be shared or comforted.

After a minute or two she stopped, wiped her face with both hands, brushed them on her skirt, then she turned and came back to the cane chair and sat down. 'So. That is that. Poor James, poor boy. The ugliest of deaths for the most fastidious of creatures. Are you content now? You have your proof . . . I have always known, *always*. It is something every woman knows the moment the heart dies. Shrivels, withers, rots . . . I told you so often, I begged you not to search, you ignored me. I pleaded with you to let things alone, to accept the fact that he wished to just creep away, die like a beast in a dark corner, but you were cruel, unthinking! He was *my* husband . . . I knew . . .'

And I cut in swiftly and angrily. 'He was *not* your "husband", but he was *my* brother. He was merely your romanticized ideal of a husband – he was as much married to you legally as I am married to Céleste or Brigitte Bardot. It was all in your mind. All nonsense, Florence! I told you yesterday afternoon, here in this very place, that I just couldn't let him fall off the edge of the world and not do something to find him. If I could have helped him I would. He is *my* flesh and blood: it counts in the end. He was only someone who took your virginity, someone you gave yourself to willingly because you had never loved anyone before, and had never expected to . . . James used you, as he used so many people, to amuse himself and give himself an illusion of security, ordinariness, normalcy. He desperately needed that, and therefore he needed you. But when his child was born he knew that he had lost. He lacked the true courage to overcome that, to handle it bravely, as you have done. Instead he took all the blame on himself and fled back to his disgusting little friends to seek punishment for his "sins". God Almighty! He *got* his punishment!'

During this tirade, and I was bloody angry, I know, she sat motionless before me, head bowed, weeping silently. The tears just dribbled down her face and chin, there was no sob or gulp. Silent, ugly misery and suppressed pain splashing out helplessly. I knelt beside her and took a listless hand; it was wet with tears. 'I'm sorry. I'm really sorry. You know it's true, and I know it's true, we have both been dreadfully hurt in our different ways, but I know that what I did was the right thing. I could never have given up. I had to find him and now that I have there is a terrible relief. He's gone, Florence. We know that now. For certain.'

She withdrew her hand from mine, wiped it across her ruined face, combed fingers wearily through her hair, blinked, brushed her eyes. Her nose was red.

'What will we do now?'

'A funeral. A cremation. Aronovich will cope with that.'

'Will you help me? With Mama, the household, Céleste. What can we say?'

'Say? That he died of pneumonia in Cannes. I traced him. We don't have to go into more than that. I'll have to notify the British Consul, which shouldn't be very difficult, and the mayor of your village, or wherever he got his papers. His resident's permit, the bank . . . Aronovich will deal with anything else, apart from money, and I can deal with that.'

'I don't have to go, do I? To a funeral . . .'

'Of course not. I'll go . . . to the cremation. After that, well, we'll see.'

She got up slowly and walked over to the fish tank, dipping a trembling finger into the bubbling water. Everything she did, and said, was as if she was half asleep. The clock in the church tower in the square suddenly jangled with its tinny clang. It was four o'clock. She looked up, shook her head, folded her arms.

'What will you do now? After? Go back to England?'

'I don't know. I might. Might not. I really don't know.'

'How long did he have it? This . . . How long did he have the virus?'

'I have no idea. No one does. Maybe Aronovich? I think that sometimes it can be a long time, sometimes a short time. I really don't know.'

'I wondered. I only wondered. About myself, really. I suppose there is a chance, isn't there? That I might carry the virus. Or Thomas? We might both be infected. It's possible?'

We stood looking at each other in complete silence. The oxygenator in the fish tank bubbled quietly.

'It's possible,' I said. 'I don't know.'

She picked a leaf, shredded it slowly, dropping little green scraps on the tile floor. 'After Thomas was born, there was nothing. Of course. Nothing. We never touched. Never touched. But before . . .' She dropped the stalk of the leaf, shrugged her shoulders slightly. 'Before, it was sometimes very fine. Sometimes. But it is, I suppose, just possible?'

'I suppose. I'm going back to the Theobalds', I left Giles

there. And I have to go to the hotel to explain things to Madame Mazine. She was off duty when I arrived here.'

'They know, at the hotel. The telephone call this morning evidently was news. She called my mama the moment you had left for Cannes. I knew too . . . anyway, something.'

'Something,' I said. 'Not everything.'

'No. Not everything. Not that he was dead. From pneumonia . . .'

'And that is all anyone has to know. Nothing else. That's how he died, and he did.'

'Mama will not weep, I fear. There will be no tears shed.'

She opened the door into the dim hall, and we walked together to the front door. She had straightened now, was crisp once more. In control. As I stepped down on to the white gravel path she said, very quietly, 'Thank you, William. Forgive me.'

I waved a dismissive hand, walked down to the gate. When I turned back the front door was closing. I wondered, as I set off for La Maison Blanche and Madame Mazine, if she knew that her mama had once tried to kill James? Tried to run him down in her car. Failed to, of course. She was a bad driver always. Florence didn't know about that little effort. Florence never would, either.

CHAPTER 2

Madame Mazine turned the ledger on her desk so that it was facing towards me, pointed to the page headed MAY. It was filled. So were JUNE and JULY, and the bookings leaked into AUGUST. I pushed it gently back towards her.

'You run a very successful hotel, Madame. And with reason.'

She nodded agreeably, closed the ledger. Giles was squirming uneasily beside me. I told him to go off to the lavatory by the bar.

'So after the twenty-sixth I am roomless? And the boy?'

'Hélas! Monsieur Forbin has your room every year, regular as the swallows, and the Doumer family always take your son's room. They are all walkers. I did warn you, Monsieur. I am desolate.'

So was I at that moment. Less than a week left of my booking, and far too much to do in the week. She was regarding me kindly. She knew the situation. I had told her my news from Cannes, and she was a close friend of Florence's mama, Sidonie Prideaux. So she would be filled in with every detail from that source. No, she said sadly, there was no other hotel near. A Novotel in Sainte-Brigitte, and perhaps I might find a room at La Source? Or . . . and she rubbed her forehead with the palm of a hand as an idea drifted towards her. Or, if I was prepared to be not very comfortable and share with my son, perhaps I would like to look at the Pavilion in the garden? It was empty, apart from the hotel linen which was stacked there after ironing. No one used it unless the hotel was absolutely full. There were two beds, a shower. Would I care to look? I would, and we did.

Eugène led us into the courtyard at the back of the hotel and opened the door into a damp-smelling void. The Pavilion had, at some time in the past, been stuck on to the back of the hotel rather haphazardly to serve as a store and an emergency 'room'. It was presently dark. The shutters let slits of light spill across piles of stacked sheets and pillowcases. There was a tumble of striped bolsters on one bed, a bundle of folded lace curtains on the other.

'Voilà!' said Eugène, wrenching at the bolt on a shutter and flinging it wide. 'Le Pavillon. We used to play ping-pong here – there was a table – in wet weather. We can clear it up for you in the next week, if you would like it? I am sure my aunt can make a suitable financial arrangement. The shower – you see? – is here. In the corner. *And* there is a toilet. But no bidet.' He was smiling to himself.

Giles prodded the bed with the lace curtains. There was a rusty squeeze of springs.

'I'll take it,' I said.

Giles shot a swift look at me, looked away, thumped one of the bolsters.

'So I'll move in here on the twenty-seventh? We neither of us use the bolsters, so can you change them for pillows. What about mosquitoes?'

Eugène shook his head, closed the shutter, we walked out, locked the door. The smell of damp and incipient mildew lingered. I put that down, charitably, to the laundered sheets. 'No mosquitoes at this height, perhaps one or two in August. How long does Monsieur intend to stay with us? A question of your table.'

'I don't honestly know.' As we pushed the door into the hotel lobby, paint flaked from the woodwork. 'I think until I can get a telephone installed at Jericho.'

Another look from Giles, this time eyebrows raised. I looked at him without expression. I was thinking hard. He looked away, but I'd seen the flick of a triumphant smile on his lips.

Eugène, standing aside to let us pass through the chenille-curtained door into the little lobby, laughed. Not unkindly, just rather wearily. 'It is cold in that Pavilion in *winter*! There is no radiator. But maybe you will come back into the house after September? When the regulars have gone back?'

'Maybe.' I realized that I had made a commitment with the telephone. Not just to Eugène and Giles, but to myself as well. The idea had just arrived: I had probably thought it all out subconsciously, but never knowingly. Perhaps it was Fate that had decided for me and forced the decision?

So, Jericho? Well, why not? It was mine for the next three years, rent paid in advance already. I liked it, I was quite adjusted to living there, even though it had only been a matter of three or four weeks since I had known of its existence. I was divorcing my wife (or she was divorcing me rather) amicably, I had handed in my last book to my publisher and corrected the proofs. I could take a year out, relax, consider my life and where to go, and indeed how to go, and start off again. It had to be a renewal of life if one divorced and severed family ties. I'd rather start off again here at Jericho than lumbering about in Parsons Green on my own. Helen had already declared that she would be moving off with her lover, Eric Rhys-Evans, who had a 'super house' in Burnham Beeches. I could well imagine it. Indoor swimming-pool, guarded by a pair of snarling pottery leopards, tasselled Knole settee, a jacuzzi somewhere, scarlet cardinals and jolly monks enjoying a drink all over the walls, and lots of buttoned silk bedheads and gold and glass coffee tables. Well, she liked that sort of kitsch. I liked Jericho.

At the desk Madame Mazine looked up from whatever she was doing. Eugène threw the key to the Pavilion on to the ledger.

'Thank you, Madame. We'll move in there. If it is not inconvenient to you?'

She shook her head, removed her spectacles, slid them into their case. 'Pas du tout!'

Eugène moved behind the desk, reached up and took our bedroom keys from their hooks and handed them over to me. 'Monsieur Colcott says he will stay until he can get the telephone connected at Jericho, so I have told him it is very *cold* in the Pavilion in the winter!' He was smiling, but his aunt was not.

'Nonsense! Things are far easier now than they were. If you have the money, Monsieur Colcott, you will very shortly have a telephone. The poles are already along the road, I think? Pas de problème.'

I took up the keys and pushed Giles in the direction of the bar. I was desperately in need of something to fortify me. To strengthen resolve. I knew that the instant we were on our own there would be a torrent of questions from Giles. There was a torrent of questions from me myself, come to that. But Giles merely said that it was a bit early to go to the bar. I agreed but went on in.

Claude was leaning against the till watching a cartoon on the television. There were two people sitting with beers at a table arguing quietly, and a sad looking truck driver, his cap at the back of his head, glass of rouge in one hand, the other thrust into his greasy overall pocket. He was staring at the yellowing map of the area pinned to the wall. It was almost quiet, apart from the turned-down volume of the television. A diffused, distant scream of brakes, clang of metal, thud of running feet, but quiet in comparison to the evenings when the men came up from the fields. I ordered a brandy and a glass of Coke for Giles.

'I just feel I need a strengthener. Okay? I'm not turning into a drunk. I know it's only half past five or something, but I want it. All right?'

Giles nodded perfectly contentedly. As far as he was concerned he didn't care if I did become a drunk. Everything in his short life had altered so much in the short time that he had joined me that he was quite ready for anything. And, anyway, he had his Coke. Suddenly he looked up, grinned. 'You remember those giraffes? Arthur says there is a wild-life park there. You can just walk about and see them. Elephants too! Awesome.'

'You quite like Arthur and Dottie now, don't you?'

'They're all right. He's a bit boring. Talks to me only in French.'

'That's why you're there. I pay for that. French.'

'I know. It's still a bit boring though. He knows more words than I do.'

'You'll learn.'

He swivelled round on his seat. The television had changed programmes. A young, half-naked woman caressed a tube of hair-spray.

'Anyway, you'd better learn if we are going to stay on here.'

He swung round again quickly. 'Are we? Really? I mean, about the telephone, did you mean that?'

'Yes. I meant that.' I finished off my cognac, made a sign to Claude to check it to my room, got up. Giles finished his Coke too quickly and belched.

'I hoped you did.' He wiped his mouth and followed me into the hall.

'I have to telephone your mother, tell her that the search for your uncle is over. She gave me her address at the airport, didn't she?'

'I don't know. Maybe. It'll be in your wallet perhaps? Was Florence very sad, about her husband being dead?'

We got into the lobby. Eugène came towards us with the menu in his hand. 'If you are dining tonight? Ossibuchi? Or just tagliatelle and chicken livers? A salad?'

'We'll be dining. I'll let you know what we'll eat soon. I have to call Spain.'

'Spain!' Eugène made a wry face as if I had decided to call Afghanistan. 'It's always a problem with the Spanish. You have the number?'

'In my room. I'll call down, if you'd be good enough to try it for me.'

He said he would, give him ten minutes, and Giles and I started up the stairs. I confess that I was suddenly rather weary. It had been a long day. And an emotional one. Trouble with having a young son at one's heels was that he couldn't be expected to understand just how emotional and disturbing it had been. One could just as easily address oneself to a pet dog, cat or parrot. Warm, kind, uncomprehending. Helen, if I got her, wouldn't be much better. And not all that kind either. Not in her nature. Warmth she kept for particular occasions. This was not one of them.

Giles went forlornly down the corridor to his room, jiggling his key, and I went into my old, almost familiar room, with its Napoleon bed, and walnut wardrobe and the view out over the vegetable garden and chicken run. I never cease to amaze myself at the amount of litter I manage to collect around myself. Even after only two or three weeks in the little room it looked as if I had been its inhabitant for a year. Papers, envelopes, the box-file with all the junk about brother James, newspapers, folded and discarded, a scatter of postcards as yet unwritten, and even though I eventually discovered the card which Helen had pushed into my hand at the airport in Nice, stuck among credit cards in my wallet, it gave me no pleasure. All it offered was an address in Valbonne where her 'chum', Eric Rhys-Evans, had a villa. There was no telephone number, and I was not certain that she would have yet finished the job she was 'putting together' in Marbella. Typically she had not, as she had promised, sent me the address of the television company there. Helen was extremely adroit at keeping distances distant.

I sat on my lumpy bed. The afternoon sun had turned the high cliffs beyond the garden to a blush of apricot and pink. I'd got myself into a bit of a jam, if I let it *feel* a jam. Giles, Jericho, a telephone, and the horror of sharing with him in the mildewed Pavilion. However, if one allowed oneself to dwell on the hurdles ahead, one would never gain the strength to jump over them.

I went to the window and leant on the sill looking down into the chicken run. Two windows along to my right Giles was leaning out of his window, apparently firing an imaginary rifle at something.

'What are you up to?'

'Shooting mammoths.'

'Really? Mammoths?'

'Something like that. Up on those cliffs. I expect there were mammoths there trillions of years ago. Don't you?'

'I expect so. If you are as bored as you sound, come along to me. I'm going to change, then we'll go down.'

But he had already withdrawn his head and a couple of seconds later tapped at my door. 'It's a bit boring. My room. And I finished the book Arthur gave me to translate.'

'Already! What was it?'

'Babar the Elephant. Honestly! *Kids'* stuff . . . it was dead easy.'

29

'That's encouraging. That's what he probably expected. Tomorrow he'll give you a chunk of Flaubert.'

'To eat?'

'No. To read, idiot.'

'I never heard of it. Did you put the call in to Mum?'

'She didn't give me the number in Spain. Clever old her, and there's no telephone number on the card she gave me.'

'What'll you do, then?'

'Take a shower. Have you washed?'

'I'm not dirty. Have you got a comb?'

The water in the shower was tepid, but cleansing both physically and mentally, except that it ran down the billowing plastic curtain and dribbled on to the tiled floor of the bedroom. Giles called out that there was a flood, and I turned off taps, grabbed the towel, and stepped out. It was hardly a relaxing event, but I felt better. Lying in a hot bath, just thinking, sorting things out, soothing the anxieties would have been a good thing. Crouched under a shower-head green with verdigris and buffeted by a sagging plastic curtain did not inspire much clarity of thought. Should I, I wondered, start the Heavy Father act and insist that the child wash? Or ignore it? I decided to make just a token gesture.

'Giles, I really think you ought to clean up a bit. You look a mess, and you've been banging about in the aviaries with Arthur – you'll be covered in bird-shit and stuff. Go and wash while I dress.'

'I did wash. Dottie made me; she always does. And I've only got one clean shirt left, so I'd better keep that, hadn't I? For tomorrow? If you like I can wash my hands in your wash basin, can't I? There's no soap in mine, Mum forgot to pack soap in my hand-grip. I think . . . I don't know . . .'

And so it begins. Life as father. I dressed quickly and we went down to the charnel house which was his room. I searched about in his meagre luggage and found, as I expected to find, a cake of soap squashed in his damp facecloth. Helen could be sluttish, but she had never failed as a good, thoughtful mother.

'I forgot it.' Giles shrugged irritatedly, pulled off his shirt, sighed heavily, and washed while I leant out of his window and considered that even if I had exercised my paternal rights over my son's cleanliness, it had cost me energy, time and probably his goodwill. The hell with it. Start as you mean to go on, they say. So I was starting.

'If we do stay here, I mean if you don't change your mind, Arthur said that one day, when I learned enough French to talk to it, he'd give me a lovebird.' He had pulled on his shirt, was buttoning up his collar. 'You wouldn't mind, would you?'

I said that it depended on what sort of lovebird. If it made a row it would not be welcome. And who would look after it when he was at school, or wherever? This last remark caused a deep scowl; he brushed his fingers through his hair. 'It'll be a Rosy-Faced lovebird, probably. He said they were easy for a beginner and make "quite delightful" pets. You *know* how he talks. The lovebirds talk too.'

'How very interesting.'

'He said I should have a pair, really.'

'If you're ready, let's go down to the bar. Come on.'

Madame Mazine called out as we crossed the lobby. 'I have been speaking to Maurice, the driver, about your car. The mayor is back from the clinic, but he's not strong enough to drive yet . . . So . . . ?' She left a question in the air for me to catch up.

'So perhaps I continue to rent his Simca? Is that it? I'd be very grateful, until I can make other arrangements.'

'Maurice is in the bar, he went to get some cigarettes. Perhaps you could have a word with him? Clotilde will start cleaning the Pavilion tomorrow.'

'But I still have a week in my room. Until the twenty-sixth?'

'Indeed. But it will be better for a little paint, and the paper is quite . . . poor.'

What she meant was that the paper was peeling off in grubby strips like old bandage here and there and would be replaced. Which was good news.

So I nodded, politely, and we went down to the bar, noisier now, with the volume up on the television and a group of truck drivers arguing good-naturedly about tyre pressures. Maurice was among them. He was affable, drew me aside to a corner by the pin-table. Monsieur le Maire was home but weak. He would be relieved if I wished to continue renting the Simca. He had it in mind, anyway, to change to another model when he was better. And was there a question of a telephone? Madame Mazine and Eugène suggested that there might be. Or had he misheard? You could never be certain with Eugène. He was always so busy rushing here and there . . .

News does indeed travel fast in small communities. But in this case it was saving me a good deal of trouble; after all, his brother-in-law was the mayor and I was paying handsomely for the use of his Simca. I obviously, from what I had been told, was helping out with medical bills, so perhaps someone knew someone who knew someone else who would be sympathetic to my desire for a telephone? Madame Mazine had suggested, quietly, that 'if you have the money, Monsieur Colcott, you will very shortly have a telephone'. So.

'No indeed! You heard quite correctly from Eugène. I am about to go into Sainte-Brigitte tomorrow to get the forms and so on.'

To my immense delight, Maurice brushed the remark aside as if it had been a mildly irritating gnat. 'Boff! Forms! Bureaucrats. Des gens *terribles*.'

I agreed warmly and offered him a refill. He had drained his glass after his line about bureaucrats, quite deliberately. We were to discuss telephones.

Sitting at the corner table, which was far enough away from the bar counter to hear oneself talk, he pointed out, with his newly charged glass of Ricard, that my brother, 'Jimmie', had once applied for a telephone, but had not been able to afford it after all. Times were hard for a painter, wasn't that so? I knew, of course, that the poteaux had already been erected along the road from Saint-Basile, past the house, to Saint-Basile-les-Pins? All that had to be done was take a line from the road up to the house . . . And so it went on. Reasonable, simple, absolutely 'pas de problème'. He took a swig of his drink and I picked up my cue. But what, I said worriedly, about the forms and papers and most important of all, how would I go about paying for this bounty? Simple! said Maurice, setting down his glass and wiping his mouth with the back of his hand. Simple, my dear Monsieur. As I probably knew, Monsieur le Maire had had a very bad time with his prostate; it was a delicate subject to bring up in public, and he apologized, but health was all. Health – malheur! – was life itself! And that cost money. The clinic had been a disastrous expenditure, eating away at his fragile resources, for a maire did not become a millionaire from his work for the community! Ah no!

This line of anguish went on for a time. I let him tell me the story without interruption for fear we'd both lose track of my telephone; but all was well with a second glass of Ricard, and it was agreed, in very low tones as if we had been planning to blow up a bridge somewhere or demolish the mairie itself, that a little 'gesture' from me, towards the ailing Monsieur le Maire, slipped 'under the table' would be most acceptable and also go a long way to securing a machine and getting it installed in the charming little house which I would soon claim as my own.

It was unthinkable, Maurice insisted, that a writer such as I should be without a telephone and unable to be in touch with – he hunted about for a few place names anxiously – New York? Washington? London? Moscow even! As a writer I had to be completely au fait with the world. Was that not so? I assured him that it was so and suggested a price might be written down on a piece of paper?

This Maurice agreed to with alacrity. It saved him the acute embarrassment of having to phrase the sum, the amount due to his brother-in-law for the kindness and the amount due to *him* for bringing us together. After all, he had suggested that I rent the Simca in the first place. Hein? It would not be amiss? I sent Giles across to Claude behind the bar to get pen and paper, while Maurice went on to suggest that he had a nephew who had a friend who would both be happy to come and install the poles which would be needed to bring the line from the road. He felt that three would be quite enough, and turning slightly, so that he was screened from any possible observer, he wrote, rather laboriously I felt, some figures on the back of a beer mat which Giles had brought across, with a yellow plastic Biro.

By the end of the session I had secured my telephone. When the instrument would be delivered was uncertain, but it was mine, for sure. The nephews and the poles and the 'tra tra la la' (meaning the cable or line) would be discussed, as would the price for them, as soon as he could find them and bring them all together. About this time, just as the third Ricard was being raised in a salute to the completion of the transaction, Eugène arrived and slid the menu for the evening across the little table and said he'd be back in fifteen minutes. Maurice, by this time, was sitting comfortably, his eyes slightly glazing with the Ricard consumed, the beer mat safe in his inner pocket, with my signature of acceptance for the sum indicated.

Giles took the menu and asked what I'd like. I suggested biscuits and cheese after this essay into financial largesse. It had not been desperately immodest, but not minor either. When Eugène returned I settled for the tagliatelle and chicken livers.

'Yuck. Will I like that?' said Giles.

'I honestly don't know, Giles, and at this very moment I don't terribly care. You are not going to your bed with a gut full of veal and saffron rice. You've been stuffing yourself the entire day. You'll be sick.'

'I might. I jolly well might. Chicken livers! Yuck!'

'Well, we'll find out, won't we? It takes about seven hours to get through your system. We'll see if you've been poisoned. The lavatory is at the end of your corridor. Convenient.'

'A convenient convenience,' he said brightly, watching to see my reaction.

I made none at all.

Aronovich was as good as his word, coped with the cremation arrangements, and left me to get on to the very understanding Vice-Consul in Nice. I sorted out the bank, and really almost effortlessly, it would seem, James and his mortal remains were disposed of without fuss or fury. I attended the brief ceremony with Aronovich. No one else was present apart from two young women whom we thought might have been nurses from the clinic. But we none of us spoke. It was simple, tidy, absolutely unemotional.

The last member of the family I grew up with was finally scattered to the four winds a few days later. I drove along the coastal road and pulled into a lay-by where I chucked the dust which had, I supposed, been James Elliot Caldicott over the cliffs near Le Trayas. There was no one there, no one saw me. The winds whipped and gusted over the sharp red rocks and the seething foam-frilled sea far below and then he had gone.

There was nothing now left of him. I'd already got rid of the shabby little holdall from the hospital and the bits and pieces it contained, even the old photograph of the family on the beach at Dieppe which he had treasured. The torn bit of label dangling on the handle was from an Hotel Amstel, Amsterdam, wherever that was. I just stuffed it all into a poubelle in the court under my window. I heard the dustcart in the early morning grinding away towards the square. And that was that.

After chucking the ashes I drove back slowly along the coast road and got to Dottie and Arthur Theobald's just in time for tea, to collect Giles. Dottie was in the kitchen setting Lulu biscuits on a plate. The kettle boiled, whisperingly.

'All done?' she said, pushing a strand of faded hair into the plait on her head. 'So easy, cremation. No fuss, no wailing. At least in this case, I suppose? Arthur and I have insisted on it. It's still not frightfully popular in France. They do so adore all that white marble and weeping angels in Catholic countries. Little sepia photographs set into the stone. Awful really. But it takes all kinds, doesn't it? They say it is burning the soul but I don't know.'

I turned in the paper flap on the biscuit packet. 'I suppose that James must have had a soul to burn?' I said. 'Must have. He was a painter. He did appreciate light, colour, design. He just wasn't very good at expressing what he felt from what he saw. Distilling, do I mean? Rendering the emotion on to canvas. Couldn't transfer what he felt from what he actually saw. Something on those lines. Perhaps he never really "felt"? His work was frighteningly angry, con-fused, often violent, or else just awful and bland. Like cheap Christmas cards for socially mobile estate agents and prop-erty developers. That sort of thing. Sometimes I wondered why he ever bothered. We're not an arty family ... I wonder where this not very gifted talent came from? Odd, isn't it?'

Dottie had set everything on a tray, told me to bring the teapot and the plate of biscuits and we went out on to the terrace. Arthur and Giles came down the dirt path from the aviaries together, this time talking in French, to my satisfaction. But of course I couldn't be sure that the conversation hadn't started the instant they heard me call up to them to join us. However, it was a short burst of animation, and they were laughing. Giles had a hand held high above his head.

'Was it very sad? Going to collect his ashes? Was it?'

I said not really, but he wasn't much interested because he had a small white egg in his hand, lying like a fat pearl on his open palm for me to see. I said it had all been very easy, and he said that the egg came from a Senegal parrot which Arthur had given him because it was cracked and wouldn't turn into another Senegal parrot. Which was a bit of a pity. After this scintillating piece of news, he shut up and got on with his tea and Arthur said he understood that we'd been moved into the Pavilion and was it awful? And I said that we had indeed, and that it was. We had spent a few moderately anguished nights there in the stench of size and cheap super gloss paint, plus the sour smell of bill-sticker's paste, because they had wallpapered the place as well, the evening before.

'Surely they didn't wallpaper the whole place, did they?' Dottie's eyes were bright with mild amusement. I said not all the room. Just the places where the old paper had peeled off rotted by damp. Nothing matched exactly. The paper had the same pattern all right, but was yellow instead of pink, but that really didn't matter because already three spanking new poteaux had been set along the wall at Jericho and all that we waited for now was the arrival of the engineer from Sainte-Brigitte with the lines and the instrument and we'd have a telephone at last. And we'd quit the Pavilion as soon as possible.

'I don't really want to leave the hotel until I hear something from my wife. She's almost bound to try and telephone me now. I got a postcard two days ago from Marbella, sent a *week* before, saying that the recce was over and that she was on her way back to Valbonne. So I have to hang about rather.'

Arthur broke a Lulu biscuit in two and dipped a piece in his tea. 'She obviously hasn't given you a number?'

'Ah, no. Helen likes her life private. She'll call when she's ready. No one at Directory Enquiries has ever heard of a Rhys-Evans in Valbonne or at the address I had on the card. So it's a matter of patience.'

Giles was watching me intently, quite still, his biscuit held in his fingers. 'Maybe she'll call tonight?' He put the bit of biscuit in his mouth, looked away. 'Perhaps she'll telephone on my birthday? She'll remember that, won't she?'

I have a feeling that I looked pretty blank. Dottie filled in my silence of surprise. 'You have a birthday! How splendid. Soon?'

Giles looked up at me with slightly raised eyebrows. 'I bet Will doesn't remember. You don't, do you?'

'No idea. None at all. Didn't even know you were having one. Sorry. When?'

'July. The second. The crab, that's my sign.'

'Very soon,' said Arthur sticking the other half of his biscuit in his tea.

Dottie said sharply, 'Arthur, I *do* wish you wouldn't do that. It is rather foul and a fearfully bad example to Giles.' And turning to him she said, 'Surely she'll call before then. That's weeks away. What age will you be? It's so difficult to guess now that you all wear these awful jeans.'

'I'll be ten.'

'Giles, are you sure? Ten? God! How the years have gone.' I set my cup down slowly.

'You weren't noticing perhaps,' said Dottie gently. 'Years do that, I'm afraid.'

'I'll be ten. I've been waiting and waiting to be ten, you know? It's quite grown up, isn't it?'

'Nearly. Not far off. You make me feel dreadfully old.'

'Well you are really, aren't you? What age were you when I was born, then?'

'I can't remember. Ten? Well, I was about thirty-six . . . about that.'

'Golly!' said Giles admiringly. Arthur snorted with laughter.

After tea we stacked the cups, Arthur and Giles went back to their birds and Dottie got a pair of secateurs and we went up to her rose garden.

'I'll give you some of my delicious Surpasse Tout. It's an old-fashioned rose and it has the most heavenly scent. For your Pavilion, to fight the wallpaper glue and awful paint smells, and, look, these Provence cabbage are glorious . . .'

'I feel pretty awful about Giles's birthday. Fancy forgetting one's son's birthday. Terribly important to him, of course. I've just had rather a lot to cope with recently. I know Helen thinks he's nine. She said so once.'

Dottie snipped away, cautiously. 'Well, he is. Presently. He'll be ten in a month, or something. He's so tall, one can't guess their ages. He's very handsome. Look, here's a smell-killer. Mind the thorns and the odd greenfly. They are brutes this year.'

We walked back to the house slowly. 'If you do stay on at Jericho, what about schooling? I mean proper schooling. Arthur can really only chat and explain grammar and so on. But he'll need maths, history and so on. Won't he?'

'He will. But just for the present, while I'm sorting out

my life, and his too, might we go on as we are? With Arthur? Is it a fearful imposition? Do say!'

She raised her hand with a swift gesture. 'Not at all! Not a bit, my dear Mr Caldicott. Look, I'm going to call you Will too. It's too silly banging on with formalities. Will, Arthur and I are childless, as you might have gathered. My fault, not his, alas. I can't carry a child. We've tried, God knows. So doing what we did, teaching, living with the young, advising, caring, even cherishing sometimes, did rather fill what might have been the dreadful emptiness of our lives. And even though we do love each other quite terribly, we both simply longed for children of our own. Isn't that silly?'

'Not at all. And I forgot my child's birthday. Until he arrived here two weeks, or whatever, ago, I'd frankly almost forgotten him. I'd grown apart from my family. Perfectly contentedly. Just forgotten they existed. Almost. One can.'

'And now? Any change of heart?' Her voice was quizzical, cautious.

'Complete. Complete change of heart. I'm getting used to it fairly quickly. I actually find that I like my child very, very much indeed. How's that?'

'That's simply excellent. He's a good fellow. Really very well brought up. He was not absolutely, shall I say, secure? Not secure, just at first . . . but I can feel that altering daily. Being taken into your confidence has had a very big effect on him.'

'His mother was a bloody good mother. Brought the two of them up marvellously. Without much help from me, I fear. I was pretty useless. Never wanted them, frankly. I was only anxious to make Helen happy. Rather like buying a puppy at Christmas to please the children and to hell with the pee stains on the carpet. Know what I mean?'

We had reached the kitchen door, clattered through the bead and bamboo curtain. Dottie filled a jug with water, stuck the roses in it, and then rummaged about for a ball of string and scissors, talking all the time.

'Yes, know exactly what you mean. So fortunate for you two. So fruitful! Oh God! I'm sounding wistful. Sorry. Well, just look after him, he does rather look to you for, ummmm . . . ? Salvation is far too strong a word. Help will do.' She tied the roses in a bunch, stuck them back in the jug. 'There you are, sweetness for the smelly room. Yes, take care of him. A responsibility, but very worth while. We'll do what we can for him. Until you decide to make proper arrangements. Don't think that it's an imposition. It's a joy. Honestly.'

'Thank you. I think that his mother finds him surly. And I think he probably was, and I know the reason now. He found that there were rather a lot of strange new "uncles" floating around. He didn't mind terribly at first until he discovered that they sometimes occupied my side of the bed when I was away. You understand me?'

Dottie put the scissors on a hook by the stone sink. She cleared her throat and simply said, 'Perfectly. That'll take a lot of forgiving.'

'I'm rather afraid it will. For both of us.'

'Perhaps Jericho will be a terrific healer? You know? A complete change-around. A new life. One doesn't often get a second try at life, does one?'

'One doesn't. No. Point well taken. As soon as Helen deigns to telephone, and I get the next hurdle, "Who Has Giles, You Or Me", out of the way, I'll move over to the house and just sit it out, with or without a telephone. We'll go over to Jericho now, poke about, see what's happening to the garden. I've not had any time since the sad discovery of my little brother. And now that is all put behind me I can worry about, well, invasive mint and seeding poppies.'

As we drove over to Jericho through the lanes in the late

afternoon, the air was sweet, the sunlight glinted and flashed on the new green of the vines, and threw deep purple shadows across the red earth ploughed and cleaned of the old winter weeds. Giles was leaning out of the window, his hair ruffling in the breeze. He was singing something under his breath.

I said, 'Look. I'm sorry about not remembering your birthday. Didn't even know you had one so soon.'

'It's all right. I don't mind. You know now. I'll be ten. Wow!'

'I know now. What about a birthday supper? A special event for being ten?'

'With wine?' He was instantly interested.

I nodded. 'With a modest amount of watered wine. Yes.'

'But who would come? We don't know anyone.'

'Dottie and Arthur? Why not? Madame Prideaux and Florence. What about that?'

He considered the list for a minute, squashing a bright green insect on the windscreen with his index finger. 'All right. They are all a bit old, but all right.'

'I can ask them. Eugène would cook anything you really longed to have to eat, providing it's in season. How about that?'

He nodded, folded his arms across his chest, leant back in his seat. 'Supposing Mum is still here. At Valbonne? She might remember it's my birthday. She always did. What then?'

'Yes, indeed. What then. We might, of course, be asked over to Valbonne, to Eric Thingamigig's house. I gather he's got a fab pool . . . so she said.'

There was a long silence. I did not break it, just let what I had said sink in. His voice was anxious. 'Do you think they'll still be here? In a month's time? Where is Valbonne?'

'I don't know. Not very far. It's a sort of smart village. Full of foreigners. He has the place there. "Villa Dafydd".

Very typical. When, if, she telephones, I'll find out all their plans.'

'But you won't say about my birthday, will you?'

'No. I won't say. If you don't want me to, I won't.'

'Because if she asked me to go, I wouldn't. So don't say. Please?'

'Fine. But any reason? Why wouldn't you go? A fab swimming-pool?'

'I don't like Eric Rhys-Evans. I don't want to go to his house.'

'Reason. You haven't said why. If I'm to make your excuses, if it should happen, I have to have a reason in my mind. Something. Not just because you don't like him.'

I had to slow down, turn right at the sign for Saint-Basile. 3 km.

'At home, when he came to stay, he took the key from the bathroom door so you couldn't lock it.'

'What on earth for?'

'Well, he said what if I was ill or something, they couldn't get in to help me. If I had a fit or something.'

'A fit! You?'

'He said. Sometimes he came in. When I was in the bath. He came in . . .' He was scratching his arm, looking away from me so that I could hardly hear him.

'Well? So what? Perhaps he wanted something, shampoo or something.' It was a pretty lame remark.

Giles knew it too. He barked a kind of laugh and then looked directly ahead, avoiding me. Suddenly he said, 'He was staring at me. Quite cross. He said, "What are you hiding there?"'

'Hiding? Were you hiding something? Come on, what?'

'No. My facecloth. I put it over . . . over me, when he came in. Then he said, "You are being deceitful! Stand up at once!" He was really cross. So I did. And he made me

43

drop the cloth in the water. And made me stand there . . .' Suddenly he wiped his mouth with a fist.

My heart had started racing. Keeping a very level voice I heard myself say, 'And then what? What then, Giles?'

'He . . . touched me.'

'Shoulders, head, where?'

'There. He touched me there. You know . . .' He was still looking straight ahead.

A goat suddenly pushed through the hedge, skittered about, I swerved, it pushed back again in a scatter of leaves. I slowed down.

'And? Anything else?' I was still calm, quiet.

'He said, "What a lucky little boy." I don't know why.'

'And did he go?'

'Yes. He went away then. I cried a bit. A little bit. I don't know why. So I only had a bath after that when he wasn't staying. Not if he was there, and Mum got furious sometimes. But I never said.'

'I'm glad that you said it to me. Thanks. I don't know why he did that. Perhaps he was just being . . . I really don't know . . . funny, jokey? What about that?'

'He was cross! His face was red. He squeezed me there hard. I hate him. You are my best friend, you don't mind I said that?'

'I'm very glad you did. I'm honoured to be your best friend. Thank you.'

'So you won't tell, will you? I mean you are. My very best friend. Of course you are the *oldest* best friend I've ever had, but you don't mind, do you?'

'Not in the very least. Thanks.'

But my blood was raging. Ahead another sign board. Saint-Basile 2 km.

We turned right with a screech of tyres. I was taking the corner too fast, but I knew that if I ever set eyes on Eric Rhys-Evans I'd end up in the Old Bailey. Guilty.

CHAPTER 3

The next morning I got up well before Giles, as I usually did in the Pavilion, and washed and shaved while he lay as if for dead. There was not enough room for the pair of us to move about with soap and razor or socks and shirts. So I got myself ready first and, knotting my tie, called him to wake up.

'I *am* awake. I've been awake for hours.'

'Why didn't you get up?'

'Nothing to do. What would I do?' He clambered slowly out of bed and shook his head. 'It's a really mouldy room this, and the lav's miles away.'

'I'm going down to breakfast. Don't take all day, I want to get over to Jericho early and I've got to dump you at the Theobalds before. Clean your teeth. Remember?'

In the trellis-and-rose-papered dining-room only Monsieur Forbin, the walker who had moved me out of my room, and I were present. He was pouring coffee, reading *Var Matin* propped against a pot of white daisies. We nodded across at each other. He set down his coffee pot, poured milk. He was about seventy, in stout walking-boots and flapping khaki shorts. Eugène came swiftly through the swing door from the kitchen with a small foil-wrapped packet and a half-bottle of Evian which he set on Monsieur Forbin's table, then brought me my coffee and a dish of hot croissants covered with a little cloth.

'The boy will come?' He hardly awaited my word of agreement, hurried away with a rustle of white apron through the click-clacking door.

A small dog careered suddenly into the room followed by two thin women with short grey hair and knitted cardigans. They were laughing quietly about something, took their places at a corner table with a scraping of chairs. One of them called the dog away from Monsieur Forbin's side, where it sat expectantly. He ignored it entirely.

'Dollie! Dollie! Viens!'

Eugène came in again with a tray of fruit juice in a jug for them. The conversation was animated, the dog sniffed about at Eugène's feet, with a little hiss he lightly kicked it. Then Giles wandered in, his curly hair now seal-sleek with water, his tie squint and the top button of his shirt undone. He thudded into the chair, slumped opposite me as Eugène swiftly came to the table, said good morning and would the young man like fruit juice or, perhaps, some tinned grapefruit. Iced?

Breakfast was eventually ordered. I told Giles to do up the button at his neck. The dining-room began to fill with a murmuring of new residents. The season had commenced with vigour. Giles watched everyone with intense interest, dropping crumbs and swinging his legs.

'Don't swing your legs at table. You're shaking everything.'

'I only do it when I'm thinking. I'm trying to understand what they all say. They talk so fast. Will you get me some more toothpaste today? If I have to clean my teeth *all* the time I use it up quickly. And this is my last clean shirt. Remember?'

Eugène came hurrying through the kitchen door with a

tray of metal coffee pots. He called across to me, 'M'sieur! Telephone! In the cabin.'

Giles looked up at me quickly. 'Mum? Maybe Mum?'

'It could be. You wait here.'

Madame Mazine nodded good morning, indicated the cabin with a bob of her head, switched something on the board in front of her.

'Attendez, Madame. Il arrive!'

In the quilted cabin, rioting with parrots in faded chintz, Helen sounded near, bright and quite unapologetic.

'*Didn't* I give you the number here? At the airport? Oh silly me! We only got in a couple of days ago. Just flaked out. God! It's a brutal job, but huge fun really. Are you both well?'

I filled her in with the barest detail. All that she really had to know and nothing more. She was kind, sorry about James (whom she had never met), and glad that eventually he'd been discovered, even though it was what she called a 'sad discovery'. I agreed.

'Well, anyway, William, now you know. I was beginning to think he'd just evaporated or something. Really! Pneumonia. People don't die of pneumonia now. They give them shots and things.'

I explained (avoiding all the true facts) that James had let things go too far, had been very run down and had become a recluse.

She sighed. 'Oh, God. I suppose because of the child? The Down's Syndrome business? Some people *can't* come to terms with that. You haven't asked about Annie, your *own* child, if I might remind you? She is very well, thank you. Mummy is buying her a pony! Quite mad. Now then, when can we meet? It's been absolutely ages. We must have a chin-wag. Lots to talk over. The house for one. *Me* for another. So when?'

'And where? I'm free, utterly free. Giles is at his tutor, I can be with you when and where you like. Do you want to come over here?'

I knew she'd rather die.

'Well, William, listen. Eric has to go into Monte Carlo today. Business. What about today? Lunch with me? So that we can talk things over alone. It really has been weeks . . .'

'Not terribly keen on coming to Valbonne, Helen. Can't we find somewhere –'

Her voice was over-willing, too hasty. False apology. 'Oh I didn't mean *here*, William! No. Eric can drop me off somewhere. What about Nice? Can you make Nice? I mean, I don't know how far away you are. He'll be back this evening, when we have to have a dinner at the Negresco for the American team. Lunch? Make lunch? Meet me in the Negresco bar half-twelve? All right by you?'

'I'm not far away. You seem pretty busy, so I'll come to the Negresco.'

'Super! Terrific! Explain to Giles, will you? That this is "grown-up time". I'll be in London in a couple of weeks anyway; we can all be together then. You'll be there too, won't you? Now that your "mission" is over and you've discovered where your little ewe lamb got to, you'll be coming home?'

'For a time. To pack up the house with you. Then I'll come back here.'

There was a slight singing on the line. A silence. When she spoke again her voice seemed to echo slightly. As if she was talking very quietly through a tin funnel.

'Back there? To *live*? You can't mean it! Anyway, let's do all the talking when we meet. Give Giles my love. Is he better?'

'Better?'

'Well, sulking, sullen, rude. He's been really awful.'

'Much the same. I can't imagine why, can you?' Lying was easy, suddenly.

'No. Hell. Never mind. I'll sort him out eventually. It's the growing-up stage, and you've never been brilliant with the children. Never mind, never mind. So! Half-twelve, the Negresco? I might take you to a super restaurant we know. It's in walking distance. L'Auralia. It's seriously expensive and wildly smart. You'll need a tie.'

'I have one.'

'Lovely, lovely. Twelve-thirty then.' And she hung up.

I stood for a second, the receiver in my hand, leant against the quilted parrots, heard the beep beep beep of the disconnected line and replaced my receiver. She was amazingly dated in her vocabulary and priorities. In her life-style too. Presumably she had found the one she wanted with Rhys-Evans? Revived it? It would make my news easier for her to take, I hoped.

Giles, in the dining-room, was feeding the wretched little dog with bits of croissant.

'Its name's Dollie. It's very funny, Will. Look.'

'Don't feed the thing at the table.' I sat down to my now cold coffee.

'The ladies over there don't mind.'

I turned and the ladies and I smiled at each other. They nodded and sipped.

'Send the bloody thing back, Giles. Get rid of it. That was your mother.'

'Oh. And? Is she all right? She in wherever it is? Valbonne or whatever?'

'Yes. I'm going over to Nice. To lunch with her. There is a lot to talk about.'

'To Nice? Not Valbonne? Am I coming?'

'No. No, you're not. She said to tell you that it was "grown-up time". I gather you are supposed to know what that means. It would be pretty boring for you anyway. We're going to a "seriously expensive" restaurant.'

'Well, I'd quite like that.'

'You're not coming. You're going over to the Theobalds'. Come along.'

'But *they* wouldn't mind. Dottie and Arthur? They wouldn't mind a *bit*. After all, I would be going to see my own mother, wouldn't I? Unless, he's going to be there too? Eric.'

'No. He's not. Come along, I've got to drop a note off to Florence. I thought I might lunch with her. Be seeing her. She'll be waiting to know about your uncle's final – well, where he's gone.'

With little grace, he got up and we left the dining-room just a little ahead of Monsieur Forbin, who had collected his sandwiches, the bottle of Evian and his *Michelin Green Guide*. I held the door for him, and he pushed through without a glance, dropped the packet of sandwiches, and got hit in the back by the swing of the dining-room door. Giles retrieved the packet and handed it to him. He nodded sharply, tucked the Evian under his arm, strode off in his boots and flapping shorts.

'Jolly rude, some people. I could have just kicked his rotten old packet all down the hall. Like a football. Couldn't I?'

'You could have. And I'd have clubbed you to death.'

He laughed and clapped his hands and we went into the lobby where I wrote a card to Florence, telling her that I had to go to Nice on family business and that James had been cast to the sea-wind, that I'd contact her that evening – could she dine this evening at the hotel? – and to leave me a message. Madame Mazine said that someone would take it over to No. 11 rue Émile Zola right away, and would I be in for lunch?

We drove over to the Theobalds' through the fresh green Provençal summer in silence: Giles because, I presumed, he was cast down by not being invited to a 'seriously expensive' restaurant or, rather more plausibly, frankly, because he had not been invited to see his mother again after almost half a month.

The sun was already high, sparkling and winking on the bonnet of the car, the fields yellow with sheets of pale narcissus tazetta, the tiny little dwarf ones, which seemed to smother the land at this time of year. There were small flocks of grazing sheep, elderly sheep dogs lying in the shade, aged shepherds sitting with their sticks, a woman in a red dress walking slowly up a track to a house, two small children loitering and pushing each other just behind her. It was a calm, serene, still summer morning. There was time enough here, and no apparent anxiety. Peace, ease, security.

How then, and when, to tell Giles sitting silent on my right, that his world was shortly to be thrown into turmoil? That his parents were about to divorce? That I would now be returning to England in order to sell up what he had always considered to be his lifetime, and pack it into boxes and storage? That he and his sister Annie were to be 'shared' between Helen and me, and that he would have to countenance a new 'uncle' who would, this time, not merely intrude into his bathroom but the rest of his life? At least, as far as I knew.

But it seemed to me wiser, kinder, and altogether essential that I should tell him all this before I went to seal his fate. He ought to know so that, at least, he would not be taken by cruel surprise when the inevitable 'grown-up time' had to be shared by him.

In some odd way, as if he almost knew my slightly anguished dilemma, he suddenly said, 'Will, would you mind stopping? I want to have a pee.'

I was so relieved to be given the excuse to halt the car and talk to him that I almost immediately pulled into a small space just along the lane under a tall cypress and a tilted calvary.

'You didn't say anything rotten! Wow! I was *sure* you'd say, "Why didn't you go before we left the hotel?" But you didn't.' He got out of the car. I waited for him to return.

Tell him straight out. That's what I must do. He was far too intelligent a child for me to evade the facts with euphemisms.

He pulled the Simca door open, shaking a hand with exaggerated pain. 'Ouch! Ouch! It's so hot already. The handle is red hot! And do you know? I think I peed right on top of a fat old toad, I think it was a toad, it sort of lumbered slowly into some nettles. It could have been, don't you think? Or maybe a hedgehog?'

'Giles. Now that we have stopped, and we're in the shade, I have to have one of those father-and-son talks. And I'm not going to find it easy, so don't interrupt.'

'About Dottie and Arthur? My French isn't good enough?' He shut his door hard.

'I said don't interrupt. Right? No. It's not about Dottie and Arthur. It's about your mother and me. I'll come right out with it, you have to know soon anyway. Mum and I are separating. We are getting divorced. Okay?'

He looked out of the car window, away from me, avoiding my, I assume, anxious face. He rubbed a finger along the edge of the wound-down window and said, 'I know. I knew ages ago.'

'*Ages* ago? How?'

'Annie. Annie told me. "They're going to be divorced." She said that ages ago. Before you came to this place. To France.'

'I see. Well, that saves me a certain amount of trouble. If you know, then, you do. How did she know?'

'She said Mum told her. They talk together, you know. They like each other. Secrets. I know they do. I don't mind.'

I sat back, slightly more relaxed, into my seat, stuck my

elbow out of the open window, picked at a fingernail. 'Has it made you very unhappy? You haven't shown any signs.'

He suddenly turned and faced me. 'Well, *you* didn't say. So I didn't know if you knew. You see I didn't know if you knew about ... about Mr McKenna, Mr Price, and Eric. But I did tell you about them. When I arrived. I didn't know if you would mind.' He looked helplessly away, stared out of the windscreen. '*Will* it be Eric Rhys-Evans? Do you think it'll be him and Mum? Do you?'

'I honestly don't know. I say "honestly" because it's true. I don't know. You know more about that than I do. You said his hair spills all over the pillows when he undoes his pig-tail. Right? And that he comes to stay at the house. Takes the key from the bathroom door. You said all that? Correct?'

He nodded very slowly. Put a hand over his mouth, looked away again.

'Well, it looks to me as if Mum quite likes him, doesn't it? More than the other, umm, "uncles" as you called them. And she's been on this trip with him to Spain, and joined his production team, or whatever, and if he stays at the house a bit more than the others I reckon that, yes, I reckon perhaps it *will* be Eric. I think he makes her happy. Does the things she likes to do. She got a bit fed up with the washing-up, the shopping, cooking, looking after us all ... all those things. Being a mum. You know?'

He nodded slowly. A slight movement. Hand still to his mouth, fingertips white.

'Does Annie like Eric? Do you know?'

He nodded again. Took his hand down. Placed it, clenched, in his lap, head lowered, and spoke so quietly that I could almost not hear him and was afraid to ask him to speak up. I leant closer to him. He twisted his fist in his other hand.

'She likes him. He brings her things. Lipstick. Once lipstick. And some scent. Mum said she was too young and he said a young lady is never too young for scent. He calls her Annie-Pannie. I don't know why. And he makes her laugh too.'

'Well, today I'm going to see your mother and we'll decide what to do about the house in Simla Road. We'll sell that, and your mother is going to move down to Eric Whatsisname's house at Burnham Beeches, she says. Did you know that? Annie tell you that?'

He shook his head rapidly, but did not speak.

'So, soon I'll go back to London, we'll clear the house, sell it, and I'll probably come back to live here. At Jericho. At least for a time. That is the rough idea anyway. Mum and I *want* a divorce. It's not because of "uncles" or that sort of thing. We decided to separate a long time ago. It's all quite friendly. We'll all settle down again. It'll be a bit of a jolt just at first, but I'm certain it'll be the best thing. Mum and I don't want to be together any more. It happens. People grow out of each other. We'll both talk it all over very carefully. Schools for you two. How to share you. Holidays and so on. We are thinking of what's best for you. Eric is jolly rich, very successful and I am sure you'll all get on pretty well after a time . . . it'll just be a bit difficult at the start. It's a question of getting used to each other, that's all.'

Suddenly, frighteningly, he gave a great cry, his arms reached out blindly to me, his face creased with grief, and howling, sobbing, he hurled himself on me, thrusting frantic arms round my neck. 'No! No! No!' he yelled. 'No!' His body hooped with rage, fists beating wildly, legs flailing, kicking, then he crushed his wet face tightly against my throat, hands scrabbling, clutching my shoulders, pummelling my back. His whole body bucked with fury or panic, and then, quite suddenly, he collapsed into my arms. Sagging against me like an empty sack, sobbing hopelessly, his strength ebbed away as suddenly as it had arrived.

For a moment he lay in my arms jerking in little spasms, whining like a wounded dog. There was no time now for theology, for parent counselling, for sophisticated reason. This was a devastating display of grief which had taken me utterly by surprise and it demanded instant smothering. Unquestioning love and strength.

I gathered him in my arms and crushed him tightly to me. He sought breath in sudden gulps, but I held him firmly until all violence had quite abated, the sobbing eased, giving way to anguished hiccoughs and, finally, his energy drained away and he lay still. I relaxed my grip, but still held him.

I was shattered that my (I had thought) fairly reasonable approach to a difficult problem should have provoked such a fearful outburst. Clearly all kinds of distresses had been building up behind an almost casual façade. I now understood that he had built his trust on me and that, unintentionally, I had kicked away the key brick holding up the scaffolding. I had never held anyone in such desperate distress before. I had never held my son before. This crushed creature cradled in my arms, eyes closed, nose running with snot and tears, lips wet, sagging open like a split fruit, was mine. I was now wholly responsible. I had betrayed his trust and must now regain it. I knew that whatever might happen to us, together or apart, that our lives would now be indelibly coloured by this moment of real grief played out in the shade of a giant cypress and a tilting calvary. In some strange way it was a Calvary for us both.

Slowly I released my hold on him, slowly he eased himself away, slid untidily back into his seat, head against the leather, eyes still shut, lay still.

'Better?'

'No. You promised. You *promised* me.'

'What? What did I promise?'

'The first time. First time you ever took me to Arthur and Dottie. That time. When you left, I asked you if you would come back . . .'

'And?'

'You said, "Always." You said that. You said that. "Always."'

'So?' I took a handkerchief from my pocket and started to wipe his face.

'Now you're going to leave me.' •

'I'm not. Hold still. You're covered in nose-snot. Open your eyes. Come on.'

'I won't go with Mum. I want to stay with you. You promised me.'

'Look, Giles. This is something your mother and I have to talk about together for your good, and for Annie's.'

'You said all that. If you go, if I have to live with Mum and . . . him, Eric, I won't. And you'll be sorry.' He eased himself up to a sitting position, pushed his fingers through his hair. 'I'll just kill myself.'

'Don't be so silly.' I stuffed the soiled handkerchief into a pocket.

'I will. I know how to. With a belt.'

For a moment we sat in silence. So still I could hear birdsong somewhere.

'Look. I've got to see this business through. Today, I mean. With Mum. We'll have to talk about everything. I'll tell her what you've told me. I'll tell her why.'

He suddenly looked at me with hopeless, bleary, eyes. 'About the bathroom?'

'No. *Not* about that. Yet. I won't say anything about that. I'll just say that you want to stay with me when we do separate and that you want me to look after you. Right?'

'Right. I do. But, I mean . . .' He started to pleat a fold on the knee of his jeans very slowly, sniffing from time to time, but otherwise apparently calm again.

'What were you going to say, Giles? "*I mean*" what?'

'If you're fed up with me? About the no soap when there was some, and all my shirts dirty, and Arthur and my French. If you are . . .'

'I'm not. Not in the least. You are going to make a hell of a change to my life and I may not altogether manage to come to terms with things, but I will have a shot at it. Somehow we'll make things work out, and I am not in the least fed up with you. You're just a bloody nuisance but I do love you. Okay?'

He allowed himself an exceedingly watery smile. 'Okay. But I won't have to go to live with them?'

'No. Not if I can help it.'

He looked up in startled pain. 'But you *can*! You can help it!'

'Yes. Yes, I can. Of course I can. I will. Now that really *is* a promise. Will that do?'

He nodded his head slowly and I started the car.

'Do you think you are ready? Dottie and Arthur? We'll have to get back to normal now. If we are going to work this out together, one of us has to be boss, stands to reason. And as I'm the oldest it's better that it's me. Agree? So let's get on with it all. We have a hell of a lot of problems to face. Together. So no more whining about dying and belts. Right? Clear?'

He wiped a hand across his face, rubbed his nose vigorously, shook his head and then nodded tiredly. I eased the car into the lane and we continued slowly on our way to the Theobalds'.

'That was bloody blackmail. You realize that? Crafty little bugger, you are.'

'It is quite easy, killing yourself,' he said calmly and with a half-smile suggesting that it was nothing now to be considered. 'Jones G.C. did it. At school. In the fourth year. There was a big fuss. But that's what he did. In the gym.'

57

'Does anyone know why, exactly, such a young boy should do that? At fourteen?'

'No. I don't know why. But it didn't really matter. No one liked him much.'

We drove on into the sunlight, spiralling dust behind us into the morning.

Dottie Theobald was planting a rosemary hedge. I was looking at my watch.

'He looks a bit weepy. You give him a whacking?'

She pushed a small spiky plant into a prepared hole. A long row of them going up the hill.

'No. Nothing as simple as that. I'm meeting his mother today in Nice to discuss a divorce and what we do with the house in London and all that stuff.'

She pushed her straw hat to the back of her head, asked me to hand her another plant, tapped the trowel on the edge of a bucket briskly.

'Always a bit of a problem, that. Fortunately I have never had to deal with it personally, but God knows I've gone through it with a mass of bewildered kids the parents have dumped on us at prep school. Whose parents are coming to the Sports Day? Whose father will run in the egg and spoon? And worse, of course, Mummy has a new "friend". Brought down for inspection. Usually a bit richer than Daddy. We were near Bourne End on the Thames, so it meant picnic hampers on glossy motor launches or shandy and smoked salmon at some smart-arsed riverside pub. You know?'

We sat down together. She had found a half-filled sack of tourbe, and made a sign that I should squat on it. She perched, not altogether securely, on the rim of the galvanized bucket and I told her exactly what had happened twenty minutes before in the car. She listened quietly, now and again pursing her lips with distress, smoothing the blade of the trowel, nodding in agreement.

'I don't know if I did it the right way. Or if I did *anything* the right way. I just did what I felt I had to do. Paternal stuff. Is that how it's done?'

She readjusted her hat, squinted into the sun. 'I don't know, yet, if it was the "paternal stuff". I do know that it was right to do as you did. He's too bright by far to try and hood-wink. I knew something had happened, so did Arthur. That's why he carted him off to what we both call the "school-room". Up there. With the round window. Keep him out of the way. They're doing *Contes et légendes* this morning. Very advanced. I am sorry for you, but we guessed that there had been a problem. You were late, and he had been crying. I thought perhaps it was something to do with your brother. But I think you managed to spare him much of that? And now his mama. Oh Lord! If she fights to keep him? What then? Clearly he wants to stay with you, but can you cope with a boy of ten that you hardly know? You write. You need a certain amount of peace and quiet, don't you? You can't be expected to suddenly go fishing, or wash his socks and neck. Or cook his breakfast. You know?'

She made it sound so idiotic that I laughed.

'No. I can't wash his socks. I'm not terribly good at washing my own come to that.'

She got up and picked another rosemary plant from an old Tide carton lying on the path, dug a small hole in the sandy soil, scattered a handful or two of tourbe in, stuck the root-ball carefully in place.

I got up and lifted the watering-can, carried it to her. She poured carefully.

'Water here is like platinum. We had a terrible drought for two years. I'm so late getting these in. You'll live here, I suppose? As you have told me. At Jericho.'

'Yes. I suppose that I have *done* the right thing altogether. For him and indeed for myself.'

'There was little alternative, was there? I am afraid, Will, that it is simply a question of responsibility. That's all.'

She handed me the watering-can, took up another plant, wandered to the next pre-dug hole.

'How long, Dottie, does it go on for?'

She looked up swiftly, her kind pale eyes glinting with wry amusement. 'How long does *what* go on? Being "Daddy"? Being responsible? Looking after them?' She did her little act with the tourbe, the hole, then beckoned for the can, which I handed her, and she stuck in the rosemary plant. 'That what you are asking?'

'Yes. That's it. How long does it go on?'

She raked the soil round the plant, patted the moist little hump, and looking at me over her shoulder she said, 'For the rest of your life, Will. Unless he does a runner or goes to Australia or the Antarctic, marries a Hottentot or something. Even then, you are never entirely free of them. Never.'

I sat back on the edge of the tourbe sack.

'Even when they get married to the most wonderful girl in the world and litter the place with their young they'll still hang around. You'll see. Bad luck!'

We laughed together. I suppose I looked rueful because she said, 'And you can't retract now. Not after this morning. You'll just have to see things through.'

'I will. Somehow. It's this bloody lunch I have to face today in a couple of hours. That's what I fear most.'

She threw the trowel into the bucket, it clanged. 'Some coffee?' I looked at my watch. 'You have time?'

We walked together up to the house.

'My first battle on his behalf. Today. Probably a fight.'

She pushed the bead and bamboo curtains apart into the kitchen. 'I hope you *won't* have to fight. You said it was an amicable arrangement? Very civilized? I feel certain that your wife will be flexible. Don't you? She obviously cares rather more for your daughter, which is unusual I'll agree. Mothers are desperately fond of their sons, sometimes dangerously so. But, of course, Giles was not first-born. That makes a subtle difference.' She turned on a tap and filled the kettle, went over to the arched doorway and called up into the shadow above, 'Arthur? Giles? I'm making coffee.' She came back and set out cups and saucers. 'I do so loathe mugs, don't you? Casual and careless, I think that they "taste" the coffee, tea . . . whatever it is. But this is only instant.'

She removed her straw hat, stuck it on the nail in the wall by the scissors. 'Ah! Now that your wife has telephoned you, I suppose you can go over to Jericho?' She put out a sugar bowl, spoons, fiddled with the plait on her head, stuck in a slipping hairpin. 'Get you both out of that Pavilion place. It sounds awful. Not a terrific help to a new father-and-son relationship. Altogether too intimate.'

The kettle boiled, coffee was spooned, and the sound of Arthur's boots clattering on the stone stairs came down to us. He was smiling, in a faded denim shirt, the baggy shorts, the laceless boots. Giles was behind him. Unsmiling. His eyes a little red, his face slightly puffy, he was quite steady. Hidden anxiety lurking. I was sitting in a rush-bottomed chair at the end of the table. I raised a hand towards him and he came, almost cautiously, towards me and took up a position of guard by my chair. He didn't take my offered hand, but leant with his full weight against my thigh.

Arthur said, 'How's the rosemary hedge?' He was filling a silence with pleasantry. I said it was starting to look like a hedge already, almost half planted. 'Eighteen inches apart? I've said to Dottie it's too wide, but she insists that's what the *Readers' Digest* gardening book suggests. A maximum five foot spread? Sounds right, I suppose?'

Giles put his hand on my shoulder. The slight movement

61

did not escape Dottie. She flicked a sharp look up, and away.

'I've got to scatter bonemeal about,' she said. 'I should have done it before, in the holes. Never mind. Coffee? Giles? Or a Coke?'

He shook his head, said nothing. Arthur dropped a sugar cube into his cup.

'I suppose you'll be off to Jericho now, eh? I mean, your wife has contacted you. So you can nip off? I know I would. But I wouldn't count on the engineer from Sainte-Brigitte arriving with the Instrument, as they call it, for a while. Tardy fellows. All telephone engineers are.'

Giles kicked the heel of his trainer with one foot, a slight movement which did not prevent him from sliding his hand on my shoulder into a more possessive position, round the back of my neck.

'I'll be out of that Pavilion', I said, 'as soon as I can get out. The sooner the better, telephone or no telephone. We'll just hunker down, as they say. And wait.'

Giles said very quietly, '*Who* says "hunker down"?'

'I don't honestly know. I've heard it. Do you know, Arthur?'

He was stirring his cup. 'Cowboys, I'd imagine? Don't they hunker down round the camp fires or something? Chewing buffalo steaks? Or is it beans?'

'Probably. Cowboys. All I mean is that we'll be patient, and just wait.'

A slightly strained little meeting. One could have considered it useless, but in fact it had been carefully engineered by Dottie. It had brought Giles and me together, allowing a moment of bonding between us, and it had given him extra time to allow the grief which had ravaged him seep away. He stood attached to me, literally, and possessively.

The conversation turned easily to Florence. And had I been able to tell her about the disposal of James's ashes? I said that it had been agreed that she be left quietly on her own for a while, until everything had been tidied away and that I'd left a note to ask her to meet. Now that things were all clear, that the winds and sea had carried the last human vestiges of James away into space, we could all restart our lives. It had been, as Arthur said ruefully, a 'quite astonishing few weeks'.

I had parked the Simca in the shade of a stand of carefully pruned bay trees, tall walking-sticks with feather-duster tops. Giles came with me to the car, wandering, as if there was no hidden urgency, or anxiety. His hands thrust deep into the pockets of his jeans, he leant against a lichened stone figure of a goddess, prodding the gravel at his feet with the toe of a trainer carefully, not looking at me. I got into the car, started up, sat there with the engine quietly running.

'I'll get you some toothpaste, all right? And a couple of extra shirts, and tomorrow we pack up. Move over to Jericho.' I opened the glove-pocket before me. Under a pile of maps and an opened packet of fruit-gums lay, concealed, the ancient key to the house: the same key which had thumped on to the doormat, many weeks ago, in Parsons Green.

Now it carried no label, no sign of what it might be used for, or what it might open and reveal. No one would be tempted to steal it: it was old and long and too heavy to carry around in a pocket, not heavy enough to cosh anyone. I held it up, wagging it between forefinger and thumb.

'Here's the key to Jericho. Want it? Take charge of it for me? It might just get pinched in Nice . . . in the *parking* or wherever. Lots of villains there. Mafia. Don't want to risk that, do we?'

He straightened up, then a very small smile broke at the corners of his mouth. He took the key and held it in his fist.

'I'm only ten, on the second. Not twenty-one! And I've got the key of the door.' He laughed suddenly, easily, joyfully.

'Cor, what presumption! So you have. And I forgot to say anything about your birthday supper to the Theobalds. Mention it, will you? I might forget again. Just tell them the second, informal, at the Maison Blanche.'

'But that's a month away! Ages.'

'I know. But they're pretty busy, so get in quickly, then they can't very well refuse. I'll do it formally, but in case I forget. You know? Do that?'

He stood there by the lichened figure, polishing the key slowly on his sleeve.

'You hear me?'

He nodded, looked up, smiled, waved the key.

'Now belt off to your school-room. Do a bit of work. I am paying good francs for these lessons.'

'We're not going to do any lessons. We're all going to Fréjus to the Safari Park. The giraffes and hippos. You're not supposed to know.'

'Then I don't. Tell Arthur I'll be here at five to collect you. All right? *Five.*'

I didn't wait for him to reply, pulled out of the shade of the bay trees and slowly began to bounce and crunch over the hard-packed ruts of the track to the lane. Clever old Arthur! Of course he wouldn't try to shove *Contes et légendes* down the throat of a child who had just discovered his future to be in question and his very existence in jeopardy. Giraffes and hippos. Of course!

I watched him through the rear window, saw him turn away and run back to the little house unaware that the key which he held triumphantly above his head had not only opened the door to his probable future (or the start of it at any rate), but that it would also be responsible for the overturning of a number of well-ordered apple-carts presently awaiting my arrival in Nice.

I was absolutely determined to do as much damage in the marketplace as I possibly could during the progress of the day.

CHAPTER 4

She was sitting at a corner banquette, a flute of champagne and a bowl of pistachio nuts on the table before her. She hadn't changed at all, and after only a six- or seven-week separation there was no reason to suppose that she would, except she was now very brown, trimmer somehow, her hair piled high, fixed on top with a wide black velvet bow. Guerlain scent, careful make-up, silk shirt, pearl ear-rings, good shoes. The Drab of Parsons Green, as she had called herself on occasion, had fled. Helen was back to the woman she had been before we married. She was not, I could easily see now and much, much too late, the marrying kind. Somebody's expensive mistress was her line, to hell with domestic bliss.

I ordered a flute, accepted her slightly cool kiss on both cheeks and sat beside her. She lit a cigarette, waved a thin tendril of smoke under my nose. Playfully.

'Started again. You mind?'

'Not a bit, of course not.'

'It doesn't drive you mad? You smoked so much. Three packs, was it?'

'About. You look really splendid. Work suits you.'

She raised her flute, took a sip, set it back on the table,

grinned at me. 'It suits me fine. It all started to come back to me. At first I was shit scared that I'd lost it all, lost my touch. You know? But not a bit. Everyone was very patient and kind and Eric was amazingly encouraging and I just swam in again. Terrific!'

'Great. Good. I'm really glad. And have you finished? I mean in Marbella.'

'The recce, yes. The shoot won't be until October. Cooler and the light is kinder. And you? *You* look terrific, if I may be so bold, I mean you look seriously glam! Brown, lean, boyish . . .' She laughed, smothered it with a ringed hand. 'Perhaps we got away from the London grind just in the nick? What do you think? And now you say you'll stay here? Amazing!'

'*I* think so. I agree, I think we *did* get away. In the nick. It was a lucky moment when that key fell on the doormat that morning. Very lucky indeed. For us both.'

She took up her glass, serious eyes, both hands to the flute, red-tipped tendrils curling. 'Was it all ghastly? Finding the "ewe lamb" and all that? Awful, I suppose.'

And so I told her. Carefully edited, giving her a fairly distorted view, quite deliberately, of James's life, wife and times. But when I had finished, up to and including the trip to the clinic but excluding the true diagnosis, she looked very correctly grave, flicked her cigarette into the ashtray, then apparently decided to stub it out.

'A funeral? I suppose so. You went, of course, good old loyal you. His wife? Was she destroyed? Suppose so . . . Of course, I never knew him, but I suppose, being so much younger than you, he was really very young. It seems so much more terrible to die young.'

'It is. There was a cremation, but she didn't attend. I collected his ashes and got rid of them.'

'*Rid* of them? You didn't bury them? Graveyard, flowers, all that stuff? *Rid* of them?'

'Chucked them into the sea. Scattered them. He's quite gone now.'

For a moment she looked at me in calm surprise, then she shook her head and laughed gently. 'Honestly, you Caldi-cotts. You *are* a rum bunch. Chucking your little brother's ashes into the sea. Honestly! You really are weird. I see now where Giles gets his moods from. You know, William, I don't go along with the pneumonia bit. It was something else, wasn't it? Only you don't want to say? Right?'

'Viral pneumonia on the death certificate. You can browse through the papers with the Vice-Consul. Here, in Nice.' I took a sip of my wine. 'A most caring chap.'

'I feel certain he is.' She fixed an ear-ring. 'How is Giles anyway? I told you Annie is in fine form? My mother is buying her a pony? Madness of course, as I said, but she's given up the ballet idea and now wants us to use her proper name, Annicka. Longs to be a show-jumper; first a groom, get trained properly, then she's all set for Hickstead! God! And my surly son? At a tutor? Very posh, and not before time either.'

She had obviously decided to give up pursuing the cause of James's death, using her common sense instead, so now we were moving towards family matters which she could more easily comprehend. She had never met any of my family. They had all died before we married, except, of course, James. So now that we had got over the obligatory, and polite, preliminaries, we must consider the hurdles of our own life. It was littered with them as far as I could see. A veritable Hickstead indeed. Or, I wondered vaguely, Aintree?

I briefly told her how well Giles had settled down, was doing with French, that he had gone through all his shirts and toothpaste, and then she finished her wine and said briskly not to worry about that, Mummy was back for the time being, and that she'd take care of shirts and things. She was glad that she had packed him enough to come out with, and when was I planning to return to England now that my 'mission' had been accomplished? I surely had no reason to stay on, had I? We simply had to come to terms with putting Simla Road on the market, and getting things into store, or whatever I wanted to do with the stuff. We had to move pretty quickly because the Festival started on the 26th of June, and that was not so far ahead.

'What festival?' I finished my wine and set down my glass.

'The Television Advertising Festival. It's always in June, and VideoEuropa, that's Eric's company, is a strong contender for the Golden Camera this year. It's a huge booster for whoever wins.'

'I am sure it is. But what has that to do with you? I mean directly? And with Simla Road and all the rest of it? Why the rush?'

'Well . . . Oh, don't be silly, William. I want to *be* there. Be with the company. You don't think I'd pull out on him, do you?'

'You don't seem to mind pulling out, as you call it, on me? Who's been at the house while you've been away? It hasn't been absolutely empty all this time?'

'Two weeks! And no it hasn't! Are you mad? I told you time and again. Mrs Nicholls goes in every day and Maureen Cornwall and Chris have the key and keep an eye on the place, and anyway it's like a bloody fortress! Fort Knox!' She felt about for her bag on the banquette, asked me to get the bill, and stood up briskly. She had brought this move to an end.

Walking through the marble pillars and glittering doors, she said, quite suddenly, 'We'll go up to Eric's suite. It's no use trying to discuss things with you in a restaurant. You are sliding into one of your stubborn moods, I can tell.'

She went over to the desk and asked for a key. By

number. I went with her in silence to the lifts, up to the third floor.

Eric Rhys-Evans's suite was very splendid. A sea view naturally, palms, yachts, sea, a mass of flowers, tuberoses, malmaisons, and spiky birds of paradise everywhere. The room was heavy with sickly scent.

Helen moved swiftly to close a door, but not before I saw a pair of her evening shoes spilled by the leg of a gilded chair. 'Ring for room service and get a menu? I'll fix the drinks.'

There was wine in a bucket. Ice clattering and sliding, she struggled for a moment, and I let her, with the cold bottle, then she thrust it at me to open, while she arranged two glasses.

'Of *course* I didn't leave the house empty. You knew that. You really are bloody sometimes! You knew I was going to Eric, that I was giving everything over to you, house, furniture, stuff. You knew!'

'Yes. I know that. We agreed all that a long time ago. Just seems rather a lot to do, packing up, selling houses, sorting ourselves out, all before some bloody Festival in a couple of weeks' time.'

Then room service answered and I asked for the menu.

'Certainly, Monsieur Reeze-Evans, right away,' the voice said.

'Is this your chum's permanent squat? The Negresco?'

'No, it is not. He has to give a dinner tonight for the American side of VideoEuropa, VideoUS. And wives. It's easier here than at the house. They know him here and take care of everything.'

'Obviously.'

'I don't know why it's "obviously", but I can detect the snarl. Your dry wit.'

'I really didn't mean it to be a snarl. Sorry.' I poured the wine carefully because she had shaken it up in her struggle to open it and it was mostly foam. 'Krug!' I said in a faux-reverent voice which she apparently accepted as quite normal. 'Mr Rhys-Evans must be *very* rich.'

'He is. Very. And I enjoy that.' She took her glass and went over to the open windows, leant against them, the light breeze billowing the thin net curtains. 'I know you hate him. Hate the idea of him. But he just called one evening when you were away. Just after you left. I'd met him quite by surprise one evening at the Cornwalls'. A drink before dinner. He asked what I was doing, that's all.'

'And you told him, of course?' I had settled into the twin of the gilded chair in the bedroom. Everything was Louis Quelquechose and faux-Lalique in the suite, all very sparkling. She turned and came back into the room, arms folded, the flute in her hand, her brow slightly furrowed with, I presumed, anxiety. Or else irritation? Difficult to tell at this moment.

'Yes. I told him. I said we were . . . well, separating . . . that I would need a job. Something like that. A joke really.'

'Which? The separating or the job?'

'The job. The separating has never been a joke. I have meant that ever since that god-awful discussion we had in March; the "clearing of the air", as you so succinctly put it.'

'And he had a job for you up his sleeve? Good timing.'

She sat down opposite me just as room service arrived with two large cards and the wine-list bound in red leather. He bowed and handed her a menu.

'Bonjour, Madame Reeze-Evans,' and turning to me with a faint nod handed me one as well. I asked him to give us quarter of an hour and he left huffily in a swift little patter of feet.

'Taken the vows already, I gather?'

'I've never seen that idiot before in my life. He just assumed that you were Mr Evans. William, I am going to be absolutely honest with you. I am determined to make this second chance of a job – of a life, if you like – work. Eric thinks I can make it, I know I can. I love it all, I can manage it. At the very start I thought I might have been too old, they'd want someone younger. But I fought that, and I've won. And I am going to go on winning. All I need is a bit of extra luck. Just a teensy-weensy bit. You agreed, as you must remember, that we both *wanted* to separate, that it would be by mutual consent, no ugliness, you said, just "pack it in", I believe was your exact expression, and I agreed. We have had fourteen years together. Some of it was great. Some of it has been absolutely dreadful and I want out before I am too old to start again. Is that so wrong?'

'No, it's not at all wrong. It's just that things, since we made those arrangements, have altered just a "teensey ween-sey" bit. In – what is it? – six, seven weeks, say two months, we have both managed to do something rather unexpected.'

She got up and refilled her glass, turned towards me holding the Krug bottle by its body. 'Unexpected? What do you mean, William? Be simple.'

'Well, simply put, we have both of us met someone else. We didn't expect that to happen then, did we?'

She poured wine into my offered glass, settled it back into the ice-bucket. 'Someone else? You mean, *you* have? Here?'

'Yes. I have. Here. That was not on the agenda, was it?'

'I don't think I really understand you.'

'Well, you found, or perhaps you refound, Mr Rhys-Evans, which is most fortunate for you, and I have met someone too. "Refound", you could also say.'

'Oh William! *William*. I'm amazed, but I'm *really* de-lighted! I mean it's quite wonderful for you.' She obviously was pleased, the furrows had gone, her smile was kind, warm, relieved. There could be no problem now about a speedy, mutually agreed divorce in her mind. Her chance of hooking Mr Rhys-Evans seemed more and more likely. 'It is so super for you! I really am glad. Is she younger than you? Must be. Oh, super!'

'Younger. And not a she.'

For a moment, just as she was about to sit, the menu in her hand, she froze.

'Not a she?'

'It's a boy. I'm afraid.'

She sat suddenly, spilled her wine. '*A boy!*'

'A boy. Yes.'

She put the menu on the floor at her feet. 'William! Oh God. Well, I don't know what to say, really. I really don't. But well, if it's something which will make you happy. You have – you have thought about it? What it will mean to all your friends? To the children? William?'

I nodded kindly. 'I have thought about it. Yes. I know what it'll mean. What I will have to give up. Change my whole life-style around. People will talk. It was completely unexpected, I never thought for one moment that I was the kind of man who could even remotely accept a situation like this, it just suddenly exploded and – you must know how it is, I was lost. I think I'm quite besotted. It's frightful.'

'Oh, William. It is, well, it's a bit amazing. I don't quite know what to say.' She looked away helplessly. 'But I hope I'm saying the right thing . . . I just pray that it'll be, for you, huge happiness. I mean this is seriously important. At your age, it is such a ghastly risk.'

'I know. I know. A dreadful risk. Don't think I haven't spent hours worrying about it. After all, as you very well know, I'm over forty – well over forty – and I'm not really in the habit of, well . . . you know?'

Her warmth was suddenly radiating like an electric fire, her smile generous and caring, a Botticelli Madonna. She put a hand on my arm sweetly.

'I *have* to be happy for you. I *have* to be. Simply have to be. You said that, well, like Eric and me, you had refound this person. Refound?'

'Yes. Amazing. I've known him for years. Ten almost, to be exact.'

'Ten!' Her good green eyes were wide with surprise. 'Ten! And you never said?'

'I never knew. Was quite unaware.'

'Oh, my dear. How extraordinary. Then is it anyone I . . . anyone I would know?'

'Oh yes. Very well. Giles,' I said, as the door opened and the pattering waiter asked if we were ready to order.

'A cruel and witless thing to do! Honest to God. Winding me up. You really *are* bloody, I feel a complete idiot and that delights you, I know.'

'Not in the least! Helen, dear, you simply misunderstood. I haven't lied or been underhand, I didn't try to make you feel a "complete idiot", not at all. I just told you exactly what had happened, how I felt, that's all. I admit it is a surprise. It took me by surprise. Totally. I didn't want Giles hanging around here while I was trying to discover what had happened to James. God knows I didn't. The last thing. And I'll admit, freely and with full apology far too late, that I realize now that I was a bloody awful father to them both.'

'Oh great! At last! Now we grovel.'

'I'm not grovelling, my dear, simply stating facts, I was too busy with my work, flogging the books, with trying to make a secure place for us all to live, to pay for school fees, mortgages, food and clothes – all that junk. Stuff I had never even considered before you and I met. I was a late developer, a happy bachelor, and I didn't honestly know the rules of the game. For that I am deeply contrite. I am going to do my very best now to make up for past failure. Okay?

Will you accept that? Remember, you sent him out to me. By Air France. To be collected.'

She prodded her already congealing half of an omelette, pushed it to the side of her plate, reached for the cheese board. 'Not much I can say, is there? It's a great moment to suddenly see the light. You hardly knew the children. Oh, a couple of ghastly holidays in some god-awful barns in France, the obligatory picnics on bitter beaches. You were as much fun to them as an abscess.'

'I know, and I am apologizing.'

'Ten, twelve, years too late.'

'Not too late. Just in time. Perhaps.'

'Well. The sooner we start on the alterations the better.' She cut a wedge of Pont L'Évêque, reached for the basket of sliced baguette, spread a piece with a lot of butter. Dottie, I vaguely thought, would not have approved at all, but the sharpness of Helen's voice banished reverie. 'And you had better start on your halo-polishing now. Get your backside on to a seat and start battering away at your "best friend", Mr Typewriter. You're going to have to dig deep into your pocket to pay for some more school fees, for your "refound" son, Giles.' She bit into the bread as if it had been my throat.

'Will I indeed? What have you in mind? Eton, Harrow, Gordonstoun?'

'Deadly witty! I don't remember you putting him down for any of those at his conception.'

'No. Agreed. I did not.'

'God knows you planned everything else for that event. You even got yourself pissed. Desperation time in the double bed. Talk about donated sperm! God!'

'Giles was a final effort to get us back together. Remember? Deliberate.'

'The "bicycle patch", you said. Your deathless prose, not mine, and then when he arrived hardly a glance in his direction for sodding years. You do make me *so* bloody angry sometimes.' She took a large gulp of white wine, her eyes wide with rage. She looked very fine; and was furious when I said so.

'What, then, have you in mind. Harrow, and so on, apart?'

'Eason Lodge. It's terribly good, expensive, but worth it. The Cornwalls sent Hector and Bobby there. They were very pleased.'

'Bully for the Cornwalls. Does anyone know? I mean does the school know? Does Giles know?'

'Not yet, and yes, the school does know. Dr Lang is extremely pleasant, so is his wife. He wants to see the child, obviously, as soon as possible, but I got all his reports and so on from St David's, and he was quite impressed. He also spoke with Mr Loder at St David's, who was very reassuring. Anyway, Giles has a place, all being equal, and he could start in the autumn term. September. That'll give us time.'

'Where is this school? Would I know?' I poured myself a brimming glass of Sauvignon. There wasn't very much else to do at the table. I wasn't hungry and I had to sit there listening to this tarradiddle from Helen. Until I was ready.

'I don't know if *you* know it. It's near Burnham Beeches, so it'll be very useful for weekends. He will board only during the week, and Annie is already over at Chalfont, so that's a huge help. Easy to get to for, you know, speech days, sports days, the school plays, carol-singing ... that sort of thing.'

'Wonderfully easy. And everyone will be at Burnham Beeches together then? I mean you and, whatsisname, Eric Thingummy, Giles and Annie.'

She did not flinch, just said quietly, '*His* name is Eric and *hers* is Annicka. Yes, we'll all be together. They each have a lovely room up on the top, views over the woods and fields, lovely. *And* a bathroom each, huge luxury! You must admit it'll be an improvement for them? Country air, all that stuff. Super.' She took another, less violent, bite out of the baguette. 'I have been very good and sent all my really personal things, clothes, books, my typewriter, processor, most of the children's things, down to Mummy's. She's got loads of space for storage. It makes it easier when we get to the packing-up stage. I've tentatively, only tentatively, put the house with Andrews and Fry. They're reliable, safe. It really rather depends on just when you'll manage to get back. Now that you've cleared everything up here.'

'As soon as possible. I suppose. One or two things here to set straight and then I'll get back. You really *have* been busy. Haven't wasted a moment, have you?'

'Well, it seemed the sensible thing to do, and especially now you've decided to move here. I'm a very good planner, as you know.'

'I do indeed.'

'Eric thinks so too, which is vastly encouraging. He feels that I have this tremendous flair for organization. That's what he needs, someone to organize things in the company.'

'Obviously that's what he's getting.'

'Seems a waste not to use my potential, doesn't it? I mean what else would I do? The children are pretty well grown up now, you and I have come to the parting of the ways, amicably, thank the Lord, and I really can't see me spending the rest of my days in bloody Simla Road. I have grown to loathe it.' She pushed her plate away. 'Sorry, but I do, and there is no point now in trying to pretend otherwise.' She got up and went over to the desk to press the button for room service. 'Coffee? Some tea? A tisanne, or a brandy? Something?'

'No, nothing, thank you. But there is something else . . .'

She was about to press the little button, stopped. Her hand frozen in space, index finger extended. 'What else? What "something"?'

'Well, you are right, we did agree it would all be amicable, the divorce, but I am not absolutely certain that it will be uncontested.'

She turned and looked at me, her hand fell to her side. 'What on earth do you mean? We agreed. Ages ago . . . weeks ago. We both agreed!'

'I know. But there is a small point to consider. You may not care to hear it, but Giles won't be going back to London, and he won't be going to Eason Lodge and he won't set a bloody foot near Burnham Beeches. That's all.'

She sat slowly in a Louis chair, hands in her lap. 'Have you lost your mind? What on earth are you talking about? Giles must do as he's bloody well told.'

'He won't be told to do anything. By you. And if you find that disagreeable and something you'd rather consider, then do. But he stays with me. He will not come back to you. That's quite definite. Understood? So if you want to contest any little thing just say so now. Time is getting short. Right?'

For a moment she was white with anger, then she sat back in the chair, her hands on the arms, crossed her legs casually, swung a foot. 'And who, may I ask, made this astounding decision?'

'Giles, at the start. Then I did. After he explained why.'

'What did he explain? I think you have taken leave of your senses. Try and be calm, William, and just explain to *me* what is going on. I'm rather slow, it seems.'

'He was rather distressed by Eric Whatever's pony-tail. To start with . . .'

'His pony-tail! You *are* mad!'

'The way it spread out. When he undid it. All over the pillow.'

She was still as granite, silent.

'On *my* side of the bed. Understand?'

78

She put a hand to her mouth, looked away, biting the side of a finger.

'He also found it very difficult to come to terms with other . . . little factors.'

Then she swung round. 'What other little factors?'

'A Mr McKenna? A Mr Price? I believe they are called "uncles"?'

She was visibly shaken, but managed, heroically, to sustain her cool and her dignity. 'And you believe all this rubbish? Tittle-tattle from an over-sensitive child? He's ten, for God's sake – nine. Of course I have friends, everyone does in my business. Douggie McKenna, Ian Price are good chums.'

'On my side of the bed too? And Eric?'

Suddenly she was flustered, waved a hand above her head. 'The silly little idiot should never have barged in like that.'

'Should he have knocked, perhaps? At his mother's door. In his own house?'

'It wasn't locked.' She started to flounder badly, clasped her hands on her thigh.

'Neither, I gather, was the bathroom on occasion. Am I right?'

Then she collapsed into silent tears, hands to her face, head bowed, shoulders shaking. The traffic from the promenade thundered, so I wouldn't have heard her anyway. I got up and pressed the button for room service and she fled to the privacy of the bedroom, slamming the door. Pattering Feet arrived, tut-tutted at the half-eaten meal, started to fold the table. I ordered coffee and a bottle of Heine, and he wheeled it all away. I wandered to the windows, looked down at the sparkling sea, the racing cars, skimming windsurfers, a boy running with a kite and elderly women dragging little dogs on thin leashes. Someone rolled past on skates. I'd gone too far. I had not meant to use the bathroom business until I hit a really sticky patch. But I'd just snapped and let it rip. No use now pretending anything.

Pattering Feet brought in a tray with the Heine and two brandy balloons, set all down and bowed himself away, closing the door. The balloons had a large gold 'N' on their sides. I poured myself a stiff three inches in a whisky glass, tapped on the bedroom door, called her name quietly. She was wiping her nose roughly with a tissue, dabbed at the skin under her eyes. I offered her a large brandy, in a whisky glass too, which she took silently. Then she went and sat on the high-backed gilded settee. She chucked a couple of cushions on to the floor, lay back.

'I didn't just meet Eric at the Cornwalls' for supper. Surprise, surprise. It wasn't like that at all. I remet him years ago. About four anyway. Behind your back. There wasn't a sudden pick-up. No one knew. The children. You. Least of all you. But it was very tidy, careful, it never harmed Giles or Annicka.'

'Until now. And, anyway, I knew.'

For a moment she let fall the careful guard she had erected. 'You *knew*? How, for God's sake?'

'Those little lunches you tripped off to when I was about, *not* when I was away in Rome or Boston, when I was just up in the attic working? I didn't think that those little lunches with "Muriel" or "Maureen" at Fortnum's or San Lorenzo were absolutely kosher. As far as I know they don't use the same after-shave as Eric. Do they?'

'How the hell do you know *what* after-shave Eric uses? How the hell – ?'

'It was always the same stink. After your "girls' lunches", and I was pretty certain they weren't all into Monsieur Givenchy. Right? Anyway, you don't have to tell me any more, we are only hurting each other needlessly. Let's stop.'

She pushed a bracelet up her arm, fiddled with a cuff. 'I

don't know what this bathroom thing was.' Her voice had become quiet. 'I only know I got really furious because Giles was so damned rude. Difficult. Eric didn't want any kind of problems when he was' – she cleared her throat – 'in the house. He said he wouldn't be responsible for any, well, trouble with the children. And if anything happened, a fall, something – or a bad cut – you see, Giles always locked himself in there, for ages. Refused to come out sometimes. Sulking. Silent. You can't imagine how maddening he was. He was a real little sod. So if he ever decided to do something seriously idiotic, locked in there. Well . . .' She took another pull at her drink. 'So Eric removed the lock. Simple. No problem.'

'No problem. Except for the boy.'

She shrugged indifferent shoulders. She was beaten and knew it, but her very vulnerability infuriated her. 'I detest sneaks. I brought up my children bloody well, and being a sodding little sneak was *never* on their agendas.'

'Giles didn't sneak. He just dropped a few bits and pieces here and there, quite unaware really, didn't even know he was doing so. Fragments which I picked up. There was no kind of conspiracy, Helen. Promise you. But when I told him this morning that we were going to have this meeting, to discuss a divorce, about which he already knew he said, because Annie had told him, he just blew a fuse. That's all. And if at ten you keep a whole lot of intense anguish bottled up for long then, when the bottle busts, it bloody well does. Everywhere. The whole thing explodes. It did this morning.'

'Anguish! Christ! He's a selfish, sullen, rude little boy. He needs a tough school, a boarding school. Eric should have given him a bloody good hiding, I always stopped him, but he really asked for it sometimes.'

'Over his knee? Good old fashioned thrashing with a slipper? Trousers down? That it?'

81

My anger was so obvious that she shifted about uncomfortably. 'I didn't say that. That's Victorian nonsense.'

'If you had allowed that to happen, Helen, I'd have had
Eric Whatever's *and* your guts for garters! I assure you.'

She got up, put her glass down and went over to the
windows. Stood there, silhouetted against the brilliant light
of the afternoon. 'I love Eric. I want to be with him. I want
to be Group Head of the company, and I won't let anything
come in the way.' She had raised her voice and was speaking
over her shoulder in order to beat the roar of traffic below.
I got up and walked closer to her. 'So just tell me what you
want. I don't want the divorce contested. I'm guilty, I admit
it. What do I have to do?'

'I keep the boy, you keep Annie. I'll make financial
arrangements for both of you, and that's that. We'll talk
lawyers later.'

She leant against the window, tugging idly at the blowing
curtain, not looking at me. 'I'm his mother. I carried him,
fed him.'

'I'm his father. And I don't honestly feel that you have
been the best mother he could have had, but let's not be
forced to go into that. In a court. Let's be grown up and
sensible. It's a fair division. You love Annie, don't much
like Giles. I do. Okay?'

'You don't know him. How tricky he is. You've only had
him for a few weeks, for heaven's sake. You don't know
what you're in for. It's totally idiotic. You can't look after a
ten-year-old child. You can hardly look after yourself.'

'I can try, and I'm about to. I am perfectly well aware
that I haven't taken on a gerbil or a hamster. Now, here's
what we do. I'll come back to London with Giles. I'll tell
him what we have arranged and you tell Annie. You can see
him whenever you want to, no question of that. We'll have
a very sensible, easy relationship, all of us. And I can see
Annie when I want. They can come and stay together here,

why not? There must be no kind of acrimony or stress when we are packing up Simla Road. You can tell your mother whatever you like about us. But just try to remember that once, not so long ago, we did love each other very much. It just happened to wear off. With use. Wear and tear. All right? We must put an end to the hurt and deception. For all our sakes.'

I put a hand on her shoulder, turned her towards me, tilted her chin up very gently. 'Now. No more. We have wounded each other quite enough. We both know what we each want, separately, so with the last part of our lives left to us, let's make it work for each other. I only wish you well.'

She moved my hand away from her face. 'You are asking a hell of a lot. Giving up my child. Christ!'

'Worse than giving up Eric? Group Head or whatever you said? Worse than another chance at life? Come on, be sensible.'

'Oh Lord, oh Lordy.' It was a sigh. 'But does Giles agree to all this? Does he know what you have so cleverly arranged?'

'He knows only one thing: he wants to stay with me. He is determined on that. He has been offered the choice. I won. Got it?'

She looked at herself in the full-length mirrors on the double-doors to the corridor. 'God! I look a fright. Six for dinner.' She smoothed her skirt, turned left and right, hands on her hips, patted her stomach. 'Is that all? Are you leaving now?'

I went to the desk, pulled out the little chair before it, handed her a pen. 'Not quite yet. You write all this down for me. On Negresco letter paper. Just say what we have agreed today. Date it.'

She laughed mockingly, shook her head. 'You really are lunatic. It won't be legal! It *couldn't* be legal.'

'No, perhaps not. It is just a declaration of intent. I somehow don't think you'll want to break it.'

I indicated the chair, gave her the pen, put a large sheet of letter paper before her; and, with a shrug and a half-smile, she sat down and started to write. I looked at my watch. I just had time to be at the Theobalds' by five.

Giles was sitting on a rock by the side of the track under the umbrella-bay trees. He was wearing a blue baseball cap and a yellow T-shirt with FRÉJUS ZOO in scarlet letters. I stopped beside him. He got up and came slowly to the car.

'You look exceedingly smart. Cap and T-shirt, eh?'

'You're late. Fifteen minutes late.'

'Sorry. Were you worried? I promised faithfully, you know. I had to go shopping in Draguignan. For toothpaste and shirts. Remember?'

He clambered into the back of the car, leant over the seat beside me. 'Did you see Mum? Was it all right?'

'Saw her, yes. She sent all her love. She's going back to London next week . . . in a couple of days anyway. And we'll be going back then too.'

'Going back? To London?' There was unease in his voice. 'Did you talk about things? About me?'

I told him that we had, that it was all settled, that he was going to stay with me, Annie with his mother, and we were all going to pack the house up together. There had been no problems, just that she was a bit sad if he didn't want to stay with her, but she wanted him to be happy. I chuntered on in as soothing and generous a way as I could manage. He seemed to accept it all. There was no scream of delight, no baseball cap in the air. He just sat perfectly still, a plastic giraffe dangling from his hand over the seat.

'Was she very sad? Mum. I mean, *she's* all right. It's just that . . .' He let it fade, and so did I.

Ahead the Theobalds' little house stood silent in the late-afternoon sun, the terrace in cool green shade. I parked under a giant olive, and looked over my shoulder at the yellow T-shirt.

'All right now? No worries? I think Mum will get quite used to not having you around. She's going to be very occupied with her job. With Rhys-Evans. I mean, you'd have been bunged off to boarding school anyway. She will have to be travelling a good deal. So in a way I think it has all worked out pretty well. Don't you? She loves you very much, and really does want what is best for you, and I said that you and I thought that being here, living at Jericho with me, was best for you. At the moment. Right?'

He nodded. 'Thanks. I'll see her when we go back? To pack up, I mean. I've got some things I want. My things. To bring here. But I will see her?'

I got out of the car and Dottie leant out of an upper window. We waved, Giles slid on to the gravel track.

'We had a super day at Fréjus. Really ace,' he said.

Apparently the storm had gone over. For the present.

Dottie had a bundle of clothing under her arm, a packet of washing-powder in one hand.

'I've got rather behind. Arthur's stuff. It was great fun at the zoo but it does take up rather a lot of the day. How did *your* day go? You look a bit weary.'

I followed her up to a small shed stuck on the side of the house where there were two concrete sinks. One for soaking, one for washing, she explained, turning on taps.

'You were very kind to take him off. Baseball caps and T-shirts. It was, more or less, all right with his mother; less rather than more. Fairly rocky, really. But I won. Thank God! I even got it in writing! Imagine . . .'

She sprinkled a spray of blue powder into the gushing water, steam rose, she dumped the bundle and stirred it about with a strong arm. 'Good,' she called over the rushing tap. 'I *am* glad. Well done. He's been a bit preoccupied all afternoon, as you can imagine. Really, that safari park place.' She dried her hands on her apron, turned off the taps. 'There are more wild beasts outside the compounds than inside. I can't tell you how awful Mr Marx's masses can be on holiday. Dreadful gobbling Germans with Nikons and Leicas. Fat, white British in colour supplement prints and brown socks in sandals. Overweight French from the north eating ice-creams, in curlers, throwing things at the animals. *At* them. One despairs. However . . .' She took up the pack of detergent. 'However, he liked it all. A bit surprised by the giraffes. They are rather tall, of course, if you are ten years old.'

We walked up the path. On a top meadow Arthur was pushing a giant mower. Dust and grass fragments whirled about him like a desert storm. Giles was just behind.

'He seems pretty well settled, you see.' Dottie was shading her eyes against the paling sun. 'I'm glad that you've got him. He's interesting. Far too sensitive really, but that's not altogether a bad thing, controlled and channelled. You'll see to that, won't you?'

I said I would, and realized just how tired I was. My legs felt as pliable as pipe-cleaners. Sensing this, probably because of my reluctance to speak at all from sheer exhaustion, she called up to Giles, waved arms, pointed at me, and steered me back towards the car. 'Off you go. Take him back, he's had his tea.' And then, suddenly, she leant up and kissed my cheek. 'Jolly good. I really am most terribly glad for you both. It can't have been fun, today.'

We had reached the car. I opened the door and saw the pink plastic Monoprix bag on the seat. 'I bought him some shirts. Couldn't think what neck-size he was. So he'll have to wear them open.'

Dottie laughed and pushed me gently towards the car as Giles came running down the track. 'Go back. We'll see you tomorrow. Off you go now.'

*

At the hotel, Madame Mazine handed me the key to the Pavilion and a white envelope and said how hot the day had been. I opened the envelope in the middle of the little lobby. It was from Florence. She couldn't make this evening but would it be all right tomorrow? She could be free (I assumed of Thomas) between three and five. Would I let her know? I scribbled 'Perfect. I'll be waiting' on the back of her card, sealed it in the envelope, and asked Madame Mazine to have it taken across the square and I told her that tomorrow we'd be leaving the Pavilion for Jericho. She showed no surprise, merely smiled, bowed, and put the envelope in the pocket of her pinafore, and I went out into the courtyard to the Pavilion.

'Can I go and watch the telly in the bar, if you are going to start packing and things?'

I pushed the key into the flimsy door. 'What makes you think I'll be *packing*? I'm half dead. I've been to Nice and back. It's a journey.'

He eased himself into the room while I opened shutters. 'You said we were leaving. I understood that part. For Jericho. Tomorrow. So you'll be packing, won't you?'

'In a little while. So go and watch the telly. I just want to lie down for a couple of minutes. I'm really rather bushed.'

I thought that he'd gone, and went over and crashed down on to my hard straw-filled mattress, hands behind my head, but he was suddenly beside me. He took off his baseball cap, chucked it across to his own bed, sat on the edge of mine, the plastic giraffe in his hand.

He forced it to 'walk' slowly, in staggered moves, up my chest. 'I really am glad,' he said. 'Thanks. Will it be all right to call you Dad, and not Will?'

'Perfectly all right. But why?'

'Well . . .' He fisted the giraffe and pushed it into the pocket of his jeans. 'Well, you really are now, aren't you?'

CHAPTER 5

Jericho lay still and silent, like a sleeping dog in the sun.

I stopped the car beside the mossy pillar which marked the boundary of the land, and Giles got out. We stood looking up the path through the potager, past the big cherry and the fig, to the long, low, rough-stone house, the two sentinel cypress trees (one for Peace, one for Prosperity), the green curtain of heavy vine falling from the iron trellis shading the terrace. All round the property the wall, which James and Florence had built so lovingly to secure themselves from the outside world. Their veritable Jericho Wall, breached now by tragedy and death. The little iron gate, sagging on a pair of rusted hinges, still carried the faded-paint name 'Jericho'. Almost casually, but determinedly, I pulled at the wire which held it in place and stuck the weather-silvered board under my arm. Giles watched me curiously.

'That's the name, isn't it?'

I pushed the gate open with a foot. 'That was the name. Is the name still, but I'm going to take the gate away. Leave it open, just a space. I don't think that we need protecting now behind a wall. Do you? Locked away? Seems silly somehow. Come on.'

We went up the path between clumps of marigold, purple bobbles of chives gone wild and drifts of mint. Everywhere cushions of scarlet poppies, which had sown themselves in the grasses with abandon. There were the two little tin chairs still on the terrace where we had left them a couple of weeks ago. Rust bleeding down the faded white paint.

At the door, the sign still under my arm, I told Giles to produce his key and let us in. A gesture, which he immediately accepted. We were about to take up residence at last. It would be his house now as much as it would be mine. And he had the key in his pocket.

The Long Room was shadowy. I began to open the shutters. The sun spilled softly and green through the canopy of vine outside, drowning the room in underwater light. Dust had settled everywhere in a thin film, there was a dead butterfly trapped in a window, a crumpled *Var Matin* lay hastily set down on the battered settee with its cheap Indian bedspread. It was dated the day that Aronovich had arrived to take James's paintings from the studio above, paintings which he had generously commissioned for his new hotel, the Commodore, in Cannes. An age ago it seemed. Life had concertina'd, had been crushed into a tangled mess. I'd have to sit down presently and take stock.

It seemed to me that ever since I had arrived in France, on my voyage of discovery, I had been forced to take stock every few days. I was in a constant state of vague, bumbling bewilderment. I had stumbled into a brand new, worryingly unfamiliar, existence. It was nothing remotely to do with my old, ordered, safe world of writing, alone in my Parsons Green attic.

For the moment, however, I had to get this present part of my life firmly based. At least until the next upheaval befell me. We unloaded the Simca, pushing through the lush sprawls of self-sown courgettes and thrusting nettles with what baggage we had. Not much in either case. I had brought very little with me from England in the first place, Giles had arrived with just a large blue holdall. But we seemed to have collected extra stuff and it was a good half hour, more even, before we finally got it all up the stairs and I was able to open the shutters all over the house so that clean air could wipe away the dead, mouldering smell of stale breath which always seems to loiter about a deserted house. Giles carted his stuff into his room, apparently making no effort to unpack. I had also brought a couple of plastic bags which Eugène had given me at the hotel containing a large baguette, butter, ham, cheese, a pot of cornichons and some bottled water. I confess I didn't know quite what to do at first. Stood in the middle of the newly fitted little kitchen, tapped idly, thoughtlessly, with a knife on the scrubbed table-top. Lost.

Giles said he was going up to the stream, did I mind? I told him to take off his shoes and go barefoot, which stopped him short for a moment.

'No shoes? It's all stones and things. I could cut my feet.'

'Time to start hardening them. You do with Arthur Theobald. Good for your insteps. Mind where you walk. We'll go into town soon. Get you some espadrilles. I'm going to sit in the shade under the vine. You clear off and don't drown.'

He *had* done some unpacking, it appeared. He was now wearing a pair of particularly ugly floppy swimming shorts, covered in yachts. He unlaced his trainers with ill-grace, sighed heavily a couple of times, and when I made no response, sitting on a tin chair with my eyes closed, he went away whistling. Well, well. A new life was starting: how to manage it? Simply consider it only as a summer holiday. June, July, August. A few days here to get things arranged, then off to London and get things arranged there. Then back to think in peace. Sleep, proper sleep, would be very acceptable. The nights spent in the Pavilion were hardly restful, and there was little chance of just lying flat and thinking, which is what I wanted to do.

After yesterday's collision course at the Negresco, I'd pretty well blundered about for the rest of the day in a witless manner. Just as, I supposed, one might behave having walked away from a plane or car crash. Numbed, only aware that there were minor cuts and bruises but that one's body still functioned enough to move fairly normally. Then I wondered what the new beds up in the little rooms above which I had bought in Futurama would be like. I'd only ever thumped and sat on them. Tonight I might sleep on one?

I was beginning to drift away pleasantly when there was a shattering sound, the shrill and insistent snarl of a car horn blasting. I opened bleary eyes and saw, to my mild dismay, Monsieur Maurice from the hotel coming up the path. He stopped for a moment halfway along, prodded something with his foot, put his hands in his pockets, shook his head sadly, then came on.

'Bonjour! Ah! I disturb you?'

I assured him that he did not. Not at all.

'You know? You have a little plum tree growing, by the path?' he said. 'You must move him in October. He will flourish, but not perhaps in the middle of your potager, eh?'

I agreed, wondering why he had come.

He nodded in the direction of the east wall, asked if I approved of the siting of the poteaux which his nephew and the friend had placed for me. I said that I truthfully had not seen them yet. We had only just arrived and I was trying to decide what to do next, which problem to attack first. I was finding it very difficult.

He took off his cap, scratched his head, replaced his cap and said he had a suggestion. Might he make it? Would I permit him to do so? I said that I would indeed. (What else? He had fixed the poteaux, probably fixed the telephone,

91

had fixed my Simca, courtesy of his brother-in-law, the ailing maire, so what else was he offering?) He bowed deeply, a wide smile on his bland, red face.

'You can be free of those problems! I have *anticipated* these problems! A fine gentleman, a writer, like you, cannot be expected to be the femme-de-ménage! So I have brought one for your inspection. Your *inspection*, Monsieur! *Only* for that! You are curious?'

I said that I was exceedingly curious. He stuck two fingers in his mouth and blew two sharp whistles as if he was calling a gun-dog. But it was not a gun-dog. It was Clotilde, from the hotel. The jolly girl who had cleared out the Pavilion and whom I had seen, from time to time, hanging the hotel laundry on the line under my window, and occasionally glimpsed through the click-clacking kitchen door in the restaurant. Clotilde came cautiously up the patch, twirling a poppy in her fingers with studied nonchalance.

Maurice waved a brisk arm towards her. 'Viens! Ma belle! Viens,' he called encouragingly, and turning to me he said that he now had the honour to present his youngest daughter who would be enraptured to work for me at Jericho if I so wished. She could clean and mend, wash and darn, cook and polish, she was agreeable and kind, unmarried and not at all interested in any tra tra la la and was someone that would serve me well and whom I should not lightly reject. 'Un trésor véritable!' She was also a devout Catholic. So I had no fear of employing a heretic in my house. Jericho, he knew, was a sacred house of love. He had known it all his life, he had known my brother, knew Madame Prideaux well, and was proud to offer Clotilde the opportunity of working for a famous writer, a man of the Arts!

Clotilde just stood there smiling pleasantly before me, the poppy in her hand drooping. I got up, nodded and smiled inanely. She was wearing a neat blue cotton frock, her hair pulled severely upwards on either side of her head by two pink plastic combs, arms folded demurely across her ample bosom which swelled beneath a spotless white apron. A sturdy girl, freckled, thick-legged, stubby-fingered, as strong as a fork-lift truck. Monsieur Maurice explained in a low voice that she was named after Saint Clotilde who had converted her husband, Clovis, King of the Franks, to the faith. So it was worth my taking note of her. She was a plain, but honest, creature, with, alas, little prospect of marriage, but she could split logs, wring the neck of a hen, and make a loaf as easily as she could make a bed. Surely I would be in need of such a paragon? He gave not the least sign that he was speaking before his daughter and as if she was no more to him than a brood mare or a pregnant sow. And Clotilde seemed not to notice either, merely smiled agreeably every time I looked in her direction, and nodded her head at every accomplishment catalogued by her proud parent on his thick fingers. I said (and I meant it) that I would be delighted if she wished to come and work for me, but that could only be when I had managed to get into town and purchase the things that she'd need to start her labours. Like soap, scrubbing-brushes, dusters and mops. Maurice lifted a stern finger of admonishment.

'Do not forget your Eau de Javel! Malheur! It is the life blood of any good housewife!'

I agreed eagerly, naturally. (Eau de Javel is a disinfectant used in France for everything from drains to wasp stings – of course it was essential.) So, when these items had all been bought, I'd let him know.

Maurice raised his finger once again. Alors! And nodding in the affirmative to his stocky daughter (who quickly turned and hurried off down the path), he assured me that they had thought carefully of all that, and that Madame Mazine (whose idea it all had been) was absolutely certain that I would be in need of assistance. A man with a child suddenly alone in a strange house in a strange land! All, all was considered, and she was most happy to release Clotilde from her hotel duties during the daytime in order to accommodate my more pressing needs. The language tended to get more and more flowery as we progressed, and then it was up to me to broach the subject I knew to be uppermost in his mind. What fee, I asked reasonably, would be acceptable to Clotilde? And should I pay her by the day? Or the week? How would she prefer to work? Ah, Monsieur! By the *week*! And by the hour. Six days a week, but not, of course, Sunday! Pas le dimanche! Otherwise eight until five, or whenever her duties were finished. She could be my bonne-à-tout-faire, except that he knew I had no room for her to stay at Jericho, so therefore she would be my femme-de-ménage-en-plus! A little more than that, because she would willingly cook and market for me as well!

'Her fee per hour, Monsieur Maurice,' I said in a firm voice, for I heard the vigorous slam of the car boot, and light singing as Clotilde made her way up the path, loitering a little by the gate, studying the mint and poppies with quite inordinate interest. (Obviously she was, tactfully, hanging back.) Briskly Monsieur Maurice thrust his right arm towards me, rolled up his sleeve and disclosed a scribble of figures in blue Biro on the inside of his wrist. I said, regretfully, that it was really more than I could presently afford so, as I began to show slight signs of perhaps closing the conversation, he instantly thrust forward his left arm with a more reasonable figure printed on a hairy wrist just above his Tintin watch.

This I accepted with a nod. He beamed, rolled down his sleeves just as clever Clotilde, conveniently, reached his side with a neatly packed plastic bucket of packets and cloths, a broom and a mop, and, in her free hand, a string bag containing a terracotta casserole. Madame Mazine's compliments. A little rien-du-tout for our supper this evening. She was certain I would not have thought to prepare food with all I had to do, and it was Sunday, so it was arranged that Clotilde would now tidy around, make up the beds, and begin serious work tomorrow. She'd familiarize herself with the house. He would call to collect her in two hours. Tomorrow the week would commence. We would arrange payment from then. Eh? I agreed, and with a happy smile and a clattering of utensils Clotilde strode into the Long Room and I walked Maurice down to his car. I thanked him for his thoughtfulness, but he brushed my thanks aside and said he was certain that his daughter would be satisfactory. I said I was certain that she would be, and that I would see to it that she was taken good care of. He told me not to concern myself at all.

'She is as stubborn as a mule and kicks like one too! Prenez garde!' And laughing happily, with a roguish wag of his finger, he slammed into his car and drove off down the lane.

Florence had the most beautiful feet I think I'd ever seen. Slender, small, brown, beautifully arched. She thrust supple toes into the long grass, her arms around her knees, head bowed, hair falling over her face so that I was unable to see any reaction she might have made. If she had made any at all.

'And that was it?' Her voice was cool, almost uninterested. Except that I knew very well that she was not.

I rolled over on my stomach, pulled at a long grass. 'That was it. Very simple. I just parked on the cliffs. At Le Trayas. There is a place. No one was about at all. Lunchtime. I just scattered them out over the rocks and the sea. The wind – there was a stiff little breeze – carried him away. Eddied him up and out to sea. He'd have liked that far better than anything else.'

She shook her head, brushed a hand through her hair. 'How did they . . . ? What were his . . . ?' She stopped helplessly, looked away across the neglected garden.

'That was all there was to it, Florence. His ashes were in a hideous little white plastic urn. I hardly noticed it. If they *were* his ashes. You can never be certain. I threw the urn into the sea as well. One day, perhaps, some happy child will find it washed up on a beach, use it to make sand-pies . . . and that was that. The end for James. There are many worse ways. I have done all the dull official bits and pieces, as I said. The Consul, the bank. It's over. He had no possessions, just the bag, some bits and pieces which Aronovich gave me. Apparently there was a watch which he liked. He sold it eventually. Had to. For nothing. But that was all.'

She lay back in the grass, arms beside her, eyes closed, her pale face shadowed by dancing flickers of leaves from the tree above us. 'It was a Piaget. He was given it by one of his circle in Paris. He was very proud of it. I hated it, but he kept it. How strange it all is, to suddenly realize that I will never use his name again. Never call to him. For his lunch or the evening soup, or in this garden. Never hear him laugh again. Do you remember his laugh? Very light, like a flute! And then deep, like a cello. Oh! Of course . . .' She rolled over on her stomach beside me, chin cupped in her hands. 'Of course I didn't hear him laugh for many months. Months. Ever since Thomas was born. The laughter stopped. But how strange things are. I still called him to his meals, still called his name, touched him. Even though he hardly spoke to me in the last year he was in this house, I knew the scent of him, I heard his steps, when his door shut, the bolt run in . . .' She rubbed her face vigorously. 'Well, it's done. I have his son. At least that. I still have poor inelegant, helpless, mongoloid Thomas. And I love him desperately.'

Looking at us both from across the dereliction of blowsy garden, it would have been perfectly easy to take us for a happy, relaxed couple talking idly about Bonnard or Leaf-cutter bees, or Gershwin, or simply the state of the Government. We could even, from a short distance away, just have been lovers. She on her stomach, chin cupped in hands. I lying beside her chewing a piece of grass. Discussing where to be married? Who to invite? What music should be played? But it was not at all like that.

'Florence,' I said, cautiously, with infinite care not to hurt her, 'I have told you this before. I know you understood at the time, but I don't want you to forget. I am *in* love with you. I love you very much indeed. Perhaps I am too old to use the word "desperately", but it is a strong love. I am stubborn and I'll be patient, as I promised you before, and wait. Until you are ready to consider me. Will you keep that in mind? At the very back of your mind? I will be there.'

I risked touching her arm lightly. She made no move, didn't even flinch away. Encouraged, I said, 'Your most difficult problem now is how to restart your life. I understand that.' It was a singularly unoriginal remark, and the slight hunch of her shoulders made it quite clear that she had hardly bothered to consider it.

'Boff!' she said. 'Boff!' And sat up briskly, brushed her skirt of dust and crushed leaf and said carelessly, not looking at me, 'I am going away shortly. To Marseilles. I'll take Thomas. Céleste will come too to help with him. He is so active and exhausting on a voyage. He thinks it is all such an adventure. Somewhere new, fun.'

I sat up beside her. 'When will you go?'

'I don't know. It depends on the clinic. On Dr Pascal.'

I heard myself repeat her like an echo. '*Clinic?* Pascal? What is this, darling?'

She looked studiedly across the garden, golden-hazed in afternoon sun. 'Just a few days. That's all. I can't do very much about restarting my life, as you say, until I know that I have one to live.'

Across the garden I suddenly saw Giles wandering about in his floppy shorts, a hand shading his eyes. I supposed he was looking for me. Us. I called and waved and he waved back and made a sign with his hands that he was going to get something to drink. Or eat. Drink, I think. I shouted out, 'Okay. In the fridge.' And to Florence I said, 'Marseilles? Why do you have to go there?' Although I knew what her answer would be. I had spent a long time evading the subject which was obviously in both our minds.

She was wearing a string of olive-wood beads, turned it round to find the clasp, found it, unscrewed the little silver ball, screwed it back again, rearranged the beads. 'To see if I am HIV positive. And Thomas. It is possible. I'll go to Marseilles, Dr Pascal's clinic is there. It is very discreet. If I took the test anywhere near here it would be disastrous. They make vicious gossip if you alter your hairstyle, or buy a "restaurant" instead of a "baguette". So I'll go to Marseilles. Mama has friends near there. At Allauch. It's not far.'

'Oh, my darling! I can't see that there is the *remotest* chance of you being –'

She turned to me quickly, her fine grey eyes flat with anger. '*What* can't you see? How can you even remotely know *what* situation I am in? How? Were you holding the candle during those months in this unhappy little house? What do you know about this disease? No one *knows*. They can only tell me if I am positive or not. If I carry the virus. And I assure you, my dear William, that *you* have no possible way of knowing that! Even I cannot be sure. And, you must forgive me, but I am *not* your "darling". As far as I am concerned, I have never been so, and never could be. You are good and kind, and I am forever grateful to you for everything that you have done to comfort and help me. For finding James, and sending send him into the "wind and the sea", as you have said. Your gentleness and tact have given me immense courage to continue. *But*. I loved one man. The first I ever loved, and the last I shall ever love. I love him passionately, no matter what happened to us both in the end. I always will, and I will cherish his child, until the day comes when he too must be cast to the wind and the sea. He is all that I have in my life, and all that I need. Thank you, my dear, good William, but that is all. C'est tout fini.' She got up slowly and I joined her, stuffing in the front of my shirt which had pulled out of my trousers.

'All right. I heard all that. But just one thing, please? Let me take you to Marseilles? Be with you, share this last wretched hurdle with you. Please?'

She put a hand on my arm, a gentle movement made to diffuse the anger in her words. 'You intrude, William! Don't! I make my own plans, I am quite capable. I am a colonel's daughter, remember? We are trained to cope. I don't need your help. I did not require it when you arrived, uninvited, in this place, I do not require it now. He was your brother, that I had to understand and come to terms with, but he was my "husband", however much you may mock the word. We lived and loved as man and wife. I shall keep his name and I shall cherish that part of my life for ever and ever. Nothing, *nothing*, can erase that.'

Through a giant tumble of going-over peonies Giles was waving something glittering in one hand, a bamboo pole over his shoulder. Florence and I turned and began to walk towards the little terrace where he was standing, legs apart, arms signalling.

'We don't speak before him,' Florence said. 'I will always remember your kindness to me with intense gratitude. Thank you.' And as we clambered over piles of yellow cuttings and dead weeds, she called lightly, and in English,

99

'My goodness! Giles! You are Father Neptune! So much mud, so wet! What have you caught? Whales is it?'

For a few wretched minutes we admired a glass pickling-jar of water weed and an hysteria of tiny fish. I suggested that he should throw them all back into the stream and he began to argue, so I clipped him swiftly on the head, then Florence turned and started down the path to the gate and her little Renault, at the exact moment that Maurice arrived in his car to collect Clotilde, who had come out untying her apron, waving happily to her papa, and suddenly my bosky garden had become a marketplace. People greeted each other, admired the catch in the pickling-jar, nodded and beamed, and it all broke up, and then there was nothing but a slamming of doors and revving of engines. Clotilde called something about sheets and pillowcases. As she got into her car Florence bowed politely to Maurice, who doffed his cap, and then slammed his daughter into the back of his car. Giles started to whine about keeping his fish for a little longer so that he could look at them properly if he could find a magnifying glass anywhere. And I suddenly realized that everyone was leaving; that Florence was walking firmly out of my life, talking brightly to Maurice, and that any plans, or ideas, I might have entertained for a possible future with her were now lost for ever, were fading rapidly away before my eyes in this brilliant afternoon light. I was being, more or less, abandoned. Left behind up on the beach with a ten-year-old son I hardly knew, and my dead brother's rented house in three hectares of gone-to-seed garden, and unpruned vines and roses. So much for the dreams and aspirations of a moderately successful writer. A lesson learned at last. One doesn't get to live happily ever after. That is simply a comforting invention for children.

Giles was clattering away up on the terrace with a bucket, spilling water everywhere. It seemed to me, stooping to tug up a clump of dumb-nettle, that I had lost out pretty well.

Helen yesterday in Nice, Florence today under the fig trees. The slate was clean. The shadows from the cypress trees fell like pencils across the rough grass up to the little orchard, the vine hung like a green silk curtain, cool and dark. Then cicadas started up in the bark of the olives. It would all be all right. I minded very much about Florence. However . . .

Water slopped down the terrace steps and Giles swore. I don't know what he said but it was born of furious frustration and damp.

'What are you doing with that punch bowl? It cost a fortune.'

'You got it in Sainte-Brigitte, at that stall. You said it was a bargain.'

'Even so. Why fill it up with fish and weeds?'

'It's bigger than the pickle jar.'

'They'll die anyway. Not enough oxygen. Put them back, Giles.'

'They could be grilse or something.'

'Then you're in dead trouble. Grilse turn into salmon. Come on, put them back.'

'Salmon! Wow! Can we get an aquarium then? One day.'

'When we get back from London. After that. I can't think straight at the moment. And when we get a telephone, and so on. Pour them all back. Has Clotilde done the beds, do you know?'

He began fishing out straggles of weed and watercress. 'I think so. When I tried to talk to her in French, you know, she just looked funny and went red. She's a bit batty.'

'That needn't prevent her from making up two beds.'

But she had done her work perfectly. Beds trim, pillows plump. Suitcase, hand luggage neatly stacked in both rooms. In the bathroom wash-bags, once scattered in a hurry, were tidy; toothbrushes in mustard glasses; new towels, one each, on the rail. I was glad to see that my new bed from Futurama looked comfortable and inviting in the newly whitewashed room. I had carefully set it up on the other side of the room; not where their walnut bed had stood. I would not look up at someone else's ceiling geography. All the cracks, chips and blotches were covered under two coats of fresh paint. It was my ceiling now.

I couldn't see it in the dark. Lying on my back staring into what was in effect the grey light of a half-moon, I could hear above the frogs calling and singing in the stream some distant night bird creaking and croaking down in the little orchard where Florence and I had sat in the long grasses and, more or less, said goodbye. Her agony must be intense. The dreadful uncertainty she was enduring would take all her courage, colonel's daughter or not. And I seemed absolutely unable to help her, even comfort her or take some of the strain, just by being with her and staying close.

But it had been made abundantly clear that I was not needed. I think that hurt rather more deeply than just her quiet rejection of me. Perfectly idiotic at my age to be troubled. I mean, how could I possibly have thought that she might come to me after her marriage, false or not, to my much younger brother? How could I have thought that she would have found it possible to return, with someone else, to the house which had been so filled with joy? And, eventually, pain? Those things are not eradicated by a 'new love' and it had been made very clear that I was not a 'new love' and never would be. She had 'mated' for life. Some birds and animals do that.

Obviously some humans do too if they marry (as I did not) for love and 'for ever'. Helen and I had married, rather late in our lives, for perfectly simple 'sex'. Mutual lust. Nothing much else was there. We shared no intellect. No other interests than our bodies and what we could do with, and to, them. When that started to fray away, as inevitably it does and did, then there was not even familiarity or warmth to hold us. Dislike took the place of desire fairly quickly. All the habits, personal habits, which had been amusing or tolerable in the past suddenly magnified into disaster areas of irritation. We couldn't share anything beyond our bodies.

Poor Giles, now sleeping in the next room, was the final effort to hold on to some idiot thing which is called 'family values'. It does not exist when Mummy and Daddy have no values to share. 'Sperm donor,' she had said . . .

I knew I'd never sleep. I was overtired and too alert. It had been a fraught week. My mind ran like speeded-up film, jumbled, back to front, unsteady, blurred. I'd make no sense of anything. I groped about for the kitchen matches, lit a small stub of candle waxed on to a tin lid. The room flickered into life. Shadows bounced and stretched in the soft draught from the window. I'd have to get a few pictures one day something on the walls. I almost missed my bleeding heart Jesus and the goldfish and kittens in my little room at the hotel; at least they had become familiar.

Giles called anxiously, half asleep, from his room, 'Something wrong? Dad? All right?'

I said I was all right. Just couldn't sleep. Was he all right?

'Yup. I like it here. It's nice. I'm all right.'

'Good. I'm glad.'

'Do you like it? Here I mean.'

'It's better than the last few nights. In that Pavilion place.'

'Better than that! Oh, yes. But it really is pretty good, isn't it? Just in our own place. I like that. I saw your light, that's why I woke up.'

'I know. Sorry. I should have shut the door but you wanted me to leave it open. Right? You did ask.'

'I know. Just the first night. It's a bit strange, isn't it? But I am quite used to it now, after the hotel and that place, the Pavilion.'

'Well, try to go back to sleep. And shut up and let me think. I might just look at a magazine for a bit. Okay? Shall I shut my door? Stop the light?'

'No. Leave it open.' He fell silent. I reached for an old *Paris Match*. 'Mum used to do that.' His voice was fading into sleep.

'Do what? Look at *Paris Match*?'

'No. Shut the door of her room. She said because her light might keep me awake, but she would be there, quite close, just shut her door, so not to be worried.'

'Where was this? Not at Simla Road? You and Annie were on the top floor.'

'No. At the seaside. A huge hotel, but she was next door, and she said' – he broke off and yawned – 'I would be able to see the light under her door, so it was all right. And so go to sleep.'

'And?'

'She wasn't really there at all. I heard their car going away. But her light was on under the door. But I saw them driving away out of the car park.'

'Who was them? You mean Eric Thingummy?'

'Once it was him. I knew his car. I watched them, and when I knocked at her door there was no one there. So that's why I asked you to keep your door open. You see? It's all right now. It won't keep me awake. I am going to think about my aquarium.'

'Were you quite alone? Wasn't Annie with you? Surely?'

'No, it was term time. She was at Granny's. It doesn't have to be a big aquarium, you know? You could afford it easily. All right?'

'Absolutely all right. Now go to sleep. It's tomorrow already. Off with you. It's Monday. Realize that? French lessons again.'

'Oh no!' His voice was muffled by sleep. 'Not today, Will.'

We had reverted to 'Will'. 'Dad' was to be used for more intimate moments it would appear.

'Can't live in France, Giles, and not speak the language. Stands to reason.'

He didn't answer; probably drifted into sleep. Which was more than I could hope for. I'd have a lot of repair work to do on my son. Helen had obviously used her free time, while I was away, very well indeed.

Arthur clipped a small bunch of tiny grapes and dropped them at my feet. 'This size. When they get to this size – before, if you can – nip 'em out. Otherwise you'll choke the rest. It's a deadly job, thinning. I do it every year and groan. You'll be in trouble with yours. Unpruned for years, I daresay, so you'll be knee-deep in the things. And they attract the hornets and wasps. Best get rid of them all. You see? About two inches long, three. Have them out or you'll be in trouble.'

I steadied the folding steps and he started down, secateurs in one hand, his unlaced boots scrabbling for a foothold. 'I was just showing you an example, I have done the rest. Did them early this year. Muscat of Alexandria. Nice grape, wonderful flavour. October about. Know what yours is?'

We sat down at the tiled table. He clattered the secateurs on the tiles, took off his straw hat, reached for the wine carafe and poured us a couple of fairly generous glasses.

'Get yourself some secateurs, a couple of plastic buckets – they are lighter when you're up the ladder – and, of course, a pair of steps, or a damned ladder. God! How I hate them. Can't stand heights, you see. Dottie usually has to stand at the bottom to reassure me.' He took a good swig.

I looked, I suppose, a little doubtful, because he suddenly said in his schoolmaster voice, 'What's up? Going to be timid and British suburban? Glass of wine in the afternoon? Delicious.'

'I'm driving,' I said lamely, and took a sip myself. 'But I do admit I have never seen a sign of a flic between here and Jericho all the time I've been here.'

He laughed, scratched a bony, bronzed knee. 'You won't either. Too rural here, they stick to the main roads when they aren't stuck in a bar. Helmets on the counter. No problem.'

'I need this anyway. It's been a sod of a week. I'm only just getting used to life on the farm, so to speak. I've slept for almost two days. What is it today? Wednesday? I had to hang about because a Monsieur Bourdon from the PTT was due. No one knew just *when*. Sometime. Because "he is on your route". So one waits. Came this morning, a great deal of "Mon Dieu! La chaleur! Malheur! Oh là! là!" He was as fat as a boar and shaggy as a bison. Dripping, poor man, like a sodden sponge. But after six iced beers and a flurry of francs I had a telephone! A real, honest-to-God telephone! With a number! I am reeling. I am automatic; he demonstrated proudly by misdialling his own office. But I put that down to excitement. I am in touch with the world. I was beginning, after the last three days, to feel rather isolated.'

Arthur laughed, drank again, wiped his lips. 'You may very likely wish that you still were. I hate that thing. Terrible intrusion into one's life. We had so much of all that in the UK. At everyone's beck and call. Parents worried about their little brutes. Caterers and laundry people. Tax fellows, police too sometimes, if a couple of little treasures had got pissed in the village and felt up some witless girl. Journalists . . . I really was glad to up stakes and clear off. Giles seems in good form. Chuffed with the house. Are *you*?' His eyes were blue and very bright, his question crisp.

'Very. I think. It's not something that I was really expecting. It has all come rather suddenly. Didn't expect the boy either, as you know, flown in like cargo. "Unsolicited gift".

I didn't have much option. Now I have a house, three hectares, a son and a telephone. And I don't know quite what to do. But it is getting clearer. Promise you that. It's suddenly starting to come together at last. I have a feeling it's exactly what I should have done years ago.'

Arthur reached for his tobacco pouch, began to roll himself a cigarette, the flimsy paper fluttering in his strong fingers. 'Well you've made a commitment now to the boy. You'll have to stick to it. I have a shrewd feeling that he hasn't felt very secure. Be cruel to muck him up. You won't do that? You don't mind me smoking?' He lit his rather ratty little tube with a lighter, blew a thin spiral of smoke into the vine.

'I won't do that,' I said. 'I have made a commitment indeed. Not just to him, made it to myself as well. Don't worry. I'll stick by it. I won't "muck him up". He's had enough of that from the lot of us. Not you and Dottie, I don't mean you! God! His family. We go back to the UK shortly, to sell up there. Then back here. Hence the telephone. I have to be ready to get over as soon as there is an alert. The house is on the market, but it's a difficult time. Always is. The hotel have the number, Madame Mazine clucked like a contented hen. Maurice-with-the-car fixed it all the moment I agreed to employ his daughter Clotilde. Simple but efficient. Drives a mean Mobylette, dead punctual, and does a bloody good line in pasta, and tarte au blet.'

Arthur waved away a curious wasp buzzing round his glass. 'And Florence Prideaux?'

'And Florence. But she left this morning . . . somewhere near Marseilles. A little break with friends of her mother. But they have the number.'

Then Dottie and Giles, chattering in French, halting but fairly intelligible, were on the terrace. Giles had a small glass jar. Held it reverently.

'Cherries! Look, Dad. All from three trees. These are for me.'

Arthur hooked a chair with his foot. 'Dot, sit down, my dear. Have a sip of wine. Giles, nip in and get a glass will you? There's some Coke in the fridge.'

Dottie sat down, wiping her hands on her apron. 'I've done about twenty kilos. Not bad. Ran out of sugar. Never mind. Has anyone ever given that child any sort of responsibility ever? He reacts splendidly, eager, good with his hands. He's also far more relaxed now. Easier altogether. Maybe Jericho? Certainly you.'

'I'm not sure about me.'

'I am. He's stopped clock-watching. He takes it on trust that you'll be here when you say you will. And so you are. Up till now, he began to get restless about half an hour before you were due. Like a dog before an earthquake . . .'

Arthur barked with laughter. 'Dottie! Really, what an analogy!'

'Well, *I* know what I mean. Anyway, that's stopped . . . Your responsibility, Will, but desperately important for him.'

Giles came back through the bead and bamboo curtain, set the wine glass down and swigged at his opened Coke. Arthur poured the wine, topped up my glass in spite of my cautious 'British suburban' hand which had half moved to cover it.

I said, 'Giles. Guess what? We are in touch with the world again. Monsieur Bourdon from the PTT arrived this morning just as I got back, swallowed a six-pack of Kronenbourg and left us with a glorious telephone! Pale beige, with real numbers and a bell that rings. How about that?'

'Terrific! Brilliant!' Then his smile faded. He pressed the side of the Coke can. It crackled. 'Now you'll be able to call . . . Valbonne, won't you?'

I nodded. 'Sure. But I still don't know the number. I

forgot to ask Mum on Saturday. There were other things to talk about. She'll call the hotel when she has to. They know the number.'

Arthur scratched a knee. 'When do you have to go back? To the UK.' His cigarette was a brown stump by this time. He stubbed it under his boot, caught Dottie's hopeless look and laughed. 'I'll sweep the thing up! Look, woman! Place is *covered* with vine thinnings. Been showing William what he's in for. I reckon the summer is a good time to sell in London? Right or wrong? Don't envy you at all, moving. God! As devastating as death or divorce.' He looked at me suddenly, slightly confused and embarrassed. 'Or so they say. Then back here, eh? To Jericho?'

'Back here. If I am still in one piece after it all. Back here.'

'For a summer holiday, you said. Didn't you, Dad? A summer holiday.'

Dottie laughed, began to take off her apron. 'I know exactly what you really mean, Giles. No more lessons for three months? No more Frog, eh? He speaks very well now, you know? Not perfect but not bad. Good accent. Total immersion in the house, as long as Arthur remembers.'

'I remember,' said Arthur. 'But up in the aviary it gets a bit fraught.'

'They have terrific summer holidays here in France,' Giles said. 'From now until September! Then it's called *rentrée*, right?' he said to Dottie, who nodded. He was swinging by one arm from one of the pillars of the vine trellis, his face bright with cheerful anticipation of weeks of idleness.

'What in God's name will you *do* for three months on our own? I'll go potty, to start with,' I said.

Dottie folded her apron, set it on the table. 'The rest of June! *All* July, *and* August. Rather long. But *we* chug on. Teaching. We Theobalds. You can come here now and then. Give Arthur a hand with his birds, keep from getting rusty with your Frog. Oh! And we'll have Frederick, or Freddy, de Terrehaute here. Three days a week. A nice young American boy, same age as you about. I think you'd like him. He comes to us to get a "French polish" as his mother calls it. Odd, considering how English we are? Come and meet him?'

'Why do I know that name? Terrehaute?' I said.

'You might. His ancestors used to own the château next to your house. Ruins now. In the Revolution. They got away to America. Louisiana. His mother comes back here every summer. Takes the Villa des Violettes, just up the hill. Most amusing woman, widow or divorced, not certain. But I've never seen a Duke.'

'Of course I know it. Great cedar tree? My brother pinched a lot of the stones to build his wall, round Jericho. Of course.'

Arthur started to roll another cigarette. 'Used to be the pigeonnier of the place, your house. That fat round tower at the corner. Ever been inside? Nothing to see but bat droppings. You getting restless, Giles? We boring you?'

Giles undraped himself from the pillar. 'No. I was actually thinking about my aquarium. Will said I could have one in the summer holiday. You did, Will, didn't you?'

It was obvious that my name as 'Will' or 'Dad' would vary according to the amount of charm which he felt he would need for whatever he wanted. And an aquarium, it seemed, would need an almost sickening amount. He was smiling eagerly, nearly winsomely.

'We'll see about that when the time comes.' The winsome bit had to be crushed.

'You said *after* the telephone. *After* we got back from London!'

'Well we haven't even gone there yet. Come on! Let's get Jericho set up first, okay?'

'Well, okay. But we'll have a really long holiday here anyway. Won't we?'

'We'll have a decent holiday, my lad. Let us call it a period of adjustment,' I said, and finished my wine.

CHAPTER 6

Sidonie Prideaux, Florence's mama, was what I suppose one would call an imposing figure. In her early seventies, tall, grey-haired, firm jaw, good legs, a body which had once been fruitful and strong, now running to slack. When I had been ushered into her presence (and it had always seemed like that each time), she was engaged in what she called her 'monthly cleaning'. Before her on a small, hideous, Moroccan inlaid-shell table lay a clutter of little brass pieces. An inkwell, a fish, some Algerian coffee cups, an ugly coffee pot with a long thin spout, a bell, a box inscribed with Arabic lettering. She was buffing away at an Aladdin's lamp when Annette murmured my name and I moved into the humidity of the familiar conservatory.

Madame Prideaux didn't look up, but set the duster and the lamp on the table, removed her glasses, folded them deliberately, indicated with them a cane chair in which I might sit, and then laid them among the brass junk on the table. Annette bobbed, closed herself out of the place. Silently.

I dragged the chair across to the little table's side, ducking a frilling of ferns swinging gently from a hanging basket above my head.

'My monthly chore. Remember?'

She had a pleasant voice, deep, warm almost. She tucked in some grey hairs which had wisped away from the brown velvet ribbon binding the cottage-loaf arrangement on her head. 'I seem to recollect that I was doing these same labours on the very day you came here to ask Florence about taking over the lease of Jericho from ...' For a moment she hesitated, moved the little lamp uneasily, folded her hands in her lap and, for the first time, looked up at me directly. 'From your brother. James.'

'Correct. You were indeed. And you were most kind in agreeing that I should.'

She shrugged, picked up an old toothbrush with which she applied her polish. 'Boff! What else could I do?' She picked up the scaled fish and began to brush it. 'Your ... brother ... had paid me three years' rent in advance. I had no complaint. No wish to be a cheating landlady; that is not my métier. I am a colonel's widow, an army woman. Not a commerçante, and you *did* agree that I need never be responsible for landlady things: electricity, drains, wood-worm and all that nonsense. Ouf! If you had not been quite so imprudent I assure you that, after your brother aban-doned my daughter, and "disappeared into the night", I would have let the house moulder away. I have no love for it. Had no love for it. It was merely a part of my – what do you call it in English? – dowry, my *dot*. Given to me by my papa. He insisted that land and property were far more useful in life than diamonds, or money in the mattress. I never even lived there. Never.'

She leant back in the chair, polishing, poking, fiddling with the fish. 'When the children were young, Raymond and Florence, we sometimes used to go there and picnic. Then I leased it to a man from Lyon, an industrialist alas! But he enjoyed the solitude and shooting. Raymond enjoyed shooting there too. He stayed for a day or two when he was on leave from his regiment. He took his military friends. I never asked questions. I am a sensible woman, I like to think.' She held the fish up before me, her grey eyes, agate hard when necessary, were presently kind, amused. She waggled the scales. 'This is not Moroccan? Or Algerian? Chinese or something, I'd say. Probably Hubert, my husband, picked it up for me in Saigon or Hue. We were stationed there for a while. And you? I talk like a parrot! A sign of age and solitude. You are settled in that wretched house?'

She placed the fish on the table, and looked at me with full expectation. I told her we were all installed, the telephone was connected, that the gardens and potager were my next concern, to restore them, and that I felt, and hoped, a new life was commencing at Jericho, for myself, my son, and for the house itself.

She smiled bleakly, folded the yellow duster she had used for buffing her trinkets. 'Your brother and my daughter worked themselves to death in that garden. And the wall they built! Stealing stones from the Terrehaute château ruins. Madness! The weight! The dust, the cuts and bruises. A wall for Jericho! I had not the least idea, when your brother came to ask me to rent him the house so that he could work at his painting and build a studio, that in fact he was an infant Le Nôtre! They achieved miracles in only two years. You will have a lot to do. It had been so badly neglected, and you are not exactly young, are you?'

'Not exactly old, either. I think I still have a little strength left. I'll try.'

'And why have you come to visit me this morning? I am not your landlady, you recall.'

'I do, Madame. I am returning, very briefly, to England in a day or two, to sell up my house in London, pack some stuff and ship it out here. I intend to stay on.'

'So Florence has told me. Well, that is up to you. You

know that Florence is away? She has taken Thomas for a little holiday, a change. A rest after the distress and anguish of the last months. Now that she knows your brother is laid to rest, if that is what one should call a shower of cinders wilfully thrown over a cliff into the sea, the anguish will ease. It has been a very stressful time for her.'

I shifted in my cane chair, it creaked quietly. 'For all of us, Madame.'

'For all of you. Of course.' She was agreeing only to be civil. She smoothed the brown velvet ribbon binding her hair. 'So. Alors. What can I do? Why did you ask me to receive you?'

'My address in London. And telephone number.' I fished a sealed envelope from my jacket pocket, laid it among the brass toys before us. 'I'll be away when she gets back. Just in case she wants to contact me *before* I return.'

'Why do you imagine she would want to contact you? Remember that she has gone away to think things out. To restore her mind. When she returns she will try to restart her life. She has the boy, she will have to find a job. A disabled child is an expensive joy. She will not view you, I think, or any member of your family with affection. Her grief has almost consumed her.'

'She still carries my family name. Her son is still my brother's son.'

'Thomas is the centre of her life. She has no room for anything or anyone else. A ruinous, appalling, state of affairs.' She shrugged lightly. 'But consider, Monsieur, who could accept her with the burden which she would bring him? An imperfect, incontinent creature which she must tend for the rest of her life? You understand me?'

'Perfectly, Madame.'

'It is perhaps unfortunate that you are so near; that you have taken over Jericho. I should perhaps have thought of that? Memories stirred. But we must all be civilized about it. I am certain that we can be. *I* see no reason for her to wish to contact you again, however near. Ever.'

'Except that I love her. Am in love with her. She knows that. We have spoken of it a number of times: she knows I will be patient, that I am stubborn, that she is absolutely all that I want in my life, to cherish and to heal.'

Madame Prideaux looked at me calmly. She made no move, her eyes were quite flat, unfathomable.

I sat back in my chair. 'I am not a youth, Madame. I know exactly what I am saying.'

'You are not a youth, indeed. You are a married man with children. You appear to have failed in your marriage and now attempt to restart your life in middle age with the woman your brother so brutally discarded. What impertinence! I am certain that your protestations of "love" were severely rebuked.'

'Rebuked indeed. But with infinite gentleness and sweetness. Obviously she has told you of this. I am certain she told you without anger or disdain.'

Madame Prideaux looked across the conservatory to the bubbling fish tank, then down at her lap, flicked a piece of fluff from her flannel skirt. Looked up. 'Yes. Yes, she told me. I still consider it immoral and distasteful. Your brother never even married her: fathered a malformed child, and fled away to rejoin his loathsome friends from Paris. The sodomites, those who corrupted him from his earliest days. He had no courage. He was unmanly. No courage. He abandoned my child as a spinster, with a disabled child, alone in a small, gossiping little village. What chivalry! How gallant!'

'She was abandoned as his *wife*, Madame. As Madame Caldicott, *not* as a spinster.'

'Boff! A faux-marriage on some beach by moonlight, with a tin ring! Capricious, romantic idiots. Very well, I can, *almost*, accept that, but the brutality of his desertion, and of that disgusting creature, Aronovich!'

I leant towards her, the cane chair creaking noisily. *'No!* Now I must rebuke *you*. He is not "disgusting". If it had not been for Solomon Aronovich in the first place my brother surely *would* have been destroyed by those ugly people in Paris. I can agree there. It was Aronovich who got him away from that city, from them, who got him to come here, who forced him to paint, to work, to start his life afresh. Aronovich was his patron, paid him for his paintings, commissioned him to work for him for his new hotel in Cannes. If it had not been for Aronovich, Madame, your daughter would never have had the little joy which once she did. She owes all the happiness she had to him, however brief it might have been. And then, finally, he cared for James after he disappeared. If it hadn't been for him we would none of us ever have known what had happened to him, where he had gone. That he had died –'

'Of *pneumonia*? In some *private* clinic? In Cannes?'

'That is so. You may check, if you will, with the British Consul in Nice –'

'I have not the slightest wish to do so. He is dead. And that is enough for me. But, Monsieur, do not try to cajole me into admiring Monsieur Aronovich. I know those people. I know his tribe. I detest them. They buy and sell and demand their pound of flesh. Remember your own Mr Shakespeare! He knew them ... I know them, they are parasites.' She got up abruptly, and walked with anguished little steps towards the potted palms and geraniums.

She was tugging angrily at some yellowing leaves when I said, quietly, 'You tried to kill James, didn't you. In your car. Tried to run him down. Just after Thomas was born? When it was certain that he was a Down's Syndrome child. Correct?'

She stood absolutely still. One hand clutching a scatter of dead leaves, the other rigid at her side.

'That is so, Madame, isn't it? You saw James, and he saw you, that day. C'est ça?'

'That's so. I did. But I touched him. Struck him, and he fell. I hit the iron barrier outside that wretched little bar at Saint-Basile . . . drove away.'

'Dented your mudguard. You should have had it repainted perhaps.'

'One day I will.' She dropped the dead geranium leaves into a pot on the tiled floor, wiped her hands. 'We distress each other. Life is so strange. I was almost certain that I had got him. I hit his bicycle, from behind, so I felt certain he would not see me or the car. Hélas! . . . How many people did he tell? Not Florence . . . ?' She turned towards me with a white-knuckled clasp of her hands. 'Who told *you*?'

I had got to my feet by this time, and was standing by the Moroccan table. I picked up the waggling fish, flipped its jointed tail. 'He telephoned the people up at the house where he spent so much time, the people he had known in Paris. He was unhurt –'

She cut me short swiftly. 'An American writer called Millar? I know him. At L'Hermitage. Of course he *would* run to that dreadful man. Of course. Who told *you*?'

'Solomon Aronovich. He just mentioned that it had happened. An accident at La Source. James, I think, rather waited for you to try again. But you didn't, did you? Did you try again?'

She shook her head in a preoccupied way, looking at the tiles on the floor, her hair shaking under its fixing of brown ribbon. 'No. I never did. But I wished him dead. I must confess that. I wished him dead for the wickedness he did to my child. Not *because* of Thomas, you understand – how does anyone know, absolutely, who is responsible for that fault in a child? It is all a question of chromosomes. But for his desertion, for the depravity of his life from then on, the cowardice, the terrible pain and grief he caused. I hated him for that, and . . .' She walked slowly towards me across the tiles, her heels clacking slowly and quietly, and when she had got close to me she looked at me with steady grey eyes. 'And I still do. I will always hate him for the lives he has ruined.' And then she turned and went back to her chair, sat down heavily, put on her glasses, picked up her toothbrush and a piece of brass. 'No. I never tried to run him down again. I was too shocked by the first attempt. I had never, in my long life, wished to kill another human being until then. I did not cherish the experience. But I could again if necessary . . .'

And then, as if we had never had the conversation at all, she said, in a high, light, conversational voice, 'I understand from Dorothée Theobald that all goes well with your son and the French lessons? That must be very satisfactory? They are charming people, Arthur and Dorothée . . . not terribly clever at the bridge table – they seldom win – but charming guests and good in the garden. You have seen her garden, of course? She is passionate about it, but they do find the living expensive, on his pension. There *is* a modest inheritance, I believe, and that is why I suggested that they earn a few centimes by tutoring after all those years in a school, and their French is perfect. Accented, of course, but pure. So. Excellent. I am happy it has worked so well for everyone.'

She started brushing again, rather too energetically, head down, brush flying. I knew that the meeting was at an end, and moved to the curtain which covered the door to the hall.

'All has worked very well, Madame. Thank you.'

At the door I turned. She did not look up but said, 'I will give Florence your envelope. When she returns from Marseilles.'

'Thank you.' The church clock was striking eleven, as I began to open the door.

She clattered the bit of brass on to the table, placed the battered toothbrush beside it, half turned towards me.

'You are English of course, Monsieur Colcott, but perhaps you are not a Catholic? It is possible?'

'Quite possible. I am not. Not anything, frankly.'

She took up a little brass coffee cup, polished it absently on a sleeve, eyes fixed thoughtfully far across the humid room. 'Nevertheless, I imagine that you believe in the sanctity of human life?'

'No. Really not. And as I am too young to have experienced a war I can't possibly make that an excuse.'

She raised the coffee cup in her hand, looked at it intently as if she had just discovered it. 'No need to have an excuse. The belief is all. Or disbelief, do I mean?' She placed the cup back on the table, folded her hands in her lap, still looking away from me. 'I am a general's daughter, a colonel's widow, mother of a captain, all in the same regiment, all most brutally taken from me. A military woman, you might agree?'

'I might agree indeed. And I do.'

'I was born in Algeria, I am what we call a "pied noir". We served in Indochine in '53, in Algeria again in '60, so I know enough of brutality and death, you see? It has always been about me. I cannot be expected to go through my final years encumbered with the absurdity of such a platitude. There is no such thing as the sanctity of human life in real life: that has been invented by bishops and theologians. I know. I have seen. Smelled it. I have cradled the brutally dead.'

The church clock had stopped clanging. All was suddenly still in the conservatory. I remained motionless, and then she broke the stillness with a little rasping laugh, briskly fixed a pin into the grey hair. Still looking away from me, unwilling apparently to meet my eyes, she said, 'The meek, my dear Monsieur Colcott, do *not* inherit the earth. You will see. One day. I bid you goodbye.'

I still had my hand on the door-knob, pushed the door wider. She finished fixing her hair, sat perfectly still, straight-backed, head high, hands folded before her brass trinkets.

'Good day, Madame. I shall remember what you have said, thank you.'

She slightly inclined her head, reached for the folded yellow duster, took up the brass-scaled fish again. 'Thank *you*, Monsieur Colcott, for *your discretion*.' She began polishing busily as I closed the door and went into the shadowy hall.

The stewardess slid a tray on to Giles's little table, smiled indifferently at me when I refused mine, and moved on up the aisle. Giles sat looking at his tray of neatly arranged inedibles.

'Aren't you having yours? Don't you want it?'

'No. I'll have a sandwich or something. In London.'

'If you'd said yes, and didn't really want it, I could have had a second helping. Couldn't I? It was pretty mean. It's free, isn't it?'

'Part of the price of your fare. Not free, mate. You're flying Business Class.'

He was unwrapping his bunch of knives and forks. 'Wow! Brilliant. And you're having champagne. I thought there was a cork? Nigel Mansell and all the football people, they always have to get the cork out before they can spray it on people. There *should* be a cork.'

'Well, there isn't. And I'm not about to spray people, I'm drinking mine.'

He poked cautiously at something pink. 'Well, it's pretty small, your bottle. What's this stuff?'

'Smoked salmon.'

'Will I like it?'

'Haven't an idea. Why not try it?'

A couple of evenings after the meeting I had had with Madame Prideaux I was sweeping up a pile of 'thinnings' from the vine out on the terrace when the phone rang. It was still such a novelty in the house that I automatically froze wondering at the sound and then heard Giles yelling from somewhere upstairs.

'Telly-phone! Quick!'

It was Helen, slightly irritated, on the line. 'I had to call that damned hotel to get your number. *I* didn't know you'd got a telephone!'

'It's new. I almost don't know myself.'

'Why didn't you call me? Let me know?'

'I haven't got a number for you, if you are still in Valbonne. Remember?'

'Of course I'm still in Valbonne. You could have written, anyway. It's about the house. A letter from Andrews and Fry. They've had a decent offer. £300,000. I know it's a bit of a drop, but the market's depressed. Some American firm want it for an employee. What do you think? *I* said yes, but I'd have to speak to you first. It took *ages* to get you. That damn hotel can't cope with English, so it's too late to call London back.'

'Do it tomorrow morning then. Say yes. I agree. Fine. Let's clinch things. When do you intend to go to London?'

'The day after tomorrow. I'm booked anyway. Eric has to be in New York on Thursday. So I said I'd go with him as far as London. When will you come?'

'End of the week. Got to close this place up, get the tickets, so on. I'll bring Giles, of course; will that give you time?'

'For what? And of course Giles *must* come. I haven't seen him for a month. And Annicka will come up with me from Mummy's place. We can sort things out together. I mean you and I. So I say yes, all right? Get it all over. Just make a few lists, of things you want to keep, you know, and the stuff we'll sell off.'

'I will. We'll stay at the house? Simla Road? To start with?'

'*You* will. I'll commute from Mummy's, it's no distance. I'll get on to Mrs Nicholls, to get in bread, eggs, coffee, milk, all that stuff. All right?'

'Fine. I'll call you as soon as I'm leaving. Probably be Thursday if I can get a flight.'

'Well, try. Don't let's have a weekend just hanging about. Huge love to Giles, see you.' And she hung up.

And somehow, the way that things on occasion do happen, everything turned out perfectly smoothly. I got the bookings, alerted Clotilde, arranged with my publisher to be met at the airport, told the Theobalds and Madame Mazine at the hotel, and gave her my London number and address (just in case, by some mischance, Madame Prideaux omitted to give Florence my envelope), and finally, after tremendous effort, I got Giles to pack and repack his blue holdall, an enterprise which lasted him two days, chucking things out and putting things in. Eventually we were ready and left Jericho very early for the trip to Nice and the airport.

And then there was the pleasant early-Victorian house in Simla Road, the green iron gate, faded windowboxes, dusty lilac bushes. Opening the door, my own front door, just as I had always done for fourteen years, was suddenly intensely strange. After two months away, with so much happening to cram the weeks, it didn't seem very much like a homecoming, rather an entrance into a new experience.

The house felt unused, even though Helen had only been away a couple of weeks and now had come effusively into the long hall and swept a slightly cautious Giles into her

arms with a great deal of air-kissing and little cries of
'You're *so* HUGE! God! *How* you've grown – and brown!
Aren't you *brown*!' to all of which Giles responded with
twisted smiles and twisted feet.

Annie came bounding down the stairs crying, 'Giles!
How *big* you've got! And I've got a pony, did you know?
Granny gave him to me. His name is Merlin. Hello,
Daddy, kissy, kissy? Did you have a lovely holiday in
France?'

All that sort of stuff. Family together again. I had forgotten how much I had got used to it and how much I had,
frankly, tried to join in but had really failed at the same
time. I never felt, truthfully, that I belonged in this rather
emotional overtly artificial, family life business. I had been
a lousy father, that I knew, and nothing had improved in
the time I'd been absent. I had not, I knew, been missed
by Helen or Annie, and really with fairly good reason.
There wasn't much to miss about me anyway. Oddly
enough, now that I was back in the frame, among familiar
yet forgotten things, like the wallpapers, the carpets, the
curtain which had lost two hooks and always sagged when
pulled, the Munnings prints, the bits of Helen's hideous
china, the view from the kitchen windows over the weedy,
dismal, narrow London garden, the slate sky, the stale
smell of closed rooms, in spite of all the things I remembered and could touch even, it all felt distant and faded.
A perfectly familiar stage set, awaiting demolition. And I
felt merely an observing stranger looking at someone else's
life and belongings, perfectly aware but apart, outside.

Somewhere at the very back of my head I heard
Arthur's voice saying that divorce and moving house were
as devastating as death. Looking round my dusty, still,
messy little office up in the attic, jammed with shelves,
filing cabinets, books, papers, folders, boxes and jars of
pens, rubber bands, paper-clips, gummy bottles of Tipp-Ex,

and sundry envelopes, I realized that, however lugubrious the remark, he was deadly accurate. How was I to clear this terrible chaos? How to sort, stack and pack the books, manuscripts, diaries and dictionaries?

I had spent years of my life in this room with its curtainless little window looking down over scabby gardens and the two wispy poplar trees. The greyness of it swamped me within an hour. How had I managed to live a life up here in the roof away from my children and my energetic, if irritating, wife? When I was not sealed up here reading and researching (when I was on the biographical leg of my work), I'd be abroad or anyway away from home, seeing for myself the backgrounds against which my subjects had led their lives, or talking, if I was fortunate enough to trace them, to witnesses to the events themselves. At the time I know that I found it perfectly acceptable, enjoyed it even. I had never been cut out, frankly, to be a father, let alone a devoted husband.

In the past, in my youthful prime, in between great epic feats of isolation and total immersion in my work, I got sudden violent bursts of hysteria – I suppose you could call it that – and was as desperate as a diabetic for his insulin 'fix' – in my case, female company. A wife was *not* what I desired, I was restless for 'assorted flavours'. It would seem to me that I stored up my libidinous urges until the cork exploded from the bottle, and then I just fizzed about in a glory of lust and physical pleasure which I had no intention of continuing once the body had been satiated. I did not want a 'relationship' as it was called, is still called. I dreaded possession of any kind; so my casual and satisfying encounters were only ever that, and understood by my partners to be just that at all times, until the advent of one Helen Wiltshire, spinster of Chalfont St Giles. She had happened to be just a little too satisfactory, a little too adventurous sexually. Physically she proved to be a disaster area for me. And, at a late stage in my life, I was getting older if not wiser, feeling that perhaps I should settle down. (Why, for God's sake?) We were married. And here I now was, standing in the middle of the room drained of emotion, anxious to quit, wondering how to start packing up a not altogether happy existence on which I could not look back with the slightest degree of pride or satisfaction in myself. Apart, that is, from Giles. He had been worth it.

And then there he was standing at the door, an empty hamster cage in his arms. 'I suppose I couldn't keep this now he's dead? But it seems a pity to throw it away.' He came into the room. 'Gosh! What a mess you've got to pack.'

'Worse than your hamster cage. Leave it for the men tomorrow. They'll deal with it. I've got to cope up here. You all right? Had some tea or something?'

'Yup. We've got to go down to Granny at Chalfont.'

'I know. Good idea really. Saves making beds and things. It'll only be for a day or two. You haven't seen Granny for yonks, have you? And you like her.'

'Quite. She likes Annie best. I have to call her Annicka now! Mum said so, and *she* said so. She's silly. I don't suppose that Eric will be at Granny's will he? He couldn't be. Could he?'

'No. He's gone to America for a week.'

'Mum was very nice to me. She was a bit worried that I really did want to be a, well, she said it ... a "little Frenchman". She said I didn't have to if I didn't want to, she'd seen a lovely school, and I could have my own room and bathroom at their new house. And there were lovely woods and places ...'

I was chucking used felt pens into a bin. 'What did you say to that. Tempting?'

'I said I'd rather like to be a little Frenchman. I was

getting used to it. But she *did* look sad. I felt . . . well . . .'
And he sighed. 'Anyway. She said it was up to me, and then
Annie said to come and smell her.'

'Smell her!'

'Yes. It was some awful scent from Los Angeles and she
had been allowed to wear it to welcome us back. Really
yucky . . . He gave it to her. Eric did. I won't have to stay
there, will I? You will remember what you said?'

'Giles. I'm going to be very, very busy. You are not going
to be kidnapped, you'll be at Granny's for a couple of days
or so, Mum will bring you up when we are clearer here and
you can look out the things you want to take to France, and
then we'll go off. Now *you* go off. Be very nice to Mummy,
she's not going to find it easy to let you go away with me,
so be sensible. Don't overdo things, just be polite, affectionate, and give Granny my love. Now piss off. Right?'

He turned at the door, jiggled the cage, 'And just leave
this in the kitchen?'

'Just leave it. They'll pack it with everything for storage.
Off you go.'

It took three and a half days to clear Simla Road. It was, in
spite of my acute anxiety that everything would be chaotic
and devastating, perfectly simple in the hands of five experienced men and a couple of vans. I made endless cups of
coffee and tea, provided biscuits with a willing, if tearful,
Mrs Nicholls, and generally directed operations with the
help of Helen who arrived every morning from Chalfont as
bright as polished steel and just as hard. The powers of
organization and quick-mindedness, the amazing capacity
to make instant decisions and judgements, which Eric so
admired, were brought into full display. She knew just what
should be done, how it should be done, when it should be
done. At the end of each working day she drove off again,
and I went to the comfortable Cadogan Hotel in Sloane

Street, where I stayed in peace and calm. It really wasn't such a sweat after all, and as the word 'regret' did not ever come into the scheme of things it was quite unemotional. Fourteen years of living in the one house, of births, of rows, of love, of anger, of all the other bits and pieces which go to make up a life within a handful of rooms, were obliterated tidily by the slamming and rattle of the tailboards or doors of the vans.

A dandruffy young man in a blue chalk-stripe suite and pink shirt, 'our Mr Wells', came from time to time to check that the fixtures and fittings were as agreed, admired the acres of beige Axminster, and said in what good condition everything seemed to be. Full marks to Helen there. The new owners, an American oil company, would entirely redo the house, of course, which is why they felt unable to match the asking price. None of this was in the least bit interesting to me, I just wanted out; and as crates and cartons trundled and banged past us I suggested that perhaps Mr Wells and I were in the way, and got on with stuffing black bin liners with old papers and litter from the shredder.

It really wasn't catastrophic. I would be delighted to tell Arthur when we got back. On the last day Helen arrived about noon with the kids. The house was practically stripped, a few boxes here and there, feet thudding about on bare boards somewhere, a tap trickling in the sink. A duff washer.

'Feels quite odd, doesn't it? As if we had never been here. Odd. Anyway, I'm glad that I took all my little belongings down to Mummy ages ago. You know, clothes, processor, so on . . . and the only bits of furniture I kept for myself are just sentimental really. Sentimental stuff.'

'That's really not like you, Helen dear.'

'What? What's not like me?'

'Being sentimental. The last thing I'd have expected.'

'You are a shitty bastard. There is very little you would

ever know about sentiment, or even if I ever had it. I tell you one thing, there won't be any sentiment at all when it comes to the divorce. None at all, my friend. Not a whiff . . .'

'Good. When do you want that to start up? Any urgency? I can get on to Hudson as soon as you like.'

Helen was leaning against the sink, looking through the window down into the drab little garden with its tiled patio, dried up pots, drooping may tree. She played idly with the chain which held the plug, clonking the metal of the basin. 'Eric is the one to decide really. His divorce is not final yet.'

'I see. I didn't know he was married. Sorry.'

'Nothing to be sorry about. They're splitting just as we are. Incompatibility. No children. *Unlike* us. That's all. She's a cow as far as I can gather, met some Italian fellow in Monte Carlo. Very rich. They're working on it all.' She dropped the plug into the sink, wiped her hands on a piece of kitchen paper left behind.

'Just let me know when.'

Annie came into the room behind a burly youth carrying a cardboard carton. 'Oh! Mummy! It's awful really. Everything's packed up. Will you ever find anything again? I feel quite sad, don't you?' She was a pretty child, good skin, her mother's green eyes, like Giles, and her mother's hard mouth. She had as much sentiment too. She'd be splendid with horses, hell with her men.

'You going to be a horsey lady?' I said.

She shot me a look of extreme irritation. 'I'm going to *try*. I'm learning. Eventing, one day, perhaps. There's a stables and Miss Bliss-Montgomery says I'm very good. And Merlin, my pony, is lovely; you'd like him. I'm reading *Horse and Hound* to see if I can find a secondhand coat for him in the winter. Do you think I will?'

I said I really didn't know, and watched Helen prodding

through the half-filled carton. 'What's in this? Oh, the food processor and the blades, scales and things. That's why it's so heavy. Is that the lot, young man?'

The burly youth looked at her blankly. 'The lot. Apart from that old calendar on the wall.'

There was a hint of sarcasm in his voice which Helen chose not to hear. She took the calendar and smoothed it carefully, flipping through it. 'I'll take it. It's only May, June now. Another seven months. Pity to leave it.' She stuck it into the carton. 'Seal it up, then. *That's* the lot.'

Annie said suddenly, 'Mummy said that one day I can come down to see you in your lovely house in France. I'd like that, but it would mean leaving Merlin so I couldn't stay long really. I'll come when Giles has a holiday from school. That would be all right, wouldn't it?'

I said it would be splendid and I would like it very much, and Giles, who had wandered in from the garden with a small china frog he'd just found, said the holidays were really long in France, and she'd have a lovely time except it was terribly hot all the time, and Annie sighed and said she really *hated* the heat. Giles said he knew that, and then asked me if he could put the frog in his pocket. It was an old one, he'd lost it years ago. So the stub-end of family life flickered on, guttering in the empty room of the echoing house.

'I was looking at the calendar a moment ago, the one that hung by the sink,' said Helen carefully, 'and I suddenly saw that someone I know, not two miles from where we stand, is about to have a birthday. Right?' She looked at me hard, then Giles.

Giles stuck the frog into his pocket. 'I am. It's my birthday. On the second of July.'

Helen ruffled his hair, the loving mother. 'Did you *really* think I'd forget? I never have, have I? Mummy never forgot your birthday. Did she?'

Annie, uneasy that all the attention was now on her brother, asserted her rights: 'You never forget *mine* either. Mummy always remembers mine. It's April. And next year, when I'm thirteen, we shall have fourteen candles on my cake because thirteen is unlucky, you see?'

Giles was looking at me uncomfortably.

I said, 'We're having a small supper party at the little hotel in our village . . . just local friends. It would be terrific if you could make it? He's ten, you know?'

'I *know* he's ten.' Helen's voice was sharp with irritation. 'But I don't think I can be there then. The second. I've got to be in Cannes on the 26th of June for the Festival, but I really don't know if we can stay on for your birthday. I'll see. We might have to go up to Milan, in Italy. It's not far from Milan, by air, is it?' She turned to me, a face devoid of any expression.

'Not far at all,' I said. 'Couple of hours about.'

Helen turned to leave the empty kitchen, the tailboards and doors were slamming on the vans, a couple of men came blustering into the hall with questions and papers to sign. Giles stood quite still, leaning against the empty refrigerator, the door slightly open. He was smiling, eyes bright. Annie had left with her mother. I closed the fridge door, turned the tap in the sink to stop the dribbling, smiled back at him, raised my hand, two fingers crossed. He laughed quietly, nodded.

When the vans had driven away, papers had been signed, tips dispensed and bright farewells exchanged, Helen and I went up to my stripped office, to do the absolutely final check. The children were down in the garden. Our voices were muted for some strange reason, as if there had been a death, which, I suppose, was exactly what the empty house signified. Death of a marriage, a relationship. Finished now. And the stripped house a mute symbol of that ending.

In my office some scattered paper-clips, empty shelves, a

splash of ink arced across a wall where once, in some frantic moment of correcting, I had probably flicked my pen in haste. The big room, our bedroom, bore no signs of anything. No relics of tumbled love, troubled nights, spilled pig-tails, young anxious faces at opened doors. And the bathroom, the main one on that floor, which had been the scene of Giles's distress, had refound its lock, and we didn't speak there. I just twisted taps. And so on, down through the house which now stood silent, awaiting a new pattern of life to be imposed on it.

It looked fresh, clean, tidy. Bits of string, scraps of straw, packing-bubbles, those ugly little plastic balls that one can never be rid of, were scattered here and there, but Mrs Nicholls, and her friend, had promised to 'come in and do a last tidy'.

Helen, at the top of the stairs leading down to the front door and the hall, stopped, hand on the banister rail, one foot poised to move down a step. 'Well, that's it, then. All done.' She shook her head, pushed her hair briskly behind her ears with one hand, went on down. I followed.

'Funny,' she said, 'that fourteen years leave no marks, don't you think? Nothing. Marks in the carpets where wardrobes and things have been. That ink splash; but, really nothing. You'd never know.'

I said nothing and we went down to the hall, the pleasant brass Georgian lamp hanging motionless. Fixtures and fittings.

'You brought up your family here. Very well indeed.'

She nodded with a mock bow, 'Thank you, kind sir. We had some good times, when we were young, and in love. In love. What do they say in the movies at this sort of moment? "No hard feelings." That it?'

'Something like that. Yes. And there aren't, are there?'

'Not really. It's all over now anyway. And you never actually hit me, did you?'

'No. No I never did, did I? Perhaps you might say that I was lacking in passion. Right?'

'Oh no! Your passion was my downfall. There was plenty of passion. But you were a well-mannered young man, striking women was not your forte. You were pretty too. Long legs. I remember very well.'

'And you were pretty too. Fantastically pretty. Still are, frankly.'

'We're being rather silly, you know. Talking as if we were dead. We're not! Second chance starting.' Her hand caressed the polished pine ball at the end of the banister. 'I reckon we just might make it to our fifties looking good, don't you? Still got your hair and teeth, no beer gut. I've got a few stretch-marks, a little sag here and there. Not much.' She was smiling like the old Helen I had known before passion gave way to 'permission', and that to 'perhaps', and finally 'period'. As in full stop. She caught herself swiftly, doused the flirting, mocking little smile, pulled the chain-strapped bag from her shoulder and fumbled about in a veritable minestrone of papers, lipsticks, coins, compacts and tweezers and found a scuffed cheque book. 'You'd better take this now. Cancel our joint account. I can cope.' She finished with an embarrassed shrug, the book limp in her fingers. Eric the Provider. I refused it.

'When we have settled all else, Helen. Not before. I am still responsible for Annie, and even for you, Burnham Beeches notwithstanding. Thank you for thinking of it, I'd forgotten. All right?'

She shrugged lightly, not looking at me.

Sunlight struck into the empty hall like a probing finger, dust motes rose and fell, drifted.

'All right,' she said, and then the car I had ordered for Giles and myself slid up to the kerb. I saw it through the glass panes of the door.

'The sun has come out, can you believe? And my car is

here. Would you be sweet? Go and call the children? I'll load the suitcase and stuff.'

For a split second we looked at each other with the suddenly clear, direct eyes of our youth, untarnished by time. Just a second. Like a spark struck from a flint. Nothing more, then she turned quickly away and I heard her calling the children as she went down the hall, and I opened the front door.

There had been no message from Florence on the answering-machine.

I had telephoned Dottie from the airport at Nice, and said we'd be passing in about a couple of hours' time. She came running down the driveway of her house as the Simca swung through the gates.

'How lovely! On time! *What* a treat!' She was holding her straw hat with one hand, blowing kisses with the other.

Giles waved a brown plastic bag in the air. 'Look! Your presents! Tongue! Four tins! And the sausage thing!' He got out of the car, there was a slamming of doors, a flurry of embraces.

Dottie had the plastic bag, swinging it about, her hat pushed back on her head by my kiss on her cheek. 'Oh, you are good, Giles! So lovely! We waited for lunch. It's all ready, a little cold collation, some salad.'

I protested a bit. 'We just stopped off for the tins and the Cumberland ring. Giles insisted. And this week's *Country Life*.'

'You can't have eaten! It's too early surely.'

'Breakfast,' said Giles. 'We had a *sort* of breakfast.'

'Well, come and have a sort of lunch.' She turned, one hand on his shoulder. 'The car's all right there, under the trees behind the Mercedes.'

'Mercedes? Has Arthur won at bridge?'

We were laughing, the light was bright, hot, the path up to the house and its green vine dappled with pennies of sun and shade. On the terrace, to my slight consternation, a small group of people.

'Oh Lord, Dottie, you've got guests. We really ought to get on home.'

'Nonsense.' And then she called up to the terrace. 'Arthur! They've got here, on time, isn't that amazing! A big glass of chilled Frascati for William.'

At the terrace table were Arthur in a faded denim shirt, and a straw hat, and a boy of about Giles's age, a woman lying back in a planter's chair, with black glasses and a scarlet headscarf. Arthur was on his feet, bottle held high.

'Will! Giles! Wonderful! You've been away an age. *Vous avez oublié tout votre français, Gilles. C'est vrai?*'

When we had got up on to the terrace Dottie, with plastic bag held high, swung it towards us and made her introduction.

'William and Giles Caldicott, and this' – she swung the bag towards the back of the terrace and the far side of the table – 'this is Frederick de Terrehaute and his mama, Madame La Duchesse de Terrehaute, only no one uses the Duchess bit, do they, Lulu?'

The woman in the planter's chair slowly leant forward. 'Well, no. No. Not since 1793 anyway. Isn't that sad? But it's only useful for maître d's and getting the best table, and I *always* get that anyway. I'm Louise de Terrehaute, Mr Caldicott, and I am really delighted to meet with you.' She reached for a glass at her side, raised it in a half-toast. 'Bienvenu! A new face in town, and my, oh my, a *pretty* one at last! Doubly welcome, sir.'

I felt myself blush suddenly, to my consternation, and sat down quickly amidst the laughter.

CHAPTER 7

Clotilde was what my mother (who, over the years, wrote a slew of very successful Romantic Historical novels under the pen-name of 'Harriet Rust') would have called a 'bonny creature, good, wise, kind and loving', and, one imagined (for one had only known her for a short time and at that distantly), she was. She was also sturdy, with a ripe figure, no pretension to beauty, none to ugliness. Merely plain. But the sort of plainness from which goodness and joy fairly radiated. So such a person in Jericho added lustre to the delights which were gradually unfolding there before me, and brought a sense of added stability to my stumbling efforts to rearrange my life.

With Clotilde about, with little drifts of mindless, but contented, singing meandering through the rooms, with the tidiness imposed, the polishing and washing, the arranging of wild flowers in pickle jars, or whatever she could lay hands on, and, perhaps above all, the excellence of her plain but delicious cooking, Jericho gradually started to accept us, its new owners, and the different pattern of life being imposed on it, once again. It seemed gradually to settle down, as I did, with a comfortable complacency, like a cat on a cushion.

And what was even better was that Giles had now over-come his original shyness with me, and Clotilde did the same thing once she realized that she was accepted as a member of the family and clucked and fussed about us rather like a Rhode Island Red, which, from time to time, her eyes beady with inquiry and interest, she vaguely resembled.

We had been back from the London saga only a few days when I noticed, almost in a subliminal way, that Clotilde had used a lipstick, had erased many of her sandy freckles somehow, let fall the severely dragged-back hair and the two plastic combs, and permitted it now to drift, almost tumble, to her shoulders and carried a sprig of honeysuckle or a single little rose behind one ear. I noticed this, as I say, almost subliminally. I was occupied most of the time in either unpacking and sorting the stuff I'd brought over from England and Simla Road, or digging and carting, and cutting away with the scythes. However, these small improvements to her person seemed only to happen *after* she had reached the sanctity of Jericho. She'd leap off her Mobylette, cry 'Bonjour!' and go into 'her' kitchen, after that re-emerging (usually after I had dumped Giles on Dottie and Arthur and was unloading the marketing from the Simca) as the 'made-over' Clotilde. Her ample bosom had now become two rather fine breasts by the simple expedient of a deeper cleavage revealed by the quick removal of a little modesty panel of 'frill', and an adroitly tied wide ribbon bound high under them. It seemed to me, after a little time, that Clotilde at Jericho and Clotilde at her father's house were similar, but not at all the same. Something was afoot; it amused me to speculate while breaking my back and restoring some muscle to my stomach and arms with the pioche in the potager.

In the late afternoon, when she left, all frivolity had been banished, and all that remained was perhaps the sprig of honeysuckle, or the little rose, but fixed firmly to her handlebars. We'd lock up the house together, so I was near enough to notice the change, the plastic combs, the wiped-off lipstick, which still left a faint pink stain, the 'frill' at the cleavage replaced, and then she'd bounce off down past the mossy pillar, and I'd start up the Simca and follow behind her ample body on my way to collect Giles.

This was the usual routine now. Over to Dottie and Arthur at five, perhaps a glass of wine, an exchange of any news, and back to Jericho with my 'little Frenchman', always slightly bemused to realize how quickly a boy of that age (or child I suppose) could readjust and begin to speak French almost without an accent. Something which, starting far later in my teens, I had found difficult to fully eradicate. And still did.

'You *do* speak it very well, Will. Giles must take after you. He seems to have an affinity for languages. Useful, you know? I always tried to drum it into my wretched parents. Let their children concentrate on German or French: even if they refused Latin because *"it's a dead language, he'll never need it"*. Oh God! the narrowness! However, Giles seems to have escaped that. Perhaps because of your "ear"? One really should have two languages in life now. Terribly important. Half our Government can't even say "Bonjour". Appalling, really, when you consider the responsibility they have, sitting about there in Geneva and Bonn or wherever, with a ruddy plug stuck in their ear listening to "instant translation"! Bland, accentless usually, unemotional, *no* nuance, *no* subtlety. How *much* they must miss, the idiots!'

Arthur was off, if I let him, to climb upon his hobby horse. 'The awfulness of the British Government. The British people, and their "shocking insularity".' It was really harmless, not at all vicious, but worrying because we had all heard it so often before and could only agree or disagree and keep him on an even keel so that he didn't lose his temper. Dottie had some excellent, private signals, which she made from time to time signalling a moment for changing the subject instantly and easing her adored husband into calmer waters. She did it now, and sweetly.

'Will read French history for two years at the Sorbonne, darling. I expect it was ever thus, wasn't it, Will? Or was French used far more in England *after* William, your namesake, invaded? Will, dear, have a tiny slice of tapenade . . . so good with your wine.' And we drifted away from the 'wretchedness' and 'bigotry' of the British Government. At least for a while.

'Of course,' Arthur said after a sharp look at his wife (aware that he had been deflected), 'now that Giles has Frederick to yatter away to, it's a great help. They only speak French, as far as I can hear. I don't pry, mind you, but when I do overhear them, up there with the cages and the birds, it's usually French. Odd French, archaic sometimes.'

'Archaic? Why?'

'He's from America but from Louisiana. Very old family, very proud, and some of them still use the French they came over with during the Revolution! I think it is an affectation frankly. He speaks perfectly terrible American when he wishes.'

On cue the two boys came running down the path from the aviaries, Giles with his espadrilles wagging in one hand above his head.

'Arthur! Arthur! The lory are starting to nest. The red one's tearing up huge bits of those branches.'

'Pushing them into the nest box,' said Frederick. 'And God! Is the hen ever making one hell of a racket! Listen!'

Frederick did indeed speak perfect American-English, pleasantly, as pleasantly indeed as he looked. Taller than Giles, auburn hair, a slim build, wide mouth, long legs, well-set eyes. Very like his mother, in fact, who I seemed to recall rather too vividly from our last, and indeed first, meeting a few days before.

Arthur got to his feet, pushed easily into his laceless boots, and stuck his straw hat on his head. 'You mean the *chattering* lory, I assume? Not just "the *red* one". Well, I was rather expecting that. I'll go off and see. School finished half an hour ago. Right? What's today's date? I must make a note of it. I mean the lory nesting.'

Dottie walked with us down to the Simca under the big olive and just as we got there the open-top Mercedes, which belonged to the de Terrehautes, turned in off the road. Lulu de Terrehaute was driving, scarlet headscarf, wrap-around glasses. She raised an arm a-glitter with clattering gold bracelets in greeting.

'Hi, y'all!' she called, took off her eye-shades, and for the first time looked directly at me.

I stood perfectly still as if something inevitable was about to happen. The moment before the earthquake. A flat, singing silence.

Then Frederick yelled, 'Lookie, lookie! There! On the stone.' Giles cried out, and there was a scuffling of feet and the sound of Dottie calling out to leave it alone, it was only a lizard. Then the slam of the Mercedes door and her feet on the gravel, and she called out to the scuffle, without once taking her eyes from mine, and said, 'Let it be. You'll wreck the roses!' And slid her eye-shades into the pocket of her white silk trousers.

Dottie called out about the flowerbed, but there was still a modest riot I could hear taking place somewhere to try and find a lizard. I knew now what a horse felt when it wore blinkers. I could see ahead, see Lulu de Terrehaute's eyes, hear the laughter and the scolding and the rumble of stones and Dottie saying, 'Enough! *Enough!* Go home both of you.' But I could see absolutely nothing else. Whatever was happening to left or right of me was obliterated by the intensity of the eyes before me.

Dottie's voice somewhere was still light, but now under-lined with impatience. 'Little blighters, they're trampling stuff to *death*.' And then she stopped, took off her straw hat, started to fan herself lightly (I could now just see all this beyond my blinkers), but she was aware of us and said briskly, 'Lulu, dear, cart the fruit of your loins back to your château, will you? And the same goes for you, Will.' Then she turned away and yelled out to the scrabbling boys. I heard stones fall. 'Oh! Do *leave* it! Frederick, Giles! What harm has it done to you?'

Lulu said, evenly, quietly, 'Shall we lunch?'

'Yes. But I have my son . . .'

'So have I. I can fix that. No problem.'

Dottie said, somewhere out of sight, 'Now come on, you little brutes, both of you. Look at the mess you have made.'

Frederick's voice was still high and excited. 'A lizard! Blue and green, with a yellow belly.'

And Lulu, still looking at me calmly, called over her shoulder, 'Freddy! Let's get back now,' then broke our look by pulling off the scarlet scarf so that her hair spilled down to her shoulders in a cascade of auburn curls. 'I have people for cocktails! Can you believe such a term? *Cocktails* for the Bernards, the de Rocquemontforts. Alastair Whistler and his dusky boy lover – do you know them?' I said no, I had only just arrived in the area, and she laughed and turned away and said, 'Dottie, darling, bring me my child, and the bill for any damage to your divine garden.' And, turning to me again, she asked if I had a telephone number. I couldn't remember for an instant, then did, and saw the lightly mocking smile widen as I wrote it hurriedly down on the back of a receipt from the traiteur in Saint-Basile. She took it and slid it into the same pocket as she had put her eye-shades.

'Don't lose it. Sorry. It's all I had to write on,' I said.

'I know. I know. I won't lose it.' She was still smiling, her hand outlined in the silk of her tight white trousers. She waggled her fingers, saw me drop my gaze to them, laughed and said to Dottie, 'Oh *God*! What a fuss for a crazy old lizard. Come *on*, boys. Henri – you know my chauffeur? – has trodden on a nail, do you *believe*? He was playing around in the yard and trod on this plank. I mean, the man is so thick . . . Bare feet and treads on a nail! In a plank! So I have to come and find Junior. Can you *imagine*? Walking about with bare feet in the yard of the garage? He could have slipped in sump oil, or something, broken his peasant neck.'

Dottie, brushing down her denim skirt, asked if the nail was rusty, because if it was he'd probably get tetanus unless he'd had a shot. Lulu said she really didn't know or care, but he was in bandages and that it was a good job that *she* could drive. Otherwise where in hell would she be? She directed the last line at me, and then broke the group by pushing Frederick into the car, kissing Dottie, clipping Giles lightly on the ear, never again noticing me until she slid into her seat and started up. Then she looked swiftly and directly across to me, waved, then began to back down the drive.

'Bye, y'all. Until *tamarra*! Dottie, now lissen, it's got to be *me* at dawn, don't watch out for it. Promise not to peek? I look like the wrath of God naked, at that hour. Goddam Henri!' And as she started to manoeuvre the large car round she called, 'My eye-shades! Where are my eye-shades?' I told her they were in the pocket of her pants, and she laughed, as if she hadn't known, and said clever old you for noticing, and *wasn't* she crazy, and drove rapidly away.

Dottie and I walked over to my Simca. Dusty, rusty, very proletarian. Giles got in slowly. 'It was a *huge* lizard. Like a dinosaur really. Hugh knobbly ridges down its back. You really should have seen it.'

Dottie folded her arms, hat hanging in her hand. 'She's very . . . vibrant . . . is that the word? Lulu de Terrehaute . . . Arthur and I call her the "Shrimping Net". Rather rude, really.' She laughed lightly, raised a hand in salute. 'Tomorrow? As usual?'

I called above the running engine, 'As usual. I hope they haven't *really* mucked up your roses.'

She was smiling, shook her head.

'Why Shrimping Net?' I said.

'Oh! Well, not just "shrimps", you know? You can catch all manner of things with a shrimping net. Quite large prawns, sometimes, plump little crabs, hiding away out of sight. Find a nice quiet little rock pool, poke about? You never know *what* you'll catch. Lulu's very good at it.' She was now smiling broadly, stuck her hat back on her head and with a wave turned up towards the house as I swung with a crunch across the gravel and headed down for Jericho.

Giles sighed heavily, theatrically, stuck his pen in behind his ear. 'I think it's very silly, all this writing invitations. We've got a telephone now, can't we just telephone everyone?'

'We could. But it's more polite to write, personal. It's your birthday, the cards are all ready, printed. All you have to do is stick in their names and the time and date. Surely that won't kill you?'

He was sitting slumped at the table, a scatter of cards and envelopes, his fist screwed into his cheek. 'All the addresses,' he mumbled. 'I've got to write *all* the addresses? I mean, I go to Arthur and Dottie every single day! And I could easily just walk to Florence's house when we are in the village, and give Frederick his when he comes to Dottie's – three times a week – and I can't spell "Violette" or whatever it is.'

I heard Clotilde singing in the kitchen, little bursts of

song between heavy thumps of wood on flesh. Giles looked up with sudden interest. 'Whatever's that? Clotilde banging away?'

I finished lacing my garden boots, stood up. 'She's tenderizing the veal. Schnitzels. You have to beat them hard with a rolling pin. I'm going down to the potager. When I come back I would be extremely pleased to see that you had done those cards. Tough luck! So get on with it.'

He scowled and I went out into the heat of the morning. It was Saturday, so no 'school', and I was trying now to assert my authority. Writing out the invitations was one way. I knew, perfectly well, that I could just have telephoned everyone. But that was not the right method of setting an example.

Anyway, I wasn't over-anxious to speak to Madame Sidonie Prideaux honestly. There had been no message from Florence. No card, note or call. Perhaps she was back? Perhaps she had news? Perhaps she was *not* back, and had no news, and, anyway, I couldn't very well ask Sidonie Prideaux if her daughter had had a satisfactory trip to Marseilles. And, in any case (I picked up my pioche and the heavy spade), I didn't have a number for the de Terrehaute place. She had mine. She hadn't called, and now it was the weekend she probably wouldn't.

So Giles could write the things. It made the supper table larger, inviting Frederick and his mother, but it also made it rather jollier. For Giles anyway. He had complained that his birthday was going to be full of old people. Well, now it wouldn't be. So that should please him. If they came. And that would please me: but perhaps I'd meet her before then? It was still almost two weeks away. I realized, fully, that I was far more concerned for myself than for Giles. I wanted to see Lulu de Terrehaute very much more than he did. She had said, hadn't she, 'I can fix that. No problem'?

Suddenly, down at the little iron gate at the end of the path, there was a sharp stab of brilliant-laser light: the sun blazing on a motorcycle standing just outside the wall. A bright, red and chrome, glittering Honda, with a hefty blue plastic-wrapped chain to secure it. But no sign of an owner anywhere.

I wandered back to the potager, began hacking slowly, thoughtfully. I had plenty to think about. Pleasing things, curiously erotic things. And the time passed, hacking through the dry soil, shaking earth from dead roots, watching the pile of sun-dried weeds and grass by the path grow larger, feeling the sweat run down my neck and chin, drip down my chest. A far cry from Simla Road. I wouldn't ever get a sagging gut doing this. And then Giles came wandering slowly barefoot down the path to say that he had finished the cards and where were the stamps and did I know that there was someone in the kitchen with Clotilde? I didn't. How did he know?

'I haven't actually *seen* anyone. Just heard a voice. When she had finished the thumping business, she spoke to someone and he answered her and she laughed. That's all. But I heard, not clearly, but voices anyway. A man.'

'Perhaps someone has come to deliver something from the village. There's a Honda parked outside the gate down there.'

Giles looked over to the path. 'I don't think so. I think it's Mon-Ami.'

'Mon who?'

'That's what Clotilde calls him.'

'Calls who?'

'Her friend.'

'I didn't know she *had* a friend. How did he get here without me seeing him?'

Giles shrugged, kicked a stone and sent it scuttering through the rough grass. 'I don't know. Maybe he came up through the little orchard. You were inside anyway. I think that's his bike. Must be.'

'Well, who is this friend? She tell you?'

'Nope. Just said, "Mon ami est très beau, très gentil." Pretty silly. I saw him leaving one day, far away down through the trees, and she was just going home, and I said who is that? And she said, "Mon ami," and that's all. And where are the stamps? Have we any?'

I was sweaty and curious. Who was this stranger in my house? Could he be a threat to the stability of the place, the comfortable arrangement we had come to with Clotilde and her father? Could this be the reason for the pink lipstick, the deeper cleavage, the flower tucked in her hair, the softness of her, now that the plastic combs had been removed? Anxiety pulled at me. I was hot. So I had every reasonable excuse to go down the steps to the kitchen and get an iced beer from the fridge and check the visitor out. If I lost Clotilde, God knows who I'd ever find to replace her. She ironed my shirts as if they had come straight from Jermyn Street, was starting to run my life. Sod him!

In the kitchen Clotilde was flouring the schnitzels, her face flushed from heat and labour, hands snowy from the flour carton, a single red rose pinned to her hair. On a chair, across the room, sitting with long legs wide apart, hand clasping a shining helmet between his thighs, a burly young man with tight gold curls and red and white leathers. When he saw me he instantly got heavily to his feet as I came down the little steps into the room. Clotilde smiled happily, sprinkled flour over the chopping-board, nodded brightly.

I said, 'Bonjour!' and went to the fridge for the beer, and Clotilde said, in a pretty, but unusual little-girl voice, 'Ah! Monsieur Colcott. This is mon ami. He is a very good worker, he knows all about the land, the vegetables, the trees, the seasons, he is a good carpenter, a maçon, and he has come to offer you his services. C'est vrai, mon ami, eh?'

Mon-Ami appeared to be about six foot three or four, and I began to feel like a shrimp indeed. Not even a prawn. I would not have been in the least surprised to learn that he had modelled for Greek coins or that he had once reduced Praxiteles to tears of envy and despair. He stood there before me in the modest kitchen among the pots and pans and ropes of garlic and peppers like a misplaced god. Strong, clear of eye, firm of mouth and chin, large capable hands holding his glittering casque.

Now I understood why Clotilde had taken herself in hand. Here was the reason for lipstick, cleavage, tight ribbon and flirtatious rose. This spendid specimen of about twenty-two, erect, strong, perfectly secure and quietly confident.

'Mon ami est *tellement* timide!' said Clotilde, casting flour about in a little cloud.

And shy indeed he was, blushing red, and lowering eyes, but standing his ground. Legs apart, shoulders square.

'You must say to Monsieur Colcott all the things that you can do!' said Clotilde as if to a child. 'He is a busy man, and you must unstick your tongue. He will be patient. Hein?' Mon-Ami nodded. A thread of exasperation slipped into Clotilde's voice. 'Bien. Tell him where you are working now then? At the pépiniéristes near Saint-Basile-les-Pins? Eh? Chez Gavery? Say?'

Mon-Ami turned his casque in his strong hand. 'C'est ça,' he said, and looked to Clotilde for help. He may well have had splendour between his legs but it would seem that there was precious little between his ears.

'Why', I said kindly, 'do you want to offer your services if you work for such a big firm as Gavery? You have that splendid Honda, eh? He must pay well. Hondas and leathers and casques like yours are not won at a village fête.'

Clotilde was setting anchovy fillets on to a tin plate. She looked apprehensively at Mon-Ami, who seemed not to have quite understood me. Perhaps I had used too many words and confused him? Possible.

'You are not, perhaps, *satisfied* at Gavery? Is that it?'

Mon-Ami shifted his feet, lowered his casque in one large fist and murmured, 'Yes, Monsieur. I don't like it there.'

Clotilde decided to interpret cheerfully. She was determined to keep him on the premises somehow or another. 'Monsieur, écoute! He wants to work for himself, there are twenty men at Gavery. He feels that he can better himself. Some are specialists in trees, in laying drains, in making swimming-pools for the rich in Saint-Basile-les-Pins, the people who live in the big lotissement there – the Paris-Rustiques! It is not a real existence. It is so, mon ami, eh? You want to work alone. For yourself.'

Fortunately, to prove that god-like or not he was not also mentally retarded, as I was beginning to fear, he nodded his head vigorously. 'Yes. That is true. For myself. And one boss. That is so. And to have pride in what I do.' This effort at speech exhausted him.

I told him to sit down, and to encourage him to do so sat on the edge of the table with my beer. I offered him one to ease shyness, but he refused politely with a raised hand and a shake of his head.

'Imagine!' said Clotilde, reaching for a big jar of capers. 'Twenty thousand primulas every spring to water! A thousand pots of chrysanthemums for the Jour des Morts in November! Christmas trees and *poinsettias*! He is not *that* kind of worker! He loves the soil, the land. C'est vrai, mon ami?'

'Yes,' said Mon-Ami. 'I like very much the land. Not to work for rich Dutch or Germans, to plant their patios, clean their swimming-pools. They only like concrete and pots, and little lawns. Boff!' This was the longest speech he'd made. I hoped it had not exhausted him again, but I had begun to get the picture.

As if perhaps I had not, Clotilde, spooning capers and black olives into bowls, said, 'The rich in those new villas only stay for a month in the summer and a week at Christmas! From Paris, from New York, London, Brussels. They don't care about their land, except that it is clean and pretty, like a photograph. A maison secondaire, that is *all* those places are in the woods. The people never see anything grow. Never plant a seed, prune a rose, they think strawberries grow on a cabbage! Tiens! C'est juste, mon ami?'

I was quietly surprised that Monsieur Maurice's daughter was so loquacious, so eloquent. It was a pleasant discovery. Clotilde seemed to have found her place in life, determined to settle Mon-Ami in his and, above all, share that life with him. Not a bad idea. She was certain to be a good mother and a very capable wife. She screwed the lid on the caper jar, knuckled her floury hands on her hips and looked from one to the other of us questioningly.

I took the hint and went with Mon-Ami out on to the terrace and down the path to the garden and potager all hopelessly overwhelmed by the prodigality of late June. He stooped, his leathers creaking lightly, and took a handful of soil in broad fingers, spread it between thumb and forefinger, murmured sadly, 'Fatigué.'

I said that it was *all* tired, everything needed feeding, nourishing, caring for, that once upon a time it had all flourished gloriously, had produced beans and peas in abundance, spinach and cabbage, potato and celery, that roses blazed, figs were plentiful, and almond, cherry and apple were prolific and presently burdened with fruit, in the little orchard, and were now waiting for his attention. *Urgent* attention, I added. And, for the first time, he smiled.

Then Giles, who had been hanging about all the time on

the periphery of the action, his eyes glistening with envy at the sight of the Honda, the casque and the trim leathers, eased himself cautiously into the conversation and said that there was plenty of water everywhere too, a stream up at the top, and that he'd show him if he liked, and where the well was. He knew, he added reasonably, the garden much better than his father. Which was quite true, as he spent some considerable time on his own there damming the stream, trying, in vain, to fish, catch lizards or dig out a space for the future pond.

Mon-Ami smiled agreeably, and asked if he would like to examine his casque more closely. Giles grabbed the thing and stuck it on his head, almost breaking his neck, and we all laughed. Clotilde came down the path waving some scissors.

'For some sage, Monsieur. Mon ami is also very useful in the house if the weather is bad. He can mend a pipe, clear a sink, re-lay the boards in the bedrooms, clear the chimney. There is a hornets' nest in there, I think! Mon ami can do *everything*. Even electricity.' She went off gaily to find the sage bush.

Mon-Ami retrieved his casque, and we walked together slowly up to the house discussing when and how he could come, and what salary he felt would be acceptable. We reached an agreement before we got to the little terrace. His name, he said, was Luc Roux, his parents owned the traiteur in Saint-Basile. (I had written my telephone number on the back of one of their receipts for Lulu de Terrehaute, who had still not made use of it alas.) He had finished his army training (an important point – he wouldn't suddenly be called) and no, he hadn't known Clotilde, but he knew that her father was the brother-in-law of the maire of Bargemon-sur-Yves, and therefore knew that Jericho had a new master. He had passed the place often and always felt sadness at the neglect, he said, and he would be happy and proud to try and restore it to its past glory, for it was well remembered in the area that, when the 'other Monsieur Colcott' had owned it, it was a most bountiful property. He had just wandered in one evening to look about (apparently when I left for London) and found, to his mild dismay, Clotilde mending some linen on the terrace. He had been, of course, trapped from that moment. But, naturally, did not say so in as many words. I was very pleased with Clotilde, and when she rejoined us, a bunch of blue sage in her hand, I told her the good news that Mon-Ami, as I would always call him, was now a part of the household of Jericho. At least he would be, as soon as he had given in his notice to Monsieur Gavery, and then at that very moment Giles yelled, 'Telly-phone! Telly-phone!' and I turned and raced up to the Long Room.

A gigantic terracotta plinth supporting a huge urn frothing with a bounty of white impatiens and scarlet geranium. Two enormous cedars left and right of a pleasant, unremark-able, but cared-for late-eighteenth-century house. Tall chim-neys, long windows, white shutters, a curved portico over an open front door flanked by two rearing griffins. There was also a peacock, and Frederick running towards us trailing a kite.

'Hi! So you found us. It wasn't so far, was it? I have a kite, but there's no wind this morning. We can go to the lake. There's a lake through the trees.'

Giles had clambered out of the car, had hitched his jeans, looked round at me. 'Awesome!' he murmured, and to Frederick he said, 'Can we swim there? I've brought my things.'

And then she was on the top of the steps tying the scarlet scarf round her hair, long legs apart, a cream chiffon dress light on her slim body.

'Hi, there! I'll be right with you. Frederick, you can't

swim today. Not without Henri present, and Henri has gone and messed up his foot. So *no* swimming.'

She came down the steps slowly. I was standing by the Simca, and then she was beside me, an envelope in her hand. 'But you can use the pool. I hate you to be in that lake. Henri can be Nanny by the pool, right?' She only looked at me during this, calling over a shoulder. She handed me the envelope and in a low voice said, 'This is where to meet. Full instructions. I'll follow you. Twenty minutes.'

I took the envelope. She was smiling, her eyes bright with complicity. 'I do not, at any time, believe that my right hand should ever know what the left one does. Do you? Just wait there in the *parking*: I'll be driving a little car, a Citroën. The Mercedes is too obvious.' She turned away and started back up the steps calling to the boys. 'Frederick. Take Giles to see the monkeys. We have monkeys, Giles! Don't get bitten.'

Giles turned and looked at me with a vague smile of disquiet, not about the monkeys, I felt certain, but about being left.

'I'll be back, don't worry. About five, or maybe before. Enjoy yourself. And put on your hat. Sunstroke.'

Frederick yelled, 'Come see, Giles!' But he stood watching me, still uncertain, the bundle of swimming things slipping under his arm. I crossed my heart. He smiled, nodded, waved, and ran off shouting, 'Where are you?'

She was still at the top of the steps, a tiny breeze frilled the light hem of her skirt, floating it. She stood there smiling. 'You have to do that always? Crossing your heart?' I nodded, she went into the house. 'Twenty minutes after you. Right?'

Just outside Sainte-Brigitte, in a modest block of inexpensive new flats, three storeys high with sprinkler-watered lawns, two tall imported palms, and an oval swimming-pool, deserted and tidy, I parked the Simca and sat under a spray of violent bougainvillaea to wait for the Citroën. Her envelope had contained the address and a note to say that she'd bring a picnic. 'We'll just rough it. Won't that be exciting?' It was unsigned.

I waited quietly under the ugly creeper and saw no sign of a living soul. The flats were built on a ridge looking down over the town and the soaring view below. It was a clear sign of what was about to happen to the area in the near future. Modest retirement flats. 'Studios', the large sign-board said, for modest incomes, elderly people from Paris, Lille, Amiens and places north. A pleasant, inexpensive nest for the aged, arthritic, rheumatic or just ordinary, retired shopkeepers, bank officials and insurance clerks. Unpretentious, discreet. An odd place for Lulu de Terrehaute to hang out in? Perhaps she didn't? It didn't matter one way or another, lust had risen within me once again. Long, long suppressed desire and need was swelling me, infusing my whole being as if I was a randy eighteen with spots and a bad haircut.

And then, with a soft whisper of tyres, she had arrived and driven her car into the *parking* just a discreet way from my Simca. There were no other cars to be seen. Maybe the elderly only used their Zimmer frames to get about? It looked as though no one had *ever* swum in the crystalline pool.

'No one ever does,' she said, a large lidded hamper in one hand, a bunch of keys in the other. She had covered her head with the scarf, wore the wrap-around dark glasses, no jewellery. 'This place is strictly for the aged, fat and ugly. I borrow the flat from a girl I know who is as discreet as hell and is, presently, away on a trip to Rio, or Saigon, or maybe Athens. You can never be certain of her. This is her secret place. But I have a key! That's all that matters.'

We were in a neat, unscarred lift. 'They are all empty in

153

this block. We are right on top. Great views. If we get time to look at great views.' Her hand was suddenly on the zip of my jeans, slid up to the brass pull, slid down again, caressing my growing strength. 'I guess we can find lots of other things to look at, don't you?'

The lift murmured to a stop. A light, narrow corridor, a couple of doors, left and right, one green, one pale blue. She opened the blue one and we were in a dim, shuttered room. The door slammed behind me, the hamper was dropped and she reached eagerly for me again, crushing her mouth brutishly over mine before I could even yell, which, with the force of her grip, and the suddenness of the attack, was almost obligatory. It was a greedy, vicious joining. I matched her easily. I lacked restraint too, and matched her greed now that I realized the situation. Good manners were not for today. If this was the 'lunch' she had suggested, then I was ready and able and we'd have one. It was also being made clear that we were not into *nouvelle cuisine*. This was to be a banquet and I, from where I stood, braced against the door, legs astride, was to be the main course. With a groan of impatience she pulled away. I could see her eyes in the filtered light from the louvred shutters. Diamonds, they were so hard and bright.

'Get the message?' Her voice was as hard as her eyes.

'Loud and strong,' I said.

'And so is this,' she said, and struck me sharply between the legs. I lurched forward gasping but she grabbed my belt-buckle, pulled me into a sitting-room.

Light filtered, a smell of dust. She unzipped her dress, let it slip to the floor round her feet. Kicked off her shoes, pulled the scarf from her head and, as her hair fell to her shoulders, told me to remove my shoes.

'I'm going to strip you, babe. I don't mess with shoes. Get rid of them, then come to me.' She walked into the pearl light of the room, opened a window with care, eased a shutter. The light became a little stronger, when she turned back to me I was shoe-less. Her nakedness overwhelmed me completely. Slight, smaller than I had realized, her breasts taut, shining, jutting upwards, waist narrow, firm thighs, long legs. She had no body hair; glowing, bronzed, satiny. Only white, pure aching white, at the fork. Her arms raised wide in invitation, head to one side, the cat-smile.

'Here I am,' she said. 'But *where*, my randy fellow, are you? Shall I look? Feel the package? Guess what I got? I'll look. Just you stay very, very still so I can strip you all the way down. To your "bare essentials".'

She lowered her arms, the provocative cat-smile faded. I needed no provocation. If this was how she played the game I would go along with her. She came towards me arms reaching, hands curled into predatory claws, and ripped my shirt open to the waist. Buttons scattered. 'No vest. Great . . .' The shirt was tugged roughly from my jeans, dropped. 'No hairy shoulders. I *hate* hairy men.' Her hands caressed my breasts. 'Smooth. Sweet.' She pinched a nipple roughly. I cried out.

Her hands were on the wide buckle of my belt. 'Jockey pants! You wear *those*?' The buckle gave, she wrestled impatiently with the metal button closing the zip. 'I could *feel* you.' Her voice was rough, the button gave and she ripped down the zip, split my fly. Then she sank slowly to her knees pulling the jeans to my thighs. 'Stand tall. Get these off.' Jeans and shorts crumpled round my ankles. 'Heavens to Betsy! That is all a wicked girl can desire. What have you got here? Why hide it.'

She took me in her hand, squeezed and cupped me as if she was weighing fruit. Looked up again, the little smile, teeth glistening. 'Step out, spread wide, babe.'

I complied willingly, her hands splayed on my thighs, her head bowed down, and I was greedily, furiously, engulfed. I think that I cried out, her fingers clawed my flesh, I arched my back thrusting out to her, and heard a harsh sobbing which can only have come from the depth of my guts and then I was suddenly, and monstrously, released; sweat running, gasping for breath, spent. After a moment, she pulled away, wiped her lips. 'Don't hang your head. *He's* not hanging his, look!' She rose, took my hand, and pulled me across to a small divan under the window, pushed me down on it. I lay still, drained indeed, arm across my eyes, gasping for breath. Heard her moving about somewhere.

When I looked up, blearily, she had the hamper, set it on the floor, produced a bottle of vodka, two cheap glasses. 'Refreshments, mouthwash, or whatever. To keep everything up.' She gave me a half-filled glass. I eased on an elbow to drink it. 'Not too much. You haven't touched base yet. The best is yet to come.'

She had filled her glass and emptied it easily, got to her feet carrying the hamper through a small curtained archway. I lay slumped, the glass tilted in my hand, the liquid burning into my empty stomach. Behind the curtain she was rustling about, treading softly. I reached for the bottle which she had left on the floor and she was instantly at the arch. 'No! No more. I want my "lunch".'

'I thought you'd just had that?'

She came into the room, took the glass away, 'Just the hors d'oeuvres. Now I get to have a feast. C'mon.' And taking my prick, still alert, she forced me to my feet and led me through the archway. A large Victorian bed. Curly brass, black bars, stripped. No sheet, no pillows. Flat. A tight white rubber cover. It smelled slightly of sweet chocolate. I was pushed down, backwards, on to the bed. Sun from the louvres raked her body with rippling stripes. With a quick surge of anxiety I saw cords trailing at the head and end of the bed. 'Now, look, no silly buggers,' I said.

'This is going to be silly as hell, I tell you.' Quickly, and expertly, she bound my arms wide apart above my head, moved briskly to my feet. I was spreadeagled, helpless as she intended, flat to the sickly smelling rubber. My body raged, she slapped it lightly, kissed it with pursed lips. 'I just want you to realize I am reversing the general situation. Usually the lady gets to be in your position, correct? And the gentleman gets to be where I am! Reversal of fortunes, you could say? You'd be right. This way it's not *me* who is the vulnerable one, babe, it's you. This is "Girls' revenge". Wait for it.'

'Oh God! Go easy. Please, go easy.' I closed my eyes.

'No one ever went easy with *me* . . .' A cool liquid spilled on to my belly, trickled down my thighs. I tried to raise my head from the sheet.

'Baby oil, for a smooth finish.'

'What the hell are you doing?'

'I am in the process of doing you.' She set the bottle aside. I dropped my head, tried to pull away.

'Oh Christ! Go easy – Lulu – stop. I can't hold it –'

'Don't you dare! Don't waste a drop! You have a real hard gut, you know that? This strictly does not work on flab.' Her hands were wanton, sliding, caressing, cupping.

'Don't! Don't! I'll let rip – I'll lose it –' I was writhing.

Suddenly she clambered over me, spread her thighs wide across mine, bent down and bit my breasts, the right, the left, savagely. I know I yelled, I know I heaved and pulled against her weight. Heard her laughing from a mile away. 'Don't *pull*. Silk ties. They won't budge, just tighten.' With thumb and forefinger she twisted my nipples again as if they were bottle tops. I bucked, pleaded.

'That may mark you: the ties won't.' She twisted again. I rolled in pain. This was suddenly no fun at all. Flat to the bed, head to heel. An insane, voracious woman straddling my thighs, her hands sliding, pulling, pinching. 'Lulu! Don't! No more – no more!'

'Never did this before, babe?' Her voice was rough.

'Never, never. Stop, I beg you, stop –'

In a sing-song, her voice: '*Ride a cock-horse to Banbury Cross* . . .' She had me tight in her fist, ran a sharp thumbnail over my bursting cap. 'Wow! Look what I got. A real crimson acorn just for me . . . *To see a fair lady astride her big horse!*' And then, in a very different voice, 'Let's go for it.'

I felt her weight lift for a moment from my thighs, slippery fingers pull my scorching body roughly upwards, holding it tightly she gently lowered herself down on to me and cried out in pleasure. I half raised my head, watched her slowly sink down on me, her hair spilling wildly about her face, hands gripping my hips. I yelled, matching her cry, arched up to join her, and then the ride commenced. Slowly, slowly, gathering pace as we matched the same rhythm. Her cries became sobs, the trot became a canter, the canter a gallop, and then we exploded simultaneously in a torrent of raging lust fulfilled. She crashed down on to my body, lay sobbing, gasping, half laughing.

After a while I felt her ease me out of her body, pull herself up to my belly and roughly, fingers in my hair, grabbing me by the head, force me to take her breasts. Tight, lemon shaped, firm, nipples as hard and bright as rubies, she pulled my willing mouth to each, allowing me to suckle like a greedy child, tugging my head from one to the other, judging, for herself, when *she*, not I, was satiated. She had absolute control over me, her body and everything else. She had won. Quite soon, abruptly even, she had finished the game, pushed herself from my sweaty body and slid beside me on to the rubber sheet. I lay as for dead, listening to her breathing.

'Real good. Experienced, right?' she said softly.

'I was. So are you.'

She raised herself on an elbow. 'What a big fellow you are. Sturdy friend. Play it again one day?'

'Play it again. One day. Untie me now?'

'I'm looking at him. He's still so gorgeously tumid. It's wild ... you want to go again, huh?' I shook my head violently. Begged to be untied, to get the vodka quickly and she, prudent girl, untied my feet, *then* my aching wrists. 'Remember,' she said sliding off the bed, 'this was for *lust*. Just lust. There was no *shred* of love or affection anywhere. Right? None.'

'I can believe that.'

'Men don't believe that really. Don't believe that women can have wild desires too, fantasies, mad as hell. Well ...' She leant down to kiss my thighs lightly, sweetly. 'Well ... they do. We just aren't allowed to say anything. Show it. Except that *I* have. I got used like a bloody inflatable doll just too often, no one ever asked if *I* had had an orgasm, never. Just pulled out and went to grab a shower. Well ...' She patted my still erect cock. 'Well ... I've changed the rules of the game. Okay?'

'Okay. Fine by me.' I began to rub the weals on my wrists. 'Never played it quite like that, but if it's the way *you* play it, fine. Just whistle.'

She had started to wind the red scarf round her head. 'It's called "male-rape". I just *love* it.' She tucked the ends of the scarf in neatly. 'I got married twice. Both of them rich-rich like I wanted. But, sagging butts, flabby bellies, bad breath. They had to do it that way to get things going. Only *I* was always the target, it was always little old me trussed up like some goddamned hen. And then I thought, get me some great looking *young* guy! Take my revenge. Change places?' She slid her hands across her thighs still slippery from the oil. 'So I got me one or two. You pay, you get. But they get shit scared. They all did, or else pissed or puked or spent too soon. Hated to lose their manhood or something. So *unnatural*.'

She was standing quite still, arms at her sides. Slender,

shining, ageless in the filtered light. She grinned the cat grin again. 'Then I saw you that afternoon. Just had a hunch. And *you* saw me. We locked in, right?' She stooped to pick up the two glasses on the carpet. Her breasts juddered slightly as she rose, the glasses in one hand. 'Still rubbing away? They'll go . . . You okay?'

'I'm fine, really fine. Just glad that I was older and wiser. It really was a great "lunch".'

She stood silent, rattled the glasses in her hand lightly like castanets, cocked her head to one side. 'Hey,' she said. 'Did I ever get to have dessert?' She walked slowly towards me smiling.

CHAPTER 8

I'd opened up the house and put on the coffee. Giles was still mucking around in the bathroom. I always got up first to avoid the stumbling sleep-bleary shape of my son blundering about, near sightless, hands groping for his toothbrush. Clotilde had not yet arrived to start her day.

It was the part of the morning which I particularly enjoyed. Alone. The calm and serenity just before the normal, ordinary routine of daily life commenced. There was still a light dew under the fig tree where the early sun had not yet thrust its laser beams among the tall grasses, a sweet freshness in the air which the attendant heat of the day had not yet been summoned to disperse.

Behind Jericho rose the great cliffs, riven, just behind the house, by the narrow gorge through which the infant river Yves tumbled and shouldered round, and over, water-polished boulders. The cliffs were deeply scarred at this hour in the morning by the first light, which threw the crags and pinnacles into harsh relief against the brilliant cliff faces. By noon the whole massif would be a dazzling glare of sun-washed limestone, burning the eyes; only the clumps of live oak, broom and myrtle would stand sentinel in their meagre puddles of black shade. By late afternoon the westering sun would gild those same crags and pinnacles, tip them with flame and gold and rearrange the shadows from indigo to bottle blue to black, as the orange globe suddenly slid, with astonishing rapidity, over the rim of the cliffs, dragging with it the last vestiges of day, throwing the valley and plain below into deep shade, while swallows soared and swooped into the darkening sky, and finally, as the fireflies drifted about under the figs, it would be night.

But for *this* moment, this brief pause before the sun arced upwards into the sky, exploding over the land with light, for this moment I cherished absolute solitude. Stood alone in the dusty potager wondering if my brother, James, had experienced the same feeling of peace and intense delight. It was strange, humbling even, to stand there on the earth, a silent pygmy below that wild panorama of vibrant, changing colour. Had he seen it as I did? Had it hit *him* in the gut? Found *his* soul? He had attempted to set it all down on his canvases. But had it reached *more* than just his eyes? Why should I think that I saw it differently from him because I tried to use words, and he used paint and brush?

But however he or I perceived it all, there could be no doubt whatsoever that the rearing cliffs of Jericho, with the ruined hamlet high up on the rim of their jagged lips, had the most profound effect on the observer. Soul or no soul. How one chose to interpret the emotions which that colossal sight engendered in one's mind and heart was a personal matter. One did it the way one knew best. By pen or brush, sometimes in music, often only by silence. It was the one moment of the day which I chose not to share. I stood healing in the stillness of the morning. Which one might consider very appropriate after the utter madness of the day before, but it was more a spiritual healing than a physical one. Only shattered suddenly by Giles bawling from the terrace that the coffee was boiling over.

'Then turn it off!'

'I have. It's a mess! The stove thing.' He was wandering down the path between furrows I had ploughed up, his shadow falling tall beside him in the rising sun. He saw it and waved his arms like a windmill. 'Zoom! Zoom! Zoom! I'm a helicopter!' Then he stopped before me. 'Gosh! Terrible scratches. Do they hurt?'

I had imprudently left my shirt open like a jacket. He looked vaguely curious.

'No, they don't hurt. Nothing really. I was . . . um . . . up in the orchard yesterday, by the cane-break, you know? All that tangled bramble, and that prickly stuff? With the strimmer.' I began to button up. Slowly. Not quickly: no need to arouse his curiosity further.

'Terrific bruise too. On your bosom.'

I laughed a light laugh. Or hoped it might appear to be that sort of laugh. 'My *what*?'

'Your *boooosum*. You fall over as well?'

'Yes. As a matter of fact I did. Tripped over a big log, a pile of them under the brambles. It bloody well hurt too.'

He thankfully suddenly lost interest and turned to look back towards the house and the cliffs. 'I'd like to go up there. To that ruined village. You did say we could one day?'

'One day, sure. We'll have to go up by car, but it's on the edge of the range, the military range. Red flags everywhere. It can be dangerous. Grenades, shells, bullets winging about.'

His eyes were wide with pleasure. 'Wow! Like a war?'

'Just like a war. They are all practising, you see.'

He had completely forgotten my cuts and abrasions. Lulu's legacy. I made a decision to remain covered for a day or two. We had started up the path to the house as Clotilde came bouncing up past the mossy pillar and pushed her Mobylette through the little iron gate. We all waved.

Giles said suddenly, 'You never really took down the Jericho sign, *or* the gate, did you?'

'No, I never did. I put it back. Remember? Well, people do seem to wander about here. Clotilde's little friend for example.'

'Mon-Ami? Oh, he's all right. Anyway, it didn't stop him, did it? And if we had some peacocks or something, we'd *have* to have a gate, wouldn't we?' He was scuffing pebbles on the path up to the terrace.

'Peacocks? Why peacocks, for God's sake?'

'Well, we could. Frederick has two, a cock and a hen, only she's a bit boring. He said the hens were, but they lay the eggs. He's got two little monkeys, marmosets. They wouldn't need a gate, just a smallish aviary, and they aren't expensive – easy to feed. They are really ace. He got them from a shop in Nice. Can we go there one day?'

Clotilde had hurried past us and was tying her apron when we got into the kitchen.

'No peacocks, mate, no monkeys. This is supposed to be a holiday, we aren't absolutely settled yet. Let's take things gradually, okay?'

He slid into his chair and watched Clotilde spreading his tartine thickly with jam, and we heard the blast of a horn, three short bursts.

'Postman! Three honks. That means a packet or something. I'll go.' He ran off down the path to the gate.

'The post?' said Clotilde. Giles had been speaking in English. 'Ah! He's such a timid one, that Jacob. Won't walk an inch if he thinks there is a dog anywhere.'

'But we haven't got a dog.'

'Does he know this yet? You have only been here a little time. Maybe you have bought a dog? How does he know?' She set the coffee pot back on the stove on a low gas. 'And they say there is rabies at Saint-Rémy! A German tourist was bitten by a pony at the Club des Vacances there. Ma foi! Rabies! So you can't blame Jacob for being cautious.'

I watched Giles coming up the path, a clutch of envelopes in one hand, a small package in the other. 'I'll put out a sign on the gate saying "*No* dog! *No* rabies"! Do you think that would work?'

Clotilde just shrugged indifferently and went into the Long Room. Her French logic was being questioned.

'What have you got?'

Giles spread the letters on the table like a hand of cards. 'All for me! Look, two letters and a postcard. Two for you. Postcard is from Mum. Amazing! "Lots of fun here. Miss you heaps. Love. Mum." It's one of the Casino in Cannes.'

I picked up my letters. One from Andrews and Fry with nothing to say of importance, the other from my bank, equally dull. The packet was very like the one which James had sent me so long ago containing the key to this house. 'I send you the key because it is now yours, I no longer have need of it . . .' A strange, sad, kind of faux-will. Jericho was mine. He had left it to me. For three years anyway. But what oddity did *this* little buff envelope contain? Postmark Nice-Centre, address typed. No outward clue and nothing slid about or rattled.

Giles suddenly gave a whoop of pleasure. 'Everyone is coming! They are coming to my party on the second! Wow! Brilliant. Listen "Mr and Mrs Arthur Theobald are very pleased to accept Giles Caldicott's kind invitation to supper on July second at eight o'clock." See! They have replied right away.'

I took the card, saw Arthur's neat, schoolmaster's handwriting. 'And the other one? Who's that from?'

He pushed it across the table. 'Madame Prideaux! She's coming *too*.'

Sidonie Prideaux had, indeed, accepted. Had accepted in French (I had insisted that Giles wrote his cards in French) and was happy to accept the invitation to supper on behalf of herself and Madame James Caldicott and noted that no gifts were to be expected. This was something I had written at the bottom of each invitation. 'Please, no gifts.' It made Giles ill with anger for at least three hours.

'That all? Nothing from the Terrehautes yet?'

Giles was looking dreamily, in rapture, at his acceptances. 'No. Nothing. But I told Frederick yesterday, and he said he was pretty sure it was okay but he didn't know if his mother had got the invite. And anyway, she was away all day yesterday, in Monte Carlo, wouldn't be back till after dinner. What's in that? The packet?'

I spilled it on to the table between the bowl of sugar and the pot of raspberry jam. A slim, gold watch. A Piaget. James's watch. Attached to it a card. 'I managed to trace the owner and got it back for you. A souvenir for you to keep.' It was signed simply 'S. Aronovich'.

It was rather a lot to take at the breakfast table. Two gifts, in a way. One, which caused me the most intense pleasure, was the acceptance from Sidonie Prideaux indicating, perfectly clearly, that things must be well with Florence. At least as far as I could judge. Her mother had no idea precisely *why* Florence had gone to Marseilles. It was highly improbable that the true reason was ever mentioned in that smug little house in rue Émile Zola. So, unless she was concealing anything, it would appear that all was clear. And on that assumption I felt my whole body metaphorically sag with relief. Subconscious stress tenses the whole range of one's muscles. All unaware, one is none the less as taut as a drumskin.

Although I had, deep down inside, felt that there could not possibly be any cause for alarm as far as Florence was concerned, or Thomas for that matter, how the hell could I be certain? As she herself had said, I was not 'holding the candle' in this little house during those fearful months. In any case, I knew so little about the disease: how long one could be HIV positive, or when everything could suddenly blow up into what was known as full-blown AIDS. The very vaguest thought that Florence could perhaps have ended as James had done was unthinkable. I had buried it deep in the blackest recesses of my mind, never to let a spark of light fall across it. So that now, sitting at the table, my son eating his tartine, reading and re-reading his letters, the coffee pot drifting sweet vapour into the morning, the glint of gold on the Piaget watch rescued by Aronovich, the name 'Madame Caldicott' in her mother's looped handwriting, surely that was proof that all was well? I was suddenly suffused with well-being and, to his astonishment, lightly kissed Giles on the top of his head as I got up and went out on to the terrace.

Sometimes great happiness is almost uncontainable. The gesture which Aronovich had made, tracing and securing (at some cost I felt certain) James's treasured watch, moved me greatly. I would, as soon as I saw her, hand it to Florence. She could keep it or not, as she saw fit. Sell it again, or retain it, not for Thomas, alas. He would never be in need of such a glittering prize. I'd write immediately to Aronovich to thank him.

Maybe tomorrow would bring an acceptance note from Lulu? Naturally she would have had no time yesterday. God only knew what her movements were after she had put all her things together, tidied up the rooms in the ugly little flat and driven herself, and the hamper, at some speed out of the *parking*. She had murmured something about an appointment in Cannes with some designer and possibly a 'light supper' with 'a crazy girl I know'. At any rate, she was nowhere to be seen later when I got to the Villa des Violettes around five to collect Giles. Prudently she had kept her distance. As far as Giles and Frederick were concerned, I had spent the day hacking at brambles in the orchard, and Frederick's mother had spent her usual socially busy day somewhere along the coast. We had behaved with great caution and left no signs for anyone to pick up. Apart, that is, from a few vicious scratches and a bruise or two. Falling about in the orchard with the strimmer. Nothing at all to worry about. And very soon forgotten.

Looking at my rented Simca, standing soberly in the shade of the Jericho wall, I decided that it was time for a change. Useful, sturdy, capable of carting all manner of stuff from fruit, logs, vegetables, suitcases and, on occasion, small pieces of furniture from some brocante, it had now become, to me at any rate, a symbol of staid dependence and my London existence. I didn't want that any longer. I would do better: I was still renting, idiotically, from the mayor, which was extravagant and pointless.

I came to a silent decision, dropped Giles off at the Theobalds', went into Sainte-Brigitte and bought myself the car which I felt better expressed the slowly emerging new model of myself. Younger, energetic, responsible, even daring, possibly sexually adroit? I would never dream of going further. Admitting only that limited list to myself was embarrassing enough, immodest if I thought about it. So I didn't. I knew precisely the car I wanted. I had seen it the last time I was in the town getting the tyre pressure on the Simca checked (essential on the local roads and in the heat). The car was hidden in the backyard of the garage, half covered with a stained grey tarpaulin. Not covered enough. I saw a brilliant flash of yellow, the white wall of one tyre. Lust, of a different kind, but none the less urgent, rose within me. I was twenty-four years old suddenly, and curious, as I casually lifted the edge of the tarpaulin. I knew immediately that I had to have it.

The garagiste, a pleasant, bellied man with a red face and oil-ingrained hands, shook his head, smiling kindly. It was not the car for me, he said, it was a *young* man's car. He hoped I would excuse the remark? I wouldn't. I was, as far as I was aware presently, a young man. Lulu had a great deal to answer for. If she had appreciated my performance, and it had been made clear that she had, then I was perfectly capable of dealing with this elegant, slender, sophisticated machine, now uncovered completely, glinting and winking at me in the sun. It was canary yellow, a two-seater, drop-head, white-wall tyres, polished leather seats, giant headlamps an MG of uncertain age, lovingly cared for, waiting for me. It flirted, sparkling in the sun. I played back. Ah! No! said the garagiste. *Surely* it was not what I wanted? It belonged to his son who had now – hélas! – gone off to do his military service, fathered two children and was to be forced into a reluctant marriage. Yes, it was for sale . . . but only of course to a real specialist, a collector, and fanatic car-lover. He was about to send out some photographs to two collectors he knew, one in Antibes and another, an Arab prince, in Monaco. He was desolate, but . . . He had shrugged. I had come too late, hélas!

I explained quietly that I fulfilled all the criteria which he had expected. What is more I was there, before him, my cheque book in my hand, and I would not haggle the price. I was a local man, as he knew, I would bring the canary yellow car back to him for all its servicing, he would see the love and care that I would lavish on it, and how could he possibly think of selling such a beauty into the harem, so to speak, of a rich arab in Monaco who was very likely too fat to drive it and would use it only as a background to roasting his sheep, and cover it in sand if he took it home? It was not much of an argument, but the cheque book and my presence (serious and intense, I hoped) began slowly to erode his caution and satisfy his avarice.

I still managed to remain a 'real specialist, a collector and a fanatic car-lover' even when he stated his price. I knew that I had taken him slightly off guard. The price was higher than he had expected to ask, and higher than I had expected to pay. Nevertheless, I had started, so I would go on. In his trim little office below a picture of the Virgin Mary looking appropriately heavenwards, and a fireman's calendar with a view of grazing goats, I signed a cheque which could have easily bought me a brand new Peugeot, except that I didn't want a Peugeot. I wanted, and I got, the canary car and drove it, first carefully round the streets of Sainte-Brigitte, and then out on to the main road, with the fat garagiste wedged uncomfortably at my side. I tried it out, made arrangements to have the Simca driven over to Jericho (I would, after all, still need a car for marketing and so on) and, with a glass of pastis to seal the deal, I drove through the lanes in the brilliant sun playing with my new image and my new toy, its engine purring in pristine splendour. The garagiste's son had obviously cherished the beauty of his car. Every rivet, every nut and bolt, door handle, the exhaust, glistened in lovingly polished, cared-for glory.

Dottie, who was slowly walking up the drive as I turned in with a crunch of white-walled tyres on the gravel, pressed herself against the lichened figure of her stone goddess, her face slack with surprise. I stopped precisely beside her.

'Have you taken leave of your senses, Will! Where did you get it? It's not yours?'

I assured her that it was mine. 'Do you think I've gone mad, Dottie? Male menopause?'

'Well, I begin to wonder. I mean, it's beautiful, but, well, I don't know. I think the menopause business is a little unlikely, don't you? I don't think that's caught you up yet? But, somehow, I do see you in the Simca. Not this. It's a playboy's sort of car. Know what I mean?'

'That's my whole problem. We all see me in a Simca Brake. Tweedy. Dependable. Elderly. Unadventurous. In a word, dull. Ageing in my Fair Isle sweater and Viyella shirts.'

'That's going too far, I didn't mean that. You know I didn't.'

'I've flustered you. You know that is *exactly* what you *did* mean. Well, I am altering rapidly. This is, as I said, a period of adjustment for me and the adjusting has begun. I'm enjoying it greatly.'

Dottie was smiling, hand on the yellow rim of the car door. 'It is really very lovely. All long and sleek. Look at that bonnet! You'll be polishing like a mad thing. When did this metamorphosis take place? Where exactly did you discover your road to – what is it? – Damascus?'

I know that I laughed, and I know that she didn't really know why when I said, 'In bed! The other day. I was just lying there. In bed! Feeling rather helpless, aware that there was a very strong force at work around me that I couldn't ignore, and had to deal with. And I decided to deal with it there and then. And I have. I always find that being in bed is extremely *good* for concentration and coming to decisions! Don't you?'

'It depends. I have *no* idea what you're talking about.' She opened the door and slid in beside me, slammed the door, grinned up at me from under her straw hat. 'Off we go. What fun. Have you found some delicious scented lady to drive about with you? Frightfully intimate. We are almost lying prone. Goodness! *Do* drive up and honk your horn. I can't wait to see the faces up top.'

We moved off and began the gentle climb to the house.

'Mrs Theobald, I really believe you approve of this.'

She laughed, pulled off her hat. 'It's the sort of car that brings out the tart in every woman. You know that.'

'I do. Didn't know that you did.'

'Schoolmaster's *wife*? That what you think? Granny glasses, chalky fingers, algebra, good-woman shoes? You'd be amazed how women think sometimes, Will. Deep down there at the bottom, we have our fantasies too, you know.'

'I do know. I *do* indeed. Very important to have fantasies . . . I was talking about that just the other day.'

We drew up at the terrace just as Giles and Arthur, a book in his hand, came hurriedly through the bamboo curtain.

'William!' he called, laughter and admiration lurking, his eyes blue as china. 'What *do* you think you are doing with my wife! What a glorious machine! Dottie! You'll be compromised in that. Out you get!'

She opened her door and, almost reluctantly, got out, hat in hand. 'Hardly be compromised before so many agog faces. Isn't it jolly, Giles? *You'll* fit in very comfortably.'

Frederick had joined the others on the terrace. 'Good grief. Is that ever a real old-fashioned thing! Is it safe to drive?'

'Is it for me?' Giles had come down to the car, ran a hand in a light caress along the door, just as Dottie had done. 'Or is it for you? *You* I suppose?'

'Me. All for me. You can sit in it sometimes. If you behave.'

'I reckoned it was for his birthday. A present. Wouldn't that be just great, Giles? A yellow antique automobile pre-Pearl Harbor, all to yourself!' Frederick was grinning. 'I never did see such a thing! Outside of a museum or an old movie.'

Arthur hit him on the head with the closed book. 'Enough! Impertinent youth. I think it is perfectly splendid. Can you get spares and so on for it? I reckon so. It'll probably guzzle petrol.'

Dottie had gone up the step to the house, brushed through the curtain, called that she 'was going to wash a lettuce'. We sat, Arthur and I, on the terrace, while the two boys peered and poked about the car. Frederick suddenly called up across the long yellow bonnet, 'Mr Caldicott! I forgot. My mother said to thank you sincerely for the invite, and we'll be there. Thank you very much.'

Giles said, 'It was *me* who sent the invitation. I did. I had to do them all. In French.'

'Well, so what? I told you it was okay. My mother just said to tell your dad personally. She hates to write things. Look at these headlamps! You could go elephant-stalking at night with these.' They moved about in a blur of trite conversation.

Arthur said, 'Well, a change of image, I daresay? Good thing to do, I always think. Jericho must be working its charm on you. But of course you'll wince every time you brush a leaf in that thing. Where *did* you find it?'

So I told him, and the telling took time, time enough for Dottie to carry out a tray and a jug of iced wine. 'Lunch? There's plenty. The boys do the washing-up.'

Arthur and I took a glass each and then I excused myself to set off for the splendours of Futurama.

'Good God! Why that place?' Arthur looked astonished.

'It's got a zoo-shop. There's a birthday in the offing. And there's a natty gents' outfitter in the mall there, with some quite decent things – for me. And it's a good time, everyone is either eating or going to eat. I hate being shoved about by all those women with credit cards.' Everyone waved goodbye and cheered as I drove away carefully down the drive.

Driving back from the concrete hell of Futurama, and the drifting hundreds of bewildered people pushing trolleys up and down its fearful aisles, on my way back to Jericho, I saw the little car pulled roughly into the side of the road. The out-of-date green Renault 'easy to park', abandoned with one flat tyre. The doors were locked. Nothing inside, the engine still warm. She couldn't be far down the road unless she had hitched a lift. But she hadn't. Round the second bend of the high-walled lane there she was, trudging slowly, resignedly, two straw baskets in her hands.

Hearing the car she half turned, made a signal to stop

with a raised basket, and as I drew up beside her she was squinting in the high sunlight, then sighed with relief and surprise.

'Ouf! *You!* How funny – in a yellow car! I didn't know: the sun was in my eyes. Will you help me?'

We loaded up, she pushed my bags aside, slid easily, wearily, into the seat beside me.

'How lucky that it was you! I have a flat and there was a terrible popping noise from somewhere inside, ever since I left Sainte-Brigitte. No one stopped for me. No one. One man just shook his head and went faster. The world is full of awful people.' She looked, in spite of being hot and tired, extremely well. Pretty, flushed, her hair tumbled. But I'd have known that straight military back anywhere, the determined walk, the trim elegance of Florence. 'This is new? The car? Foreign, eh? And yours? Yellow!'

'Mine. I bought it this morning. Quite mad, I suppose. Saw it and wanted it and bought it. It's English, an MG, pre-war.'

'It's very pretty. Très chic! Can you take me into Bargemon-sur-Yves? I must get on to the garage, Mama and Céleste expected me an hour ago – and Thomas.'

'And Thomas. We'll be there in a moment or two. I didn't know that you were back, apart from the fact that your mama accepted my invitation. Giles's invitation. So I suspected you were home.'

She nodded, looking straight ahead. 'I'm home. All was well in Marseilles. All was clear.'

I felt an enormous inner slump of relief, but let nothing show. 'I *have* wondered. I was a little bit concerned that there was no message.'

'Why should there be?' Her voice was perfectly reasonable. 'It was unpleasant, a strain, naturally. Waiting. And Thomas was not exactly easy. We had a big battle with him. Céleste was wonderful. So calm, so firm. But all was fine. Thank you.' She still did not look at me, sat calmly, arms folded in her lap, looking ahead.

'And Dr Pascal ... was he helpful? Obviously. Your mind should now be at ease?'

She brushed her hand through her hair, rested her chin on her hand, elbow on the rim of the door. 'I am at ease. Be sure. So you remember his name? Pascal?'

'I remember everything you said that day under the fig trees.'

For the first time she looked up at me. She was, as Dottie had suggested that *she* was, prone there beside me. 'And you have been to London? Was that all settled? Is *your* mind at ease now? You are back at Jericho?'

'The house is sold, my wife is somewhere with her rich lover, Giles and I are installed, with telephone as you must know, in Jericho, and *you* are coming to his party. So all is very well indeed!'

She may have laughed – I didn't hear her – but she had a slight smile on her lips when she said, 'The invitation! I was away, but Mama decided that we must accept. Not me. That was her idea entirely. I gather that you went to see her?'

'With my address in London. In case you needed help.'

'I did not. Thank you. She spoke kindly of the meeting. Amazing. You must be a magician.'

I laughed at the absurd formality of her attitude. 'Sometimes, my dear Florence, I do believe that I am. It was a useful meeting I think. It cleared the air. But I am really happy that you will come. It's not important to me or to you, but it is to Giles. You are his only "aunt", remember? Thomas is his only cousin, he cares about that. And he's celebrating his first decade and he'll be doing it in French, in his new home, with his French friends. That's very important to me. I want to open up his world.'

'Is Louise de Terrehaute French? I thought American?'

She had turned to look at the vines flashing past. *Now* what was she up to?

'American. French ancestors. She's from Louisiana – they really hardly think of themselves as Americans. Frederick, her son, and she are coming. Yes. Do you know them?'

'No. Really not. But of course everyone in the area knows Louise de Terrehaute. Before the Revolution, can you imagine! So absurd! They did own all the land about here.'

'They owned Jericho. I know that. How did you know that I knew them?'

'We all met years ago, when Raymond was still alive. She and her new, at the time, husband had come to look round. They bought a house on the hill. My mama plays bridge, Dorothée Teeobald plays bridge, they are often partners. Et voilà! There is little that is private in a bridge club, you know? Everything is sifted and sorted. I didn't know that she had accepted. Amazing! She is very "bon chic, bon genre". Really does not involve herself with local Society.'

'But she knows the Theobalds.'

'The boy goes to them for tutoring. As Giles does. Is that how you met? Of course, it must be.'

'You have answered for me. Correct.'

'The Teeobalds are very useful for busy parents in the summer holidays. They *always* accept their unwanted young to give the poor parents some time for ... amusement.' There was a fine edge of sarcasm in her voice. Unusual in Florence; whatever else she might be, I had not experienced sarcasm before. Nor ever bitterness. Anger, hate, but not female sarcasm. Against Dottie or against Lulu? Difficult to tell at that moment and then she changed the conversation. 'He is well, Giles? He is still fishing? Clotilde is still with you, I know, and *very* happy ... so that is comforting. And she cooks, too, I hear?'

'She cooks too. I am never surprised about anything that circulates in this little town. God! The gossip and chatter which must go on over those hands of cards. I am just so surprised that they all managed to clam up as soon as I arrived and began asking questions about James. It was a wall of silence or mis-information. Loyalty to you, I suppose?'

'Loyalty to Mama. But loyalty. Against the nosey foreigner,' and she laughed. She settled back in her seat, hair blowing, smiling.

I was extremely glad that I had not unbuttoned my shirt on this hot afternoon. Florence would have had a clear, uninterrupted view of my battle scars as she was very close, and rather below me. Try to convince the bridge club that I had just fallen flat in the brambles with my strimmer? Fat chance.

It was almost three when we rounded the church and drew up outside her smug little house. As she started to get out of the car and make some murmured thanks for giving her a lift, I put my hand on her arm and stopped her.

'Florence, I have a small gift I must give you. Can I bring it over. Maybe tomorrow sometime?'

'A gift?' Her brow was furrowed. 'A gift? From you?'

'No. Not from me. From Aronovich. Solomon Aronovich. Remember him?'

She pulled away from me gently. '*Very* well. *Very* well.' She took her baskets and, with one of them, slammed the car door shut. 'I want nothing from him, nothing. I would accept no gift from him ever. Thank you.'

'It's really from James, as a matter of fact. It's his watch. The Piaget. Aronovich managed to trace it, bought it. I have it.'

She was ice cold, rock steady. The lace curtains in the bow window of the house were being lightly adjusted. 'I prefer not to know about it. Please don't speak of it again.' She started to go to the little iron gate.

I called quietly, 'It's worth money, Florence. I only think of Thomas. We could sell it . . . *I* can?'

'Do as you choose,' she said. 'I would rather die.' She pushed through the gate and walked up the white pebble path. She did not look back and I started up, drove slowly round the church, and headed home to Jericho.

The gigantic terracotta plinth, the bounty of white impatiens and scarlet geraniums, the sun blazing through the branches of the two sentinel cedars, by the steps the peacock frilling in full display, his dull little hen prodding in the gravel of the drive. Giles grabbed my arm and cried, 'Dad! Look! All his feathers are up. Couldn't we have one? *Couldn't* we?' I said no, and swept in a curve to the foot of the steps. '*Why* not? For my birthday? Next week? Why not?'

Frederick came running across the sprinkled lawns, dodging the shower of glistening diamonds spilling in gentle arcs waving backwards and forwards in gentle rhythm. 'Hi! Hi! Giles, it's going to be real hot. We are at the pool. C'mon, c'mon.'

Giles opened his door and got out, carrying his blue hand-grip with his bathing things. Frederick was almost naked, and very brown.

'Why not, Dad?'

I got out and shut my door gently. The yellow bodywork shimmered pleasingly in the heat. 'Because *I* don't want a bloody peacock, that's why.'

Behind Frederick, limping painfully, a tall young man with a bandaged foot, a white thong and dark glasses. He stood with his fists on his hips and greeted Giles with a flick of a hand.

'This is Henri. He's hurt his foot,' said Frederick.

I nodded to Henri, who just scowled back.

'Yes, I know. He can't drive so I brought your pal over. Is your mother about?'

Frederick was scratching his leg. 'She's someplace, maybe in the house. You want to see my shark? It's a huge thing. You blow it up, it's great. Henri is very good at blowing things up, he's got a pump. C'mon, Giles, we'll go down to the pool. Henri will show you.' He hurried off, and Giles, after a bleak look of anger about no peacocks, went after him.

'About five?' I called crossing my heart. He turned, nodded, and went on. I was trusted.

I followed Henri slowly, on account of his wounded foot, up the steps into the house. A high arched gothic hall, white, cool, with an old flagged floor. At the end, a vast gilded console table with a jasper top carrying an alabaster jar stuffed with tall white stocks. Henri, unwilling to enter the house naked, indicated a door far across the hall and hobbled away.

Lulu was standing in a vast shady room thrusting spikes of blue delphinium into a square glass tank. She saw me, waved a spike of blossom above her head. 'I'm *so* sorry, you having to drive all the way! But I am going crazy. Seven for lunch, a sullen cook, and a lame chauffeur. I just could *not* make the time to get to you.' She was wearing a blue and white butcher's apron, a wide-brimmed straw hat and not much else.

'It's very good of you to have the boy.'

'No trouble for me.' She stuck in a couple more blooms. 'Anyway, you found me. Sit down, anywhere, I'll be just a moment. How did you get in?'

'I followed Tarzan, easy.'

'Oh. Poor Henri. Tarzan! Isn't he great?'

'Carries all before him. Unblushingly.'

'Oh God! Naked again? I keep telling him . . . He's down at the pool, keeping an eye on my offspring. And yours. He was pool-boy at the Beau Rivage. I thought he was just wasted there. So he's here. Right?'

'Right. You don't waste time, Lulu, I know that.'

She laughed, wiped her hands on the apron, started to untie it. 'You look very chic this morning. My, my! White pants, a very classy shirt. What happened?'

'I had to hide my wounds.'

She removed the apron over her head and her hat fell off. 'Wounds? What wounds? What happened?' She retrieved her hat, threw it and the apron into a chair.

'You did. Those claws of yours. I just say I fell in a bramble patch.'

'A bramble patch!' She snorted with laughter. 'You are too much! Who asked?'

'Only Giles. So far.'

'They *can't* be that bad. Let me see?' I backed into my chair. 'Oh, c'mon. A little love scratch! It was days ago.' She was wearing a thin silk shirt, short shorts. Eminently desirable, standing above me, legs astride. I got up quickly.

'I only dropped by to say thanks for accepting the invitation from Giles. It was very, very good of you. It's not exactly your kind of scene.'

'Oh, it'll be fun. Freddy wants to go, good for him too, and we get to meet *tout* Bargemon-sur-Yves.'

'No. No you do not. It's strictly provincial, not Hôtel du Cap. The Theobalds you do know, and the Prideaux, mother and daughter? Florence and Sidonie. You know them? Of them?'

'Oh God, everyone knows everyone, or about everyone, in this place, even if we don't get to sit at their tables. Sure I know who you mean. Florence is your very own sister-in-law? Right? All that agony about your brother? That has not been a secret here for years. Long before you arrived in town to look around. That was really tragic. Maybe we did meet? I don't recall. I know we met the mother and a very pretty fellow, the son? A soldier, cadet? I came here with my second husband on our honeymoon, because Bobbie wanted to see his "ancestral" plot. I ask you! The Terrehaute inheritance did *not* exist.'

'You know it all. Where I live, Jericho, was once part of that inheritance.'

She was slowly pushing her shirt into her shorts. This involved a certain amount of physical display which only went to prove how gloriously well she had kept her body into her early thirties. And she knew it, knew I was watching. She pulled the shirt tightly across firm breasts. 'The inheritance is some god-awful rockery. Piles of boulders. Rocks. We found this place anyway. Are you looking like that because of my tits?'

'Yes. When was all that? The arrival at the château?'

'Oh, years ago. I hadn't birthed Freddy. Ten years? The mother was quite pleasant, I remember, and the son was divine. He liked shooting things. Got killed in an auto pile-up a couple of years later. We only ever came here in the summer. Sometimes at Christmas. But I prefer New York for winter.'

'A week ago I didn't know you existed.'

'Now you have scars to prove I do. I don't know many people here. Not at all my kind of life, small-town meanness. I hate the gossip and intrigue. Why do you imagine I behaved like Mata Hari the other day? Secret addresses in envelopes, separate cars, that crappy apartment? Les Palmiers. Hideous, but divinely anonymous.'

'Is that its name? Les Palmiers?'

She pulled her hair up into a bunch to the nape of her neck with both hands; the movement, slow, deliberate, thrust her breasts towards me. 'Les Palmiers is where you got "wounded". My room without windows. Got it?'

'I wish like hell you wouldn't do that.'

She twisted slightly. 'Do what?'

'Display.'

She let her hair fall about her shoulders. 'I will behave

like a country milk-maid. Sweetness will flow from me at your party. I *can* behave. I know how. It's just that I really love to screw. But I know where and when and' – she moved towards me smiling her little cat-smile – 'with whom.'

'Is there still a Bobbie de Terrehaute? Does he still figure in your life?'

'As a signature on the bottom of a cheque is all. There was an utterly, utterly ugly little scandal a while ago. He was caught with a brother and sister act. Both minors, pubescent Chinese. He has unusual tastes in sex, as you gather? So I just skipped away; with a settlement. He is still my husband, in a distant kind of way. Lives in Rome now and doesn't fuss me one bit. He wanted an heir, can you believe? I provided Freddy. At mortal risk to myself. He sees his father sometimes, and if there is anything more you simply can't wait to know, you will *have* to wait until the next session at Les Palmiers, Perry Mason.' She was standing before me, hands on her hips, a silent signal that the session was at an end.

I said suddenly, 'You haven't seen my new car. To go with the white pants and the classy shirt. Come and look.'

We walked together across the high, cool hall.

'I'll behave beautifully at the supper. Lot's wife. But animated. I won't wear Chanel. Maybe something very demure? Floral? But not woollen, or flannel? You wouldn't want *that*? And it's summer.'

'I wouldn't want that. No.'

We reached the big door. She stood on the top of the steps looking down into the gardens, shading her eyes with a hand. The car dazzled in the sun.

'That it? A phallic symbol if I *ever* saw one. And I'm responsible for that too? It is divine. Sexy as hell. White-wall tyres. But it isn't the kind of car you can take to Les Palmiers. No way. It's as anonymous as a squadron of tanks. No problem! We'll think of something.' She put her fingers to her lips, mimed a little kiss, turned and went back up the steps, then she turned again, her hands caressing her thighs, leant forward conspiratorially.

'Ciao, babe!' she whispered, and went away.

CHAPTER 9

It was with a mild degree of relief that I heard from a radiant Clotilde that Mon-Ami had given in his notice at Gavery and was presently down in the potager digging. Although I rather liked my image of becoming a Vita Sackville-West or yet a second Harold Nicolson, in time, I had to confess to myself that I knew very little about gardening at all. The rebuilding of my dull character was to include, apart from the flat gut and firmer muscle, that of a man of the soil; someone like Arthur who could dig and plant and sit after his labours in the shade of his vine, glass in hand, and survey his work knowing that it would be quite in order to say, '*I* did all that. *All* my own work.'

But as I had hardly ever lifted a finger in the gardens of the family house in Faringdon, or put more than a tentative hand or offered encouragement to efforts in Simla Road, it was unsurprising that all I was really capable of doing was digging (any fool can do that) or dead-heading a rose or two, and planting a few bulbs from time to time. Although I could very well see what the land at Jericho must have once looked like under the passionately youthful energy and vision of James and Florence, I had very little idea how the reconstruction of what they had achieved should be done.

So, with Mon-Ami to help, and he was obviously keen and knowledgeable, we might together (providing I did the odd bits here and there) get a little of the place back into shape. At least for the part of the summer which remained. We were already tipping into July, the heat was reaching its height, the sun blazed, the light blinded, the shade beckoned constantly. But Mon-Ami seemed impervious to heat. Without his leathers and the bowl-like casque he, regrettably to Giles's eyes, looked 'just like anyone else. Quite skinny, really.' Tall, strong, wearing old jeans and a faded cotton T-shirt, he no longer passed as an extra from *Star Trek* but just a perfectly ordinary labourer. Albeit with classical features presently running with sweat.

Clotilde had taken everything at Jericho firmly in hand: I was extremely pleased that she had, but at the same time I *was* aware that my own comfortable existence as boss was subtly being eroded. However, it was good not to have to cope with Giles and his filthy shirts, underpants and shorts, to arrange meals, to cook and pull up the beds. Clotilde seemed to thrive on this kind of work like a diligent bee, buzzing and zooming about the place singing happily. She had 'her men', as she called us, under her thumb; we needed her and she knew that, and relished it.

The house-keeping money had to be increased now that we had an extra mouth to feed, and Mon-Ami ate prodigiously. No longer could Giles and I take lunch in the kitchen – we had to eat on the terrace under the vine so that Clotilde and Mon-Ami had the kitchen to themselves. In the winter, or in rain, she said, she would put a small table in the Long Room and we would lunch there. Supper, as she called it always, was our own affair and was to be taken when we wished and where we wished. She would leave something in the oven and there was always, always, potage. She rejected nothing that might be the basis for her soups;

every scrap was utilized and a large pot always sat ready simmering at the edge of the stove.

However, we all gathered together round the kitchen table for the morning break, while Clotilde prepared the lunch or chopped vegetables. It was informal, easy, slightly Impressionist. Her bright, plump face, the sun streaming through the open windows, the rough white walls, the rugged, bronzed arms of Mon-Ami holding his glass or mug, the scent of thyme and oregano, of hot cut grass, the blaze of wild flowers stuck in jars on the table and at the window; it all looked a little like a Vuillard or, with Clotilde's ample rosy splendour, a Renoir.

I now had time to drive about the country in my splendid yellow car without worrying about locking doors and windows. Not that I ever really had at Jericho. It was very much a country world. Tight, trusting, safe. I spent one morning over at La Maison Blanche arranging the menu for the birthday feast. At Giles's own suggestion, and as it was his event, he was to be allowed to have what he best liked, provided it wasn't baked beans, 'crusty-chicken' or fish fingers. In the event he decided on a couscous. Partly because he so relished the dish, and also, in some odd way, he thought that it would be 'very nice' for his 'aunt' and her mother. After all, he reasoned, they knew what a *real* couscous was like because they had lived in Algeria and Morocco, and Eugène knew all about couscous, so we'd have that. Eugène looked slightly taken aback at my suggestion, but accepted the situation gracefully and said we would have a perfect couscous and then we planned the rest of the supper.

He was aware, as was Madame Mazine, of the importance of the evening. A first decade. Very much something to celebrate. They would put up a round table, Clotilde had insisted on coming to serve, and everything would be comme il faut. I must have no fear, even though it was high season for the hotel. It was also, he said quietly, most impressive to be entertaining the Prideaux. They had never been seen to dine in public together before, so it was cachet for the hotel. Madame Prideaux and the Colonel had been very important in Algiers, very important figures, but this I undoubtedly knew? I said I did. Easier than enduring the detailed histoire which I knew must follow should I say no.

A frisson of controlled excitement became apparent when the name de Terrehaute was casually mentioned. Did I know that, many years ago, before the Revolution, the family owned all the lands in the area? That once my present house was just the pigeonnier of the great château whose ruins lay on the boundary of my land? I said that I did, and chucked in a few extra details, gleaned from Lulu and Dottie, that the eldest son, his bride, two children and their bonne, had fled before capture, reached Bordeaux, bribed their way on to an American frigate and after enduring a fearsome voyage eventually reached New Orleans. This caused great interest, and when I said that the present heir, one Frederick, would be attending the supper, even Madame Mazine, who usually showed the interest and disdain of a dromedary, cried 'Oh! là là! Quel plaisir! Le petit Duc *lui même*!'

I hastily added that he was not a 'Duc', but it made not a whit of difference. Madame Mazine was a great deal more pleasant than she had ever been in the past from that moment on. The French, whatever else they may be, are basically royalists and corking snobs. The fact that Frederick's father, the true heir, was drugged to the eyeballs and living in Rome I decided to ignore.

Giles had obviously seen me coming back up the track to the house. The yellow car burned and sparkled in the sun. He came hurrying down from the stream, bathing-trunks, hair flattened by sweat, muddy arms and legs. 'Did you arrange it all? Supper?'

I turned the car and eased into the shed, the engine murmuring sweetly. Stopped. He was picking his way barefoot across the dirt floor.

'Did you? See Eugène and all?'

'Saw Eugène and all. It's arranged. A round table, couscous, tomato, basil and mozzarella to start with, Cherries Jubilee to finish. And I've chosen the wine.'

'What's that? Have I had it? The Jubilee stuff?'

'I don't know. Hot cherries on ice cream? You'll love it.' I slid out of the car and hitched my pants. 'Why are you covered in mud? I have asked you not to muck about up at the stream unless I'm around. You are a little sod.'

'Mon-Ami is with me. We're damming it with rocks.'

'I didn't employ Mon-Ami to bugger about with dams. He's got other things to do.' We went out into the heat, and I shut the shed door.

'You swore, Will. Bugger. That's a terrible word. Eric Thingummy said it once and Mum really screamed at him. *And* sod. You said both.'

'Oh shit. Sorry . . .'

'You just said *another*! I don't mind.'

'Thanks. But I don't want Mon-Ami mucking about.'

'He's terrifically strong. He can lift the stones for me.'

We were walking up through the almond trees towards the cliffs and the stream, a tumbling twist of the river Yves which wound across the top of my land. I saw the naked back of Mon-Ami moving slowly in the ripples of heat.

Giles suddenly said, 'I know a really *terrible* word. Shall I say it? No one will hear, just us. It's really pretty bad.'

'Well, why say it? If it's so terrible? I don't want to hear it frankly.'

'Well if I say it aloud, to you, I won't want to say it aloud to anyone for quite a long time. You see?'

'Getting it off your chest, is that it?'

We were almost up to the stream which was softly

bickering and shouldering over its rough bed. Mon-Ami was staggering about with a boulder the size of a sheep.

'All right. Say it if it'll help you. What is it?'

He turned his head away, thrust his thumbs into the top of his trunks, suddenly, looked skywards, avoiding me deliberately.

'Suppository,' he said.

We walked on in silence broken only by the stream.

'There. It's pretty awful, isn't it? You'd be furious, wouldn't you? If I said it in front of anyone? Wouldn't you?'

'Yes, I would. You shouldn't even know such a word. Now forget it. Right?'

'Right. I just wanted to say it aloud so you'd know I knew it. Willwood Minor told me. At school. He told quite a lot of us. Very secretly. I knew it was very bad. He said it put a curse on people if you said it *to* them.'

'I see. Well you said it to me. When do I get cursed?'

'Oh no! I didn't *say* it to you! I said it to the sky, just out loud. That's all. I'm quite glad, you know.'

'So am I. But never say it again. Not ever. In front of me or anyone else. Just try and forget it. Willwood Minor was just showing off. And I don't want you to do that. Right? I loathe show-offs. So remember!'

We pushed through a small cane-break. Giles suddenly yelped. 'Ouch! Ouch! My foot!' I stopped and looked at him hopping about on one leg, holding a bloody foot. 'I'm bleeding!'

'I can see. It's a scratch. Barefoot: you're mad.'

'You said to. To walk barefoot. You said!'

'Not through a cane break. Clot. They'll harden.' I turned away (he wasn't harmed) and went on. He came hopping after me.

'Dad!' (Change of name. This was serious.) I stopped. 'Dad, you aren't angry, are you? About the word I said? I did ask you.'

'No. I'm not angry. It was very good of you to say it. Tell me. Get it off your chest. Shows that you trust me.'

'Well I do.'

'Fine. Great. But it's a really silly word. Not *nearly* as terrible as whatever his name is says it is. Just forget it, okay? Let's see how many boulders Mon-Ami has carted about. And we'll do it all in French. Got it?' I wondered quite how I'd cope as father the next time we went into the pharmacy. He'd be so swamped by the word that he'd lose all faith in me as a parent. Well, cope with it when it happened.

Meanwhile Mon-Ami straightened up and saluted across the stream. He was standing very tall, running with sweat, a bit of cloth round his throat. 'Et violà! This is almost finished. You see? Only two more to fill it.' He had caught my concern. 'You can see, monsieur, it won't be deep, just up to there.' He measured a vague line somewhere in the region of his knees.

'And when the winter comes? The rains?' I said. 'The river floods, it's so? What happens then? Does the water pour down into the house at the bottom there? Where does it go?'

Mon-Ami's expression was, as always, scrupulously polite, no smirk, no impatience at my ignorance or sarcasm. 'Monsieur! You see! Look. This is the barrier, these big rocks, but they are not *so* big . . . hein? The water will get to this height and then fall over the top into the stream below. It is not solid, monsieur. No cement. You will not be flooded.' And then mild exhaustion took over – it had been quite a long speech for him – and he bent down to manoeuvre a final rock into its place in the barrier.

Giles was shifting about on his bare feet like a hen on chicken wire. I told Mon-Ami to finish off as soon as he could, that I'd change my shirt and pants and give him a hand down at the potager, told Giles not to play about alone up there. He shrugged and said, in English, 'All right. I'll come down when Mon-Ami finishes. We'll just put this big stone in here.'

Walking down the rough track to the house I heard them laughing together, and realized that the role of father could be a bit limiting: standards to set, values to maintain. I wondered vaguely how Lulu coped with Frederick, who had, ostensibly, no father. Single-parent family. You really had to have one of each. Mummy and Daddy. What, I thought, was to become of me? Having just chucked one wife I was really not over-anxious to take on another just for Giles. Just for Giles? Was it really only for Giles? What about Florence? And thinking of her I started to whistle and was in a buoyant mood as I passed Clotilde pegging out tea-cloths on the drying line. She nodded happily towards me, flapped a cloth. Florence. Yes. I'd be seeing her pretty soon. At the supper.

On the morning of his birthday Giles gave an extremely convincing impersonation of someone having a catatonic fit. He suffered a severe attack of cataplexy and just stood rooted to the floor of the Long Room after he had ripped the paper away from the large carton I had lugged from the Zoo-Parc of Futurama the day I had gone to alter my own image with too tight jeans and classy shirts.

The picture on the glossy box, like all pictures on glossy boxes, did not exactly match up to the contents. However, overlooking glittering shoals of brilliant fish, luxuriant water weeds, mermaids and chunks of unlikely coral, what he had before him was his long-desired aquarium. Not too large – a good beginner's size – plus oxygenator, lights and a handbook on 'How to Maintain Your Underwater Magic-Land' in a frantic French translation from the Japanese. I felt compelled to help him open everything up, as he had clearly gone into a temporary decline. I waved the handbook at him, to try and break the glassy-eyed stare.

'This is what you wanted? Isn't it? You asked for it that day in the garden when Florence was here. Remember? Giles? Move! *Do* something.'

He brushed his hands over his face roughly. 'I'm trying to. It's just brilliant! You remembered. Oh! It's brilliant! And it's really *quite* big.'

The spell had broken, and he was suddenly a small boy again, joyous and gay. 'Wow! Wow! Oh, this is great. I'll have to get rocks, and sand, and weeds and – oh! *Wow!*'

The morning was still cool, the sunlight had not yet probed through the denseness of the heavy vine, did not, as yet, play across the cool tiles of the floor, and the sweet air, fresh and clean, was suddenly warmed by the scent of coffee and hot croissants as Clotilde came in carrying a heavy tray which she set down on a small table.

'Voilà! Bonjour! Félicitations, Gilles, et regarde! Des cadeaux, de la part de mon ami et moi-même.' And she handed him a tube-shaped package by a string handle. For a second it swung between them, Giles's eyes bright, hers sparkling with pleasure at his apprehensive delight. He ripped off the jazzy wrapping-paper to disclose four small goldfish nosing and gasping desperately up and down the sides of a screw top Nescafé jar. He started at the frantic little fish, set the jar carefully on the floor amidst the wreckage of the aquarium wrappings, and threw his arms tightly about her waist, his head beating lovingly against her breasts. '*Just* what I wanted! You *knew*! Thank you! Thank you! Look at my aquarium!' Clotilde detached herself gently, began setting out cups and saucers, the confiture and croissants. 'From Monoprix, yesterday. So they will be good value. In a little plastic bag. I had to carry them on my moto. So pretty. Look at their little veils, like children at confirmation. Don't let this get cold.'

But breakfast was forgotten. He carried out the fish to put them in a bucket on the terrace. Clotilde cleared up the paper, murmuring and laughing, stuck it under her arm. 'Oh là là! Such deceptions.' She had picked up the glittering, gaudy container. 'It is like a picture in a magazine.'

I buttered a croissant. 'Like the Great Barrier Reef.'

She dropped the carton, stooped to take up shreds of multi-coloured plastic 'straw'.

'I do not know this place, but I do know we live in the Var. Not where women have tails. Mais, quand même, he is happy?'

And he *was* happy, radiantly happy, and I was pleased with his show of unclouded delight. The fact that he had been able to embrace Clotilde so warmly, with so much confidence, gave me deep satisfaction. A sign of trust, of acceptance, a demonstration of affection. There hadn't been much of that in his life in his first decade. Perhaps now, almost certainly now, he was easing out of his strict British reserve. He was already freer, less introverted, than the child who had arrived in my life only a couple of months ago. He had been easy, to be sure, correct, apparently *almost* at ease with himself. But gradually the bricks which had restrained his true personality in a closed room of caution were being eased away and his true spirit was breaking out. He was beginning to trust. And show love.

This delighted me, it would do him no harm at all to be demonstrative, tactile, completely free with his emotions – with cautious but sensible restraint. Arthur and Dottie had been a tremendous help in this, Jericho had provided him with his frame of reference (anyway for the time being) and the presence of Clotilde and Mon-Ami within that frame, secure, uncomplicated, firm and affectionate, had started the healing of the subconscious bruises which he had sustained in an unsatisfactory existence in Simla Road, and, frankly, up until the day he had arrived, bewildered but excited, at Nice airport, with a mother who was on the point of letting him slip his lead. (To put it more politely than she deserved – she was chucking him away. Probably unawares – but, equally probably, not altogether.) She had known, that day, exactly where *she* was going: off to join her chum in his 'Harrods Antiqued' new villa in some suburban village. She hadn't really given much of a thought to what might happen to her son, beyond the fact that somehow 'Daddy' would cope. Would have to cope. *Did* cope. Liked coping. It was my 'birthday' today, as well as his. I felt pretty good about it. Before complete complacency overwhelmed me, and above the sound of water splashing into a bucket somewhere, I heard the three blasts of Jacob's signal that the mail had arrived (and that he was still being cautious about rabies).

The splashing stopped on the terrace, Giles shouted, 'Bonjour! Bonjour!'

I went on to the terrace. Jacob was pulling his Mobylette on to its stand, began to unstrap a package from his carrier, waved to Giles who was hurrying down the path to meet him. Some letters were held up, the package handed over, heavy, requiring two hands to carry it; a brief exchange of conversation, a doffing of a cap and then Giles came slowly back up to the house.

'Terribly heavy! What can it be? It's for me. It says *Master* Giles. Is that me?'

'Must be. What else does it say? There's printing on the paper.'

'*Hédiard*. It says Hédiard, rue des Serbes, Cannes, AM.' He had reached the terrace, set the package down, ran curious hands over it. 'It'll be from Mum, I bet.'

I said, 'She was in Cannes, she's had this sent to you. Hédiard is a very famous luxury grocer's. She probably did it all by telephone, before she went off to Italy or wherever

194

she was going. But she remembered! She *did* remember, and on the right day!'

He had started to tear away the elegant logo-paper, discovered a stout cardboard box stuffed with more red and green plastic straw, which spilled and drifted across the terrace as he produced one 'treasure' after another to his slightly startled gaze.

'Everything's in French. All the labels. Look. Is this ginger?'

'That's ginger. In syrup . . .'

'And these? What are these? P-ê-c-h-e. That's peach, isn't it? Peaches in cognac?'

'That's right. Don't chuck the straw stuff everywhere. It'll be hell if it flies into the roses and things. These are dried figs. Right?'

'What are p-i-s-t-a-c-h-i-o nuts?'

'Just that. Pistachio nuts, and those in your other hand are artichoke bottoms in salted water.'

'Wow,' he said, without much enthusiasm, and rummaged about a bit more producing yet another jar, bottle or packet, all of which confounded him utterly until he recognized some cheese straws and, with a soft crow of pleasure, a small white bar studded with nuts, angelica and cherries.

'Montélimar nougat! *That's* all right. A bit hard to chew really. But I can give it to Frederick, can't I?'

'Your present. You do as you wish. Better start clearing the cellophane muck. Up! Come on.'

We scrabbled about on the terrace, brushing little piles of trembling plastic into handfuls. 'Will I like these things? "Artichoke bottoms"? Quite rude really. I don't know what they are.'

'I don't think, this time, that you *will* like them. Much. But you haven't found a card. There must be a card somewhere in this stuff.'

He found it after a bit of rooting about in the tumbled

box. Helen's generous, looping handwriting on a Hédiard business card. 'Sweetie-one: now you are a real little French-man, grown up today, so here are some delicious goodies for your supper party tonight. I will seriously miss you, but think of you. Love you heaps and heaps. Enjoy!' It was signed with a huge looping 'Mummy'. There were two kisses.

'That's jolly good,' I said. 'She remembered. I was certain she would . . .'

'Yes, she did. That *was* good.' He was glumly satisfied.

I pushed on and asked him for the letters I'd seen Jacob give him. A card for him from Dottie and Arthur, neat, affectionate, a detail from a Manet of a faintly supercilious youth in a straw hat from *Luncheon in the Studio*. Arthur had written in his immaculate handwriting, 'Happy Birth-day! This could be you, Giles, the *next* time you are ten!'

Giles looked worried. 'I already am ten. Today.'

'That's what he means. Idiot. The *next* time you are ten again you'll be twenty. Understand?'

'Awesome. Twenty? Oh yes. I see. Ten and ten. What age will you be then?'

'Ah . . . umm. Fifty-six.'

He looked at me with thinly veiled pity.

'Never mind,' he said and started repacking the jars and bottles.

One letter for me from the EDF, a bank statement, another from my editor in London suggesting a new photo-graph for the next dust-jacket. 'We've been using the last one for two years. A change a good idea?'

A change was a very good idea. It was already taking place.

On the terrace of La Maison Blanche a tall youth dragged himself into his back-pack, his booted feet scraping about on the tiles. He had pronounced knee-caps, sloping shoulders and round tin glasses. His friend, a thin, sallow girl with the same kind of glasses, corn white hair and battered khaki shorts, swigged the last of their Coke tin, crushed it, hitched straps and buckles on her pack, took up a folded map and muttered, '*Yah? Horstie?*' and he nodded '*Yah, Schnoodie,*' and they clattered down the steps into the square. They were the last of the day-trippers and, as Eugène bitterly remarked, occupied a table, drank a Coke between two, changed their socks or removed their boots, rested a little and left. No money. No profit. And German – to add deeper insult to the trivia of their being there. He tidied up the table, his apron flapping in his haste to restore cleanliness and order for the evening arrivals. It was seven-fifteen: the hotel residents were about to descend from their rooms to take up their regular tables and order their Cinzanos or citron pressés from Claude.

However, this evening there would be less space than usual for them on account of the round table at the far end of the terrace, lavishly set for eight, chairs all around, a big jug of fat white garden roses in the centre, candles ready to be lit at strategic points. Giles's birthday feast.

Above me, as I sat beside the table, guarding it from thieving sparrows, and two white doves, the sky was fading to the pale blue of evening which would, in time, give way to the saffron yellow and pink of the setting sun. Across the square, beyond the church, a green neon light suddenly sparked on spelling out 'Le Sporting', only the 'o' was fusing, blinking now and again. A lewd wink. On, off. On, off.

High over the jumble of roofs and chimneys of the town the swallows swung and soared, spiralling upwards, a fluid, twisting comma in the fading sky. The church struck the quarter just as Arthur and Dottie drove slowly up the hill into the square and parked, with a wave, beside my yellow car. I went into the bar to get Giles away from the TV.

'Your guests are arriving. Come on. Out.' and I pushed him on to the terrace. Dottie looked startlingly pretty as they walked towards us. She had very good legs, a neat figure which I had never really paid attention to, concealed as it always was in a swirl of denim skirts or old jeans. Tonight she was trim, slim, hair shining, tightly braided. A thin coral necklet, white shirt, a silk scarf slung over a shoulder, a good bag on her arm. Arthur was dressed for safari, in a jacket with huge pockets, a red spotted handkerchief at his throat. Coming up the steps, shaking hands, wondering if they were the first, and perhaps too early?

Moments later, as the clock clanged the hour, precisely and on the last beat, Florence and Sidonie Prideaux appeared at the end of the square from behind a flying buttress of the church, walking from their house. I saw them the instant they passed the little buttress, lost them for a moment as two elderly residents scraped into chairs and set down their drinks, caught them again as they came abreast of the hotel cut-out of the chef with his pink hand upraised, the menu pinned to the palm, and then they came up the steps, slowly, carefully – Madame Prideaux's first time, one knew.

I was on my feet to greet them, lugging Giles with me. I felt a surge of quiet elation at the sight of Florence. Slender, calm, smiling, easy. The same simple frock with little cuffs and the floral tie that she had worn to dinner the first time she had ever come to the hotel with me.

It was evident that Madame Prideaux was a little shy, which imposed a vague formality on her, but then she saw Dottie and Arthur, affectionately touched Giles on the head, and, moving uncertainly through the little tables, let herself be led to our large round one, where we all sat. There really was no alternative.

Full season at the hotel meant full tables: we had nowhere else to sit. But sitting, as we did, brought us all together. Even though we all knew each other, had passed time with each other, there was still a slight feeling of the importance of the perfectly trivial event. A boy's tenth birthday: nothing more. However, at the crisp linen table, with the jug of white roses, the candles in their storm-glasses, the shining cutlery, the glasses – all these things combined to give an impression of an Event, until, with a loud sigh, Madame Prideaux relaxed, eased herself back into her rush-bottomed chair and placing her hands flat on the table declared herself content.

'We speak in French, all of us. I was anxious that we would have to speak in English and my knowledge of that is very – what did you once say it was, Monsieur Colcott? – "Rusty"? And it *was*. "Rusty". An odd word?' Ice cracked, shyness began to melt.

Giles made a face and said, 'I have to be a little Frenchman. Mother said so. But I think she was being a bit rude.'

Madame Prideaux folded her arms. 'Quite possibly. And we are two short? Two empty places here?'

Arthur said quickly, 'The de Terrehautes. They are a bit further away than we are. A longer journey.'

Eugène appeared with the Bollinger in a white cloth, eyebrows raised to me in question. I nodded and he began to pour, Madame Prideaux first, who almost instinctively put her hand over her glass and then, as quickly, removed it. Realizing.

'A toast?' she said. 'To Gilles. And he will have but a sip. A true *little* Frenchman would *not* take a full glass. Not at all!'

Giles scowled; Dottie laughed; Florence said pleasantly that she knew a lot of *real* little Frenchmen who would easily take a full magnum, and we talked and began to raise our glasses at exactly the moment that Lulu swung into the square in a haze of dust and the open-top Mercedes. We lowered our glasses. She crunched to a stop beside my yellow car, waved across to us up on the terrace.

'Hi Giles! Happy, happy Birthday! We are late because of someone's goddamned cows wandering back to their barn. Hi, y'all!' And, opening his door, she pushed Frederick into the square. 'Get out, little one, save some wine for Mama!'

There was an instant lifting of mood on the terrace. I got to my feet, Giles ran to greet Frederick, the hotel residents lowered their *Var Matin*s and *Le Monde*s and watched as Lulu parked easily, slammed doors, took off her dark glasses and swung elegantly up the steps towards us, arms outstretched to embrace Giles, who this time around didn't duck, and running her fingers through my hair said how pretty it all looked, gay and festive, and were we speaking English or French?

'French,' said Sidonie Prideaux mildly, adjusting a bracelet. 'If you *can*?'

Lulu regarded the Colonel's widow calmly. 'I can. I have a terrible Ammurican accent which will possibly amuse you, but the grammar is good, and the slang even better, and . . .' Moving slowly towards her victim, taking an unoffered hand in both of hers, she said in a sweet and low voice, 'You won't remember at all, but we did meet, years ago. At your country house, Jericho? I was with my second husband. We were on a kind of "Return to the Ancestors" kick. I met you with that very handsome son of yours. Remember? He was just ravishing . . . Richard? Robert? I forget, it was the briefest of meetings.'

Madame Prideaux sat quite still, her hand held firmly in Lulu's. 'Raymond,' she said. 'His name was Raymond. He was killed.'

Lulu leant down swiftly, intimate, caring (I was fascinated watching her play). 'I know. I *know*. I was *terribly* sad to hear that . . .' And looking directly across the table at Florence, who was sitting between Arthur and Giles, 'You, you are his sister, Madame? Florence Caldicott? Raymond's sister, Giles's aunt? That is correct? I don't remember if *we* actually met, but I can see so astonishingly how similar you are. The same *lovely* eyes, grey, his eyes were unforgettable, the same straight back. An amazing resemblance, eh, Madame? You were fortunate in your children?'

Madame Prideaux's hand had relaxed in the steady hold of Lulu's two. She nodded. 'I *am* fortunate indeed. I do recall our meeting with your husband. He found French difficult, I remember. But it was a pleasant meeting. He enjoyed Raymond's new motorcycle.'

Lulu, sensing a modest victory, eased smoothly away, in a drift of Mitsuko and pale blue chiffon, waved at Dottie and Arthur, and said where did she sit? She sat across the table, beside Arthur, one removed from Florence, and Eugène filled her glass deferentially.

We re-toasted Giles, we smiled pleasantly, he and Frederick sipped cautiously at thimblefuls and said that Coke was better and we laughed in that stupid, immoderate way that adults do if they are slightly ill at ease and use childish utterances as a relief from temporary awkwardness.

But it all passed quickly enough. Dottie began to chatter across to Madame Prideaux, on my right, about some new disaster she had had with white fly; Arthur and Lulu were laughing; Florence, chin in her hand, talked with Giles, and across to Frederick, about the possibilities of going up to the hameau of Jericho when the range was not being used by the military. It was all general chitter chatter, easy. Wine was a help and then Clotilde and Eugène arrived carrying the first course and the supper commenced as the evening slowly began to drift into the square, throwing shadows across the terrace, deepening the shade beneath the little striped awning under which we sat.

Candles were lit, and in the laughter and general murmur, the sudden barks of laughter from Frederick and Giles to each other – amidst all that I could see that Florence, although occupied apparently perfectly happily with Arthur and one of his stories about something or other, hardly ever took her eyes from Lulu, who was sitting beside him and looking, from time to time, with half-concealed amusement, across at me. Quite well aware that she was under close scrutiny at every move. But it was all perfectly pleasant: pleasure spread with the Domaine d'Ot, a chilled rosé, the candles veiled us in gentle amber light, smoothing lines and wrinkles, glinting softly on silver and glass, throwing the wine glasses into cornelian globes, bringing a general sense of comfort and ease.

Across the square, in the now gathered darkness, the Le Sporting sign still winked its fusing letter 'o', a turquoise scrawl of neon script in the dark, a slightly mocking commentary on the performances taking place round the table on the terrace. And then, her sleeves rolled to her elbows, white apron crackling with starch, great silver platter held high, Clotilde arrived and set down the steaming, golden couscous to cries of delight from Giles and Frederick and a stifled moan from Sidonie Prideaux.

'Mon Dieu! At *this* hour of the night!'

I murmured to just take a forkful, that Giles had ordered it especially as a compliment to herself and his 'aunt', because of the Algerian connection, and Eugène put the silver jug of harissa on the table with unnecessary warnings that it was very, very hot. We ate, we drank, we talked. I don't recall much of it really, and when the Cherries Jubilee had been dealt with the two boys asked, and were instantly given permission, to leave the table because there was a Clint Eastwood film on the TV and they still had time to see half of it.

'Who is this Clint Eastwood. Does he sing?' said Madame Prideaux.

'No, Madame. He shoots.'

'People, I imagine?'

'People. Yes.'

'Of course. The young. I thought maybe that he was black. And sang that awful stuff with bongo drums, guitars and things. I used to hear it so often in Casablanca. Wails and moans. Now the children all dance to it. Shimmy, *we* called it.'

Lulu closed ranks, taking Frederick's place beside Dottie, whom she leant across to place her hand on my arm, which she pressed firmly. 'You have made your boy so happy! Really so happy. You saw his face? Great! You are making a *perfect* papa!'

I laughed and Florence suddenly turned from Arthur, her eyes as shining and hard as flints. For a second, a split second of a second, we held each other's look and then she looked away, and Dottie cried quickly, 'Oh! What a *splendid* evening. It's so difficult to keep a balance when they are that age. Ten. But you were right to let them go to see Mr Eastwood. They had been very patient. Eat and *then* treat!'

Lulu gently removed her hand from my arm, smiling across at Florence, who had turned back to Arthur.

'No. I have never seen a nest. A weaver bird's nest . . . I'd like to,' Florence said. 'Can you show me one perhaps?'

Madame Prideaux took up her napkin and idly polished an unused knife, having noticed this tiny exchange, under lowered lids. 'It is a long time, you know, since Thomas saw his cousin. I would like very much to bring him over for another tea party. You remember? The last one? That was long before they went to Marseilles. For that little holiday.'

'I do remember. He must come again.'

'I wish that. It is important for him to be with people who are not . . . who are not disturbed – I can say? – by his appearance. Gilles was very good about that, you remember they were hand in hand? And the fresh, clean air up there . . .'

'I do. Let us arrange things. Giles is on holiday. When?'

'It is a question of Florence of course. She has to be in Sainte-Brigitte next week. A job. She must get a job, you know. There is a charming person there, a Monsieur Jouvet. He is a veterinarian. There is a position there for her, if they are compatible. But . . .' She shrugged. 'Sainte-Brigitte. It's a journey, every day.'

'I'm not very certain, you know, that Florence will care to return to Jericho.'

'She will. I am a stubborn woman. She will. And in any case *I* want to see just what you have done to my property! Clotilde says you have made it a *paradis anglais*! It is true?'

'Not exactly. But it is pleasant. Come and see.'

'And the garden. Clotilde says that you work day and night. I think that you are a determined man. Is that so?'

'That is so. I'm just beginning to realize the fact for the first time.'

She smiled suddenly, a warm, gentle smile, nodded her head. 'I *too* am determined. It is a useful quality, so many people give way . . . It is a quality I much admire.'

And then suddenly Madame Mazine, squashed into a tight button-through dress, a corsage of carnations on her shoulder, hair lacquered, shining as cheap porcelain, beaming through her glasses, brought in the cheese platter and set it down, with a nod and a bob, before Lulu.

'Madame,' whispered Madame Mazine. 'Your presence is *such* an honour for my modest house. An honour!'

Lulu (as I knew that she would) accepted her 'aristocratic' role with alacrity, bowed gently back, murmured words of thanks and said it 'had been quite delightful'. At which, before a slightly startled table, Madame Mazine backed away and only turned to steady herself when she reached the shadows.

Arthur cut himself a piece of Cantal. 'We are going to take the boys to Marine Land. Antibes. Next Thursday. An added treat. I know Frederick longs to go. That's all right, I suppose, with the parents?'

The parents declared themselves delighted.

'Can you bear it? All that water, dead fish, dolphins and stuff. You are really amazing, both of you,' said Lulu.

'We ran a school,' said Dottie dryly. 'You have to get used to the brats. And here they come.'

Giles racketing in from the bar firing imaginary guns: 'Pow! Pow! Pow! Stick up your hands!'

Arthur said mildly, 'What is that in, French? You appear to be speaking a foreign language. Was the film dubbed?'

And then, in a muddle of light laughter, chairs scraping back, the tinkle of a fallen spoon, we edged towards the terrace steps. Lulu took Frederick by the arm and pulled him to the Mercedes. 'If the dew has fallen you'll have a damp ass, in you get.' And as she slammed the door she said to me, under her breath, 'Next Thursday then? Two-ish suit you?'

Dottie and Arthur were chirruping away up to Florence and her mother, who were still standing by the table with Giles.

Arthur called out, 'Next Thursday! Marine Land, Giles, okay? Be with us about ten-thirty. We'll get lunch there.'

Giles shouted, 'Great!'

I eased Lulu into her seat, shut her door carefully. 'Fine. Two-ish. *My* way this time?' Laughing, and with a gloriously extravagant wave and a shout of 'Thank you' echoing across the deserted square, she reversed, squealed around and drove in the dark, car radio blaring Air-Inter Jazz. 'A really happy, happy evening, Will! Thank you.'

Dottie was smiling, eyes sparkling. 'I do so love the little undercurrents, don't you? Irresistible.' She slammed her door, Arthur switched on his ignition and lights. 'Thursday then? Bring the boy over about ten-thirty, as you heard. Not too early for you?' And they inched cautiously back, eased away, and as they began to move down the hill Dottie leant out of her window. 'There's a killer whale at Marine Land, and dolphins galore. No shrimps though.' She was laughing.

Arthur said, 'Oh, come on, woman. Chatter, chatter.' They drove away, their rear lights bouncing over the cobbles, headlights raking the blind façades of the shuttered shops and houses.

Up on the terrace Eugène and Clotilde, accompanied by a girl I had never seen before, were starting to clear the table and douse the guttering candles with a little tin conical hat.

Walking Florence and Madame Prideaux back to 11 rue Émile Zola, Giles said, 'You know, that was a very happy time. I am most content. Really very content. Did you like it? I am so glad you came, thank you.'

I had rehearsed him in the latter part of his speech, but not in the first. That was his own voluntary addition, and it pleased me because obviously he *was* pleased, and even in stilted French his happiness was apparent.

Madame Prideaux put a hand on his shoulder. 'It was most kind of you to invite us to celebrate with you, Gilles. Did you get some good presents. From your mama, perhaps? It is sad she could not be with you, eh?'

Florence looked at me and smiled, remembering, I suppose, my outburst of joy when Helen had called once before during our first dinner together at La Maison Blanche, and when she had made it clear that I was now a 'free man'. We crossed under a street-lamp to the little iron gate of No. 11.

'She's in Milan, or somewhere in Italy,' I said easily. 'It's a very demanding business being in commercial TV.'

Madame Prideaux nodded. 'I imagine.'

'I got a beautiful aquarium from my father. Its brilliant! And some fish from Clotilde and her friend. Will you come and see it? When I have got it all working.'

Florence had opened the garden gate and was standing

aside to let her mother take the lead up the path. Madame Prideaux was searching in her bag, obviously for her keys. I had a shrewd feeling that the delay was deliberate and then she said, '*Thomas* will come to tea with you very soon. He will be enchanted to see the aquarium. So you must make it *very* pretty!'

'Tea?' said Florence.

'I have agreed that we all go to Jericho for tea. Again. It has been such a long time since Thomas was with his new cousin, hein? When you have decided on the work with Monsieur Jouvet. Or not.'

She had found the keys, closed the flap of her bag. 'If you prefer not to accompany us, Florence, then Céleste and I can go over. My driving is terrible, but it's not far. And I am curious!'

She started up the path, Florence smiled at me ruefully, shrugged her shoulders. 'Curious indeed! Thank you. We will arrange a day. Next week? I have your telephone number now, of course. Goodnight, Giles.' She ruffled his hair, took his offered hand. 'That was a very happy evening. I hope you will remember it.'

'I will,' said Giles. 'And I'll have to remember that Dad has to buy ginger snaps.'

'Some *what*?' A puzzled smile trembled under her wrinkled brow.

'Ginger snaps. They are Thomas's favourite. Remember?'

CHAPTER 10

She came in from the ugly little bathroom slowly, drying her legs with a cloth as thin, and as mean, as a handkerchief. 'Marcia', she murmured almost to herself, 'doesn't exactly "spend" on her little love nest. Can you believe?'

Behind her the sound of water dribbling from the shower-head, a swirl and glugging as it wound down the drain. Her hair was now spiked, wet, like a brush or a hedgehog, her body glistening, shoulders beading with droplets. Little beads of mercury glowing in the soft louvred light.

I said, 'You look, from where I lie, as if you'd been dipped in mercury.'

She smiled, rubbed her arms. 'Maybe *you* are Mercury? He's the messenger of the gods, am I right? Maybe I've been sprinkled all about. By you? Possible?'

'Not really. Not "about". Elsewhere. Not about. Your haircut is amazing: wet. It was a very savage decision you took.'

For a moment she looked as if she might be concerned. 'You don't like it? My Louise Brooks cut? It's wrong?'

I shook my head. 'It suits you. Great. Really.'

'I got so bored with all that curly-wurly bit. I looked like Deanna Durbin. Know who I mean? So I asked Etienne just to give me bangs. You'd say fringe. I like it. It's better in the heat.'

She threw the threadbare towel on to a chair, clambered up on to the rubber-sheeted bed beside me. 'You know something? You look really wanton lying there. Arms behind your head, legs crossed. Naked as Mercury himself.' She stroked my thigh. 'You know? That was really neat. A really neat afternoon. I like "your way", I really do. You know a trick or two, in the gentlest way, really neat.' She ran her hand across my chest and laughed when I flinched in apprehension. 'Don't be so crazy! I wouldn't dare. Your son and heir won't have a moment's curiosity. No need for lies about falling in the bramble bushes. I wouldn't do that. Mind you . . .' She traced a finger along my lips. 'Mind you, I'd quite like to, quite like to. Guys like you don't come with the breakfast cornflakes.'

I took her hand, cupped it, opened it, pressed the palm to my mouth, bit it softly, thrust my tongue between her fingers.

'For Christ's sake, stop,' she said, and pulled away.

'You didn't call me "Babe" once, not *once* all the afternoon,' I said.

She was lying on her back beside me, pushing her fingers through the new severity of her damp spiky hair. '"Babe" is strictly for fantasy land. For male-rape time. A term of cruel endearment. It comes with the kind of sex I sometimes need. No love. No possession. Simple lust. And angry revenge. Can you have "revenge" without being "angry"? I guess not. Anyway, your way is sweet and good, and I go for it. With you. "Momma and Poppa" love. No aggression. And three orgasms in two and a half hours! Heavens to Betsy!'

I kissed her forehead. 'Who's got a stop-watch?'

She stroked my face, fingers as light as a prawn's whiskers. 'You know, sometimes I was just overwhelmed by having a sort-of "half-flash" about every two years. No one ever wanted to *really* know, "How was it for you?" Can you believe? Bobbie wanted his child. Fine, I went along with it but there was no pleasure, no joy, absolutely no rapture. Only, eventually, Frederick when he arrived. I enjoyed birthing him. Not his conception. Bobbie just heaved off and said, "That should do it, Louise." Believe it? Went off to his dressing-room. I cleaned up. And held on to Frederick. When I did, finally, experience the delight – not, I hasten to add, with either husband, just a sexy guy I met at some airport hotel, we'd got grounded at O'Hare by fog and so on – it was nothing. Except it was *everything*. And I realized, to my misery, how badly I had underplayed my faux-orgasms in the past. Wild! And somehow, that time at Dottie's, I kind of knew you'd make it with me. And, my shining knight, you did. We did. Thank you.'

I put my arms round her and for moments we lay together, her head on my chest, damp, sweet-smelling, soft and tender. 'I love your new haircut. I can see your ears.'

'And now you'll say they are just like shells. Pink, like shells.'

'They are like shells. Pink, like shells.'

She turned her face towards me, kissed me lightly. 'Idiot. You are an idiot.' She sat up slowly, pulled at her hair thought-fully. 'It really did look so good dry. When I saw your sister-in-law – Florence? – at supper last week, she looked so damn cool. Crisp. It's sensible for July, August . . . the heat. God!' She laughed softly. 'She really *hates* me.'

'Doesn't hate you. Far too strong a word. Jealous? I'll give you that. She's a bit possessive, that's all.'

'I thought she was wrapped up in her memories . . . your brother. No?'

'Yes, and no. I think she considers me to be part of her "family fiction".'

'Do you love her? I think that you do?'

'I do. Yes. In a very middle-aged way. It's love. I've gone over the brink, you could call it besotted. Protective, you know? But no lust. I lust for you, love her. Understand me?'

'Not very well. But I can imagine. Only don't be too middle-aged about it. We have just started getting you out of that phase. I reckon *she* loves *you*, but doesn't quite realize it yet. I know the signs – very spinsterish.'

'You are being a bit tough on Florence. She's just jealous. Good old female jealousy. That's all. I don't think she loves me. Yet. I'll wait. There is no big rush, and she knows that. She's had a bloody time. A really bloody time.'

'Well, she's in love with you. I know *that*. It's a woman thing. We can tell.' She slid off the bed, reached for a shirt thrown on a chair. 'Ah well, I just hope she goes along with your new image. Tight jeans, the Hechter shirts. Not to mention your yellow auto. It's hardly middle-aged. Does Giles notice the change in his pa? Frederick will freak out when he sees *me* tonight, wearing this, what you call, "savage decision". He'll probably notice that. Otherwise I'd have to be dead for a week to get a proper reaction.' She pulled the shirt over her head, found her thin skirt.

I put out an arm. 'Don't put it on. Wait a little. Must you?'

She came over and sat on the bed, the skirt in her hands, across her thighs. 'I haven't got a stop-watch. But we have to go. We can't stay here much longer.' She bent down, kissed my shoulder, flicked her tongue across my chest, a little adder's tongue, flicking and darting, but when I reached for her she pulled quickly away. 'C'mon now! Be good. Lust and revenge have faded. You have worked your magic. Leave it there. Okay? We have to go pick up the children from Dottie, do the "Mom and Pop" bit. Back to normal. Back to Life.' She got up, wrapped the cotton skirt round her hips. 'C'mon. Go take a shower, I'll get my hair right and we'll lock up for Marcia. Okay? Up.'

I got up and went into the bathroom, ran the shower.

'My chauffeur, you remember? Tarzan? Well, Henri is fine now. He'll be driving in a day or two, so we can't make a habit any more of sneaking away like this, and anyway, this hideous place, Les Palmiers, won't be empty for ever. Someone is bound to notice we park our cars and never open the shutters. Right?' There was a note of sharp anxiety in her voice. 'I hate to hear that water running. Can you hear me? Washing off all that salt from your body. You tasted *so* salt. Don't be too long. We have to –'

I turned the tap to 'Full', drowning her voice. Didn't hear any more. The water roared, I found a piece of soap as thick as a penny, dried myself on a fragment of towel. She was standing at a little mirror brushing her hair. 'Did you really wear knitted ties and brogue shoes?' A cool voice now.

'I did. Yes, I did. English gear. I lived in London. Not the Var.'

'And grey flannels and smoked a pipe?'

'Never that. I did wear flannels. I won't ever again.'

'But were you quite amazingly successful? I mean, *are* you? Should I know who you are? You a part of the "glittering set", or whatever they call it? I don't know these things. You're never in the *Times*, the *New Yorker*, *Vanity Fair*, papers I read. You know?'

'No. Never been in them. As far as I know. Not part of the "glitterati" or whatever you called it, just comfortable middle of the road. A book a year, faithful list of readers. Steady sales. Not at all dramatic.' I pulled on my shirt, reached for my pants.

She sighed. 'Pulling on his pants. So sad to see it all go, like that. Tuck in your shirt. Round your ass. In those pants it leaves a ridge. And that looks just awful.' She began to push a foot into a white flip-flop. 'Do you have a publisher in America? Someone very grand? I only read extracts and things, so it doesn't really bother me. But as we know each other so well in bed it seems strange not to know, well, the rest of you. Never mind.' She shook her cropped head. 'I'd better go wipe the bathroom floor. I'll take this rag that Marcia imagines to be a towel.'

'You don't drive in those things? Flip-flops. Do you?'

She turned slowly at the door, the rag in her hand, both feet now shod, frowned. 'I drive barefoot. *Always* here. Okay?'

She went into the bathroom and I went with her. 'I'll give you a hand. We didn't use any linen, apart from these things. No picnic, this time. No empty glasses.' We began mopping the wet floor.

'Are you writing something now? Some tremendous saga? Maybe about your long-lost brother James? That it? About brother James?' Her voice was high, suddenly quite cool, uninterested. Turned off. It was as if a window had been silently opened in a warm room and a chill air wreathed about. Lulu was deliberately dismissing me. I sloshed the rag round the inside of the shower-stall.

'About San Francisco, actually.'

She hung her wet towel on the edge of the little bath. 'You know San Francisco? I mean, really *know* it?' She pushed gently past me into the bedroom, I hung my towel next to hers, wrung out. 'Sure I know it. Months there. It was fun, in a hellish sort of way. Research always is.'

'What kind of book are you writing about San Francisco?' She was smoothing the crumpled pillows on the rubber sheet. '*Travels with My Uncle*. Something?' She took up a pink candlewick bedspread. Unfolded it roughly.

'It's all finished. Delivered, corrected. It's called *Five-Twelve*.'

She looked at me in mild surprise. 'Just that? Nothing more?'

'Just that.'

'What is it? On maths? Geographical? A science thing?'

'It is the exact moment in the morning when the 'quake hit the city, in nineteen-six. I spent weeks talking to people. Did you know that Enrico Caruso was there? At the Palace Hotel. He actually sang in the ruins.'

She snorted. Then a thin laugh. 'What a gas! You mean the opera singer? *That* Caruso? Anyway, that was all in a different movie. That was Jeanette MacDonald.' She threw the pink bedspread across the rubber sheet.

'So you spent months in San Francisco wearing your grey flannels and knitted ties and talking about poor old Caruso. What a wild thing to do! Can you just smooth out your side? Tuck in the end . . . fine.' She looked round the ugly little room. 'What haven't we done? Left untidy? Nothing, all is fine. Just fine and I have the key right here.' She had opened her straw purse, fumbled in it. I went across to the windows, closed the slightly opened shutters, turned off the air-conditioner. It whined softly to a stop. There was no sound. A flat, dense, muffled air. She rattled the little key on its chain, to break the silence. 'Ting! Ting! Ting! I said Henri's foot is just fine now. He'll be able to drive in a couple of days.' Suddenly she looked shy, lost, rattled the keys again. 'He's really *much* better now. It was not so bad after all. No poison.'

'You told me that. So he'll be driving you again? You won't be able just to sneak off on your own any more. Right?'

'I said all that. I told you.'

'Yup. You also said that the people here, at Les Palmiers, would start to get a bit suspicious if we came here . . .'

'And just parked? And never opened the shutters. It could be difficult.'

'I know. You said.'

'And Marcia. I don't want to get her in trouble. You know, she'll be arriving back soon. At least, I suppose so.

214

You never can tell with Marcia. Rome today, Athens or maybe Malibu. Never know. Doesn't know herself really. Where she is . . .'

'Drop in at any moment? Catch us by surprise? That it?'

'That's exactly it. And then, well, there is Freddy. He has to go see his father. We have to go up to Rome. See Bobbie. It's all part of the deal, you know? Not Rome, really. Outside. It's quite pleasant. Lago Bracciano, cooler than the city in July and August. But I do have to take him up.' She stopped and pulled off a flip-flop, examined the sole with care.

'When do you go? Exactly?'

'Pretty soon . . . I trod in some chewing-gum. Disgusting . . . Soon. I want to avoid Ferragosto, the big holiday, in August.'

'So soon.'

'So soon.' She slid her foot into the sandal. 'We really have to go.' She was not looking at me, jingled the little key.

I took her face in my hand and tilted it towards me. I was vaguely surprised, chastened, to see that her eyes were brightly rimmed.

'Not tears?'

'Almost. Silly. Yes.'

'This is all just concealing one simple word, isn't it?'

She drew her head away from my hand. 'I'm not that clever. Can't write books and things. Don't know about words. What word?'

'Goodbye. That's it. Isn't it?'

We stood together in the filtered light in the drab little room, a splinter of sunlight sparked for a moment on the rail of the brass bed.

'It sounds awful. Just like that.'

'But that's what it is, okay?'

She suddenly brushed the fist holding the dangling key

across her eyes. 'I guess so. Wiser. Did you turn off that tap in the shower? Really hard?'

'I did. Yes.'

'It drips.'

'Sure.' I leant down and kissed her on the forehead. She stood motionless. 'Now, Lulu, remember. What we did this afternoon?'

'I got my hair done at Etienne's, had lunch with Véronique at her studio. She'll confirm. She's all right.'

'I was over at Saint-Jeannet at the co-operative. Two blades for the scythes. They're already in the car. I got them yesterday. Then to Draguignan to look at the Allied Cemetery outside Muy.'

We had crossed the room. I reached up by the door, straightened a cheap print of Antibes harbour.

'You go on down,' she said. 'By the stairs. I'll wait here, then I'll take the elevator. You never know . . .'

'Like two felons.'

'I'll come down when you've driven away.'

'Will you hear me? Drive away?'

She looked deliberately across the room. 'I'll hear. Oh yes. I'll hear you go,' she said.

Standing at the far end of the studio, unfazed by the steep climb up from the Long Room, Dottie clapped her hands with delighted surprise. 'But it's huge! The whole length of the house, isn't it? I'm amazed, it's really marvellous.'

I pushed open a shutter which had swung closed. 'It will be. When I have got it all sorted out. This stuff, the desk, chairs, the crates all arrived from London yesterday. A half-load, they call it. Sharing with someone else, I think at Le Foux. Come and sit down.' I pulled a rush-bottomed chair into the centre of the tiled floor and she sat among the tea chests and as yet unwrapped stuff from Simla Road. 'Poor

216

old Arthur!' I screwed up a mass of old newspaper. 'I loathe dentists.'

She pulled off her straw hat, fixed a hairpin in her plait, curled tight on the top of her head. 'I call it my whipped-cream walnut, this hair-style. Arthur won't let me cut it. Idiot. It's his own fault, the dentist. He hasn't been for months and yesterday the throbbing started again. An abscess, of course. Maddening.'

'But a good excuse for you to come here?' I chucked the paper bundle in a corner.

'Oh, yes! Fearfully good. Well, he was passing on his way. Just dropped me off.' She looked round the long white-walled room. 'In all the years we've lived here, before Arthur retired even, I have often passed Jericho but never been inside. Was it like this before? I mean with your brother and Florence?'

I sat down on one of the tea chests. It had 'office books' chalked across its side. 'More or less. After he disappeared, I rather think she stripped it out. It was pretty Spartan when I first saw it. I've tarted it up since April.'

She put her hat on the floor beside her, looking round with obvious pleasure. 'I wouldn't say "tarted". The whole house feels "lived in". It all feels very personal to you. Your house. And you've even got an aquarium! My word. I thought one only found them in dentists' waiting-rooms and Chinese restaurants.'

'Well you've found one here. It's Giles's, need I say? My present for his tenth last week. He was almost sick with delirious joy, and then went into sullen rage when I insisted it was put here. Not downstairs, or his bedroom. I had a hell of a time. But I've won, as you can see.'

'Far better. It's rather noisy.'

'Oxygenator. I'll switch it off, kill the fish, when I start work here. But he has done it all himself. Landscaped it.

Can you landscape under water? Rocks and pebbles and so on. The fish were gifts from Clotilde and her chum.'

'Clotilde served us that huge couscous at the party? I had never eaten there before, the Maison Blanche. Really rather good.'

'She also appropriated the blond god you admired working in the garden.'

'The Donatello? Very fine. She found him? Is he French?'

'Yes. We call him Mon-Ami, he's really Luc Roux. His parents own the traiteur in Saint-Basile. You know it?'

She nodded, picked up her hat, settled it on her knees. 'Yes. Yes, of course. He's obviously a by-blow from the Occupation days. A few of the local girls suddenly gave birth to corn-blond children in the late forties. No one was desperately upset down here. Far more easy-going than up north. I assume that Papa is also blond?'

'And getting fat. Thinning blond. Pity if his son follows on. Being fat would put an end to his labours here. What an odd world it all is.'

For a little time we sat up in the studio in the cool, idly talking. It was just after three o'clock, too soon for tea, too early for wine. L'heure verte. Giles was over at the Villa des Violettes with Frederick. His time with his new friend was rapidly running out. In a week or so he'd be off to the 'Lago' and his father. Ferragosta was the fifteenth of August. I'd miss him too: when he left I'd be firmly on my own with Giles. A daunting thought. How to amuse him?

As if she had sensed that my scattered observations were prompted by some family problem, Dottie got up and wandered slowly across to the aquarium. I followed her, hands in my pockets. She was wearing a thin cotton shirt, a blue and white striped skirt, tiny pearl ear-rings. No denim now. 'It's very pretty. All the bubbles. What happens to Giles when the summer ends? Back to the UK? He's ten now. You can't leave it too late.'

'I know, I know. It haunts me, don't think it doesn't. I'll cope with that a bit later, not today.'

She traced a finger along the glass side of the tank, fish swung away, startled. 'No shrimps in here?' she said quietly, not looking at me.

I half laughed. Caught it, suppressed it. 'No shrimps. Sharp as a box of knives, you are.'

She put a hand on my arm without looking at me. 'I am being perfectly idiotic.'

'No. I know you, Mrs Theobald. You weren't far off the mark at the very start. The only shrimp there is stands beside you. Simple.'

'Into the net were you?'

'Into the net. Willingly. No regrets. The only regret I might feel is that next week there won't be a "shrimper" around.'

'Oh? She is so attractive. Wildly attractive, alive, fresh, gay. Don't blame you for a moment. She was, *is*, good for you. Got you to shake yourself up, change your attitude, what you wear, who you are, that absurd yellow car! Simply marvellous, huge fun!' She turned and we walked through the stacked packing-chests, the wrapped bits of stuff from Simla Road waiting to be unpacked. Picked her hat from the floor where she had left it.

'Dottie?' I touched her shoulder. 'Isn't it amazing just how often one can go trundling through life being absolutely convinced that how you are existing is exactly, and precisely, how you have always wanted to exist – and be quite wrong? You discover you have made a very grievous error, and you shouldn't have been existing as you have at all. Your new existence could be just across a room or, as in this case, just across your terrace one afternoon. I was losing out slowly. I was forced to reconsider my life.'

She laughed, shrugged, went towards the door, leant against the jamb. 'The extraordinary thing is that she had much the same effect on me. She forced me to reconsider *my* life. Ever since she arrived with her child, last summer, she brought a beam of dancing light along with her. It sounds quite silly, but she did. I'd become such a frump. Flopped about into indifference, wore my gardening gear all day. One suitable dress to play bridge. She forced me, by her own attitude, to reflect on mine. To make an effort to change. Not for Arthur, God bless the man: he wouldn't take note if I started to prune the roses in a crinoline. No, the effort was for my own self-respect. Woke me before the cobwebs smothered me, and it was too *late* to change. Easy to let things slide . . . easy, and quite fatal.' She turned and started down the stairs. I followed her, keeping one step behind; it was a steep descent.

'All that I can say', she called over her shoulder, 'is that we were most fortunate in your guest. That evening, at Giles's party, she looked so vivid, so alive, naughty, so attractive . . . it was splendid. But, of course, *you* knew that already?'

We had reached the bedroom floor, went on down to the Long Room.

'I knew that already. Yes. I know very well what you mean.'

She smiled lightly, stopped at the door of the Long Room, raised a finger.

'Listen! Your femme de ménage? Clotilde. Singing like a lark. How pretty it is: "*J'attendrai, le jour et la nuit. J'attendrai toujours, ton retour.*"' Her voice was sweet, young. She smiled again and we moved into the cool of the room, shadows dark in the corners, slits of light striping through the shutters. 'A silly popular song, long before she was born. "J'attendrai" meant such a lot during the German Occupation. It was almost a secret thing: people sang it all the time. Whistled it. I am waiting. Waiting for the return of their men from the deportations, for the Germans to be driven out, for us, the Allies, to arrive. For liberation. It was a sort of symbol, of courage, of holding on. Perhaps *she* sees it as a sort of "holding on"? Possible?'

I thought of Mon-Ami. 'Quite possible,' I said. 'But we were talking about Lulu de Terrehaute, remember?'

'Ah, yes! The shrimping-lady! Let's go into the air.'

On the terrace we took the tin chairs and sat under the vine in the cool. Cicadas chiselled in the olive tree near the house. In the long grass down the path crickets scissored and sawed, and beyond the fig trees, in the shimmer of afternoon, Mon-Ami swung gracefully with his scythe, a gentle, rhythmic movement.

'Frederick is her only child, I assume. By Robert de Terrehaute? And he's in Rome?'

'They go up next week. The boy has to spend part of his holiday with his father. Reasonable but tiresome. It's all this ancestor crap. He has to keep his "ancient French" polished. I can't imagine why. No one can understand it and no one uses it any longer.' Dottie stretched her legs before her, turning an ankle to the left, then right. 'I gather from Lulu that her husband considers that the Louisiana Purchase was evil and corrupt? Which it very probably was, but since it all happened in 1803 I can't imagine what he thinks poor Frederick will gain from it. He's unlikely to become Duc or whatever in the democratic USA after all this time! And the family house here is in ruins, the land's split up. No one gives a toss.'

'Madame Mazine at the hotel does. Almost swooned that night. Remember?'

'Oh, she would. Some do still. Precious few.' She looked at a little gold watch pinned to her shirt. 'Arthur's going to be late. That's a bore. The aviaries and so on. Watering to do. But she did look so pretty in candlelight that evening. It made Florence rather irritated, I felt. We are a funny lot, we women.'

'Funny indeed. Lulu's had all her hair cut off. Like a boy.'

'Oh Lord! Oh well. I reckon she still looks quite lovely. That exquisite head . . .'

'*Looked*. I shan't be seeing her again.'

'I see.' She folded her hands, pursed her lips gently as Clotilde came out with a glass jug of iced lemonade, two glasses and a little bowl of icing sugar. Set them down with a bob and a nod.

'It's hot, eh, Madame? I have a cold flask here, for mon ami, regardez!' She patted the big pocket of her apron, there was a chink of glass, and she went off down the steps to the scything figure.

'She looks quite different here. Why?' said Dottie pouring lemonade.

'She doesn't look like this at home or in town. No bosom, no rose in the hair, no lipstick. That only happens when she's safely away from her papa. Maurice-the-taxi, you know him? An old hypocrite. Knows nothing about her life at Jericho. Thank God.'

'Well, she looks marvellous. What love can do . . .' She faltered for a moment, then resumed briskly. 'Watering tonight! Be dry as old bones. Takes me hours. Then I *do* have to put on gardening gear. You were good to ask me over. I have rather talked myself to silence. You may be glad to hear.'

'I'd have been solitary otherwise, just unpacking all that junk up in the studio.'

Dottie sipped her drink. 'Delicious. Clever girl, Clotilde. She'll help you with that. And her friend, he looks strong and capable . . .'

'I need all their strength for tomorrow. Madame Prideaux, Florence *and* Thomas all come to tea. I've had to remember the ginger snaps.'

Madame Prideaux's rather battered Renault swung to a halt

by the front gate. As with most women drivers that I know, it was accurately driven, strongly, decisively, and parked a good metre and a half from where she had intended to stop. Doors opened, with a great flurry of activity, old papers, an empty juice tin, plastic bags fell to the ground, Clotilde and Céleste embracing, Giles hopping about, Thomas, held in a sort of leather harness, screaming joyfully and flailing his arms about. Madame Prideaux descended slowly from her driving-seat pulling down her corset, smiling, the brown ribbon sagging round her piled hair.

'Here we all are! Safe. You see? I can still drive. If I take *enormous* care. Are we late?'

No one was late – a little early as a matter of fact – and we all bundled up the path through the potager, Thomas waving and beaming, his large head wobbling, his mouth sputtering with little bubbles of pleasure.

'I think he remembers me!' said Giles. 'I know he's only three but I really think . . .' Hopping along beside the straining child he said, 'Thomas! I am your cousin! Do you remember? Want to see my aquarium?'

Céleste, smiling in spite of being wrenched about by the struggling child in his leather reins, said she didn't think he'd remember and, anyway, what would he make of an aquarium? We got to the terrace and Clotilde's neatly laid table, a white sheet slung over its battered tin top, cups set about, wasps already dancing round a jar of Tiptree's strawberry I'd brought from London. Clotilde said she'd get the tea, and Céleste seated herself and started to undo the reins. 'I have to use this sometimes. To restrain him. He is so energetic, and it doesn't really trouble him, round his chest . . . Ouf!'

Madame Prideaux sat on a tin chair, rearranged the ribbon in her hair, tucked in the velvet bow at the nape of her neck. '*Florence* is late. She's in Sainte-Brigitte. With

Monsieur Jouvet the vet. This is her *second* visit to him. Perhaps he is considering her for the position.'

'I hope so. Does she like animals?'

Madame Prideaux looked at me flatly. 'Not as a child. I don't recall. No white mice or rabbits and nothing here.' She looked vaguely round the terrace and the land beyond. 'Nothing here. But she is extremely patient with her *own* little animal, there. Patient beyond a saint. And, anyway, she needs the salary. Apparently. I can't imagine exactly why, she spent so much when they were in Marseilles. I didn't know Marseilles was so much more expensive than here. But . . .' She shrugged, and pulled her skirt about her firmly. 'But it is. I did not wear my tweeds today! You recall? The last time we had tea with you, the first time indeed, I was most unsuitably dressed, I remember. But that was May, this is mid-July. We shall be having an English tea again, I hope?'

Giles was standing beside Thomas now released from his reins. 'Come for a walk with me? Like last time?' He put out his hand, Thomas looked at it, looked at Céleste, who told him to accept, then the child cautiously allowed Giles to take his hand. Together they walked, carefully, slowly, towards the steps. 'I think he *does* remember me.'

Céleste was close behind, waiting for a fall.

Madame Prideaux, bolt upright in expectation, slowly relaxed, hand to her head. She sat back slowly. 'I really *do* apologize for the state of my car. You noticed? So dirty. But you see, with all that I have to do, running errands, there is no time, and the garage charge is absurd. No time! One day I'll clean it all out. Throw everything away, papers, beach towels, plastic bags . . . one day.'

'And get the dent in the mudguard bashed out?'

She turned and looked at me sharply. Eyes hard as jet. 'One day. That too.' She brushed her brow, smoothing away an abhorrent image.

The three figures at the steps were starting to make the descent slowly. Thomas suddenly screamed out with joy.

'Otherwise,' I said, 'the rust will really take hold and you'll have to have the whole thing replaced. Or just paint it? For the time being?'

She nodded, watching Giles support his cousin down to the white pebble path. 'Paint it. Of course. Protection. *Protection* is so important,' and smiling lightly at me, 'in an *inclement* climate? You would agree?'

Clotilde arrived with the teapot, plates of cake and biscuits, hot water, set it all down with a scatter of *Voilàs* and *Bon appétits*, darting shy, swift smiles at Madame Prideaux.

I called down to Giles that it was 'sur la table', Céleste turned and waved acknowledgement, and at that instant Thomas appeared to fall, sprawling into the pebbles.

Madame Prideaux was instantly on her feet, Clotilde hurried to the steps, but Giles turned back to us and yelled out in triumph. 'He *does* remember me! He *does*! He's found another shell. This time, he's giving it to me. Remember? I found him one last time! He remembers!'

He eased our tensions. Clotilde went back to the kitchen. Thomas was crowing with apparent pleasure; Giles laughing; Céleste calmly turning everyone around for tea with murmured admonishments.

'The money is becoming rather desperate frankly. Your brother, of course, settled the rent for this place for three years. Impeccable. But . . .' She shrugged as I handed her a cup of tea. 'But we seem to spend it rather quickly. Everything is so expensive. Can I have lemon?' I put the slice of lemon in her cup, she reached for a biscuit. 'Here they all come. Thomas,' she called. 'Come quickly! Lovely English biscuits for you.'

Giles, who had now apparently appointed himself guardian, carried the clumsy child in his arms and sat down with him, offered a biscuit. 'Ginger snaps? I know you don't know what I am saying really, but I expect you will when you put this in your mouth ... there! You see? Do you remember?'

Thomas screamed again, his face creased with delight, lunging joyously, his eyes slitted with pleasure, then he pushed the biscuit into his mouth and sat quite still suddenly, sucking noisily.

'You have a magic touch, Gilles. I think, as I said before, he must realize that you are his cousin. That's very nice,' said Madame Prideaux. I told Céleste to help herself and went into the Long Room to get myself a can of beer. James, I knew very well, had paid his rent three years in advance before he had 'gone into the night', but the trip to Marseilles, apart from fares and all the rest of it, must have cost dearly. Or, at any rate, enough to make life difficult. It was only consoling that Madame Prideaux didn't apparently realize exactly why Florence had gone there. I hoped that she never would, and as I opened the beer she was suddenly there, at the door, a silent, heavy figure, her shadow thrown hard across the tiled floor.

'You know that I am curious! So where is this "Arcadie anglaise"? This "paradise" that Clotilde has spoken of. Show me?'

I waved the can about the room, softly lit now through the shade of the vine and the half-shut louvres. 'Here is Arcadia! All my bits and pieces from England; pictures, the sofa, everything you see.'

She looked quietly around the room, her teacup in her hand. 'I see. I see what Clotilde means. Félicitations. It is quite changed, it is all *very* different. You brought this furniture from England? From your house?'

'Monsieur Simone and his sons – you know them, the log merchants? – they helped to unload and move it in. To surprise you and Florence. Do you approve, Madame?'

She nodded, set her cup down on a small table by the

window. 'It is very "cosy", très anglais. You appear to have settled down at Jericho.'

'I have. I am staying.'

'For three years? I agreed to the three years which your brother leased.'

'I meant longer. I mean for good. For ever.'

She looked at me mildly. Brushed her hands against her long linen skirt. 'For ever! Pray, Monsieur Colcott, how could that possibly be? For ever is longer than you have paid me for.'

'If I paid you for *ever*? Would you consider?'

She tilted her head slightly, as if listening for a distant sound. 'Do I quite understand what you are trying to say to me? Can you be more precise perhaps?'

'Paying you "for ever" means that I wish to buy Jericho, and its land, from you. I want to live here permanently. To be here for the rest of my life. I want Giles to have it too. To live here. That is as precise as I can get, for the moment. Will it suffice?'

She looked about, found the arm of a chair, sat, perched uncomfortably, on it. 'Go on,' she said, and started carefully to adjust her hair ribbon, a certain sign to me that she was considering things. What things I couldn't as yet tell, but she was silently thinking away. So I took courage.

'You tell me that you have never lived here? That you dislike it? That it has sad memories for you? That your father only gave it to you as part of your dowry. So, if you have no regard for it, if Florence, as she says, never wants to be here again, if you are in need of money, if Thomas is to be secured, and Florence with him, *if* you have to afford Céleste and Annette, cars and petrol, if you have so many demands, then won't you let me try to be of assistance to you? This house has, I know, seen one Caldicott here and it was not, in the bitter end, an entirely happy arrangement.

Can't I try to erase some of that sadness? At least try to? If you firmly decide *not* to sell it to me, then I would ask you to extend the lease, for my lifetime. That is all.'

Madame Prideaux was motionless. There came a burst of laughter from the terrace and Giles's voice. 'Céleste? *Please?* Let him come up to my father's studio to see my aquarium. It's not far for him.'

'*Your* studio now, hein?' said Madame Prideaux quietly. 'You *are* taking hold of the house, is that it? You really mean this nonsense?'

'Not nonsense. Not to me. Something simply for your consideration, that's all.' She moved her head, either in acceptance of a modest reprimand or, perhaps, as an acceptance of the suggestion? Impossible to tell, and she was not about to make any commitment just yet. I pushed on gently. 'You have time, of course, I do not press you. I would not dream of doing that. Three years? My lease is for three years. After that I would be grateful to know if you would think favourably of my suggestion. My offer. Understand, Madame, I do not, and will not, press you.'

Sitting uneasily on the arm of her chair she waved an impatient hand about in little flutters, as if brushing aside some tiresome bee. 'You may not "press", as you say, you may not. But my bank very well may. I find that as I grow older the banks grow less lenient. They will pressure me very severely. They will "press". That I must consider seriously. It is beginning now. I have a modest inheritance plus Jericho, from my papa. But . . .'

Giles suddenly barged into the room. 'Céleste says it's too far to go up all the stairs. So we can't see the aquarium. So we'll go to look at the new pond instead. It's not so far, and it's all flat, and he'd like it. He really would. All right?'

I had set aside my can of beer and was standing. 'All right. If Céleste is with you? Someone? Mon-Ami can go.'

Giles had ducked back on to the terrace. 'We can go!' he shouted. 'We can go. Céleste is coming. Come along, Thomas.'

Madame Prideaux looked up at me, smiling. 'You are making so many changes already. Tiens!'

I thrust my hands into my pockets. 'I didn't bother to ask your permission. Not permanent. You might be interested to know that I have a watch, a gold Piaget of some value, which belonged to James. I managed to get hold of it. Florence refuses to touch it . . . look at it . . .'

'She does? But if it is valuable?'

'It is worth something. Not enough to solve any problems which you may have at present, but it could be useful pocket money for you. For Thomas.'

She was fanning herself gently with one hand. 'For Thomas, you say? And what will it provide, this pocket money, for Thomas, pray? A new head? New limbs?'

'I was thinking of practical things. Clothing, dentists, general bits and pieces . . . A toy of some kind? An animal? A pet?'

She was smiling pityingly, but pleasantly. '*A toy? An animal?* A pet for a "pet"? Boff! Monsieur, you fail to understand. Thomas would not be capable of appreciating your kindness to him. No. No, no . . . I shall accept this watch, not for Thomas, but for Florence. She may have a new job, you see. With Jouvet. She will need a new dress, something pretty. She has one "good" one, she wore it at your supper party. I can get her to accept something. Something pretty, simple, useful.'

'As you wish. You know best.'

'I do. And Céleste, Céleste needs a little financial encouragement . . . It will be most useful. Yes. Thank you, Monsieur Colcott. I am interested.'

'How shall we proceed? I ask your advice, Madame. You have an idea?'

She nodded, rose majestically, again pulled at her corset. 'You could sell it, perhaps?' She was tugging at her skirt.

'I could. I'll try. And put the cheque into your bank? Would that be acceptable?'

'Greatly,' she said dryly. 'Beggars, Monsieur Colcott, cannot be choosers, they say. It is true. I lost pride a long time ago. And I am fast losing my wits.'

'Hardly a beggar, Madame, hardly. You own this house, you own your own, I assume. But if it makes any difference, and it won't be a fortune understand, I will sell it on your behalf for Thomas, and Florence need never know. Agreed?'

'Agreed,' she said. 'We are accomplices.'

Outside there was a scrape of chairs and clatter of cups and china, Thomas crying out with some barking noise of delight, Giles shouting, Céleste chiding, Clotilde, who had obviously joined them, calling that she would show the way. Madame Prideaux began to cross towards the terrace in short, sudden little jolts of movement. I wondered, for a second, if she was unwell. But it was soon clear that she was moving in such a manner because she was in fact 'considering'. At the door she turned slowly.

'You have given me much to think about. Unexpectedly, to be truthful. I was not certain that you were, and this you must forgive me for saying to your face, a man of honour. Was uncertain. I have had a life of cruelties, not all my fault . . . some, no doubt, but not all. And one becomes untrusting. Do you follow?'

'I do. I follow. I understand exactly.'

'Will you accept my apology, then?'

'I will. I will, very gratefully, Madame.'

She suddenly began to pluck nervously at a button on her shirt.

'My husband was murdered. In 1962. You did not know that, eh?'

'No. I did not know that.'

'By the FLN. His car was ambushed. Outside Oran. They mutilated him and nailed him to a door.'

I was quite still and silent. She brushed an imaginary hair from her cheek. Her fingers trembled. 'One learns hate so easily. When I saw him . . .' She looked away, out through the door.

'I think I can imagine, Madame.'

'*Can* you!' There was a half-smile on her lips, her eyes hard. 'There have been cruelties in my time. My son was crushed to death by a speeding truck. Cruelties. Not my fault. All that I have left to me now is Florence. She is my life.'

'And Thomas?'

She looked at me sharply, shrugged. 'And Thomas . . .' She took up her cup and saucer and turned away swiftly.

She went out on to the terrace with her empty cup, stood silently by the scattered chairs and the disarranged table. 'You should put a lid on the confiture. It is full of wasps.'

I flapped about, screwed the top on the jar in a swarm of angry insects. Far down the path Mon-Ami had straightened up and was talking to Florence, who had just come through the gate. She laughed, he nodded, she laughed again and Mon-Ami pointed up towards us on the terrace. She came up the path, throwing a backward remark to him over her shoulder. I heard him call, 'Ah si, si, Madame. C'est vrai.' Then Florence, seeing us, waved brightly.

'I have a feeling that she got the job,' I said, cupping the now tepid teapot. 'I'll leave you both, and put the kettle on. I can do that. Amazingly.'

I went across to the kitchen. The telephone suddenly rang, a shattering sound, totally unexpected on this 'family' afternoon. I set the teapot down quickly and raced to get to it before it stopped, barked my shin on the corner of the Simla Road sofa, swore, grabbed the receiver and shouted 'Allô! Allô! Oui?'

At the other end a high flustered voice. 'Hello? Hello? Is Mister Caldicott there? Is it his house? Do you speak English? *Anglais?*'

I pressed the mouthpiece to my chest, shut my eyes. The voice was blurred now but still shrill enough to be heard.

'Hello? Hello? Oh *God*! *Is* that his house? Bloody hell!'

It was Helen.

CHAPTER 11

It had just finished raking up the grass which Mon-Ami had been scything all afternoon when I noticed (because I was right up beside it) the door of the round, squat, tiled pigeon house which stood at the very end of my land. Hanging on the handle, a supermarket bag, a bottle neck sticking out, the bulge of something or other thrusting against the shiny yellow plastic. Mon-Ami had forgotten his refreshment.

I pushed the weathered door wide, stepped into the gloom of the little round tower-like building. A floor of hard beaten earth, untouched for years, sunlight slanting in long fingers of light through hundreds of small openings in the stonework, holes for the birds to come and go. There were one or two broken perches, a scattering of mildewed straw, bat droppings, some planks high up in the beams. It smelled cool, musty, forgotten. No one had been in this place for years, not even, it would appear, James or Florence. There was almost no sign that it had been used since the de Terrehaute château, far across the rough fields, had been burned and pillaged. I thought, instantly, of Lulu. Banished the thought. Considered idly that the building was too small for a house, but quite large enough for a room. A round room? Perhaps two round rooms? A useful place to have.

I went out into the sunlight. The intense heat of the day was ebbing, shadows had begun to steal across the potager, a hoopoe was making plaintive little calls, gritting up at the top of the path, crest flicking up and down, alert, its scimitar beak probing deep, and then, in a light ripple of laughter, Clotilde and Mon-Ami came down from the house together and the bird sped away in alarm.

Clotilde had dragged her hair back now, replaced the pink combs, stuck a frill of lace in the cleavage of her plain blue dress, removed the silver ribbon, lipstick and rose, and waved. 'You should leave it all,' she called. 'Better for another day in the sun, M'sieur.' Mon-Ami was almost beside me, his grotesque helmet swinging from a calloused hand.

I said, 'We don't want the hay. I'll burn it away sometime. You left your water bottle and stuff on the door here.'

Mon-Ami went across and took it up. Clotilde had started to steer her Mobylette carefully through the gate, a wilting white rose on the handlebars.

'A happy day today, eh? Poor little child. He loves to be in the air, in the sunlight. He is trapped in that house in Émile Zola. Trapped in his little body. Trapped.' She bounced the front wheel carefully up over the stone step.

'It has made you late, Clotilde, I fear. All the washing-up . . . more than usual.'

She laughed, shook her head, and said it was nothing, 'Pas de problème'. It had been such a happy day for every-one. Eugène at the hotel would have to be patient. Dinner was never served until seven-thirty anyway. 'Mon ami had English tea too! And one of the biscuits for Thomas. You didn't like? Hein?'

Mon-Ami was fixing the strap of his helmet about his throat. He shook his head, smiling.

Clotilde suddenly gave him a quick little kiss on his chin,

the only part of his face available to her at that moment. 'Deceit! We live in deceit,' she said. 'I don't like it, I don't like it.' And then with a wave she straddled her bike and, tying a handkerchief round her head, told Mon-Ami to be careful, called goodbye to me, and rattled off cautiously down the ruts of the track.

Mon-Ami pulled his Honda from its stand, started to unchain the wheels. 'She turns to the left. I turn to the *right*! You see that, M'sieur? It is crazy. Her father is a stupid man.'

He was squatting, fiddling with padlock and key when I said, 'Mon-Ami, I've had an idea. Just this moment. This very moment. The pigeonnier . . . empty, useless. You know what I mean?'

He got to his feet, wrapping the heavy chain round his arm. 'I know. It is empty. It has always been empty. No one keeps hundreds of birds for the table any more.'

'I was thinking when I saw your bag hanging there what a good site this would be for a maison de gardien. Built on to the loft, to the old tower. You know? After all, we never use the grass, the hay. It's a lot of extra work, we don't cultivate the land and it is level, beside the track, beside the gate, and in view of the house. Do you see what I mean?'

Mon-Ami removed his helmet, pushed a hand through his hair, looked about with a considering eye. 'Yes. A good place. Full sun too, near all the services as well . . .'

'Water and electricity. All near at hand. And what would you think? A half-hectare? To go with it? Surround the house with its own land. For a potager, a dog . . .'

Mon-Ami pursed his lips, shook his head. 'Protected land, all this. It is protected, M'sieur, a half-hectare is a lot of land.'

'But if we built carefully, included the old pigeonnier in the fabric, used ancient tiles, stone, left all the trees. I *need* a maison de gardien. I intend to remain here now for as long as I can, at least for three years. And Monsieur le Maire would probably be understanding? For a "consideration"? Eh? It is possible?'

Mon-Ami started to show signs of stirring interest. He walked into the centre of the plot, looked about him, nodded, dug the heel of his boot into the earth, kicked up a clump of red soil. 'Si, si. Possible. If you can get the permis de construire . . . difficult. But for a maison de gardien . . .' His voice trailed away, he squinted about him, hands on hips, the helmet swinging. 'And chickens? There could be chickens too? Eh?'

'Of course! Chickens. Maybe a goat even? A goat. Good idea? But it's a bit far from the village, that's the trouble. From Saint-Basile and Bargemon-sur-Yves. Pretty remote. Unless they could drive. Can you think of anyone in the area who might accept a job like that? If I get permission?'

Mon-Ami started to adjust the helmet on his head, fingers at the buckle beneath his chin again. 'I can ask,' he said, with a slight flicker in his eyes. 'I can ask. Clotilde knows people – in the village, or Sainte-Anne-le-Forêt.'

I took up the rake, handed him his plastic bag, and began to move, slowly, away. 'Think about it, Mon-Ami. I shall talk to Monsieur le Maire this week. Try and get some reaction from him. But, of course, it is useless to build a maison de gardien without a gardien. Eh? Idiotic.'

He called out. I had just got to the path up to the house. 'A couple?' he called. 'Would a couple be acceptable, M'sieur? Perhaps you could think of a couple?'

'Of course! Let us consider a couple. Without children. To start with. Okay? Now, you get on to your supper, you are late this evening. We'll talk when I have been to the mairie, shall we? When you have spoken to Clotilde.'

For the first time since I'd known him Mon-Ami actually grinned. A conspirator's grin. Then strode down to the gate swinging his bottle in its plastic bag.

Giles was sitting on the terrace steps fiddling with some tubes and a screwdriver. He looked up as I arrived.

'What were you doing? Down there?'

'Getting things to work, Giles, that's what.'

'I wish you could get this to work. I can't.' He was holding a grey plastic figure of a deep-sea diver, masked, booted, a plastic tube wriggling from its helmet.

'What is it?' I sat beside him resting my back against one of the iron support pillars.

'It's the diver Florence brought for me today. For my aquarium. It's an oxygenator, you see? When I get it all wired up, the tubes and everything, it'll stand in the water and look quite real . . . all bubbles.'

'Looks awful. A dreadful bit of kitsch.'

'It's brilliant! The air all comes bubbling out of the helmet, you see? It shows you on the box. But I can't join it all up. Will you help me?'

'You know me and screwdrivers. Put it all back in the box. We'll look at it tomorrow. I've had enough for one day. Tea parties . . . God!'

He started repacking the bits of his diver. 'Are you still angry?'

'What do you mean angry? When was I angry? *I* haven't been angry.'

'When Mum telephoned. You were then. I could see.'

'Saw wrong. I was just a bit surprised. Everyone here, and you all up at the stream. How did you know I looked angry?'

He had fitted everything together, stuck it back in its box, put the screwdriver on the stone step. 'Well, Florence thought you were angry. She said you *looked* angry; and you were, when we got back here. Was it something about Mum?' He was not looking at me, fiddling with the box, avoiding my eyes.

'Florence merely said, "You look cross, William." She

didn't say anything about being *angry*. Anyway, I *was* cross
... right in the middle of all that ... Florence had just
arrived ... I *was* a bit cross. Of course nothing more.
Irritated.'

'Is she in London? At Chalfont with Gran?'

'No, she's here. At Valbonne. And Eric's in Nice on
business. She was bored. That's all.'

He was suddenly rather quiet, hunched up on the step,
his elbows on his bare knees, chin in his hands. Then, 'She
want something?' He was still looking away from me, as if
by looking at me he might find confirmation of his worst
fears in my face. That she would be coming to see him, or
asking to see him, or deciding to take him back to England.
Which was precisely what she had wanted. So I, partly, told
him.

'She wants to see you, Giles. It has been a long time since
Simla Road you know. And she's a bit worried about ...
well ... about what you are going to do about school. You
know?'

'It's the holidays! Why is she worried about that?'

'Can't be holidays all the time. She is right. We'll have to
discuss it all very seriously soon. School, I mean.'

He got up, picked up the diver, wandered slowly towards
the Long Room door. 'So when do I have to see her?' He
was standing with his back to me, running a finger up the
hinges of the open door.

'You don't *have* to see her. She is your mother, Giles.
You *want* to see her. She longs to see you, and Eric
Thingummy won't be here, don't worry. I made that clear.
She's coming over to have lunch on Friday. I'll send Maurice
and he can take her back after. Her idea. So just be civil,
well behaved, look forward to seeing her. She loves you,
even if you think she doesn't. It's been difficult for us all.
We'll have to be very grown up and sensible and polite. No
good in sulking.'

'I won't sulk. But I won't go back to school in England. I really won't.'

'When it comes to it, you'll just have to do as you're told. You aren't twenty yet. In ten years' time maybe . . .'

'I'll be dead!' he said and went into the Long Room. From somewhere in the gloom he called out in a fractured voice, 'You *promised* me!' I sat perfectly still.

Helen had said, 'Fine. Tell the taxi-whatever, anyone will direct him to the villa, it's right at the end of the village. Friday, eleven-thirty, I'll be ready and waiting. *Ciao!*' And hung up.

I replaced the receiver, rubbed my shin, took up the teapot and went into the kitchen. What a time to call. Tea. Kettles to boil. Her voice, strangely, had unnerved me slightly. It was an intrusion. Apart from with Lulu, and now and then Giles, I spoke only French. Apart, of course, from Dottie and Arthur, but theirs were familiar voices, I was attuned to them. Helen suddenly sounded abrasive, angular, sharp. I was irritated, uneasy, and all at once anxious.

The kettle boiled, I filled the teapot. Somewhere up the garden calls of pleasure and excitement from a blur of voices. On the terrace, Florence, cool, smiling, hands clasped on her lap.

'You get the job?' I set the teapot amidst the clutter of cups and plates.

'She has the job!' Madame Prideaux nodded and answered for her daughter. 'Isn't that splendid?'

Florence found a clean cup, poured her tea. 'Is there lemon? Ah, yes! Yes. I got the job. Jouvet is a charming man, very serious, which I like, and I answered all his questions to his satisfaction, it would appear.' She stirred her tea.

Madame Prideaux took a custard cream biscuit. 'It is

odd, to work for a veterinary surgeon and not like animals very much. Don't you think?'

Florence shook her head, as I sat down beside her. 'Maman. Don't be silly! I *do* like animals. I am very compassionate. *Really.*'

'You never had an animal as a child.' Madame Prideaux spilt crumbs on her skirt, swiftly brushed them off. '*I* never saw you with a cat or a puppy, did I?'

Florence shrugged. 'There was hardly ever time, was there? We never settled anywhere really long enough. A military life is not conducive to a child having pets. Then there was that school. Years of weary school – no pets there.'

The sound of laughter and Giles calling, 'You liked that, Thomas? You did? You liked that adventure . . .'

And then we were suddenly engulfed in the chatter and cries and general reaching, the taking, kissing and stroking, as mother and child were reunited and a slightly breathless Clotilde and Céleste, brushing hair from foreheads, pulling down sleeves, bobbed and bowed and went off together to the kitchen.

'Did you have a lovely time, Thomas? Where did you go?' said Florence.

Giles was standing, hands on his hips, legs astride. 'We went to the dam. He liked it. I don't think he'd ever seen water before.'

Florence looked up with slightly amused eyebrows. 'Gilles! Thomas sees water every evening! In his bath, be sure!' And she laughed and Giles said he hadn't meant that sort of water, but *real* water with rocks and all spilling down to the stream, and, because I had not spoken, or hardly at all, Florence suddenly said, 'You look cross, William. Are we very distracting with all our adventures and cups of tea?' Thomas was wriggling and stretching on her lap. She put down her cup and held him with both hands. 'Don't pull, what is it that you want?'

240

Giles took a ginger snap and held it aloft and the struggling, wrenching little buddha shrieked and bubbled, hands opening and closing like a pink sea anemone. 'He wants this, hein? This, Thomas?'

'Give it to him, Giles. Let him have it. I don't mean to look cross, sorry! Just flustered; rather unlike me but all is well. An unexpected telephone call, that's all.'

Madame Prideaux laughed a short, soft laugh. 'I always tried to resist having one. They are terrible things. Usually bad news. Like telegrams. I used to hate those too. Never good news. I was sure you might come to regret having one installed. Sure.'

Thomas sat back against his mother's body, sucking his ginger snap, eyes wide, vacant in pleasure, seeing nothing, only turning slowly at a sudden movement, or the rasp of a chair dragged across the tiles.

'It wasn't bad news, this time. Just unexpected really. And somehow I never quite get used to the telephone ringing here in Jericho. Especially on a blistering day, at this sort of time. People usually wait until evening. They have other things, or nothing, to do in this heat.'

'As long as it wasn't bad news,' said Florence, wiping dribble from her child's chin. 'How many of these has he had? He'll never eat his supper.'

'You must see the house before you go, Florence. The Arcadie anglaise which one has heard about. It is really very charming, very "cosy". She may look?'

'Of course, Madame.'

Florence indicated, with a nod of her head, a package on the table among the tea debris. 'Gilles. That is for you. A present for the aquarium. I wanted a treasure chest, but this was all the shop had. Take it.'

Giles grabbed the package, ripped off the paper, and crowed with pleasure. 'Look! A diver. It's an oxygenator! Oh, thank you, thank you, Florence.' With a cheerful lunge, he threw his arms round her neck, knocking Thomas on the head, who beamed happily, and caused a mild ripple of laughter.

Madame Prideaux got up and took the child from his mother. 'Florence, you go with M'sieur Colcott and he will take you to the Arcadie anglaise. I can sit with this one for ten minutes, I am quite strong and perfectly capable.'

I got up and moved across the terrace, waited at the open door. From down in the kitchen a burst of laughter. Florence came slowly across to join me, arms folded, a thin silver bracelet on her wrist.

'Now where is Arcadia?' she said.

In the cool of the room she ran her finger across the polished surface of a small Regency card table. The light was soft, gentle after the glare on the terrace. She looked quietly, carefully, about her, stroked the faded striped fabric of the sofa, traced her finger round the frame of a small John Piper, looking intently all about, a light smile on her lips.

'It's *very* changed. Very. This is all yours? And the pictures? From England?'

I nodded, leaning against the door on to the terrace, my shadow, like Madame Prideaux's before, striking hard across the red tiles of the floor. 'Bits from there, some bits I bought here, in the market at Sainte-Brigitte and an antiquaire in Draguignon.'

She laughed suddenly, a happy, relaxed laugh, without irony or any trace of bitterness as, sometimes, there had been before. 'Oh là là! Are you a millionaire perhaps? Antiquaires in Draguignon! Next will it be Monte Carlo?'

'Not a millionaire. No. And I bought modestly. This, the swan, you remember him?'

She shook her head and sat down in the sofa. 'This is soft, *very* English, eh? What did you do with the few pieces I left? That disgusting old thing which was here, you covered it with a terrible Indian cloth with bits of mirror in it? I can remember that, but not the swan . . .'

We laughed together, easily. I sat in the small chair by the door. 'I had to cover it with something. But it was almost worse than your sofa, if you understand . . .'

We sat smiling easily at each other, not shy, in the soft, green-reflected light filtering through the vine. It was the first time, almost, that we had sat like that. Her smile had never been quite so open, so clear of apprehension and suspicion.

'It is pleasant sitting here. The English are very good for "comfort". We French are always more formal. It's a relic of the Court, did you know? The straight backs, thin legs, upright, brocaded, elegant. It suited the dress of the day. They did not wear jeans and trainers then, in the days of King Louis.' With feline suppleness and grace she changed course. 'And Madame Louise de Terrehaute? How *is* Madame?' Her eyes were smiling, her face gently amused.

'She is very well. I believe. I haven't seen her since . . . well . . . since the party for Giles. She leaves for Rome shortly. The boy has to stay with his father for some of the holiday – part of their deal.'

She stroked the arm of the sofa against which she sat. 'And your son? Gilles. Does he stay with you? Does he not see *his* mama?'

'She has been away on business, back now. Actually it was her who telephoned just now, she is back from Italy. In Valbonne. She comes to see Giles at the end of next week for lunch. But he will stay with me after the divorce. We have agreed that. The division of the spoils.'

Madame Prideaux's voice suddenly called authoritatively, 'Céleste! Céleste! We shall go to see the aquarium. Come!'

Céleste came hurrying up from the kitchen and almost ran out on to the terrace. 'Take Thomas, Céleste. Gilles will accompany me up to the studio.' She was on the threshold,

Giles behind her. For a moment she stood still, adjusting her eyes to the soft light. 'We go to inspect the studio. You recall last time? I told you that it would make a splendid room? Come, Gilles, let us see.'

Together they started slowly up the stairs and I heard her heavy tread on the floor above. Florence smiled, sat forward, her hands lightly clasped together. 'I think Mama is being tactful. Giving me time to look about in peace. It's very pleasant, William. So changed. And *you* are so changed! A yellow car! Where is the yellow canary?'

'In the shed up at the top. It doesn't stand out in the sun. I treasure it. My symbol.'

'Symbol?'

'Of readjustment.'

'Like your jeans, eh? And, what do they call it, "designer" shirts? You look so different. I imagine,' she said, looking at the tiles at her feet, 'I imagine that perhaps Louise de Terrehaute has had an effect? Would that be right?'

'The royal association! You linked her name just now automatically with Louis and the furniture. Louise de Terrehaute is a perfectly simple American girl from Louisiana, just married to the fag-end of a once aristocratic French family, that's all! You really mustn't be scornful of her! I know that you are. I can sense it.'

'Boff!' she laughed really happily, leant back. 'Boff! I do *not* scorn her at all, William. I am so *grateful* to Louise de Terrehaute! Shall I tell you why? It is curious and it will amuse you. Louise de Terrehaute actually made me aware that my emotions were not entirely frozen, as I thought that they were, like a mammoth in permafrost! At supper that evening at La Maison Blanche, I was suddenly, wonderfully, aware that I was not entirely dead. I was alive because I discovered that I was *jealous*!' She stretched her arms along the back of the sofa, nodding, her eyes filled with amusement. 'Jealous! Can you imagine! Of you! And of her effortless control and power over you, and the table in general. Even Mama! Madame Mazine, remember? They were almost fainting with reverence. Dottie Teeobald actually almost chic! Because of *her* influence ... Your yellow car in the square, your elegant white trousers, the Laurent silk shirt! Mon Dieu! The changes since I went to Marseilles!' She laughed softly, amused, but lightly mocking. 'What if I'd gone to Santiago! Or Peking!'

'It is perfectly possible, Florence, that you are right. Even Dottie agrees. It is the usual cliché: a peacock lands in the hen-run and everyone becomes flustered, clucks around anxiously and rearranges their feathers. You know? She did a lot of good!'

'I am most grateful to her personally. It is not very agreeable being frozen in permafrost. I was. For almost three years. Until that evening. Ouf! Will Gilles ever know just how important his birthday supper was, I wonder?'

'Probably not. But I am very happy for you.'

She leant forward quickly. 'Oh, that little spurt of envy or jealousy is over now. But it was proof to me that I was not entirely dead yet, that my reflexes still worked. She was being overtly possessive of something which I considered to be my property alone.'

'You mean *me*?' I let my astonishment show deliberately.

She waved a calming hand. 'My property as my "brother-in-law", if you like. *Nothing* more, William. Just that. But I was released.' Briskly changing the subject, she got up and went to the stairs. 'I must call to Mama. We must all start to go. It is late and Thomas has his bath to get, and Céleste must be weary. Ordinary life must continue.'

She called up the stairs that they had to move homeward, and I walked out on to the terrace where Céleste was glumly trying to buckle the straining Thomas into his reins. I squatted down to assist her and Thomas clobbered me on the head, laughing, bubbling, dribbling, wrenching about, the unseeing eyes flashing with furious joy. Florence was not released entirely.

Maurice gave his traditional two blasts on the horn. I saw the sun glittering on the bodywork of his car over the wall.

'They are almost on time. Now, off you go. Greet Mum, be polite, affectionate, and remember it's *your* pad this. Make her feel very welcome. Okay?'

He nodded, shrugged hopelessly, ran off down the path through the rows of beans and spinach and reached the gate just as Maurice, cap in hand, bowed Helen through. She smiled and said something to him and then stood with open arms, packages hanging from her wrists. 'Giles! My little Frenchman!' she cried, and engulfed him in an apparently joyous swoop.

Maurice called to me, in French, over the wall, that he'd return at three-thirty, d'accord? And I shouted back in agreement, as Helen started carefully up the path in her white stiletto heels. A short tight, expensive white lace dress, a wide gold belt, flash of gold bracelets, swinging earrings, hair high, secured with her usual velvet bow. This time white.

'William! Long time no see! My word! Lean and brown we all are. Have you all been on a diet? Or do you only eat salads? Everyone just eats salads in this country.' She sat easily on a tin chair, discarding a giant Hermes crocodile bag, a straw hat with a bunch of cotton wisteria on its brim, a folded white cashmere cardigan, and handed Giles two gold-and-green-wrapped packages. 'You *did* get my box from Hédiard, Giles, I hope?'

'Yes, thank you. It was great. Especially the nougat.'

'I hadn't *heard*. So I just wondered. It would have been infuriating if it had not arrived. Your old ma went to a hell of a lot of trouble to get it to you on the very day! I am glad. Thank you for telling me, sweetie.'

'We didn't write, Helen, because we didn't know exactly where you were in Milan. You were in Milan at that time? You said you would be?'

She crossed her splendid legs, reached down for the crocodile bag and put it on her knee, found a gold lighter, a packet of Lucky Strike. 'Yes. Milan! God! That's a noisy city! This is *very* peaceful. So silent up here!' She blew a little flute of smoke into the hot, still morning. 'Aren't you going to open your packages? All the way from Italy?'

It seemed not to have occurred to her that 'all the way from Italy' wasn't really that far, about the same as, say, Margate to Brighton; but Giles, squatting on the terrace, murmured pleasantly and ripped off paper and found a glass jar with a ribbon round its neck and a long, slim packet with a Swatch inside. This, at least, he was able to react to, and with an affectionate kiss.

'It's such a wild thing, isn't it? It's called "Breakdance". All the colours, and it'll look really jazzy. I bet not many boys you know have a Swatch!'

Giles was just about to blurt the name 'Freddy' when I cut in swiftly and admired the glass jar.

'What are these, Helen? Chocolate truffles, right?'

She nodded brightly. 'Only one shop in Milan makes them, but don't eat too many at once. Just one after dinner, you know. They are frantically rich, seriously delicious and death to Weight-Watchers!' We all made amused noises and Giles fitted his Swatch on to his wrist. 'So this is home, then? I hadn't really expected it to be so – you know? – utterly *rural*. It's a huge change from London, but I know that you always liked solitude. Well, you've got it here. It's simply *miles* from anywhere, isn't it?'

'No. Not miles.' I was mixing drinks which Clotilde had organized at the table by the door. 'It is vodka, still?' I said.

Helen nodded. 'Vodka. Still. Ice. And lemon. If you have

it?' She snapped her bag shut, set it on the terrace beside her.

'From the tree next to you.'

She looked vaguely over her shoulder. 'Amazing. Goodness. Have we tonic too?'

'And tonic. It's very good to see you. You look terribly well, relaxed, and now *you* are the one who's brown. Very, very becoming. You really do look quite marvellous.'

'Well, don't go on, William! God! Did I look a freak or something before?' She laughed gaily to show that she was not quite at ease and only joking anyway. And that is how we went through the pre-lunch period. Except that she did come in and look about the house, up to the bedrooms, the studio, exclaimed at the sight of the aquarium and remembered bits of stuff from Simla Road, said how different it all looked in this light. Then we all sat down and Clotilde, beaming, set down a deep glass dish of salade niçoise, the bread, and I uncorked the Domaine d'Ot which had been chilling in a plastic bucket.

'Voilà!' said Clotilde happily. 'Bon appétit, Madame.'

Giles thrust his arm towards her. 'Look what I got, Clotilde,' he said in French. 'A Swatch. From my mama, from Milan.'

'Oh là là! So chic! Mon ami will be very jealous. You must show it to him.'

'All Froggy stuff! My goodness, you really *are* my little Frenchman, aren't you? It hasn't taken *you* long to mug it up. Frankly I can't seem to get my tongue round it, French, I mean. Or Spanish. I mean, Spanish is the *pits* – impossible. I leave it all to Eric, the same with Italian. I just haven't got the hang of languages; your old ma hasn't got the hang of them, Giles. Oh! You know I *loathe* anchovies.'

She forked two offenders on to her side plate. Giles cheerfully took them from her. Lunch progressed. She was gay, animated, glittering, scented. We had all altered radically since that April morning in Parsons Green when the key to this house had fallen on the mat. But I didn't bother saying that, it was self-evident, and she was talking, easily it would appear, to Giles, who was polite, agreeing, and only gave his utter lack of interest away when he suddenly waved happily across the table and called 'Bon appétit!' to Mon-Ami walking up from the potager, naked apart from a pair of rather short shorts and a red handkerchief round his throat.

Helen sat back, her glass in her hand. 'Who is Rambo? Someone you know?'

I explained who Mon-Ami was, and who Clotilde was, and that we now were a household, and did she want a little more? There was only fruit and cheese to follow. She accepted some more wine, said she'd let everything just 'settle, all that tomato and onion and olives', and then perhaps a teensy-weensy bit of cheese. For bulk.

When Clotilde had cleared away, we went inside and had our coffee served there. It was, Helen said, rather 'glaring' under the vine, and she didn't want to keep screwing up her eyes against the light. She'd foolishly forgotten her dark glasses. Wrinkles, I knew, were devastating after a certain age. Then looking about, patting the sofa beside her, she asked where Giles had gone to. I said probably down to the kitchen to show Mon-Ami his Swatch, and she smiled thinly. 'A good idea? Familiarity? A small boy? With the staff? I know things are a bit freer here in the Med. But still, one must keep an eye on it all. Servants get so damned bolshie if they are given an inch out here. I *know*. God! The sods I have to work with sometimes! In Italy! You can't believe . . .'

'I think we are all managing pretty well. I like Giles being about in the kitchen, and they like it too. Anyway, the "holiday period" is nearly over now.'

Helen leant forward, stubbed her cigarette in a glass dish

at her side, shook another from the pack, lit it with a sharp flick of her wrist, bracelets and chains clinking and clattering. 'I wanted to have a little word with you about that. It is about time that we considered the child's future. School. You know?' She drew on her cigarette hard, snorted smoke down her nostrils, an old habit which usually meant intense concentration or anger. 'I have been thinking it all over very, very carefully. I remember, have no fear, that ugly day at the Negresco in Nice. Remember it well, and don't want to go into that again. But Eric and I do, honestly, feel that it is utterly wrong to deny the child a proper *English* education. We feel that very strongly: I know you don't, I understand your, rather trivial, worries, but we do think he should be able to take advantage of Dr Lang's offer at Eason Lodge If you remember where that is. Do you?'

'Very well. Burnham Beeches.'

'Where he will live, at weekends, in a family atmosphere, with his sister and with me.' For a split second she floundered, tapped the cigarette on the rim of the dish. 'In a close-knit family. That's all. He can't potter about France for the rest of his life like a sort of vagrant. I don't think you realize that children do need security. The security of a family.'

'And you feel that you can offer him that?'

'Definitely. I'm his mother, remember? Did it slip your mind?' She was smiling pleasantly, head tilted on one side. Coquettish, you could say.

'What about this "trivia" which you have said you understand? Has all that "trivia" been tidied away? Your chum isn't curious about my son's genitals any longer?'

She blushed scarlet, either with embarrassment or with rage, difficult to know just at that moment. 'Don't be so bloody obscene! You are inferring that Eric abused him? Right? Is that the fashionable word? Abused? How dare you! How dare you suggest anything so vile.' She leant back in her chair. 'I really do think you have taken leave of your senses. Sun's got to your brain. Chuntering away about –' She shrugged, avoiding words which might trap her. 'You really have to try and understand, as I've told you before, that I am his mother. I know. Can't understand that basic feeling, can you? Men don't give birth, do they?'

'No they don't. If you have come here today to try and take the boy away, just forget it. We've agreed all this. More or less amicably. He stays with me.'

'He'll come to you for the holidays. Easy. So can Annicka. Remember, we agreed? But he gets a proper English education, he has a place at Eason Lodge, a proper family life. He *has* got a sister, after all. We are a unit.'

'Helen dear, if you are brightly playing Solomon today, drop it. He stays with me, you are not getting him back. Got it?'

She crushed her cigarette in the glass dish. It rattled lightly. 'Some quite absurd idea that he was, what, spied on? In a bathroom. Something?'

'Something.'

'He's just ten. Under age. Hysterical emotionally, they all are at that age. Easily swayed, accept wild suggestions.'

'He's not a bit emotional, in that manner. He's settled with me, he has friends, feels that he belongs to this place. He loves it. I am, Helen, *trying* to be fair!'

'So am I. Maureen Cornwall, who suggested Eason Lodge, her boys go there, is a social worker, for her sins. Marvellously supportive, loves helping, she's very bright, and frankly, William, she is a tiny bit uncomfortable about Giles here. All-male society? Running about, as I can see, half-naked. Half-naked gardener – all hugger-mugger, to use a phrase. And well, there *is* the mother and son business, but equally there *is* the father and son thing. Unhealthily close. But if I even whispered my concern to Maureen, well. You

251

can imagine how difficult it would be? For us all. Take ages. Investigations, so on. Eric and I do rather worry for him, honestly. Not that *I'd* ever *dream* of making a sound. But you do see? The situation?'

I got up, went to the kitchen door, and called for Giles. She flinched, put up a hand to secure the bow in her hair, drew on the cigarette. 'Oh, don't drag the child in . . .'

Clotilde shouted, 'Il arrive . . . une seconde . . .'

Helen stabbed out her cigarette. 'Really, William. Don't make a meal out of everything.'

I sat opposite her. 'My goodness, Helen, you must want him back very badly? To risk all this in public. That, subtly, I may, as his father, be "too close". That it? That it might be "unhealthy". That's the implication, isn't it? Want to drag us all, willy nilly, headlong into misery, harry us all through the courts, through Maureen Cornwall's concerned, meddling hands? The tabloids?'

She shook another cigarette into her hand, dropped the package into her bag, twisted the lighter. A flash of gold in the cool room. 'I merely want my family. What belongs to me. I have had time to think, and I am not ready just to hand him over to you. How do I know how you will cope? His hair is halfway down his back.'

Giles clambered up the stairs from the kitchen, puffing as if he had been running. 'I was going up with this to see Mon-Ami at the stream. He's made a place for it.' He opened his palm and offered up the small china frog he'd found in the garden at Simla Road on our last day there.

Helen was perfectly in control. Her voice was measured, warm. Motherly, interested.

'Giles, what on earth is that? It's got a broken leg.'

'I found it in the garden. Dad said to keep it. It's my lucky frog.'

'Giles, a bit of a problem here. Your mother is a bit worried about you, she feels that, after all, you *should* perhaps have an English education, you know? There is a jolly nice school near her new house, Burnham Beeches. She feels that you and Annicka have been apart for a bit too long and you do need to be together again as a family. Understand? It's for your good. She feels that you ought to start, at Eason Lodge, in September. New term. I gather she has arranged it all. The Cornwall boys, Hector and Bob, go there. Remember them?'

He looked at me with despair. Moving only his eyes, he said dully, 'You promised.'

'Yup. And I'm about to keep the promise. But you have to help me. Right? It seems the only hope you have. So, tell Mum exactly what you told me, all of it, in the car that day. Remember? Everything.'

He clasped the frog in his fists, lowered his head. 'Do I have to?'

'You have to. The bathroom. Right?'

He told his wretched little story, with a bit of prodding from me to remind him of things he would have preferred to forget. When he had finished, head bowed, voice almost a whisper, I said cheerfully, over-noisily, 'That it? Nothing more?'

Helen blew a furious bayonet of smoke high into the air. 'I don't want to hear another word. It's nonsense. Hysterical rubbish. You are imagining the whole silly thing.'

The boy's head snapped back. 'I'm *not*, Mum! I'm *not*. Really, I hate him! The next time he came in and said the water was getting cold, I'd been there too long, and he'd help me to dry myself. He did, Mum. I got out. And he did, and touched me, and I didn't say anything. But I never had a bath while he was there again and that's why you got cross with me. But I never did again.'

Helen, I was glad to see, was white. The cigarette between her fingers just very slightly trembled. The ash fell. 'You have a vivid imagination, Giles, take after your father, be a writer. Great.'

I got up and told Giles to go. He got out of his chair, ignored my offered hand and walked to Helen slowly. 'He did, Mum. He *really* did. I'm sorry.'

Then he turned and went back down to the kitchen.

'Helen?' I said. 'Want a cup of tea?'

She laughed dryly. 'Christ, no. No tea, thank you, the English panacea for everything.'

I called down to Clotilde that we would not require tea, and that Madame would leave as soon as the taxi arrived. When I turned back, Helen had gone out on to the terrace under the vine, the crocodile handbag loose in her hand. She spun her cigarette butt into the air; it fell on to the white pebble path. 'An edifying little moment. You have him word-perfect, William. Congratulations.'

'Nothing, I assure you, to do with me. I had no idea, until this moment, that he had had *another* "meeting", with your chum. That was unexpected. It happens, I suppose, but it isn't going to happen again.'

She turned slowly towards me, her face devoid of any expression, not even anger. 'I don't like you, William. Not one little bit. If that gives you any satisfaction at all. You'll have to reimburse us for Eason Lodge, the cheque for the term has gone in. They like it in advance now.' She sighed, took up her hat with the wisteria. 'Then it's up to Hudson and so on. Lawyers and all that boredom.' Maurice, promptly on the half-hour, swung up to the gate, reversed to face back the way he had come, sounded his horn twice. 'I fly back on Monday . . . Annicka will be with Mummy – I hope. She's been pony-trekking, or something, in Snowdonia. Don't bother to see me out, I can find my way. Right down the path . . . don't call Giles. I detest farewells and this one really *is* the cruncher. Goodbye.'

She turned away sharply, walked down the path on her

high white heels. Just before she got to the gate she put on her hat, tilted it to a rakish angle, moved elegantly through the gate on to the track. She said something to Maurice, who nodded, looked at his watch, saluted her and closed her door. He waved to me, drove carefully over the hard ruts, then accelerated away.

I walked slowly back to the house, feeling a bit gutted. An ugly, unnecessary encounter. Perhaps things weren't altogether serene in Burnham Beeches? Was that it? A last bid for a security she felt uneasy about? I dragged one of the chairs into a patch of sunlight. Giles came out on to the terrace. For a moment we just looked at each other in silence.

'Sorry, Giles. About that. But I had to do it.'

He was standing quite still, arms at his side. 'I know.'

I sat down slowly. 'Put on a hat if you are mucking about up there. You'll get sunstroke,' I said.

A couple of distracted humming-bird moths zoomed and crashed about the oil lamp I had set on the table. Apart from the lamp, it was dark on the terrace, a faint glow from a second lamp down in the Long Room, a wash of soft moon flooding the land, silvering the olives. At the stream the frogs sang and fiddled, and far away, on the de Terre-haute land, probably in the giant cedar, a little owl called. Otherwise all was still. This was another part of the day which I relished, as much almost as the early dawn.

Giles in bed, Clotilde and Mon-Ami long gone, and nothing but these familiar, gentle sounds and the soft shadows of the moon giving way to darkest black under the trees. The anguish of the day with Helen almost faded. Fourteen years of my life were ebbing away.

I took a sip of whisky, the lump of ice tinkled like a bell, and then I saw the headlights of a car pencilling over the wall, wavering across the cypress trees down at the bottom by the gate. They were extinguished as I got to my feet. A door slammed, then another, and then there was the wagging light of a torch coming urgently up the path. I called out, and taking up the lamp moved down the steps on to the path and saw Dottie, her hair unbound, a denim jacket slung over her shoulders. She was coming towards me stumbling, the torch jigging about. Behind her, Arthur.

'What is it? Dottie? Arthur?' I raised the lamp high. We stood bathed in soft amber light, silent for a moment. Moths sped about, whanged into the lamp chimney.

'Will. It's bad news. Terrible news.'

'What? Say it. What has happened?'

Dottie extinguished her torch; now we all stood alone in shadowy lamplight. 'Lulu is dead. Lulu and Frederick are both dead.'

I heard myself, as if from a distant place, say come and sit down, and we moved up to the terrace. Dottie suddenly bowed her head, covered her face with her hands and began to sob quietly.

'What happened? Where?'

Arthur cleared his throat. 'The chauffeur – Henri? Name like that – called about half an hour ago. They'd just called him. The police from Grosseto on the autostrada. She'd hit a broken-down tanker, Will. There was no chance, they only found out who they were because part of the boot, trunk, remained, part of a suitcase . . . numberplate. I'm terribly sorry.'

Dottie was wiping her nose on her sleeve. 'She was driving because the chap's foot was still not right, and she wanted to get to Rome before the weekend. She always drove so terribly fast, you know that. She telephoned this morning, early, to say they were off, taking the Mercedes . . . about five-thirty . . . wanted to avoid' – she was suddenly wrenched with sobs, shook her head in misery – 'to avoid the *heat*.'

'We wanted to tell you right away. Really because of Giles, and Frederick. I mean it could be all over *Var Matin* tomorrow. Local people, well known socially in the area. Unthinkable to read something like that. So we came right over. We didn't telephone you. Dottie wanted to be with you, to break the news.'

I murmured something about getting us all a drink and went into the Long Room, and uncorking the malt I remembered her voice: *I drive barefoot. Always here. Okay?* I carried out the glasses. Dottie almost refused, decided not to, took a good slug.

'How brutal. Oh how brutal. Two such vibrant creatures.'

'Tanker had broken down. She must have lost control and just swerved into it ... at terrible speed, just sort of blew up they said ... Witnesses.' Arthur looked up suddenly: 'Giles! Oh my goodness –'

He was standing in the door in his pyjama bottoms. I put out my hand and he came towards me slowly, hair tousled from sleep. 'I heard the car, then the lights ... I heard you talking ... Dad.' Suddenly he crumpled into my arms like an unstrung puppet, weeping silently, his body shaking.

Dottie wiped her eyes firmly. 'It was terribly *quick*, Giles. They would never have known. Quick as quick.'

Those bloody white flip-flops.

I'll hear, she had said. *Oh yes. I'll hear you go.*

CHAPTER 12

On a hot and cloudless morning I drove over to Sainte-Brigitte and sold the yellow car to the bellied garagiste from whom I had bought it. He was irritatingly unsurprised, but delighted, and of course I lost out on the deal. But that didn't really worry me. I just wanted to be rid of the thing.

'Comme j'ai dit,' said the garagiste holding my cheque in sump-oiled hands. 'It is a young man's car.'

Although I denied it, I knew that he was, infuriatingly, correct. The whole silly business was impulsive, an impulsive caprice intended to show off: to prove my masculinity (if proof were really needed) to one particular person. I was simply trying to impress. The sixth-former with his muddy trophy. The bower bird offering his display.

Lulu had only been mildly amused. 'Ciao, Babe!' she had murmured on the steps of her villa the day that I proffered my yellow virility symbol. The word 'Babe' almost had a gentle 'y' at its end, trailing softly in the still morning, drifting in her low, mocking, 'silly-little-guy' voice.

Now that she was brutally dead my vanity gaped like an open wound. I wanted it stitched quickly. It shamed me because it was as hollow, and echoing, as a cheap brass gong. No one (except perhaps Dottie) had been as impressed as I had hoped.

Giles was curious and interested at first, but lost both after we made a few trips around the countryside and then just lay slumped beside me. It felt exactly like a tin clockwork toy, wound up with its key missing. Mon-Ami was very clearly pleased to have his shed back (it usually stabled the large mower I had bought, plus scythes, garden tools and the log pile). Now he had his space returned and didn't even ask where the car had gone, or why. Giles, subdued after his double slamming (Helen first, and then on the same day the acute distress of losing Frederick), merely said that 'It was a bit silly really. Wasn't it?' And that was that. End of saga. I did not, however, revert to tweeds, flannels and brogues. Kept my jeans-and-chic-shirts image. I liked it, it was appropriate, cost a modest fortune and Lulu had been almost entirely responsible. I would remain this way. A reminder to hold on to my new standards. In her memory.

The only person who had shown the vaguest interest was, strangely enough, of all people, Maurice-the-taxi in the bar of the Maison Blanche that afternoon. (Madame Mazine had bowed to me in blank silence from her desk, a mourning band round her arm.) He was leaning against the bar staring up at the soundless television flickering and jumping up on the wall. The place was almost empty.

'Sold your MG! *Re-sold* it! Mon Dieu, so soon? You will have lost on that transaction, Monsieur. I know only too well that villain Vincenti at Sainte-Brigitte. Malheur! His son is no better. So, you will remain with your good old Simca, eh? Solid, safe, reliable. It is more appropriate at your age, Monsieur.'

'No. No, I think that it is time to return it to your brother-in-law. I have an idea that I will remain here, at Jericho, for some time. Long time. It is not sensible to continue renting, so I think I'll purchase a new car. Perhaps a Peugeot? Something robust, faster for the autoroute, you know?'

Maurice drained his glass, set it deliberately on the counter, wiped his mouth with the back of his hand. Blinked, shook his head sadly. 'Ma foi! A double blow for poor Bertrand! A double-blow in one week! Malheur.'

'I don't think that I quite follow you, Monsieur Maurice? Bertrand? A *double* blow? Will you accept another glass, or do you perhaps have a journey to make?'

'Volontiers! Volontiers! No, no journey this afternoon. I have need of comfort. I have need!' His sullen, red face had cleared swiftly on the word 'another'. A cloud crossing the sun. 'Bertrand is my brother-in-law, from whom you once rented the Simca. A sorry day today for his family! For my little sister, Odile, a sorry day. This very morning, Monsieur,' he leant towards me like a conspirator, 'Monsieur le Maire had been diagnosed as having cancer of the prostate. You recall? He had the operation and it was a success, but now, examinations, biopsies. Terrible things. Today we got the result! Voilà! The diagnosis is très mal, *très, très* mal.' He took his refilled glass of Ricard from Claude. 'Santé! And on top of that, on top, you *reject* his Simca.'

'I don't *reject* it. I simply want to buy my own car. I've been renting since April. It has been wonderfully useful, but now . . .'

Maurice took a gulp of his drink. 'Ah! It was the renting which was comforting to him at a difficult time. That little extra – indeed, Monsieur, it *was* little! You got a bargain from my brother-in-law. Nevertheless it was a comfort to Odile, that little, tiny, bit extra each month in the bank. Such comfort. Now, with everything falling about her ears, this news on top will be hard to bear.' He swigged down the rest of his Ricard and stared mournfully across the bar at his own reflection between the bottles in the scabbed, fly-speckled mirror.

It was quite clear to me that the amount which I paid to rent the wretched Simca each month would not have kept them in baguettes. It wasn't going to make any difference to their life-style. The only useful thing I had done was to run the car, rather than leave it on blocks to gather rust and dust while he was in the clinic. There was clearly something hidden away in this nonsense which I should explore. Maurice was excellent at undercover suggestions, wheedling, making deals, 'fixing things'. At all kinds of mild corruptions and even, at a pinch, bribery. All this was, of course, smothered in false humility, goodwill and a great quantity of Ricard. I was certain that something was afoot. He was about to make some covert suggestion. I'd be ready. Play him at his game, let him show me the opening and I'd go in. I had need of a rascal at that moment, plus one or two concessions from Monsieur le Maire before he had to hand over power to another. A new maire would be tiresome to deal with. I moved gently, pushing at the slightly open door Maurice had offered.

'Monsieur! You surely cannot be suggesting that your brother-in-law is undergoing some desperate financial embarrassment which my renting of his Simca has so far helped to ameliorate?'

Maurice looked at me (as I had hoped he would) with bovine incomprehension. He hadn't quite got there yet. It would need another gentle push.

'I apologize! I fear that I embarrass you? Family concerns . . . excuse me . . .'

'No! No!' he cried. 'No! *I* am not *embarrassed*, not I!' He was waving his empty glass uneasily before him, drained the dregs, and I had it refilled. 'Ah! Merci, très gentil . . . No, I am not embarrassed. But it is a difficult situation. Voyez? How long will this disease take? Where will it spread? How will Odile manage? Will he be able to remain in office and for how long? We have a deputy maire, certainly – but the problems! The specialists, the doctors, the pharmacists all the tra la la of illness. It mounts, Monsieur, it *mounts*! It is like a river trickling down the mountain.' Confusing his metaphors he took a pull at his Ricard. 'And the duties! Oh, là! Cartes de séjour, de résidence, de travail? Permis de construire – for *building* you can understand? The local fêtes, the banquets. Mon Dieu! Funerals . . .' He wiped an eye with a fist. 'Eyee! Eyee!'

The final important phrase, permis de construire, had been placed deliberately. I was not supposed to overlook that. I didn't. How did he know that I had, possibly, an idea to obtain a permis de construire? A coincidence? Or more likely a careless murmur from Clotilde? I decided on another move.

'I feel certain that, at the back of all this, Monsieur Maurice, this tragic business for your sister and her husband, that there is a worrying financial problem on top of the duties he has to carry as Monsieur le Maire? Is that so?'

He took another sip of his drink, set his glass on the counter, bowed his head sadly. 'You have guessed? Ah, there is always a financial problem in this life. When can a man ever feel secure in this cruel life, eh? When? You tell me, Monsieur Colcott, that you have an idea to remain here, at Jericho, but can you be sure that you will? For "some time" you say. What is "some time"? How long will it be?'

I ordered another beer for myself from Claude and, behind his back, measuring the amount with finger and thumb, another Ricard for my friend. Claude nodded understandingly, quickly, opened me a beer. 'I intend to stay at Jericho for from years. At least the three that my brother paid for from Madame Prideaux – at least. I will therefore need permits for myself and for my son. We will no longer have tourist or visitor status. We will wish to be resident. My son will remain here with me, naturally. And this' – I lowered my voice and looked behind him so that he would feel more of an accomplice – 'is not for general information. *Please!* I intend to approach Madame Prideaux and ask her if she would be willing to let me extend the lease there for the rest of my life! Voilà!'

Maurice looked at me with a suddenly slack jaw, finished his drink, muttered, 'Ma foi! Ma foi!' His jaw may have been slack but his eyes sparkled with avarice.

'So you see,' I went on in a normal voice, 'I try to be secure for myself but also for my young son. I love France, I wish to remain in France for the rest of my life, to work here *and* to pay my taxes. Therefore my fears for security are very real. Very real indeed.'

Maurice nodded wisely. 'Very real, Monsieur Colcott. You will have to be certain of your security. But, tell me, how can you manage in that lonely house all by yourself? How?'

I turned round deliberately and leant with my back against the bar facing the flickering silent television up in the corner and the abandoned football table. The bar, at this time, was always relatively quiet. 'I shall have to build a maison de gardien. I will have to have help there, of course. I write. I can't be on holiday all the time. I will need assistance.'

'Ah bon,' he said thoughtfully, tilting his emptying glass about, squinting at its base.

'So that means a permis de construire as well. You follow? Jericho is in a protected area, difficult to obtain a building permit, I know.'

Maurice shrugged, licked his lips, raised his glass. 'Impossible,' he said and drank.

'Well, I have a plan to add to the existing pigeonnier, use old stone, old material. Very aesthetic, sympathetic, you know?'

He looked only vaguely interested but was admitting nothing. 'And who would *live* in this maison de gardien, eh?

You will bring someone from England, I suppose? Someone from London? That would not be at all attractive in the area. Not at all.'

I turned again and leant on the bar close to him. 'Ah no! I am thinking of the boy who works for me. Luc Roux. His parents, as you will know, are the traiteurs in Saint-Basile, and he lives, like so many of the young today, with them. He cannot afford a place of his own. It is tragic!'

Maurice had frozen, clenched fist on the counter between us, knuckled with shock. 'Roux! Luc Roux! He is a *Boche*! There was a *disgusting* scandal in this place many years ago. He is one of the results. You can see he is not like us! Fair hair, blue eyes! Boche!'

'Ah. Then perhaps it is this tiny amount of German blood which makes him such a good worker? He is a splendid young man, not a slacker. I am very lucky to have him.'

Maurice swallowed his drink, put down his glass, leant towards me. His breath smelt like a still-room. 'You know, I imagine, that my daughter, Clotilde, is behaving wickedly? She does not say, but I know that when she goes to work at your house she is different! Her lips are stained pink! She *sings*! He works for you, she works for you. Voilà! It is obvious, they are together at Jericho! The good Lord knows what goes on there. I do not approve. Not at all!'

'Nothing "goes on there", as you say. They work together for my son and me, they work hard. They have secured me a life there, *entirely* due to them. My happiness, my future works, writings, my books, are in their hands. I will say to you that I will do everything in my power to assist them, I am almost certain that they love each other and I suggest, very politely, that you should not show hostility or intransigence towards them, otherwise they might do something very foolish and bring shame on you. They could elope! Imagine!'

He looked at me now with red-eyed bewilderment.

'Intransigence' had hit him. 'What do you say, Monsieur? You *approve* of this . . . blond "error"? *Approve?*'

'I do. Very much. Look, just suppose that they elope, go off and live in some cheap hotel locally or in Toulouse, or Toulon, anywhere. Or, if they wished, they could come to live with me. They could. There is space . . .' (There wasn't, but he didn't know it.) 'They are, I am certain, in love, and what is more they are adults. You cannot prevent it, Monsieur.'

He looked bewildered, stared at me cautiously. 'You think it is true? What I think myself?' I told him that I did, that I was very much in favour, that I needed them, would pay them a respectable joint wage and that, if I could get a permit, they would be welcome to live in the house that I would build. I added, quietly, that if Monsieur le Maire was really worried about his future security, and had need of immediate funds, that there was almost no limit to which I would (within reason) not go to assist him during a financially troubling and anxious time. We both, in fact, I said, needed each other. If the 'children' got married, which one day I felt certain they would, two very 'distinguished families' in the neighbourhood would be brought together for their mutual benefit. I thought all this nonsense might provide him with a morsel of bait. He need not see the hook. And there was one. He slowly raised his eyes from the slightly bewildered search of the floor which they had been making. 'You think this? But she is not pretty! Ma foi! She works . . . I told you . . . but she is not a pretty one. *Not at all.*'

I pushed his empty glass towards Claude. 'She is far prettier than you guess. I know the uncertainty of illness, the stress and the strain. Wouldn't it be interesting if Monsieur le Maire could think, perhaps, of a voyage? A little cruise? To rest and heal? If he felt he could go off to, say, Guadaloupe, Mauritius. Or Tahiti! Surely that would be a great boost to morale? Would it help to diminish the distress of the dreadful *double* blow of today? One blow, for I could buy the Simca to use for the market. Why not?'

As his fourth Ricard came to his trembling fingers I could see the ideas I had presented being sorted, shuffled, arranged in his cunning mind ready to be dealt as a 'hand'.

'Perhaps you and your wife could accompany them? For company? Your sister would be happy to have her family close to her, wouldn't she?'

He looked up blankly. 'Close? Close? Close where, Monsieur?'

I slipped the final card into his 'hand'.

'Tahiti?' I said, and took up my beer.

'A total and disgraceful bribe!' said Dottie cheerfully. 'Goodness, Will, you really *do* stoop low.'

We were sitting on her terrace in the shade. The August heat overpowered, the air was as thick as felt. Moving was almost agony, so everyone sat, or sprawled as Giles and Arthur were doing, while the cicadas chittered relentlessly, and she and I slowly shucked beans for her pistou.

'I wonder if he'll manage to cope with it all, this Maurice? He sounds a terrible old rogue.'

'He is. Which is why it might work out. I didn't actually offer money. Just the price of four air fares to wherever they decide on, *if* they decide to go anywhere. Anyway, you're right, I do stoop low sometimes, rather surprise myself at times. With Helen the other day I really did go very low. I might have just found it easier to give up and clear off, once upon a time. But now I've got *him* . . .' Giles lay flounder-flat, one fist supporting his chin, over an open book.

Dottie scooped up a pile of white haricot beans, dropped them in the colander. 'He's all right now. Isn't he? It was a dreadful, dreadful thing for him. I mean, Lulu and Frederick. Oh dear God. Dreadful for us all.' She took another handful of the white and pink-speckled beans, changed the subject swiftly. 'The thought of soup on a day like this is perfectly absurd. All I want is iced tea.' She called out across to the pair at the end of the terrace. 'You both all right? Arthur? I'm going to get some iced tea. Want some? Giles?' There was a general mutter, murmuring and slow movements. Giles had been reading aloud some translation to Arthur, who lay supine in a planter's chair, hat over his eyes, arms at his sides, trying to gain as much cool air around him as he could.

'Good idea, if you can make the effort, Dot.' And turning his head slowly in answer to Giles lying at his feet: 'It's a *fish*, boy. Stands to reason surely? Didn't have to ask . . . Poisson, *fish*, perroquet, *parrot*. Ecco *parrot-fish*.'

Giles looked up vaguely. 'Which is what, then?'

'A tropical fish. Many colours. From the *Scaridae* family. Parrot-like jaws. Okay?' Pushing his hat from his eyes he said, 'At times, Giles, you give me the distinct impression that you are dense. Thick. Lazy. Both. Honestly! Parrot-fish. Easy!' He got up, kicked Giles affectionately, came across to us on bare feet, his toes curling. 'Shelling beans? Busy bees. I'll take over Dot, nip off and get the tea!'

Dottie got up, a handful of bean shucks in her hand. 'I won't "nip off" anywhere. You get very common in the heat, Arthur. "Nip off!" It affects people in strange ways.' She went through the bead curtain into the house and Arthur, grinning, took her place. 'Nip off! Really! And cut your toenails, you look like a Yeti.' Her voice, light with amusement, faded as she went to the kitchen. He sat beside me, reached for a knife, started topping and tailing some thin green beans. 'Now, tomorrow we go over to the Anglo-American School at Annapolis. All right? I have spoken to Howard M. Buffer, as you know, the Principal. I have coached, crammed, some of their curious pupils. He's an affable man, he'll show us round. I think it'll do for you.

Giles, rather. Mind you . . .' He took another little scatter of beans. 'Mind you, Will, it's not Eton or Millfield. It *is* fairly easy-come easy-go. Mixed, of course, all sorts. Children from that scientific research place in the woods, Annapolis. God knows what they all do there . . . track things in the heavens? Make atom bombs? Amazing place, buggered up the woods, but it's all supposed to be for the good of humanity, although I wonder. I really do.'

Giles came up to the table, hair rumpled, his book in a hand, reached out for a raw bean, bit it.

'We're talking about school. You know that, I should imagine. Arthur's taking us over tomorrow morning. Eleven.'

He nodded vaguely, spat the bean out. 'That's disgusting. Yes. I know. Where is Sainte-Anne-le-Forêt? Miles away?'

Arthur threw his pile of chopped beans into the colander and Dottie came through the curtain with a tray of iced tea. 'Kilometres. Not miles. *Kilometres* now that you are going to live here. And it's about ten from us. Twelve from you. Iced tea! Iced nectar!' The cubes chinked and clinked in the tall glass jug, dew sparkled down the sides, rings of lemon and a tall spike of mint jostled in the amber liquid. 'Lapsang Souchong. You'll probably hate it, Giles. Too good for you. You'd rather have kitchen tea, or Coke, but I think this is delectable. Someone set out the glasses.'

We sat about in the still heat, conversation in a vague mutter. Dottie chopped and shucked, Giles sat on the terrace step, all energy sapped, Arthur spread bony legs in floppy shorts and leant back in his cane chair. 'If you stay here long enough, Giles, you'll be conscripted. I suppose you know that? Called to the Colours! Ten years' time they'll have you for a soldier, you see.'

Dottie laughed and said what nonsense, he was a resident, or would be, not a national. Foreigners don't get called into the army. Giles, who obviously had not lost his hearing in the heat, said he didn't mind, his grandfather was a soldier. In India. Arthur looked at me with mild interest. 'Your father? A soldier was he? In India, where?'

I put down my glass of tea and said not *my* father but Helen's. He had been a colonel, like Florence's papa, but in the Royal Engineers, in Calcutta. Helen still used a few of his phrases, like 'chin-wag,' and so on, but, I reminded Giles, *my* father had been a very successful headmaster in his day, so there should be some academic skills in his genes, but he was bored with the conversation, and we drifted off into generalization. In time, I thanked them both for taking in my child while I was in Cannes all morning and said we had stayed far too long and as soon as it got just a little cooler we'd leave. Eventually we did and drove slowly through the late afternoon to Jericho.

I had gone to Cannes with the Piaget watch. Aronovich had recommended a jeweller on the rue d'Antibes who could be trusted to be fair, which (as far as I could tell) he was. I mailed a cheque to Madame Prideaux's bank in Sainte-Brigitte and the receipt from the jeweller to her. Duty done, I told Giles, when he asked, that I had been to meet 'someone about a book', which he accepted easily enough. Sitting out, having the cold supper which Clotilde had left us, a salad with tuna and pasta, we talked about school, the visit the next day, and I asked if he was worried about going. He shrugged and said it would be better than Burnham Beeches. And I agreed to that.

'Who will look after my fish?'

'You will. You are a day pupil, mate. You aren't boarding. And I am not scooping dead fish out of green slime. That's your trick.'

'It's algae.'

'I don't care what it is. I'm not doing it. Bring your plate and glass into the kitchen when you're finished.'

And that was that. The next day we went over to Sainte-

Anne-le-Forêt and the huge complex which housed a thousand people in a mass of hideous glass and concrete boxes in a wide area hacked out of the virgin woods. Tall pines, chunks of limestone, raw wounds of the bulldozers, chain-link fences, asphalt paths, sodium lamps, ugliness. This was Annapolis. Giles looked apprehensive, as was only reasonable, but brightened up when he heard that everyone, or nearly everyone, spoke English.

Howard M. Buffer was tall, youngish, prematurely balding, with a paisley bow-tie, rimless glasses and a wide expanse of cosmetic teeth. 'We have everyone here, it is *truly* international. Truly! We have American, Italian, Korean, German, English, Japanese, some French even, and quite a few Hispanics. It is a full, all-round education in basics. French is compulsory in class. You can all speak what you like out of class. And here is Ma'm'selle Nadine Goldbaum, who will take care of you. Nadine, this is Giles Caldicott, he's English and is joining us in September. *We* all had our vacations in June. Now we all prepare for the *rentrée* – four weeks to go!'

One evening I saw Mon-Ami and Clotilde far down by the pigeonnier with a pocket measuring-tape. There was a certain amount of striding about, pointing, head-shaking, head-nodding. She had a small pad and pencil and scribbled things down. Something was afoot. Someone had made a suggestion. I kept my distance, and when they had collected themselves, and their modes of transport together, they shouted up to say '*Ciao!*', both smiling. Mon-Ami even waved, put on his helmet and clumped off to his bike. Clotilde pushed hers out into the track. They called affectionately to each other, he turned to the right, she to the left as was usual, except, and this did surprise me, she had not replaced the bit of lace in her bodice. Or removed the rose at her ear. Or, as far as I knew, her lipstick. Defiance?

I went up to the terrace as the sounds of their bikes faded and Giles came out of the house holding a bulging plastic bag.

'Greengages. From Clotilde, or perhaps from him? They are from our tree. Did you know we had a Reine Claude tree? That's the French name. Did you?'

I said I didn't and suddenly, just as I sat down, he leant across and kissed my cheek. I looked, I suppose, as surprised as I felt.

'And the other one. You have to have two, Dad.'

'Two what?'

'Kisses. From Clotilde. She said to give them to you and say, "Merci très, très bien!" I don't know what for. Do you?' I accepted the second kiss. He was smiling uneasily. 'Is it something you gave her? A present or something?'

'Something like that. I am glad she's pleased. Thank you, Giles.'

So, something might be coming together from my 'disgraceful bribe'. It was just about time that the effects were due to be made apparent. I wondered when I might hear the magic word 'Tahiti', but kept perfectly calm and let the days slip into each other seamlessly until August was almost used up. Very gradually it became a habit (intensely pleasurable for me) that Florence would come over to Jericho and, as she said, 'take advantage of the calm and the air, away from the heat'. She brought Thomas, Céleste and, occasionally, Annette. They carried a 'pique-nique' with them, at her insistence. She wanted no 'favours', and they usually went over to sit in the shade of the giant cedar in the château ruins and spread themselves out. I saw, but never intruded. Sometimes I heard Thomas yelling, a voice calling, sounds of admonishment. Florence wasn't starting work with the vétérinaire in Sainte-Brigitte until September, so she was here often, on account of having to drive them. I was

extremely happy about that. Giles was irritated because I
made him keep away.

'I can't see why, Will. It's a bit boring all by myself now.
I'm very good with Thomas, he likes me. I could take him
some of the biscuits. Masses of them. Ginger?'

'Stay where you are. If they want you they'll come
for you. Don't push yourself, leave them in peace and if
you are bored, go and have a swim in your pond . . . cool
off.'

He mumbled and waved his arms about. 'I already
have . . . so did Mon-Ami. Only he couldn't. It's too small.
He just sat. He looked very funny, he's really big.' Then he
turned quickly, arms akimbo, listening, a finger held high:
'A car! I heard a car, Dad . . . Someone's here.'

Madame Prideaux pushed the iron gate and began to
walk up the path towards us. Giles went down, slowly, to
welcome her. She took his hand lightly and they came up
together. She wore a long flowing flowered dress, a wide
straw hat with a frayed brim, white ankle socks and criss-
cross, leather sandals. In the crook of her arm swung a
battered raffia bag.

As I stood, and as she drew near, she waved to me that I
should not move. 'Ne bouge pas! Don't move at all, it is far
too hot. I have come to see my family. They are in the
château grounds I imagine? Their car is here.' I pulled a
chair into the shade. 'I detest August. I have a blinding
headache. There is no air to breathe. Giles? Why do you not
go to see your cousin, Thomas, hein?'

Giles looked at me resentfully but hopefully. 'Dad said I
must not push myself. He said . . .'

Sidonie Prideaux removed her large hat and some pins,
smiled approvingly, 'Quite right. But I say this time that
you *may*. So go along, I want to speak to your papa.' Giles
sprang away to get biscuits and she put her hat, hat pins
and bag on the floor beside her. 'This frock which I wear is

272

unusual you will think? I wear it only in extreme heat. It was made for me in Algiers many years ago. There was a "little woman", you know? It is formal, of course, to wear on ceremonial occasions with the Colonel. I spoke to you about the Colonel? My husband? Murdered . . .'

'You did, Madame.'

'He so liked this frock. It was most suitable.'

'It is very becoming.'

'It was useful. You will never tell Florence? About her papa? It was a confidence between us.'

'I understand. I'll never speak of it. I promise.'

She smoothed the flowered voile over her knees, shook her head sadly.

'Too good to waste, so I wear it here. I am still too hot.' Giles slithered across the terrace, a tin of biscuits in his hand and raced down to the gate. 'The energy! I so hate being my age. Now . . .' She eased herself in the chair, plucking at the ridge of steel which was her corset, poking through the thin floral voile. 'I am alerted, by my notaire, Monsieur Duvernoise, that a sum of money has been paid into my bank. I imagine that you know what that is?' I nodded. 'And I have the receipt from a jeweller in Cannes. Thank you. I am always amazed how much people value these vulgar trinkets. A gold watch! So much! Boff! . . . It is disgraceful.'

'It had a jewel for each quarter. A ruby, a sapphire, an emerald and a diamond to mark mid-day. It was rare. Especially commissioned.'

'I prefer not to know. But I am not proud. I accept the money for Thomas.'

'Not a great amount, Madame. The best I could do.'

'I am grateful.' She looked up into the heavy canopy of the vine above. 'I am sorry about the de Terrehaute affair, he seemed a pleasant boy and she was, I imagine, quite charming. Ah well . . .'

From far across the garden, behind the motionless fig trees, a clatter of laughter, a voice calling, Giles shouting, 'Pow! Pow! Pow!'

Madame Prideaux picked up her hat and the raffia bag. 'To hear laughter again at Jericho is very pleasant. Florence likes to be here, after all.'

'To my astonishment and pleasure.'

'She would not even come over to check the fabric of the house after a mistral. The place filled her with dread. Astonishing indeed.'

'She laughs now, you know?'

She got to her feet, set the hat on her head, moved to the steps. 'I know. I am aware of it. Thank you, Monsieur. Ah look! Above! The swallows are very high. A change in the weather, we shall have a great storm, a wind is coming, it is so still. No air, the sky is like copper.' She skewered the pins into her hat, patted her hips, the bag swinging from her wrist. 'Ah! I almost forgot this: most important. I grow older and sillier.' She fished in the raffia bag, brought out a sealed envelope, handed it to me. 'From Duvernoise. We have discussed the situation, Florence and I, and he has been most helpful. A good man. You and I do *not* discuss anything, you must do that with him at his convenience. My husband trusted the firm implicitly . . . I hope that you will also and we never speak of Oran? Good day.' She turned and started down the path to the gate. As she pushed it open she called up sharply. 'This needs oiling.' Then she closed herself out and was lost behind the wall of the pigeonnier.

I went into the shadow cool of the Long Room, ripped open the envelope. Jericho could be mine in permanence if I wished, no rentals. At a reasonable price. Monsieur Fabrice Duvernoise, Notaire, was 'at your disposal when convenient'.

In the kitchen Clotilde was singing, shutting drawers,

closing cupboards. 'Every little breeze seems to whisper Louise . . . birds in the trees . . .' I went out on to the terrace. The vine above was heavy, motionless, in the heat. 'Can it be true, someone like you could love me . . .'

I sat down on the top step, the letter in my hand. Folded it, refolded it, tapped it on my knee. *Monsieur le Propriétaire.* I said it aloud, just to try it. It sounded good.

My relationship with Madame Prideaux had always been as crisp and fragile as a brandy snap, but it had held. In some odd, and unexpected, way we had come to terms with each other. I liked her, and obviously it had shown. She trusted me and I had made it clear that she could. The story of Oran and her husband's brutal death was proof. My behaviour towards Florence, her adored only child (now that Raymond was dead), my ease with Thomas, the determined changes I had made to Jericho, the behaviour of my son, Giles, my tact about mudguards and the full awareness that I *knew* what she had set out to do, and why, all these things had added up to this unexpected gesture: the offer to sell me her house and land, the admission that she was desperate to have the money. She had delivered herself into my hands. She was concerned not with *her* inheritance, not with her 'land', but with securing some kind of future for Florence and her unhappy child. It was fortunate that, through Helen, I had become aware, and sympathetic to, that overwhelming oddity in women, the arbitrary, unexpected, often wild, mood swings. They all seemed to manage it with ease. Florence, Lulu at our last meeting, Dottie herself even and, without any question at all, Madame Prideaux. Guarded, hostile, cold at first, changing to become a close accomplice in conspiracy, almost with a shadow of respect? At least I chose to see it that way. Selling one's land to a stranger *and* a 'foreigner' was, for a Frenchwoman, a devastatingly extreme gesture. She had made it today. I would accept willingly. My whole future and Giles's lay shimmering ahead in the blazing sun. In four rather bewildering months my entire life had altered for ever.

Florence suddenly appeared down at the gate, came slowly up the path, walking cautiously barefoot. She offered me a battered biscuit tin (a bit of junk from Simla Road) with one hand, an empty Evian bottle with the other. 'Biscuits! Almost finished. Now he'll be sick . . . Then Giles was showing us all how fast he was with a gun, being Clint Eastwood and upsetting the last of our Evian water. Pow! Pow! Pow!' She sat beside me, leant against the trellis. 'We are all parched! Can you give me another bottle?' She was smiling, her hair sticking to her brow with the fine beaded sweat from her walk.

I got a fresh bottle, took, and rattled, the biscuit tin. 'Two left? Three? Goodness! This water isn't chilled. It's cool enough in the room though.'

She reached up and took the plastic container. 'I am sorry, William. I didn't say it to you before. It is perfectly appalling about Louise de Terrehaute. It is the cruellest, cruellest thing . . .'

'Yes. Cruellest. At least it was instantaneous as far as we know . . .'

She nodded slowly, moving bare feet in the heat of the sun, arching her back against the trellis. 'I hear that someone has already been to the villa, clearing it. It's going to be on the market, they say in the village. So, that is that . . .' She stood up slowly, pushed the hair from her brow. 'I'll take this over. They are so thirsty. You have a letter from Mama, it is so? She didn't forget? Perhaps you will think it over?'

'No. I have it. Thought it over. Tell her yes. Absolutely yes. I will speak to her notaire tomorrow. Will you, also, say thank you? I understand what it means to her.'

For a moment she stood quite still, then looked slowly

around her, down to the gate, back to the house, across to the still, brooding cluster of the fig trees. 'How strange it is,' she said quietly. 'Another Caldicott at Jericho! I will tell her.'

'You are not cross? Sad? You don't mind . . . Florence?'

She shook her head slowly. 'Not cross, why? Not sad? What for? If you will be happy here . . .' She shrugged.

'I will . . . I will. I am overwhelmed, rather.'

She smiled a very little smile and turned down to the path. Enigmatic, calm, but certainly more familiar than she had ever been before. Another example of her change of mood? But this, I reckoned, had been almost entirely due to the news from Marseilles. The intense relief from desperate stress, apprehension and fear. I took the biscuit box down to the kitchen.

Clotilde was washing the floor, a final swing with her mop. 'Mon Dieu! It is hot, there will be a storm. It is *too* still! I hate it when it is still like this, and it is getting so dark. No air, nothing moves, even the birds don't fly. You see . . .' She wrung out her cloth in the sink, spread it out to dry, started to untie her apron. 'Gilles has said thank you, eh, Monsieur? My papa was very . . . pleasant . . . very shy! He said that he would go to Saint-Basile, soon, to speak with the papa of mon ami.' She hung her apron on a hook behind the door. 'Now *that*, that, Monsieur, is like the tiger walking with the lamb! You are a writer! You have a way with words! It is magic. *Truly* magic.' She leant out of the window over the sink and called out to Mon-Ami, who was carrying a pile of cut grass and garden rubbish on a pitchfork. 'No more! It is time to finish. There is some cold beer here.' She had deliberately turned away from me to avoid, out of shyness, any further comment on the 'tiger and the lamb' situation. She had, in her few words, thanked me fully, and that was accepted. We discussed, instead, what she had left us for supper and then I got a list of things I had to buy the next day when I went into the market. I left her singing again, and laying up our evening tray.

In the Long Room I re-read my letter, almost in disbelief. The first letter I got from my publisher accepting my third attempt at a book had had exactly the same effect. One of amazed, but doubting, joy. I had to return to read it constantly just for reassurance that it really was true, and that I had not made some grave error, or that perhaps there was some dreadful hidden clause tucked away in the sparsely encouraging prose. But all was well. It was a clear and simple statement. Jericho was mine. If I wanted it.

I looked up, probably with an inane smile on my face, and saw Florence coming back up the path. Behind her, down at the gate, Giles and Madame Prideaux, with the straining figure of Thomas in his reins, were crossing the garden.

'Come on! Come on! You can, you can!' Giles's voice was light with encouragement and laughter.

Florence put the half-empty bottle of water on the tin table. 'We are leaving. It's late, and Mama fears that we shall have a terrible mistral. It's so still, do you notice, oppressive? Annette is stealing from the de Terrehaute land. Can you believe it! Marjoram! There is a big patch there. She can easily buy it in the market for a couple of sous, but it is more attractive to steal it from the field! The peasant mind . . .' She stooped and started to ease into her old espadrilles which she had stuck under her arm. 'I must go and help Céleste, she's struggling with all the pique-nique things. Annette is so stubborn.'

'I only hope that if this, shall we call it "transaction", between your mama and myself goes through, there will be enough cash for you to afford *another* Céleste. That's the idea, isn't it?'

She smiled, fixed an ear-ring which had fallen. 'Correct. A Céleste for the *night*! It is a night-time job often. That is difficult.' Céleste passed the open gate carrying a couple of plastic sacks. Florence waved down to her and shouted that she was coming to help. 'I must go. She is a saint but not a very young saint. I'll have to call for Annette too, silly woman. What a funny day, William! Do you feel strange when you think that you never knew that this house existed until a few months ago? There was no Jericho! No de Terrehaute! No Teeobalds even!'

'No Giles *even*! And no Florence . . .'

She looked at me steadily, the smile fading, her eyes kind, 'Ah yes! There was always a Giles and a Florence. It is just that you didn't know . . . But this is an old, old house, it has seen many, many hundreds of people. We are only fragments, shadows, in its existence. It will outlast us all . . . the Prideaux and the Caldicotts! Voilà!'

'And all the others since – when? Sixteen-whatever. Since the first cornerstone was set into this hillside. All the children who were born here, the people who have died, whole generations long before us. And it'll go on, Jericho, sheltering new generations. We only rest here for a little time, then others move in. Maybe Giles? I hope . . .'

Down at the gate stood Annette, laughing. She called up waving a fat bunch of green leaves, under her other arm a bundled travelling rug and a paper parasol. 'Voilà, Madame Florence! C'est tout fini.' Hurried to Céleste and the car.

'A new dynasty, do you think that?' Florence was still smiling.

'I think of that. Yes. Sure. I think of that, starting again, then I think of all the ghosts that there must be watching us –'

Swiftly, suddenly, she placed her hand over my mouth, shaking her head. 'No ghosts, William! No ghosts. *I* see no ghosts.'

Leaning towards me she kissed my cheek at the exact moment that Clotilde's voice cut into the still heat of the darkening afternoon, high, harsh with terror. 'M'sieur! M'sieur! At the *back*! Vite! Venez vite! Vite!'

Florence froze, arms half raised. I turned and raced to the back of the house, up towards the rearing cliffs and the red earth path. Running towards me, hair flying, arms waving frantically, face flour-white, Giles, mouthing silently, agonizingly. He saw me, screamed, '*Don't* look! *Don't* look! He fell – *he fell in!*' Then he crashed into my side, burying his face into my body, burrowing, clutching. I thrust out my arm to stop Florence as Mon-Ami came down towards us, in his arms the swinging sodden body of Thomas, arms and head bouncing, jigging, water dripping, mouth agape.

Florence screamed, 'No! No! No!', broke my hold, tearing towards Mon-Ami as he slowly lowered his burden to the grass.

'C'est trop tard,' he said. 'Trop tard.'

Florence was on her knees grabbing, pulling, cradling the wobbling head with its sagging mouth, water-spiked hair. 'No! No! *Thomas!*'

Behind me somewhere the gull-cries and mewing of the terrified women. Crushed against my side the shuddering body of my son. Standing far up, by the cane-break, hair tumbled in a frayed silver rope, her skirt muddied at the knees, the tangled harness bunched in one hand, Sidonie Prideaux. For a shocked instant we looked across the terrible tableau of grief between us. She dropped the leather reins loosely, and with an almost obscene gesture of benediction, raised her empty hands towards me. Smiling gently, head high, eyes wide, fingers spread.

No one had fallen.

Dirk Bogarde
10.5.93
28.12.93